The Urbana Free Library

To renew materials call
217-367-4057

Also by Rebecca Miller

Stories and Film

PERSONAL VELOCITY

Films

ANGELA

THE BALLAD OF JACK AND ROSE

The
Private
Lives of
Pippa Lee

Rebecca Miller

The
Private
Lives of
Pippa Lee

FARRAR, STRAUS AND GIROUX · NEW YORK

Farrar, Straus and Giroux
18 West 18th Street, New York 10011

Printed in the United States of America
First edition, 2008

Library of Congress Cataloging-in-Publication Data
Miller, Rebecca, 1962–
    The private lives of Pippa Lee / Rebecca Miller.— 1st ed.
      p. cm.
   ISBN-13: 978-0-374-23742-4 (hardcover : alk. paper)
   ISBN-10: 0-374-23742-5 (hardcover : alk. paper)
1. Middle-aged women—Fiction. 2. Housewives—Fiction. 3. Marital
conflict—Fiction. 4. Drug addiction—Fiction. 5. Neurasthenia—Fiction.
I. Title.

PS3613.I55P75 2008
813'.6—dc22

                         2007047321

Designed by Charlotte Strick

Pill art © 2008 JupiterImages Corporation

www.fsgbooks.com

10 9 8 7 6 5 4 3 2 1

To D
And for Barbara Browning

Part One

Wrinkle Village

Pippa had to admit, she liked the house.

This was one of the newer units, they were told. Dishwasher, washing machine, dryer, microwave, electric oven, all new. Carpeting, new. Septic tank. Roof. Yet the floor of the basement had a crack in the concrete, and some of the grouting between the tiles in the bathroom was turning dark with mold. Signs of decay, like in an old mouth with gleaming caps glued over the stumps, Pippa thought. She wondered how many people had died in this house. Marigold Village, retirement community: a prelude to heaven. This place had everything: swimming pool, restaurants, mini-mall, gas station, health food store, yoga classes, tennis courts, nursing staff. There was an on-call grief counselor, two marriage counselors, a sex therapist, and an herbalist. Book club, camera club, garden club, model boatbuilding club. You never had to leave. Pippa and Herb had first encountered Marigold Village when returning to their Long Island beach house from a lunch party in Connecticut twenty years earlier, when Pippa was just past thirty, Herb sixty. Herb had taken a wrong turn, and they found themselves on a narrow, winding road lined with clusters of dun-colored, single-story houses. It was five o'clock in April; the late afternoon light cast a golden filter over the perfectly maintained lawns. The houses looked identical; a hive of numbered mailboxes stood at the end of each shared driveway. Some of the numbers were in the thousands. Herb had been confident that a couple of left turns and a right would put them back on the main road, but every turn he made seemed to suck them deeper into the development.

"It's like one of those fairy tales," Pippa said.

"What fairy tales?" Herb asked, exasperation in his voice. Pippa was always seeing poetry in everything. Leave it to her to turn getting lost in a housing development into something out of the Brothers Grimm.

"You know," she said, "where the children enter the forest, and everything shifts, all the landmarks magically change, and they get lost, and then there's usually a witch of some kind." The trees rose to hide the last of the sun. The light went dull.

"At least a witch could give us directions," Herb grumbled, turning the steering wheel. His massive hands made it look like a toy.

"I think we passed that fountain before," she said, looking back.

A futile twenty minutes later, they found themselves at the Marigold gas station. A friendly teen in a navy blue uniform showed them the way out. It was so simple: two rights and a left. Herb couldn't believe he hadn't figured it out. Days later, when they heard Marigold Village was a retirement community, they laughed. Wrinkle Village, it was called by the locals. "We were lost for so long," Herb would say when telling the story, "we almost had to retire there."

That story got the biggest laugh yet at the housewarming party Pippa threw on their third Saturday in Marigold Village. Many of their dearest friends were there to quizzically usher in their new life in the development.

Sam Shapiro, an angular, balding man in his fifties, was probably the finest fiction writer in the country. The massive advance Herb had shelled out for his last novel had made the papers. He stood up and raised his glass to Herb and Pippa, his words firing out of him rapidly, in staggered clusters.

"We all know Herb Lee can be a bastard, but he's usually right. He hates self-pity more than anything, in writing and in life. That makes him a great editor, and a damn tough human being. I can't believe you're eighty, Herb. I guess that means I'm not thirty-five anymore. But I tell you. When it comes to words, Herb's instincts are pitch-perfect. With women, not so much. I think we all know what I'm talking about." Uneasy laughter rippled through the group, and one man guffawed. Sam continued: "So when he first told me he was going to marry Pippa, I thought, Here we go again! She seemed like . . . radioactive jam. Sweet, but deadly. Herb, however, disregarding my advice, followed his nose, as usual—a significant nose, I might add, not one of these trivial little noses we see all over town these days—and somehow he ended up with the most spectacular woman. I've known Pippa Lee for a quarter of a century, but I'll never really know her. She's a mystery, a cipher, something nearly extinct these days: a person not controlled by ambition or greed or a crass need for attention, but by a desire to experience life completely and to make life a little easier for the people around her. Pippa has nobility. Pippa has style."

Pippa's lips compressed slightly, her brow furrowed in a private signal of disapproval. She wanted him to glorify Herb, not her. Sam's quick bird's glance rested on her for a moment; reading her signal, he smiled and went on. "And Herb had the sense to recognize her for what she was, when it was damn hard to tell. So he can't be all bad. I drink to a man who, even at this late stage of his career, remains entirely unpredictable. I can't decide what I think of your choice to move from Gramercy Park to Marigold Village, Herb. If it's humble, or practical, or perverse. But as long as Pippa keeps making that butterflied lamb, I'll even caddie for you, if that's what it comes to."

"I don't think you'd be much of a caddie, Sam," said Herb, his mouth creasing into a lopsided grin, as it did whenever he made a crack.

"Never underestimate a hungry Jew!" called out Sam Shapiro.

"I think it's sort of amazing," said a hurt, adenoidal voice. Moira Dulles was a poet who had been living with Sam for the past few years. She was sitting cross-legged on the floor, at Herb's feet. "I mean, you left everything behind. Pippa, you are so courageous to just get up and go, start a new life . . ."

Pippa watched her fragile friend with concern. She hoped Sam didn't hear the tears in her voice. "It feels free," said Pippa. "No more big households to take care of."

"Don't wreck my illusions," said Sam. "You are the icon of the Artist's Wife: placid, giving, intelligent, beautiful. Great cook. They don't make 'em like that anymore." Moira Dulles gave him a black look, which he ignored. "And Herb doesn't even deserve her, he's not an artist. I never thought of that before! The one true artist's wife left in the modern world, and she goes to a publisher!" He cackled, then scraped his breath in with a donkey's bray.

"She wasn't like that when I married her," said Herb. "I tamed her."

"Oh, shut up." Pippa smiled, drifting into the kitchen and wondering if Sam was teasing Herb too hard. Ben, Pippa and Herb's son, was scouring the roasting tin, glancing up at the party through the hatch that looked out on the dining area. Still in law school, he already had the bad posture and good-natured pessimism of a middle-aged man. He scrutinized his mother through round, professorial glasses.

"I hope Herb is okay," Pippa said, lighting a small blowtorch and turning it on fifteen pots of crème brûlée. The layer of sugar on each one bubbled and darkened to the color of molasses.

"Mom, he's fine. Nothing could put a dent in his ego."

"That's what you think."

"It's you I'm worried about."

"Oh, I'm fine, sweetheart."

"Your problem is, you're too adaptable. The adaptable cipher." Pippa patted Ben's arm. He was always protecting her from harm, whether she wanted him to or not. In the next room, Herb was talking intently to Sam, hunched forward in his chair. He was still so handsome, Pippa thought. Eighty years old with a full head of hair, his own teeth. When was it all going to implode?

"You should do it, too," he was telling Sam. "If you manage to get old. I recommend it. Turned my whole life into cash. Giving it to them in increments. Otherwise it takes years for the estate to be processed, and then the state takes half."

"I thought you loved paying taxes!" interjected Don Sexton, a screenwriter whose elongated vowels made him sound like he belonged in *The Philadelphia Story*.

"That's right!" said Phyllis, his sharp-witted wife. "You always said you wished the government would tax *more*."

"I'm not funding this fucking war," Herb said.

"Ah—so it comes down to ethics, after all," said Sam. "I was rooting for perversity, myself."

"Stop boiling it all down," growled Herb. But he was enjoying being kidded. Pippa suddenly adored Sam Shapiro. He was hitting just the right tone of jocular disrespect with Herb. She had been so worried that people would start to act differently now that the invincible man was in an old people's facility. Treating it like a crazy joke—that was just the thing. The great Herb Lee, heroic owner of one of the last independent publishing houses in the country, virile champion of the Great American Novel—admitting to being old. It seemed unreal to everyone in that room. His frailty made their own middle age palpable. They were up next.

Moving to a retirement community was the last thing Pippa had expected from Herb, but then again, she had learned to accept swift changes in tack from her husband. Beneath Herb's steady-handed, unflappable demeanor lurked a profound impulsiveness; he had bought manuscripts, left publishing houses and even marriages with sudden, lurching decisiveness all his life. Pippa knew that Herb trusted his own instincts deeply, to the point of superstition; perhaps that was all he trusted. Once his internal compass needle moved, that was it—something was going to change. So when he came home, laughing, a pamphlet for Marigold Retirement Village in his fist, saying, "This is that place we got lost that time!"—then spent the afternoon flipping through the glossy pages in his study, she sensed something was brewing. In the end, he sold the idea to her as a practical solution: "I've got five, ten years at the most. What do we need the beach house for anymore? The kids are gone. Manhattan is a pain in the ass. We're hemorrhaging money you could use down the line. We liquidate our assets, Pippa, and then when I go, you have most of the money in your pocket. You can travel, buy a small place downtown. If we sell everything, you'll be free." But Pippa smelled a whiff of fear in this bluster; Herb had had two heart attacks in the space of a week the previous year. For the six subsequent months, she'd had to do everything for him. He couldn't make it up a flight of stairs. Now he napped more than he used to, but he was vigorous again, stronger in some ways, what with his near-perfect diet and all the exercise he was doing. But those excruciating days, when sudden, extreme age was foisted on him and Pippa, had made an indelible mark on their lives. Herb was, Pippa knew, terrified of having her become his nurse. Marigold Village was a sort of preemptive strike against decrepitude, cutting to the chase. It was, in fact, pure Herb: he was unsentimental, realistic, and utterly unwilling to be unmanned.

The fact that Sam Shapiro, who had become Herb's best friend over the past three decades, happened to live fifteen minutes away, was both a boon and a bit of an embarrassment, Pippa knew. Because Sam had followed Herb from one publishing house to another for years before Herb started his own press. Sam had been so loyal to Herb, in fact, that people began to wonder if the great Shapiro needed his editor a little too badly. The air of triumph that Sam exuded upon learning of the move—as if Herb had moved to follow *him*—irritated Herb, even if he *was* just ribbing. In all his relationships, Herb was the master, the desired one. To topple this pyramid would shake the foundations of his personality. Pippa watched Sam carefully for any evidence of a shift in the dynamic of the friendship. She, too, needed Herb to maintain his aura of strength. Tending him in the months after his heart attacks had been confusing. She had loved him perhaps more deeply than ever before, but the shape of their relationship had begun to warp in troubling ways. When they met, he had been her rescuer. For him to be dependent on her embarrassed both of them.

So they sold the house in Sag Harbor with its gray shingles, its cozy rooms layered, decade by decade, with paintings, rugs, objects, photographs. The children's rooms, still cluttered with horse jumping medals and band posters, the expansive master bedroom with its vast bed, the picture window Pippa sat in front of every Sunday, reading the paper or gazing at the birds—the whole of it snapped up one rainy Tuesday by a real estate developer and his wife. The apartment on Gramercy Park went to a couple of childless ophthalmologists. Though Pippa was heartsick to lose these places she had loved, she was surprised to feel released as well. To shed much of what they owned, to be free from superfluity—the impulse had rung out faintly within her for years, like the occasional beep of a cell phone lost deep in an apartment. But it was muffled by the joys, the comforts, the dilemmas of everyday life as a happily married, well-off woman, a dedicated mother, generous hostess, a woman who seemed to those who knew her to be among the most gracious, the kindest, the loveliest, the most unpretentious and most reassuring ladies they had ever met.

Pippa returned to the dining room carrying the tray of crème brûlée. Herb wasn't meant to have so many eggs and so much fat, but she figured that once in a while he should have what he loved, the way he always had, before the doctors caught up with him. Besides, Pippa loved giving pleasure, and every cook knows that lamb and crème brûlée elicit more sighs at the table than flounder and fruit salad. She watched as the guests broke through the little rinks of caramelized sugar with their spoons, bringing the thick, vanilla-scented cream into their mouths.

Cake

Next morning, Pippa was alone in the living room, supine as an odalisque in a turquoise raw silk kimono shirt and jeans. Her rather flat, feline face, with its high cheekbones and almond-shaped, upturned gray eyes, was framed by hair tinted the color of rose gold. Even in middle age, she resembled a Madonna in a Flemish painting, but rounder, juicier. Her head resting on a Moroccan pillow whose geometric pattern was intended to break up the monotony of the taupe Swedish Modern couch she'd bought to go with the clean lines of the condo, she surveyed her living room with satisfaction. Nothing here was extraneous. She had deliberately rescued each vase, bowl, painting from the morass of belongings that the family had built up over the years, most of which she had given to the children or donated to charity with uncharacteristic abandon when they moved to Marigold Village, storing only the few important pieces she thought she or the kids might one day miss. Each object Pippa had selected to survive this merciless culling now seemed charged with memory, isolated as it was from its peers in this sterile backdrop devoid of associations, walls painted dove gray: the luminous red glass ashtray Herb and Pippa bought in Venice on their honeymoon; her mother's treasured heart-shaped candy dish decorated with tiny shamrocks; the conch shell that her children had held up to their ears long ago, transported expressions on their faces, as they listened to the rush of the sea.

This house makes me feel strange, Pippa thought languorously, propping herself up on her elbow and taking a pair of brand-new binoculars from the coffee table. The sliding glass doors were open, and Pippa squinted through the powerful lenses at a wall of emerald green lawn with an opal of sparkling blue, a tiny, artificial lake—one of the many that dotted Marigold Village—at its center. She jerked the binoculars back and forth until she spied a bird, an oriole, nervously hopping on a willow branch. The bird had a black hood and saffron yellow chest feathers, fading into white at the abdomen. It looked precisely like the glossy picture of a Baltimore oriole in Pippa's manual, *Birds of the East Coast*, which she had bought at the Marigold bookstore only a week before.

On the day she purchased the manual, she noticed a sign on the bulletin board in the bookstore: "Marigold reading group meets every Thursday evening at seven. New members welcome." This caught her interest. It might be a good way to meet people. The following Thursday, she was knocking on the door of the prescribed unit, wearing one of Herb's shirts and a loose linen skirt. She felt she should hide her still solid body from the old women. It seemed only kind. A tiny lady with the tight white curls and pull-on trousers of the nearly aged swung open the door. "Another young one!" she pronounced rather loudly, half-looking over her shoulder. "Come on in. Very exciting, us old crones like new blood." Pippa introduced herself, walked into the living room, and saw a group of women in their sixties, seventies, and eighties seated in a circle like a witches' coven, purses tucked by their sides; in each of their laps lay a paperback copy of Sam Shapiro's latest novel, *Mr. Bernbaum Presents*. Pippa nearly bust out laughing. This was too much.

"I'm Lucy Childers," said the woman who had answered the door. "This is, let's see . . . Emily Wasserman, Ethel Cohen, Jean Yelding, Cora O'Hara, and— Where's Chloe?" Just then, the other "young one" came out from behind the bathroom door. Chloe was of an indeterminate age; her taut face was frozen in a semi-smile, having been ratcheted up several notches and enhanced by prominent cheekbones that looked like Ping-Pong balls under her skin. The two swollen halves of her upper lip drooped suggestively, like a set of red velvet curtains tied at the corners of her mouth, Pippa thought. The tip of her nose was pinched, as though a pair of fingers had squeezed a clay sculpture as a prank. Her eyelids seemed Krazy-Glued open a little too wide. She spoke in a very quiet, level voice, as one might speak to a child having a tantrum.

"It's lovely to meet you," she said, her startled eyes staring out of that approximation of a face like a prisoner peering out of a chink in a stone wall. Pippa said something polite and looked away, feeling a mix of pity and repulsion.

"This is Chloe's last meeting with the club," Lucy Childers said. "Her husband has recently passed, and she's moving back to the city."

"I'm sorry," said Pippa.

"Thank you," whispered Chloe.

Lucy Childers perched herself on the edge of the couch, back straight, her small feet in their white leather nurse's shoes lined up beside each other neatly, and opened the discussion with her own erudite thoughts, one tiny, stiff hand chopping the air each time she made a point, then moving it swiftly to the side, as though scraping peelings off a table. Lucy admired the symmetry of the book, the careful pacing, the slow but steady drip feed of information—not too much, not too little; she called it a "mystery of character." Then she turned to Chloe, who murmured, "It's a mean book, but I liked it." Pippa tried to shrug off the unwelcome mix of dread and kinship she felt with this person.

The oriole flew off. Pippa moved the binoculars down a bit, found Herb's red Converse sneakers. She followed his brown, skinny legs, the little hill of his belly, until she came to his rugged face, lower jaw clamped over front teeth in a grimace of concentration as he read a four-inch-thick manuscript on the lawn chair. The truth was, Herb hadn't retired. He was running the company from here, buying manuscripts, making deals.

A household list filed through Pippa's mind on an endless loop, the way the breaking headlines run under the TV news: *dry cleaning . . . toilet paper . . . plant fertilizer . . . cheese . . .* She had been lying in this luxurious position dreamily for half an hour, having cleaned the house and planned dinner by ten. The circle of the artificial pond, Herb's legs, the brilliant, green lawn . . . Pippa wished she could paint it. It was an odd desire for her; she always said of herself, almost proudly, surrounded as she was by creative folk, that she had no talent of any kind.

The buzz of the doorbell startled her. She sat up and swiveled around to see Dot Nadeau waiting behind the screen door. Dot was a bleach blonde with leathery skin and a sultry New Jersey voice. She lived just across the artificial lake, in 1272. In their late sixties, Dot and her husband, Johnny, were among the younger residents. Pippa, at fifty, was practically a child bride.

"Do you have a minute?" Dot asked in a muted tone. She looked harried.

"Sure. I'm supposed to be doing errands. But who cares," said

Pippa. They sat down in the kitchen. Pippa poured out a cup of coffee and handed it to Dot. "Is everything okay?" she asked.

"Well, we're fine, but . . . my son, Chris. Remember I told you about him?"

"In Utah?"

"Yes. He's thinking of relocating, and . . . he might be coming east."

"Oh, well, that would be nice, if they would move near you."

"The thing is, he's having trouble . . . It's just a mess, Pippa, a real mess." There were tears in Dot's eyes. Pippa checked to see that Herb was still ensconced on his lawn chair and fetched Dot a Kleenex.

"What is it?" asked Pippa. She felt awkward. She didn't know Dot very well. They'd had coffee a couple of times, but they'd never gotten past the pleasantry stage.

"He's had some kind of crisis with his wife, and he's left her, and he's lost his job—it wasn't even a real job, he was working in a men's shelter. How do you lose a job like that? I think he's living in his car. Thank God there are no kids. I don't know what to do."

"Well, he's an adult, I mean . . . what can you do?"

"He was always sort of half-baked, you know what I mean?"

Pippa wondered what Dot meant. Was the boy retarded? A drunk? Stunted in some way?

"It's painful, but sometimes you just have to accept that they are who they are. I mean, I feel that about mine." Tender Ben and tyrannical Grace. Now and forever. Nothing to be done. As if on cue, Ben walked in pulling a well-worn seersucker jacket over his sloped shoulders. Whenever Pippa saw him, she was amazed he was no longer a boy. "Hello, darling," she said. "Dot, this is my son, Ben."

"The lawyer!" said Dot, gazing at him admiringly.

"Not yet," said Ben.

"Columbia, right?" asked Dot. Immediately Pippa felt a pang of guilt for having a son in law school when Dot's boy was unemployed and possibly homeless.

Dot turned to Pippa. "You're right," said Dot. "I knew I should come to you. I had a feeling. I'm just going to let him cry it out on his own. He can't come running to me every time his life falls apart. It's no favor to him."

"Of course he knows if he's ever really in trouble . . ."

"He has me." Dot hugged Pippa and left.

Ben bit into an apple. "What were you right about?"

"I have no idea," said Pippa. "She said her son was half-baked, and I said sometimes you have to accept things the way they are."

"Well, she left satisfied, anyway."

"Half-baked?" said Herb, who had come in when he heard Ben's voice. "Is that code for half-wit?"

Pippa took a blood pressure cuff from a drawer, Velcroed it onto Herb's arm, and started pumping it up. Ben stood to read the dial with her.

"Since when are you two on the staff of Mount Sinai?" asked Herb.

"Don't get mad," said Pippa. "Your blood pressure goes up."

"How about if I hang myself?" said Herb with a grim smile. "What happens then?"

"A little appreciation for your ministering angel, Dad," said Ben in a jocular, warning tone.

Herb slid the local paper across the table, scanned the front page, frowning. He hated having his blood pressure taken in front of people, even the kids. Pippa could feel his petulance rise up in her like a tide. She should have waited till Ben had gone. Shit, she thought. Oh, well. She poured Ben a bowl of Grape-Nuts cereal and listened to the swift animal crunch his teeth made when he ate it, the same crunch they had made when he was five. She loved that sound.

"Oh, by the way," Ben said. "Stephanie brought a cat home from the pound."

"Another one!" she exclaimed, laughing. Ben's girlfriend couldn't resist lame animals. She was a dear, earnest person. Pippa was sure they would produce a fine family, as long as Ben didn't get distracted by someone more exciting. But he didn't seem to crave thrills, strangely enough.

Ben stood up. "Back to the salt mines," he said.

"Are you still working on that same paper?" she asked.

He nodded, pushing his glasses back up his nub nose. "The paper that ate Ben Lee."

"You're just thorough," Pippa said.

"I actually think I might be onto something," he said.

"Isn't that great?" she said, beaming. As she walked him out to his car, he put his arm around her.

"Mom," he said. "Come to the city next week and we can have lunch. Or dinner. You can stay over."

"We're having lunch with Grace on Wednesday."

"Oh. Right. If you want to get together another time, call me, okay?"

"I will," she said. "Of course I will. Stop worrying about me, will you?"

"I just want you to have a little fun," he said.

After Ben drove off, Pippa stood quietly staring after him. The list, which had rolled by under Dot a couple of times while she was talking, came into full view now: *cheese . . . dry cleaning . . . plant fertilizer . . .*

It was only three minutes to the mini-mall. Pippa drove over, picked up all the things she needed at the grocery store, dropped off the dry cleaning, then eased herself back onto the searing car seat and started creeping through the parking lot. She was in terror of mowing over one of the aged people, dressed in pink and pistachio, their tanned faces collapsed, shriveled skin coming away from knees and elbows.

✳ ✳ ✳

The relentless buzzing of a lawn mower dragged Pippa from a black sleep like a body from a river. As she opened her eyes, she felt a dull pain in her temples. She wanted water, and coffee. Sitting up in the bed, she glanced at Herb. As a rule she tried not to look at him when he was sleeping. Eyes shut tight, mouth slack, he looked like an ancient, fragile old man. She turned away and stood. She knew that when his icy blue eyes, with their conquering stare, opened, she would feel reassured again. She loved this man so much. It was a condition she had tried to cure herself of many times; the symptoms could be painful. But she'd given up the fight long ago. She was the woman who loved Herb Lee. Oh, and many other things besides, she thought to herself as she pulled on her cotton robe the color of new leaves. Mother. Two decent, productive human beings living in the world because of me. That's not nothing. She walked into the kitchen, squinting in the blinding light. Everything was white. Formica table, counter, tile floor, lost their edges, bled into a field of light, their perspective flattened. Shadows from the window casings threw a blue grid over the room. With her vision blurred from sleep, the effect was so dazzlingly abstract that she had to take a moment to get her bearings, and when she did she was so confused by what she saw that she questioned her own memory.

The table had been set chaotically, plates scattered at random, as if tossed by a furious domestic. Some of them had chocolate cake on them. Others were bare. Pippa noticed something the color of peanut butter spread on one of the slices of chocolate cake. She sniffed it cautiously. It was peanut butter. Yet she distinctly remembered sponging down the table the night before. The place had been immaculate. A chill went up her spine, and she swiveled around, imagining a malevolent pair of psychotic eyes staring at her from the living room—some escaped lunatic, brandishing a dirty cake knife. Seeing no one, she went to the kitchen door, tried it. Locked. She walked around the house, checked every door, every window. All locked. No one had come in. It must have been Herb. But they had gone to bed together at eleven. Herb had fallen asleep first. She tried to imagine him getting up to let people in, after midnight, for chocolate cake and peanut butter. It was out of the question. Then how had the cake gotten there? She cleared the table, scraped plates into the garbage, and stacked them in the dishwasher. Made coffee.

She was sitting at the table drinking a cup when Herb walked in, opened the front door, and dragged the local paper off the mat.

"So," she said. "I can't believe you had a party and didn't invite me."

"What are you talking about?" he said, putting on his reading glasses.

"You left all the plates out."

"What plates?"

"Herb, there were six plates with chocolate cake on the table this morning. Or there were six plates. Two of them didn't have any cake on them. One of the slices had peanut butter on it."

Herb sat and looked at her. "Have you gone stark raving mad?" he said, laughing.

"At first I thought someone came into the house, but the doors are all locked." There was a pause as this sank in.

"Does anyone else have a key?"

"Well, I guess the maintenance people. And Miss Fanning."

"The cleaning lady? She lives in New Milford. Why would she drive all the way over here for chocolate cake? We better check if anything is missing." Nothing was missing. Pippa called Miss Fanning and pretended she was confirming her for Monday. Then she casually asked her what she'd been up to the night before. There was a pause. "Bowling?" the woman answered tentatively. Herb called the administrative offices to register a complaint. They asked if he wanted to call the police. Herb declined. "I suppose you could call it a victimless crime," he said, his nostrils expanding slightly. The man on the other end of the phone chuckled politely.

Pippa called a locksmith, had the locks changed. This time, they gave no one a key. A week went by. Pippa kept thinking about the cake. It had to be Herb. He had forgotten. He was losing his mind. Pippa watched him with special care now. Every time he misplaced his glasses or forgot someone's name, she felt her suspicion grow. Then, the next Sunday morning, she walked into the kitchen and found carrot sticks planted in a bowl of vanilla frosting. A frying pan with the remains of fried ham cemented to the bottom. More dirty plates. This time she woke Herb and showed him. They looked at each other.

"Maybe you should see a doctor," she said.

Herb was furious. "Okay, if I have Alzheimer's so be it, I'll kill myself. But first I need to see the evidence." He drove straight to the electronics store in the mini-mall and bought a small surveillance camera with a wall mount, then paid the man from the store to install it in the corner, where the wall met the ceiling. The guy was up on a ladder, sweat pouring down his face. Pippa turned on the air conditioner. "This must seem a little strange to you," she said.

"You'd be surprised what people do for entertainment in this place," said the man.

"Really?"

"Yeah, but I've never seen it in the kitchen before."

"Oh. No. It's not—it's—" Pippa let it go. She'd rather have him think they were filming themselves humping on the kitchen table than chronicling her husband's descent into inanity.

An hour later, Pippa was straightening out the living room when she looked out the plate-glass window. Across the pond, in the Nadeaus' driveway, a U-Haul was hitched up to a bright yellow truck with an orange shell clamped over the bed. The shell had windows with ratty blue and red gingham curtains pulled shut inside. Pippa could see Dot gesturing to a dark-haired man who was carrying a cardboard box. Pippa picked her bird-watching binoculars off the coffee table and trained them on the young man. He had a T-shirt with "What?" printed on the back of it. So the half-baked son was moving in after all! It was funny about Dot, she thought. It felt so natural, talking to her. It made Pippa feel like a different person. Dot knew her out of context. A few months ago, in her old life, she would no sooner have had a friendship with Dot Nadeau than flown around the room. Their friends were editors, novelists, critics, poets. Yet Pippa had never felt fully at ease in their hypercivilized company. Only with her twins, when they were young—only then had she felt fully secure in who she was. Grace and Ben had looked up at her with such certainty in their little faces, and called her Mama. They knew, so she knew. Now her babies were gone. They called sometimes, came home to visit. Occasionally they all went out to lunch together. But they didn't look at Pippa the way they once had. Ben was still so sweet to her. He had always needed little, expected everything, received what he expected. He was born thoughtful but secure. Pippa's feeling for him was simple, ample, easy. But Grace—that was a real fuckup. Pippa felt stupid and bumbling in her daughter's company, and somehow guilty, as though she had let Grace down by amounting to so little. And there was something more.

As a very young child, Grace had been needy, clutching at her mother like a baby monkey. Her love for Pippa was possessive and competitive. Though she adored her twin, she tried to edge Ben out of her mother's embraces, desperate to bask in her love alone. The day after her fourth birthday she sat down at Pippa's feet, opened a book, and read the whole thing out loud. Pippa was astounded; the child had been completely intractable when it came to reading, refusing to sound out letters at all. Little Grace looked up at her mother then and, with furrowed brow, asked, "*Now* do you love me more than Ben?" Pippa swept the girl up into her lap and hugged her, feeling a sting of guilt like a poisoned needle in her sternum. Because she knew what Grace was getting at. There were flashes of jealous intensity in her daughter's love that Pippa found domineering, devouring, even repellent in moments that came and, mercifully, dissolved again into the otherwise sunny landscape of their daily lives. Once, watching a ship disappear over the lip of the ocean, Grace said to Pippa, "I own you as far as the eye can see." Though she did not recognize it, in some secret part of Pippa's mind, her daughter's wish to possess her utterly echoed another love, a deadly, sweet, and voracious passion that had all but suffocated Pippa in her youth.

Yet, never mind, in spite of it all, now that Grace was grown she was a triumph! So sophisticated, so courageous. Pippa found herself watching her sneakily, out of the corner of her eye. And occasionally, in her daughter's recklessness, her lust for adventure, her desire for experience, she recognized herself, a self that had vanished long ago. How had it happened? How could she have changed so much? She remembered the morning she looked in the mirror and saw three white, bent hairs sticking out of her head. They had looked obscene to her, like stray pubic hairs escaping from the crotch of a bathing suit. Now, beneath the reddish blond tint, her hair was white. Pippa was a placid, middle-aged woman. And Herb was eighty years old. The thought of it made her laugh. Life was getting so unreal. More and more, the past was flooding into her, diluting the present like water poured into wine.

Herb walked in then. Pippa turned. "Do you need anything?" she asked.

Herb sat down and patted the pillow beside him. "How's my pal?" he asked.

"I'm okay," she said.

"Are you sad that you're living in Wrinkle Village?"

"I have to fill up my days more. But I'm not sad. I think it's sort of romantic, starting again like this, with so little stuff." Herb smiled sadly and lay back on the cushions. His skin, bronzed from all that time on the patio, was creased like a rock face, his eyes points of light.

"Always looking on the bright side," he said to her.

"Why can't it be?" There was a pause.

"Maybe we should move back to the city," he said.

She laughed. "We just sold our apartment!"

"So we buy another one."

"Really?"

"No, of course not. It's just hard thinking this is the end of the line."

Pippa put her hand on his knee and looked around the room. She wondered what she could make for him. Maybe a glass of carrot juice. She had begun to feel a kind of desperation when they were alone sometimes, as if everything that they could possibly say to each other had already been said, and now language was useless.

"That was good cheese yesterday," Herb said.

"It was Vacherin—I was so excited to find it."

"I love that cheese."

Another Woman

A week later Pippa woke up with one arm asleep, pinned beneath her side. She felt as though her body had been crushed into the mattress through the night, her face mashed into the pillow. There was a rotten taste in her mouth. She sat up stiffly, shaking the blood back into her numb limb, which flopped helplessly from side to side like a separate being.

In the kitchen, a thick, yellow continent of what looked like scrambled egg was congealing in the center of the Formica table. A box of chocolates lay open and ransacked in the middle of the mess. A fork was balanced on the edge of a chair.

Remembering the surveillance camera, Pippa snapped her head back and looked up. The thing stared down at her with its cold glass eye, the red Record light blinking ominously. She couldn't bear for Herb to witness himself like this. Every day she would wake up extra early; if there was evidence, she planned to clean it up, erase the tape. He would never know. Pippa wiped up the mess as fast as she could, scraped off a smear of dried egg yolk with her fingernail, her vision blurred with tears.

She went into the den and shut the door, then shoved the tape into the mouth of the VCR. Her heart was pumping wildly in her chest. Seen from above, in black and white, like so many holdup videos Pippa had watched on television, her kitchen seemed sinister, like a crime scene. Pippa fast-forwarded the tape. Nothing. Nothing. Then a figure in white sped by, right through the frame. Pippa rewound the tape and hit Play. The room was empty again. A muffled, banging sound emerged from the TV. Then, a woman shuffled into the kitchen. It was Pippa/not Pippa. The stranger walked with an eerie, graceless gait, her posture slumped, her gaze downcast. This creature disappeared from the screen, came back into the edge of it, and started stirring eggs in a frying pan. She then dumped the eggs on the table, sat down in a hunched position, and scraped forkfuls of them off the Formica, shoveling them into her mouth with mechanical motions. Pippa watched herself with incredulity and revulsion. There was something inhuman about the scene.

She smashed the bedroom door open with her fist. Herb sat up, stunned with sleep. "What—" She was next to him, burrowing her head in his chest, her cheeks wet with tears. "It's me," she said. "Herb, it's me—"

"Slow down, pal. What are we talking about here?"

"The chocolate cake. And the eggs, and— I saw it on the video, oh, it's horrible." He held her like that for a while, stroking her head.

"I must be walking in my sleep," she said.

"I don't remember any eggs."

"This morning there were eggs. All over the table. She—I— dumped them on the table and— Oh, my God, this makes me feel insane."

"Didn't you do it when you were a kid?"

"That was just a couple of times I walked around." At fourteen, she would pace the upstairs hall of the rectory, her pillow under her arm, till her insomniac mother led her back to bed.

"You sleepwalking is a hell of a lot better than me being senile,"

Herb said, rolling onto his side and drawing Pippa in, raising his knees so she was resting in a little chair of him. She felt his warmth along her back, tucked her feet between his warm, furry calves.

"I guess so."

"Sleepwalkers are a dime a dozen, honey. You can't even get off a murder rap with that defense anymore. So don't get any ideas." She was already feeling reassured. Herb had a way of casting light on muddled thoughts, dissipating the shadows. This rational viewpoint was inherited from his father, a darkly funny man who despised religion, all exaggeration, and musicals. He was the embodiment of deadpan. Herb's mother had died of cancer when he was two; for years his father was a loving, if gruff, protector. He owned a profitable appliance store in Queens until he lost his business in the spending vacuum of the depression. With economic ruin came a darkening of Mr. Lee's humor. Ribbing of his intelligent son turned to bullying and, finally, a bitter, brutal dismissiveness of Herb as an effete intellectual, a fag even. For much as he pitied the dupes that looked to God as a balm to their wounded spirits, Mr. Lee reserved his special disdain for those who thought they were better than other people just because they read books. Herb was hurt by this rejection at first, but mercifully it absolved him of feeling guilty for bettering his old man. He left for college on a scholarship at nineteen, alone in the world, determined never to be bullied by another human being for the rest of his life, his taste in literature already formed by the very man he had come to hate so much. He mistrusted extravagant metaphor, favored the driest prose. As Herb saw it, he was always having to dehumidify Pippa's mind.

She felt a touch against her tailbone, and then it was gone—then back again, insistent, like a creature pressing its nose against her back. She turned, closed her eyes, and kissed him.

She was lying beside Herb, her eyes still a bit puffy from crying, when there was a knock on the door. She knelt on the bed and peered out the window, pushing the curtain aside. It was Dot. "Doesn't that woman have a phone?" Herb asked. Pippa pulled on her robe and walked into the kitchen.

"Hi!" purred Dot, standing on the threshold. She looked different this morning. Beneath the crazy network of sun worshiper's lines etched into her deflated skin, Pippa could discern the sweep of a strong jaw. Her brown eyes were sparkling. Dot must have been a knockout.

"You look lovely," said Pippa.

"Are you kidding? I'm on my way to the beauty parlor. Have you been crying?" asked Dot.

"It's just allergies," said Pippa. "Would you like to come in?"

Dot's eyes rose to the surveillance camera, then back to Pippa. "I came to invite you over to meet Chris," she said. "Herb is welcome too, of course, only I don't want to disturb him."

"Chris?"

"My son. He's moved in with us. It's perfectly legal."

"Of course it is."

"I mean, in the charter it says you can have relatives under fifty stay for up to six months. I'm just inviting a few neighbors, you know. I don't want anyone to think we're sneaking around."

"I would love to meet him. When should I come over?"

"Around four would be good. We can all have a drink and be home in time to make dinner. I hope you don't think it's rude that I'm not inviting everyone over to eat."

"Not at all."

"It's just, I hate cooking in large quantities. It never comes out."

As Pippa closed the door, she tried not to wonder about Dot.

She sensed a tragic shadow there, a wound. Pippa suffered from an excess of empathy. Sometimes, she found the mystery of other people almost unbearable to contemplate: rooms within rooms inside each of them, an endless labyrinth of contradictory qualities, memories, desires, mirroring one another like an Escher drawing, baffling as a conundrum. Kinder to perceive people as they wished to be seen. After all, that's what Pippa wanted for herself: to be accepted as she seemed.

Motherhood and Cigarettes

A little after four o'clock, Pippa meandered over to Dot's house carrying a bottle of wine she had been keeping in reserve and wondering if she could possibly be pregnant in spite of the vestigial coil still lodged in her uterus like astronaut litter abandoned on the moon. Yet, no, rare as sex with Herb was these days, precautions were still necessary; eggs were meant to be fulminating inside her in this twilight of her fertility. The thought of a new baby now seemed absurd, even suffocating, much as she had loved being pregnant, addicted as she had been to the smell of her babies' necks, the soft crowns of their heads. That room was shut and locked; she couldn't pry it open.

Herb had opted to stay home from the party. Visiting a former dentist, his wife, and their half-baked son was not his idea of a good time. Pippa walked slowly, looking up at the gnarled branches of an oak tree, dark leaves shivering against the flat, blue sky. She felt hollowed out in a pleasant, staring way. The nightmare of the videotape seemed far off, yet it had left an aftertaste: wind flattening a patch of high grass by the side of the road with a hiss, an old man straining to pedal by her on a bicycle—everything that happened around her seemed to be gathering portent, like a fluffy white cloud augmenting itself, building up into a mountainous, darkening tower that threatened aircraft and frightened house pets with its ominous rumbling. She stopped and looked at the number of the house behind her. 1275. She had overshot the Nadeaus'. She backtracked and went up their front walk, identical to her own but for a large ceramic toadstool in the center of the front lawn. It was painted glossy red, with yellow spots on it. She knocked on the metal frame of the screen door. There was no answer, so she pushed the door open and walked into a layout just like her own but with a strikingly different décor.

The Nadeaus' living room was a visual explosion. Red ivy crawled up the wallpaper, the couch was paisley, the armchairs were various shades of pastel. A miniature Victorian town was laid out on a mahogany dresser: tiny, cast-metal buildings—dry goods store, church, train depot—lined a sinuous railroad track. A glossy red steam engine shuttled along the track in a joyless mechanical loop. Every other usable surface in the room was jammed with photographs. Faces upon faces crammed up against one another: generations of babies, schoolchildren, old people, soldiers, brides from every decade since 1910. Pippa tried to take it all in, her eyes darting around the room like an alarmed bird seeking a place to rest. At last her gaze alighted on Dot herself, sitting stiffly in a peach silk armchair in the corner, her chartreuse blouse and white slacks ironed, her hair a single, shining blond wave. She was staring ahead with a fixed expression. Pippa came up to her.

"Hi, Dot," she said.

Dot looked up at her with a steady, glittering stare. "Everyone is out back," she said hoarsely.

"Is everything all right?" Pippa asked.

"He won't come out," Dot said.

"Your son?"

"He's staying in his room. Can you imagine? A man of thirty-five

locks himself in his room when his parents throw him a party?"
Someone laughed outside. Pippa glanced out the plate-glass window. A few people were on the patio, talking. Johnny, Dot's husband, was listening to an ancient man, a drink in his hand, his head
cocked. Johnny was short, bullish, slightly bowlegged. He had rosy,
healthy-looking skin.

Dot stood up unsteadily and took the wine bottle from Pippa.
"It's cold! You shouldn't have. Let's open it." Pippa followed Dot into
the kitchen. Dot pulled out the cork and poured them each a glass
of wine. "To motherhood," Dot said, knocking back half the glass.

Outside, Pippa met a few of her neighbors. There were a couple of retired dentists, a saxophonist, a former chiropractor, a tiny
woman who had written a book on child psychology. The sax player,
a widower, was clearly hitting on the voluptuous wife of the chiropractor. They were both in their eighties. Pippa took it all in, stored
it so she could tell Herb later. Pippa was a little high from the wine.
She leaned back against the Nadeaus' trellis and felt her hips loosen
up, her left leg swing open. Living in Marigold Village made her feel
youthful. She was once again the youngest woman around, just as
she had been when she and Herb had first been together. Watching
a bent old woman laugh a few feet away, she flexed the strong muscles in her calves, stood up straighter, pressing her breasts against
her thin blouse. She felt the familiar arrogance of youth, as if her
age made her superior, as if it were to her credit.

Johnny Nadeau ambled over to her with his stiff-legged walk.
"Hello, Pippa, glad you could come. A little eye candy," he said,
winking.

"Thanks for having me, Johnny."

He leaned in to her and whispered emphatically: "I'd appre-
ciate it if you could keep an eye on Dot." She could smell pretzels

on his breath. "She's having a hard time. I know she talks to you."

"Sure," said Pippa, glancing at the spot where Dot had been. "Where is she?"

"She went back inside. I told her this was a bad idea," he said, shaking his head. Pippa started walking toward the sliding door. Again, the stage whisper: "Get her to drink a Coca-Cola."

Pippa walked into the living room. It was empty. She peeked into the kitchen. No Dot. She heard arguing, crying, coming from somewhere down the hall. She followed the sound, walking gingerly. Pippa imagined Dot and the half-baked son locked in a murderous embrace, Dot trying to drag him out to the party, the doughy son resisting, squeezing the breath out of her till she hung, limp and immobile, off his pasty arm. Pippa came to a bedroom door. They were in there. She could hear them. She knocked tentatively. The voices went silent.

"Dot?" she said.

"Who is it?" It was a man's voice.

"It's Pippa Lee. I . . . was just looking for Dot."

There was a fumbling noise, then the door swung open. A powerfully built man in his thirties, with a thin, ashen face and broken nose, stared through Pippa with a look of blank aggression, his mind on something else. His meaty, naked torso was tattooed with an intricately painted Christ. The Lord was portrayed in color, from the waist up; he was bare-chested and had very large wings. Pippa peered behind the son and saw Dot sitting on the bed. Her eyes were red from crying.

"Dot," Pippa said, struggling to keep her voice even. "Johnny asked me to find you."

"Look at me," said Dot. "I can't go out there." She blew her nose into a large tissue.

Pippa gamely held out her hand to the son. "I'm Pippa Lee," she said.

"Chris," said the son, taking her hand with a surprisingly gentle grip. "Pleased to meet you. I'm sorry you had to be party to our little . . . thing, here . . ." He now began rummaging through a duffel bag and pulled out a wrinkled shirt. Pippa noticed that the Christ's wings extended over the man's shoulders and partway down his back. Dot watched her decorated son with a sly expression as he tugged on the shirt, buttoned the buttons. "Take care of my mother," he said, fixing Pippa with an alarmingly frank gaze and backing up toward the wall. "I have to go." And with this, Chris climbed out the window and strode away. He had a rocking gait and leaned far back as he walked, chin tucked in, arms slightly curled, as though ready to be attacked. He opened the door of the yellow truck, swung himself onto the driver's seat, and sped off.

"He was such a sweet little boy," said Dot helplessly, shaking her head. "You can't imagine."

✳ ✳ ✳

Several days passed, and, though Chris Nadeau's bright yellow truck sped by Pippa on the road a few times, she heard nothing from Dot. She thought that perhaps shame about the scene at the party had made their friendship impossible. The son was scary. Poor Dot. To her surprise, Pippa found herself missing Dot a little bit. She wondered if she should call and see if she was okay, or if that would be awkward. The sleepwalking seemed to have evaporated. No new messes had appeared in the kitchen. Pippa felt a calm wash over her. The days passed in the quietest possible way. Ben called from the city every Sunday. Grace was in Paris, recovering from two weeks photographing in Kabul.

Pippa was still baffled as to how it had happened. One minute, it seemed, Grace was photographing dog shows for the *Hartford Courant*. The next, she was capturing horrendous images of maimed children, screaming women that showed up in *The New York Times*. Pippa was amazed by Grace's fierce pursuit of the truth at all costs. Yet a part of her wondered, as she stared into the eyes of yet another terrified person running through a sea of dust, if there wasn't something a little bit ruthless about photographing people in such distress. She hadn't asked the question of her daughter, but there it was anyway: Was there a moment when you had to choose between photographing a person and helping him? But at least she was doing something, Pippa thought. Drawing attention to. Herself. No. Not fair. To conflicts, injustices. As opposed to Pippa. Oh well, she thought as she thumbed through a luxuriously illustrated cookbook: osso buco. Lamb Milanese. Spaghetti alle vongole. At least Herb was appreciative. He loved being taken care of.

He had found a book written by an unknown, a high school history teacher in Idaho. It had come to him in a plain manila envelope, the address typed on a manual typewriter. When he saw it, he said, This is either a lunatic or the real thing. As it turned out, the book inside was that rare beast every publishing house is always praying for: an Easy Read of Quality. It was a historical romance, told in excruciating detail. Deeply moving. Expressive language. Would make a sweeping, epic film. Herb was serious about literature. He published most of the few giants left. But he was also a businessman, and receiving a novel like this in the mail was like winning the lottery. He could publish ten poets with the money this behemoth would bring in. It needed work, sure, but Herb was confident that, with some cutting and reshaping, it could be damn strong. He read the last of twelve hundred pages, folded his hands on the manuscript, and closed his eyes. He felt Pippa leaning over him as she bent to pick up his empty glass.

"I found a book," he said.

"Oh, great," said Pippa.

"A real cash cow," he said.

"Since when do you say 'cash cow'?"

"I never found one before, so I never said it."

"What's it about?"

"War. Romance. Bad weather."

"Is it good?"

"It's a certain kind of good. It's lowbrow for highbrows. Or highbrow for lowbrows. It's perfect summer reading for people who own multimillion-dollar beach homes."

"That used to be us."

"Not us," he said.

Pippa brought the glass into the kitchen. It was so strange, she thought. The closer Herb got to death, the more he thought about money.

Grace

Grace's jolt into the rarefied world of reportage photographers was unforeseen by everyone in the family, especially Grace. In college, she majored in Spanish with a minor in photography. The summer after she graduated, Ben took off to backpack through Europe with his girlfriend, Stephanie, also a future lawyer. Though the twins had gone to different colleges, Grace had assumed that, when they both graduated, she and Ben would live together—at least for a summer, to recapture the gleeful conspiracy of their life at home. But Ben felt he ought to grow up, become a man, be sane, not frolic around with his sister. So off he went to Europe with Stephanie, that loyal hound. Grace knew that Ben loved Stephanie for what she wasn't (neurotic, blunt, alluring, hilarious) as much as for what she was (constant, sweet, accommodating yet intelligent—a sort of modern-day Olivia de Havilland in *Gone with the Wind*). In essence, she knew her brother had chosen a girl as unlike herself as possible.

So, after graduation, uninterested in rooming with any of her college friends who were swarming into Brooklyn, Grace rented herself a one-bedroom apartment in Spanish Harlem with high, arched windows and mucus yellow linoleum on the floors, hoping to improve her Spanish and think about what to do next. She had enough money from her parents to avoid a job, for the summer anyway, if she lived frugally. She spent the first two weeks wandering around the neighborhood, picking through tag sale items laid out on the street: used communion dresses, worn paperbacks, the occasional comb—and eating rice and beans with fried plantains at the counter of her local restaurant while reading biographies of Lee Miller and Lawrence of Arabia. She furnished her apartment with two beanbag chairs (one maraschino red, one Fanta orange) and an ornate white wrought-iron bedstead. She didn't talk much to anyone. She enjoyed this removal from her surroundings even as she was immersed in them. She felt mute and contented, loaded with potential, yet entirely unproductive. She came to know every nook and cranny of her block; the dusty windows of the Assembly of God meetinghouse on the second floor of number 1125, the musty used bookstore in the basement of 1130, the botanica on the corner, which advertised cures for lovesickness, homesickness, and "most ailments of the soul and body." The bodega on the corner of 120th Street was run by a puffy-eyed, garrulous Dominican man and his taciturn grandson, a melancholic who moped behind the counter, his haunted, dark eyes, wasted face, and pointed goatee making him look like a figure out of an El Greco painting. The same five old men sat on folding chairs outside the bodega every day watching pedestrians, making bets on everything from the racetrack to who was going to step on a particularly large crack in the sidewalk as they passed by. Young women and girls walked proudly down the street in tight clothes, glossy hair scraped back from their exhausted faces, pushing strollers with babies or toddlers lolling inside. The wizened, high-haired lady who ran the Laundromat stood outside smoking and chatting with her neighbors when she wasn't folding sheets inside the picture window.

Grace came to think of that stretch of pavement on Lexington between East 120th and East 122nd streets as a world of its own. Though some people on the block had come to recognize Grace and said hello when they passed her or when she walked into their shops, she still felt relatively invisible. She was not a part of the life of the block; she was an accepted observer. Looking at her, you couldn't say she blended in, particularly. She had wild, blond hair that fell in angry ringlets around a pointed, intelligent face. Her body was tall, thin, and athletic, her breasts small and compact. Men always noticed her but rarely approached her; there was something mannish in her movements. From behind, with her slim hips and muscular shoulders, her relaxed posture, she could have been mistaken for a long-haired boy.

One night late, a bottle shattered in the street and woke Grace up. A man called out in Spanish; another man answered. Their arguing voices echoed in the cavernous apartment. Grace walked barefoot across the linoleum, trying to make out what was being said. A young woman was pleading; she had tears in her voice. Grace stood inches away from the windowsill, so she could not be seen, and peered down into the street. The three protagonists of the fight were leaning against two cars parked a few yards away from each other. She recognized the El Greco grandson of the bodega owner. She had never seen him so animated. He was flailing his arms, gesturing, calling the other man, an older, stocky fellow with his feet planted very far apart, "a liar and a fool" in Spanish. A slight girl of around fifteen, whom Grace had seen pushing her baby up and down the block, was hanging on to the grandson's arm, trying to pull him away. Several onlookers had gathered in a semicircle to watch the proceedings.

Grace stood transfixed by this dangerous and real drama unfolding below, as though in a box at the theater. For a long time, the two

men were in a stalemate, the El Greco grandson shrieking hysteri-
cally at the thickset stranger, the girl alternately trying to calm him
down and yelling at him to shut up, the stranger walking up to the
pair menacingly, then returning to the hood of his car, only to be
pelted with a new round of insults from the El Greco grandson. In
spite of this posturing, the stranger didn't seem very committed to
the argument; he even looked around him a few times, as if for a
more comfortable seat. But finally, the grandson said something that
got his goat. Grace didn't catch the meaning, but whatever it was, it
was the last straw. The stranger charged the grandson, flinging the
girl aside like a doll, and laid the boy flat with one punch. Then he
walked away, shaking his head. A few people gathered around the
grandson, who sat up slowly and, shaking off their solicitude, limped
away in the opposite direction. Grace felt very tired then and went
back to bed.

The next morning Grace woke up thinking about the Minolta
her parents had given her for graduation. She took the camera out
of its case and loaded it with film. That was the morning she began
to photograph in earnest. She spent the next two months document-
ing every waking hour of her block. The people already knew her, so
they tolerated her lens poking at them, even invited her into their
apartments occasionally. She photographed everything, everyone
she could—the Assembly of God Sunday service, the affable bodega
owner, the El Greco grandson, the old men sitting outside the
bodega, the Laundromat lady. She built her portfolio up image by
image, photographing day and night as if pursued. The resulting
stack of pictures showed obsessive commitment and a sharp eye.
She got an appointment with the editor of the *Hartford Courant*, a
paper she had heard was open to hiring young photographers. They
took her on. She spent the fall and winter chasing fire trucks

and photographing orange tape stretched around suburban houses where murders had occurred; by the following summer, she was on a plane bound for Louisiana to cover Hurricane Katrina for the *Courant* with a senior colleague. She slept just a few hours a night for the entire two weeks; there wasn't a moment of that tragedy she wanted to miss. The trip was oddly blessed for her; images of horror and hopelessness spiked with humor seemed to cohere inside her lens again and again. She couldn't seem to help being at the right place at the right time. The pictures she brought back were surreal: three children wearing rubber Halloween masks of George Washington, Elvis Presley, and Chucky discover the corpse of an aged man in an alley; a shivering dog stands perched on an island of garbage, surrounded by floating dolls; a big woman dances around in the remains of her decimated living room, wallpaper hanging from the walls like shreds of skin. Grace returned to the *Courant* a star. Within two years she was working for the Getty Photo Archive, touching down in Kabul.

Grace was perplexed by what seemed to others to be talent yet felt to her like something else. Her luck was uncanny to her. It was as though she herself was creating the images, dreaming them onto the emulsion. It was, perhaps, the way she was able to forget herself, to disappear, to become transparent when she photographed, that made it so hard for her to take credit for her own work. Sometimes, she was swallowed up by the experience so completely that she could not remember having taken the pictures at all. Yet she had, of course, and anything paranormal about her new chosen profession was, she knew, adolescent hokum she would never have shared with a soul, except her twin, whom she treated with the brutal frankness, the mocking acuity she reserved for her own internal life.

Ben was, for Grace, an extension of her self. Some of what she was doing by working so hard, she knew, or rather saw dimly in some back room of her mind like a mouse one perceives scurrying along a wall out of the corner of one's eye, was getting away from Ben by surpassing him. Their relationship was absolutely perfect. It was so perfect, in fact, that Grace needed no one else. She had not, as the psychotherapist she saw for a few months in college, Dr. Sarah Kreutzfeldt, put it, "individuated completely." Grace's chief complaint, when she first availed herself of the University Health Services, was that she couldn't fall in love. She thought there must be something wrong with her. There had been one obvious opportunity: an intelligent, interesting, funny boy with sparkling eyes and a caved-in, question mark–shaped torso. She kept teetering on the brink of love with him, and even spent blissful hours in the zone of extreme fondness. But all it took was one flabby joke, a botched allusion, a moment of strained sincerity, and she felt a leaden seal forming in her gut, cutting her off from the suddenly former object of her affection as swiftly as a pair of scissors severing two sausage links. Back to square one.

She blamed Ben for it all—smart, funny, endearing, infuriating Ben. No one would ever make her laugh so much; no one could peer at the world with the same good-natured, even loving derision. After a couple of weeks of looking at this same observation from different angles, her sessions with Dr. Kreutzfeldt were drying up. Grace was embarrassed by the triviality of her problem. She chided herself for even initiating the therapy, but now she felt obliged to keep it up. She began to resent Dr. Kreutzfeldt. She became sullen and uncommunicative during the sessions, staring out the window at the students walking from the library to the dorms, the dorms to the math building.

This behavior piqued Sarah Kreutzfeldt's interest. She had always sensed some subterranean explosion in the girl, a mine going off so far inside her that even she was unaware of it. When Grace first stomped into her office, she was surprised. This girl did not seem like Larken material. A very small university, Larken catered to the privileged painters, writers, critics, poets, and performance artists of the future. The teaching was not so much rigorous as expansive, the teachers stretching their courses to the point of deformity in order to encompass the whimsy of the students. Terms like *participatory* and *student-centered* took top billing in the school brochure. Most of the students had a vague, haunted look, like possums disturbed from their burrows in the middle of the day. They walked through campus slowly, in a haze of half-digested ideas, each convinced of his or her own inherent flair. By contrast, Grace had a sharp, intense countenance. Her eyes were very focused; her walk was a march. She seemed hyperawake.

Dr. Kreutzfeldt knew there was something besides her twin at work in this girl's psyche. She wasn't sick; she was stuck. There was some knot in her that needed to be loosened. Not sure where to begin, Dr. Kreutzfeldt started with the obvious: the parents. Grace shrugged and spoke of Herb with affection, Pippa with a mix of regret and disdain. This mother was clearly a doormat, Dr. Kreutzfeldt thought, internally shaking her head. She never would understand some women. The kids grow up, and then what? Yet she sensed strong emotion in Grace when she talked about her mother. Her cheeks flushed, she looked away. Kreutzfeldt sensed an emotional morass obscured by irony cool as a blanket of metal filings. Something had happened with the mother.

Over the weeks, gently, shifting her weight slightly in her

armchair, her attractive, full face tilted slightly as she spoke, Dr. Kreutzfeldt guided Grace back, again and again, to what she saw as a kind of crossroads of character. For the first few years of her life, Grace had been extremely close to her mother. She remembered screaming when Pippa went out to dinner, craving her smell, her embrace, treasuring the time they spent together playing on the beach or just staring out the window. Yet by the time Grace was eight or nine, a vast, arid divide had opened up between them. Dr. Kreutzfeldt kept returning to the period she had come to refer to as "the turning point" in Grace's relationship with her mother, hoping that some illuminating memory would spring from the girl's mind. But there was nothing. And then one day, out of nowhere it seemed, after a long silence, Grace looked out the window and said softly, "I don't think my mother likes me very much."

Dr. Kreutzfeldt was taken aback. "But she seems to be almost slavishly devoted to you," she said.

"She is," said Grace. "But there's a part of her that she always held back. Not with Ben. Just with me."

"And you are angry with her for rejecting you," offered Dr. Kreutzfeldt.

"I suppose," said Grace with a slight sneer. And then, turning, half-laughing, she said in her mocking tone, "Am I cured now?"

* * *

Pippa stared out the window of Herb's Mercedes and thought about Grace. It had been three months since she'd been to see them, before her trip to Afghanistan, her second in a year. Pippa had butterflies in her stomach. She always did, these days, when she was going to see her daughter. Seeing Ben was like putting on your favorite old pair of jeans. Seeing Grace was like . . . like bumping into someone you had a crush on. No, Pippa thought, that can't be it. And yet it was, a little.

Herb had chosen the Gotham Bar and Grill so he could have a decent duck breast. The kids had loved to go there around Christmas when they were little. It was absurdly expensive, but there was something reassuring about the heavy cloth on the tables, the superfluous busboys, the quiet conversations, the fine silk and wool of the customers' suits. It felt like going back in time. Herb and Pippa were early, as they always were, and Pippa was teasingly trying to distance the bread basket from Herb's big hands. She saw Grace through the window as she approached. She had cut her wild blond hair short. It looked like underbrush. Her nose looked sharper somehow, a little beakish, Pippa thought, as Grace shoved the heavy door open with too much force, walked up the steps, and stood raking the room with her cool gaze. Pippa waved at her, and Grace approached with long strides, unwinding a scarlet silk scarf from around her neck. Herb stood up and hugged Grace hard. Grace then leaned across the table and brushed Pippa's cheek with her lips.

"Am I late?" she asked.

"I had time to eat all the bread," said Herb.

"Your hair looks wonderful," said Pippa.

"Thanks," Grace said, running her hand through the light blond mop.

"So. Tell us," said Herb.

"Oh, Dad, give me a second. Ben said to start without him. He's stuck in the library. He'll be here as soon as he can."

"It must be that paper," said Herb.

"Yes. *That paper*," said Grace, making loving fun of her brother. "Can I have lamb chops, please? I'm starving." They ordered for themselves and for Ben, then Grace put her portfolio on the table.

"These are just work prints, but anyway it gives you an idea . . ." She set the pile of photographs in front of Herb. Pippa had to look at them upside down. As Herb finished examining each picture, he slid it over to her. In one, a little boy bent over another, prone child, as if protecting her, his face pinched with fright. In another, a man pushed a bicycle, his large, dark, haunted eyes staring into the camera. The front wall of the house behind him had been entirely torn off; on the second floor, a bed, chair, and mirror were arranged like a stage set, open to the world.

"Were you alone when you took these?" Pippa asked. She could feel Grace bristle.

"No, I hitched a ride with Giles Oppenheim." Two-time winner of the Pulitzer Prize, Oppenheim was a legend among war photographers.

"How did you manage that?" asked Herb.

"It's pretty common, people look out for each other there."

"Well, you've got courage, we know that much," said Herb. He was nearly exploding with pride, and Grace knew it.

"These are the best yet," said Pippa.

"Thanks," said Grace, little red spots appearing on her pale cheeks.

Ben arrived, pleased to have his lunch laid out for him. "Has she told you about the bomb?" he asked pleasantly.

"Ben," said Grace.

"What bomb?" asked Pippa.

"She was with that Oppenheim fellow, and the translator, and they heard a bomb go off down the street, and Oppenheim tried to drag her left, but she ran down an alley to the right, and he and the translator followed her, and a van exploded right where he was trying to take her; if they had gone left they would have been pulverized. So now she thinks it's destiny."

Ben was lighthearted in his delivery, but he was furious with his sister, who was becoming, he felt, dangerously, arrogantly brave. Herb and Pippa just sat there, taking in the story. Pippa felt sweat coming up on her brow, a wave of nausea.

Grace looked at Ben, her face set. "Can't you ever just *not say* something?"

"Well, it seemed kind of important," said Ben.

"Just use your common sense," said Herb quietly. "That's all I ask." Then, turning to Ben: "So when are you going to let me read this famous paper?" Ben began to talk about his course work. Grace listened to their conversation in a distanced way, her chin resting on her fist, and Pippa observed her daughter. In spite of the camaraderie Grace seemed to have with her colleagues in the field, Pippa sensed a growing remoteness in her that she found alarming. It seemed to be harder and harder for Grace to return from her photographic odysseys. She was entering other, mirror worlds so violent and intense that the West must seem cold, trivial, and meaningless in comparison. Grace was sealed inside her own experiences, unable to relay what she had seen and felt; the photographs bore mute witness to stories Pippa would have loved to hear every detail of, but she didn't dare ask for fear of the silent rebuff she knew she'd get from her daughter in return for meddling. And to think—such a short time ago, Grace had been a little girl! Within this severe young woman, Pippa could discern, flashing in and out like an image in a hologram, Grace's former, child selves. It was so lonely, knowing things about her children that they no longer remembered. Layers of experience eroded from their minds but petrified in her own. As often happened when she saw Grace, Pippa remembered a day that, she had come to believe, had changed her daughter's life.

The twins were eight. She had decided to take them to the Dairy Queen on Sixth Avenue, after their piano lessons. It was the first spring day after a frigid winter, and the warm air felt liquid against Pippa's skin. People on the street moved languorously, as if drugged with relief. Pippa looked down at the twins, their messy, light blond hair shining in the sun, and swelled with gratitude for her good fortune. When they drifted into the ice cream store, a lady of about sixty in a blue skirt and loafers, white socks pulled up past her ankles, gray hair held back in a ponytail, stood at the counter beside a dark-haired girl of about the twins' age. The lady was saying, in broken English, "How much is a milk shake?" The bored man behind the counter told her. The little girl beside the woman had a tight, embarrassed smile on her face as the older woman counted out her change. When the lady saw that Pippa and the twins were waiting, she moved aside to let them order, scraping her coins a few inches to the left with her cupped palm. Pippa asked for two vanilla cones and gave the man a twenty. As he made change, Pippa noticed Grace gaping at the lady as she sifted through her little pile of coins, squinting up at the board with the prices on it anxiously, the little girl by her side stiff with shame. Pippa poked Grace, but she wouldn't look away.

"And how much is a soda?" asked the lady, smiling. Her dark eyes were shining with kindness and a hint of apology for the fuss she was making. The man gave her a price, and she went back to counting her change. Pippa could feel tears coming to her eyes. This poor woman had taken her granddaughter out for a treat, and now she couldn't afford it. The clerk gave Pippa her change, and she crammed the bills into her wallet furtively, wondering if it would humiliate the lady if she offered to pay for the little girl's dessert. She decided against it; it would be condescending.

The man handed the children the cones. The soft white cream looked perfect, plastic, shiny, like ice cream in a commercial. Ben licked his hungrily, but Grace didn't touch hers. Pippa began to move toward the door. Ben followed. Grace stood stock-still, glaring at the ground, clutching her cone. "Grace," Pippa said softly. Abruptly, Grace bolted toward the little dark-haired girl, stood a foot away from her, and offered her the ice cream. The girl stared at the gift, uncomprehending. Grace stood still, the ice cream cone in her fist raised like a sword in the hand of a statue. The lady said something to the little girl in some foreign tongue, and the child took the cone shyly, casting her eyes to the floor. Then Grace turned and fled the Dairy Queen. Pippa rushed out behind her. She could hear the woman calling out a thank-you as the glass door sighed shut behind her. When Pippa finally caught up with Grace, halfway down the block, the child's face was flushed, her gray eyes clouded with fury.

"That was a lovely thing to do," Pippa said.

"No it wasn't," Grace said. She didn't want to talk about it after that. She was quiet on the cab ride home and all through dinner. Pippa knew that something had changed in her child that day. She'd become angry at her own good fortune.

✳ ✳ ✳

Sponge, spray cleaner, water, mop: time to clean the kitchen! Pippa liked things neat, but she was naturally chaotic. She had to use all her concentration to bend her mind to the task of cleaning, like a high wind forcing a tall tree to the ground. One stray thought and she would wander away from her scrubbing, end up staring at hummingbirds through her binoculars or checking a recipe for spaghetti

alla primavera, only to return to the kitchen forty minutes later, surprised to see the dishes still piled high. This morning, however,
Pippa was keeping an image of a perfectly neat kitchen in mind, trying to replicate it in reality. She took everything off the counter,
sponged it down, then replaced the vitamin bottles and condiments,
carefully lining them up. She wiped down the stove, scrubbed the
pan encrusted with Herb's chicken sausage, emptied the dishwasher,
putting away clean dishes and flatware, then filled it again with dirty
dishes and flatware. She poured blue and white speckled dishwash-
ing powder into the little rectangular box, slid its door shut till it
clicked, turned on the machine, selecting "heavy duty wash" because there was a pan in there. She swept the floor, mopped it. She
wiped out the sink, even opened up the fridge and threw out everything that looked sad or rotten. She made a list: eggs, soy milk, yo-
gurt, aluminum foil. Grape-Nuts. She folded the list, tucked it into
the zip-up compartment inside her purse, and walked out onto the
patio. Herb was on the phone. He looked at her expectantly.

"I'm going shopping. Is there anything you need?" she asked.
He shook his head, waved, and went back to his phone call. He was
talking about the book. Pippa wondered who the author of the cash
cow might be. She walked through the living room, out the door, got
into the car, and froze.

The floor of the car was littered with cigarette butts. There
must have been ten of them, stamped right into the carpeting. Pippa
had quit smoking twenty years ago. The smell of smoke made her
throat close up. Herb had never smoked cigarettes, and he had
given up cigars on the advice of his heart specialist. So what the hell
was this? She picked up the butts, dropped them into a Baggie she
kept in the glove compartment, and hurried back into the house to
tell Herb. He was still on the phone. She lingered in the living room

for a few seconds, waiting. The car had been open. It could have been teenagers, some kids from the nearby town, out having fun. It could have been Chris Nadeau, in an oblique act of revenge for coming upon him as she had. Or it could have been Pippa. She felt her cheeks growing hot. And if it was she, if she had walked in her sleep, and smoked in the car, she might have driven the car. She found this thought terrifying.

Where did she get the cigarettes? A feeling of bottomless panic came over her; it felt like she was standing in an elevator with the cord cut, going down—down—down. Herb, unaware, continued: "Well, Phil, you can do two things," he was saying. "You can get an agent, I can recommend an agent to you. You'll need one eventually anyway, you're a writer now. Or you can hold off, make this deal on your own, forget about their cut. The good news is, you get the entire advance. The other side of the coin is, an agent will be more interested in you if he has this book, and he'll be loyal, because you're gonna make him a lot of money."

Pippa, feeling slightly dizzy, turned and walked out of the house, got into the car, then drove a very slow mile to the convenience store. They stocked simple groceries, and it was the only place in Marigold Village that sold *The New York Times*. She walked in, still wearing her sunglasses. Forgetting about her list, she distractedly picked up the newspaper, eggs, a packet of pancake mix. Her hands were shaking. She walked to the register and looked up. There was Chris Nadeau, his hair wet and slicked back, face freshly shaved, thick brows like dark brush marks on light skin, lips chapped. He smelled of aftershave. There was something hulking about him, strength coiled so tight it looked like relaxation. "Pippa Lee, right?"

"Oh, hi," she said, taking off her glasses. "You got a job already."

"I'm working my way to the top," said Chris.

"It's a beautiful day," said Pippa.

"I'm trying not to notice," he said, punching in the items on the cash register; his fingernails were bitten down to the quick, Pippa noticed. Her eyes then wandered to the wall of cigarettes displayed behind him; she felt a sudden impulse to smoke clutching at her chest.

"Oh, and, ah—a packet of . . . Marlboro Lights. Please."

Chris turned around and found the cigarettes. "Costly habit," he said.

"It's just— I don't really smoke," she said. And then, a thought dawning, "You don't work here at night, do you?"

"I haven't yet," he said. "Why do you ask?"

She felt relieved. "It's open all night, and I always thought it would be a terrible job, just waiting . . . all night, for someone to buy . . . you know, cigarettes, or something." Tears were starting to come to her eyes, the breath catching in her throat. Chris looked at her with a patient, listening gaze, his face expressionless. She felt completely exposed before him. His total lack of mannerisms was almost offensive in its directness. Mercifully, her emotion began to recede.

"Matches?" he asked.

"Please. How's your mother?"

"Recovering," he said. "I'm sorry I skipped out on you the other day. I'm not a big party person."

"I shouldn't have—I shouldn't have interrupted," she said. A man in line behind her cleared his throat. She put some bills down, fumbled through her purse for exact change. "Well," she said. "Tell Dot to call me, if she wants to."

"You'll have to call her," said Chris. "She's too mortified."

Pippa left the convenience store, got into the car, ripped open the cigarettes, pulled one out and lit up. As the smoke filled her lungs, she felt a tingling in her hands and lips. Everything she looked at—the steering wheel, her hand, the gas pump outside— seemed saturated with color and detail. She hung her arm out the window. Why am I doing this? she thought. Her eyes wandered to Chris, tallying up someone's purchases. What a strange young man. Seems bright, but . . . She was beginning to know what Dot meant. There was something not quite right about him. Chris looked up and saw her through the glass. She waved at him cheerfully, put out the cigarette, and drove away.

Sam Shapiro and Moira Dulles were coming over for dinner again. It was too hot for warm dishes, so Pippa poached a salmon, made potato salad with vinaigrette dressing, and served it all on the patio. After dinner, the four of them sat quietly eating strawberries, looking out at the small artificial lake in the golden light and listening to the crickets. "Delicious strawberries, Pippa," said Sam.

"I got them at the farm stand," Pippa said, looking at him and thinking how he had changed over the years. The skin on his long neck had loosened and trembled now like a turkey's wattle. The point of his hawk's nose had been dulled, rounded somehow, as if worn away by the grindstone he'd kept it to for the past thirty years, writing twelve hours a day almost without fail, hounded by the stories in his head like Orestes by the Furies. His eyes, once liquid black like molten tar, now looked dead as coals. It was as though, by writing all his life, he had consumed himself, chunk by chunk, and now he was a host, a husk. Time and again, Sam took his life and the people in it, boiled it all down—skin, bones, all of it—till it was a paste the color, Pippa imagined, of whale blubber. Then he built up an image with this paste, a kind of complex frieze, a story made of human beings, human feelings, human memory.

The main problem Pippa had with Sam (much as she loved him as a friend) was that she suspected he needed his relationships to fail so he could use them later. He would be a monster, she thought, if he wasn't more merciless with himself than with anyone else. But it was he who jumped into the cauldron first, every time. To be cooked down and rise again; that was Sam's endless, exhausting destiny. A writer, and no more. The hopefulness had gone out of him, she thought sadly. But that was the deal he had made: in exchange for a real life, he had been given nine novels, two of them classics, the rest excellent, his immortality almost assured. Still, she pitied her old friend. And she felt sorry for Moira for having fallen in love with him; he would never give her what she wanted. She was too needy. The trick with Sam, Pippa knew, would be to make his life so appealing, such a pleasure, that he could not but turn toward it and away from himself—at least a little bit. But then, she thought, Moira is a writer, too. So maybe they understand each other. She sighed and noticed Chris Nadeau's yellow truck parked across the way. She wondered what was going on inside the Nadeau house at that moment.

"How's the novel coming?" asked Herb.

"I'm only a hundred pages in," said Sam. "I don't even know if it'll work yet."

"Excuse me for a minute," Pippa said. She went to the bathroom, locked herself in, opened the window, and took the cigarettes out from behind Herb's blood pressure medication. She blew the smoke through the screen, watched it expand and disappear into the dark air. Then she brushed her teeth.

She came back to the patio with a slab of pistachio halvah, feeling toxic from the cigarette and berating herself for smoking. Moira sighed deeply and craned her neck to see the sky, drawing her knees up to her heavy bust and clutching them to her, her large, black, kohl-rimmed eyes glazing over with wonder. All of Moira's gestures and reactions had an element of self-consciousness. At twenty-four, she had won the coveted Yale Younger Poets prize. From there she'd gone on to publish a few volumes of surprisingly vitriolic poetry, her private life a brushfire of failed romances. In her middle thirties now, she clung to the demeanor of near-constant astonishment that had clashed so beautifully with her intellect in her early years. Not that Moira was old. No, she was a good deal younger than Pippa. Among the aging literary set she circulated in, she was a bombshell. Pippa found her endearing—and occasionally pitiful. She was irresponsible and neurotic, a grown woman without children, without health insurance even, still searching for love with the reckless hopefulness of a twenty-year-old. Yet occasionally, Pippa found herself envying Moira's chaotic, self-centered life.

"Is that a bat?" Moira asked, squinting.

"Yes," said Herb.

" 'Like a glove, a black glove thrown up at the light,' " said Moira. "Who said that? What's his name . . ."

"The sex fiend," said Sam. "Mr. Lawrence."

"You should talk," said Herb.

"And he got it wrong, too. Look at that. Does that look like a black glove to you?" asked Sam. They all looked up. "It's a fucking *bat*."

"Ben used to subscribe to a magazine about bats, remember?" Pippa said to Herb.

"Oh, yeah," he said, squinting in recollection.

"Look how frenetic the fluttering wings are; that's how you can tell it's not a bird," said Moira.

"No," said Sam. "It's the way it changes direction so fast—like a stunt kite."

"That's good." Herb chuckled. "A stunt kite." Sam tucked his chin into his neck, content; Herb never said anything was good unless he meant it.

"Do they really get in your hair?" asked Moira.

Sam tossed his head. "Could you maybe just once come up with an idea that isn't a cliché?" Moira looked at him, an incredulous expression on her face. "Just kidding," he said. "You're an original, baby, and don't you forget it."

"Fuck you, too," said Moira.

Pippa stood up. "Decaf, anyone?" she asked in mock-stewardess style.

Moira stood up as well and followed Pippa into the kitchen. By the time they got to the stove, she was sobbing. "Every time I open my mouth, he puts me down. I can't take it anymore. He's such a *prick*."

Pippa sighed. Sam was cruel to his women. Everyone knew that. She'd seen him gnaw through a handful of them over the years.

"That's just the way he is sometimes. He has a mean streak. Maybe if you just laughed along?"

"I've been laughing for four years. Now I'm crying."

"Are you talking about breaking up?"

"We're not talking about anything. Sam is so involved with his novel, he barely looks up. I'm having all of our discussions with myself."

"Have you found . . . someone else?" Pippa knew Moira well enough to guess she wouldn't think of leaving a man as powerful and desirable as Sam Shapiro unless she had a replacement in the wings. Gifted as she was, this poet needed big men.

Moira looked down at her hands. "No . . . I mean—" Then, pressing her palms against her eyes, "Oh, Pippa, I'm so confused!"

That night in bed, as Herb tried to read and Pippa rubbed cream between the backs of her hands, she mused, "I bet you Moira's having an affair."

"What makes you say that?" Herb asked.

"She's talking about leaving Sam, but she's terrified of being on her own. It just adds up."

"Maybe she wants you to think she's having an affair so you'll tell me, and I'll tell Sam, and he'll pay more attention to her."

"Do you really think Moira is that conniving?"

"That's what women are like."

"Devious?"

"It's instinct. Survival of the fittest. Of all people, you should know."

"Never mind."

"Does that mean I get to go to sleep now?" Herb said, yawning and putting his reading glasses in their case. "Since reading is clearly out."

"I still think she's having an affair," said Pippa, turning out her light.

A Little Death

The office of Maxwell, Lee and Brewer Publishing was in New York, seven surprisingly shabby, glassed-in rooms choked with books. In Herb's absence, the company was being run by Marianne Stapleton, a muscular, somewhat manic person with excellent taste and a penchant for self-doubt. She called Herb at least five times a day with questions.

"If I have an office," Herb told Pippa, "I give that maniac three hours a day when she can call me. The rest of the time, I'm retired."

Though Marigold Village was a retirement community, there was office space available. Mostly rented out to businesses that catered to the residents, the smaller units were modestly priced. Pippa found Herb a room with an adjoining toilet that looked out onto the mini-mall. She got him a sofa, a desk, a chair, a coffeemaker, and a small fridge. Though Herb kept justifying the office, telling her why it would allow them more quality time together, Pippa was actually relieved to have him out of the house a bit. She wasn't used to their new constant proximity, and she felt the need to be by herself these days. Since she'd discovered the cigarettes on the car floor, flashes of apprehension would surge through her body out of the blue, like electric current. She was having alarming dreams. In one, a body was carried out of her neighbor's house on a stretcher. Someone unzipped the body bag, and it was Pippa, her face gray. In the dream, she wasn't actually dead, but she wasn't able to open her eyes or speak. As they carried her away, she realized with horror that she'd be buried alive. She didn't mention the dream to Herb. She didn't tell him she had been smoking, either. Every time she was about to mention it, as a sort of joke, she felt ashamed.

* * *

Pippa was just coming out of Why Not Furnishings in the mini-mall, carrying an almond-colored throw for Herb's new couch in an over-size shopping bag, when she heard a squeal of brakes, the heart-rending scream of an animal, and the sickening crash of a car. She stood on her toes, craning her neck to see the road, then walked toward it uneasily. When she arrived, she saw that a tan Toyota had smacked into a lamppost. Its front end was crumpled. The driver, a man in his seventies, unhurt but dazed, was opening his door. A few old people were already clustered on the sidewalk outside the convenience store. Pippa walked toward them, made her way to the front of the crowd. There was Chris Nadeau, kneeling on the sidewalk, cradling a big white dog. The animal had a glistening, six-inch gash along its side. It was yelping. Chris was stroking its long white fur. When he saw Pippa, he looked up at her with such naked, beseeching sadness that she dropped to her knees beside him, then instantly regretted it. It was too intimate a thing to do. And now she was stuck there, crouched beside Dot's half-baked son, a dying dog in his lap.

"Is he yours?" she asked. He shook his head, looking down at the dying creature. "I saw it happen through the window," he said softly. She looked at the dog. It was whimpering and shaking. She found it unbearable to watch. She turned to Chris. He kept his eyes on the dog's face. The man who had hit the dog kept insisting, "He jumped right out at me." The dog started panting, its clear, light eyes fixed, white froth like whipped-up egg whites foaming at the corners of its mouth. Chris bent over and murmured something into its ear. Pippa couldn't see the dog, just the back of Chris's head. When he sat up, the dog was still, its eyes clouded over. Chris still didn't move. Neither did Pippa. They sat there, heads bowed, as though it was their pet that had died.

A van arrived with "ASPCA" written on the side. Two men got out. Chris let them lift the body off him, then, without glancing at Pippa, he stood up and walked back into the convenience store. One of the men from the ASPCA asked her if it was her dog. Pippa shook her head, brushed off her knees, picked up her shopping bag, and walked unsteadily to her car. She felt shaken and strangely moved.

* * *

Moira was late. Pippa leaned back in the aqua leatherette banquette and scrutinized the small oil paintings that were hung at regular intervals on the walls of the restaurant. They were all dutifully painted, humorless landscapes. She thought about her old artist friend Jim, how he would have looked up at them, his head slightly bowed. He would have nodded slowly. "Ah, yes," he would have said, smiling grimly. She wondered if Jim was still alive.

Moira appeared, out of breath, kissed Pippa, strands of black hair escaping from her ponytail. She smelled pleasantly of milk.

"I am so sorry I'm late, I was writing and I looked at the clock and—"

"Don't worry," said Pippa, "I was just relaxing, enjoying the art. That's a great buckle," she said, fingering a silver sheriff star below Moira's belly button.

"Thanks," said Moira, covering it with her hand and sliding into the opposite bench, her large suede handbag clutched to her side. An effeminate waiter appeared. "Oh! Hi! Can I please have, um, an iced tea? The one with, um, melon in it?" Moira said to him with involuntary flirtatiousness. Then she looked back at Pippa, tucked a strand of hair behind her ear girlishly, and smiled, a dimple indenting her left cheek. No wonder she had been her father's favorite of seven kids, Pippa thought. She must have been a magical child, with that heart-shaped face, those enormous, Indian orphan eyes—and that imagination. In her messy, breathless, self-obsessed way, Moira was adorable. There was no getting around it. You could think her sincerity was ridiculous, you could lampoon her overblown sexuality, her exaggerated appreciation of life, but finally, you just had to throw up your hands and love the absolute purity of her confusion. Disarming. That was the word for Moira.

"You look *so beautiful*," Moira said, scrutinizing Pippa's face. "What are you doing different?"

"It's the indolence," said Pippa.

"I wish I could be so peaceful and good like you."

"*Good?*"

"You seem so . . . beatific."

Pippa laughed. "If only you knew."

"Knew what?"

"Oh, a variety of things. I'm like one of those used cars that have been in a terrible accident. They look perfectly fine on the outside, but the axle is bent."

Moira smiled, puzzled. "You're so mysterious about the past."

"You think?"

"You never say anything about your life before."

"There are things that happened that I don't dwell on."

"What, like what happened to Herb's first wife?"

"Second."

"Second. He said she was already crazy."

"Not that crazy."

Moira sighed, put her head in her hands, and sniffed.

"What?" Pippa put her palm on Moira's shoulder.

"I'm just a rotten apple," said Moira, wiping the tears off her cheeks. "I'll never have a normal life."

Pippa was used to her friend's sudden episodes of self-flagellation. She always used humor to bring her out of her maudlin spirals.

"Oh, come on," said Pippa. "What's normal? You mean marriage?"

Moira nodded, blowing her nose. "It's over between Sam and me. Oh, Pippa, it's all so completely fucked up. I—I've gotten myself into— I'm going to be forty with no man, fifty, not that it matters but it *does*. I—I just wish I knew how to recognize the right man."

"Oh, pish tush," said Pippa. "You can be married to anybody, if that's what you're worried about."

"What do you mean?"

"Pick any man in this room, in the right age range, I could be married to him."

Cheered up by the game, Moira surveyed the room, then pointed to a thin man wearing glasses, looking at the menu with distaste.

"He just needs his routines, that's all," Pippa said. "I bet you if you anticipate his needs before he knows he has them, he'll be docile as a lamb."

"What about that one?"

"As long as you stick your finger up his ass when he's coming, he won't give you any trouble at all."

"Pippa!"

"Sorry, it just slipped out."

"You make it seem like . . . so unromantic."

"Courtship is romantic. Marriage . . . is an act of will," said Pippa, taking a sip of water. "I mean, I adore Herb. But the marriage functions because we will it to. If you leave love to hold everything together, you can forget it. Love comes and goes with the breeze, minute by minute."

Moira shook her head, smiling, baffled. "I can't get my head around that one," she said.

"You'll see," said Pippa, amazed at this act of complacent cynicism she was playing. When in God's name had she started saying "pish tush"? When had she even heard it? Did she really believe what she was saying, about marriage being an act of will? Yes, she realized sadly, she did. After all she and Herb had been through together, after what they had lost to be with each other—their very souls, perhaps—being married ended up being *an act of will*. It made her want to tear through the dull present, claw the vivid past back into herself, devour it like a bear busting into a camper's stores. She wanted to run out of the restaurant, to find Herb and kiss him violently on the mouth (she could imagine his surprised, bemused expression as she crushed herself on him), to burst into tears, scream even—lose control at last. Instead she waited, smiling, for her lobster sandwich, and wondered if she might be on the brink of a very quiet nervous breakdown.

Part Two

Pippa Begins

I emerged from Suky's womb fulsome and alert, fat as a six-month-old, and covered in fine, black fur. After a brief look round the delivery room, I turned my face to my mother's swollen little dug and latched on, sucking so noisily that I sounded like a litter of piglets. My mother burst into tears at the thought of having given birth to this beast. The doctor's reassurances that I had merely been gestating a little too long, and thus had time to grow a dusting of vestigial hair, harkening back to the days when human beings belonged to the ape family, did nothing to calm her down. Being the wife of a pastor, she was ambivalent about evolutionary theory, and couldn't help feeling that my bestial looks, explicable as they apparently were by science, somehow reflected a basic flaw or sinfulness in her own character. Handing me back to the flabbergasted doctor, she launched herself off the delivery table, her legs still rubbery from the anesthetic, and ran down the hall, slipping on her own blood and screaming, *"I had a monkey!"*

It took two nurses and a doctor to subdue all five feet, two inches of Suky Sarkissian. They injected her with a sedative, then gave her a private room, which our insurance didn't cover but the hospital threw in for free.

* * *

The sense that her daughter magically embodied all that was wrong in herself never left my mother. Long after I had lost my furry coat and grown into a pretty, chubby little girl, she thought she discerned in me a deviousness, a lustiness, a general *badness*, which was, in secret fact, her own. At the age of two, I would clamp myself to her leg like an amorous dog. She always shook me off her, shrieking. One time, desperate to be freed from a crowded Greyhound bus, I scratched her face until it bled. She wept for my cruelty. I even took a crafty little poop in one of her favorite shoes, hoping to foil her plan of going out to dinner one night. It was one of a pair covered in pink velvet that matched her new dress perfectly. When she saw what I had done, she tried to be furious, but she couldn't stop laughing. For, in spite of the flaws in my character, or because of them perhaps, Suky loved me fervently, even ardently. She just couldn't get enough of me, couldn't stop cuddling, sniffing, kissing, nipping at me. I remember at the age of six or seven struggling to emerge from one of her embraces, not because I did not enjoy her affection but because I actually could not breathe.

I was the first girl after four boys. Suky mothered my predecessors fine; she herded them into and out of the bath as if it were a sheep dip, then shooed them into bed like a flock of pigeons. She ferried them conscientiously to their endless sports competitions. Yet I had the feeling, growing up, that Suky saw only me. Being the only girl, I had my own bath every night, and Suky would sit on the lid of the toilet, legs crossed, languorously watching me as she filed her nails, or stand at the mirror plucking her eyebrows. We would chat about this and that—the other girls in my school, who was friends with whom, who was planning on running away, what hairdo was best for which occasion—while in the next room my brothers shouted and teased and bashed one another over the head. At bedtime, she gave all the boys a swift kiss good night, but she lay down with me, tenderly stroking my head till I was asleep. We would dance to Bobby Darin in the kitchen, my feet on hers, holding hands, round and round and round.

I was the youngest, and for a few years, this lavishing of attention made a certain amount of sense. But once I was six and could fend for myself, the boys began to resent Suky's clear preference for her only girl. She even bought a camera, the sole function of which was to take pictures of me. She dressed me as angels, cowgirls, movie stars. Occasionally she photographed me naked. She was the most passionate of mothers.

Suky was a diminutive, peppy woman with bright red hair and a high, squeaky voice with a slight southern lilt, a shadow of her mother's viscous Mississippi drawl. Her waist was so tiny, her ankles so slim, she had to shop in the teen section of the local department store. I was proud of Suky's Tinker Bell figure; other people's mothers, with their rounded, fleshy bottoms and jiggling breasts, struck me as bovine and sloppy compared to my lithe, lively, tireless mother.

Suky smiled easily, wore her hair in a low beehive, and nearly always kept her eyebrows up in an expression of bemused surprise. In spite of this, I think she was a closet pessimist. I could tell by her driving. As she maneuvered our fat-assed station wagon around the narrow country roads, she sat bolt upright, her little hands clamped to the steering wheel, knuckles white. Every time we approached a turn, she whacked the horn, warning the eighteen-wheeler that was surely barreling round the bend, making ready to spin out of control and flatten us. An insomniac, she would stay up deep into the night, baking cookies, paying bills, or just pottering around. I remember waking from a bad dream in the middle of the night. The house was dead quiet. Knowing she'd be up, I walked downstairs and found her trimming the withered leaves off the plants in her pajamas. She was happy to see me. She made cocoa; we snuggled up to each other and watched TV till five, when we both passed out on the sofa, her arms around me, my head on her breast.

Suky slept there often. She'd say she was up so late, there was no point going to bed. We'd come down and find her huddled under the blanket she kept for watching TV. I would shake her awake, and she'd shuffle into the kitchen, drink a glass of orange juice, look at the clock. At seven on the dot, she'd take her medication—she was always muttering about her thyroid being off-kilter. By the time my dad came downstairs, she was dressed and cheerful, masterfully fixing everyone's breakfast, packing lunches, organizing book bags. She cooked nourishing meals but rarely sat with us at the table for long, preferring to stand by the stove spooning rice pudding from a china cup into her endlessly chattering mouth.

But then there were days when my chirpy, talkative, cheerful mother went quiet and staring, seemingly deaf to even my requests. She would dump the dinner on the table and rush away from the teeming mass of us to lie down and eat toast with butter in front of the television that stood at the foot of her bed. My father, Des, sighed when this happened, but he didn't reproach her. He knew there were times when his wife quite simply shorted out, went limp and affectless as a run-down robot. Des would rally then; singing in his painful rasp, he washed dishes, supervised baths. I relished these evenings being overseen by my father, because he would ignore me a little. I was just part of the other kids, not a unique and special creature, not the apple of anyone's eye. It was a relief. I roughed around with the boys, wrestled, kicked, giggled. But inevitably a sense of guilt overwhelmed me on those nights and, wish as I might to simply go to bed with a rough kiss from Dad, skipping the elaborate affections of my mother, I felt her pull me toward her; her will had infested my own. I walked into her room then. She was always fully dressed, on the bed, her plate of toast on her abdomen. She looked at me with a mix of joy and apprehension, as though at any moment I might renege on my affections. I had such power over Suky; it frightened me and made me bold. Sometimes I let my face go cold and stony just to watch the fear flash in her eyes.

Des

An impassive Hartford Armenian, my father had a thick, gravelly voice that made him sound as if he had just eaten a large spoonful of peanut butter. He moved his powerful, squat body with a deliberate, oxlike slowness. The russet circles surrounding his kind black eyes made him look perpetually exhausted. Father Sarkissian never got too happy, but then he never got too sad, either. His unlikely choice to become an Episcopalian minister had been made against the wishes of my grandfather, a fervent Armenian Orthodox who never forgave his Protestant wife for luring their only son from the church of his ancestors.

As it turned out, Des was a born pastor. He worked on his sermons scrupulously, kept the rectory open late for lost souls who needed a sympathetic ear. Yet one sensed, beneath the folds of his holy robes, not the airy, bodiless expanse of the spiritual man but the squirming flesh of a man all too much alive. Des always emphasized Christ the man in his sermons, to the point that some of his parishioners wondered aloud whether he actually thought Christ was also God, seeing as he nearly never mentioned it. To be honest, I don't think my father cared much about the God part. The miracle was the reality of Christ, his it-ness, the *fact* of him. I remember at dinner he once said that what really mattered was what people did to each other here on earth. The Holy Ghost could take care of itself.

Des was a compassionate man. He listened with a concerned, interested look as people with porridge-colored complexions and red-rimmed eyes told him their troubles on their way out of church or at our house in the evenings, when they had put their children to bed and had a few hours' respite before their daily obligations kicked in again. He seemed to enjoy us kids, in an abstracted sort of way, cocking his head and watching us as we did our homework, argued, played. He was always tender with us when we were hurt or sad and would sit with a weeping child for an hour, well after the crisis had passed, holding a small hand, in no rush to go anywhere. In that sense, he was the opposite of Suky, who skittered around in a flurry of activity eighteen hours a day. She relaxed only when she lay down with me to put me to sleep, humming wisps of songs into my ear in her high, breathy voice and curling a strand of my hair round her finger.

The truth is, I never got to know my father very well. Suky eclipsed him; the fire that burned in her day and night blotted him out in my imagination. He was a shadow figure, a refuge at times but not fully real to me as a man. I find this sad, because now I realize that, of all my traits, the ones I got from my father are the most valuable; it was the Des in me that allowed me to survive.

It didn't seem strange to me that my parents barely spoke to each other. Their exchanges were almost entirely confined to talking about the children, or simple requests, such as "pass the milk please." As far as I could tell, Suky spent any free time she had with me. She got most of her affection from me, too. I wonder what my parents' life together was like before I was born, or when they were newlyweds. In one early photograph, they seem shyly happy together, holding hands and smiling outside my father's first parish in Hartford. My mother is wearing a flowered housedress. Her face is young and round. Growing up, I was fascinated by this image, because Suky was not tiny then. She was almost plump.

Dolls and Husbands

I was always a housewife when I played, a little mother pushing my toy vacuum cleaner, a fussily dressed baby doll on my hip, or primly taking messages on a pink pretend phone for my husband, a tall, shadowy being I called Joey. Sex with Joey was a swift, choreographed movement. I would lie down, flap my legs open and closed, and stand up again, returning to my chores. I think I got the idea that you lie down from my friend Amy, who was, at nine, already a bit of an aficionado.

"You know what the worst word in the world is?" Amy asked me one day as we played in the dark corridor of our second floor.

"What?" I asked.

Amy stood against the window, pensively swiveling the head of one of my dolls round and round. A web of fine, shiny brown hair tumbled to my best friend's waist. Her cornflower blue, crescent-shaped eyes gave her an old-fashioned, wistful air. "Fuck," she said flatly. Then she turned to look across the street at her older brother, Andy, who was mowing the town green. Amy's family was rich compared to ours, yet all the kids but Amy had summer jobs, to teach them the value of money. I watched Amy from behind: her arms rested on the crossbar of the window frame. Her lilac dress was cinched at the waist by a slender belt and fell in neat little pleats to just below her knees. Her bare feet were crossed at the ankles. I felt awed by her elegance and her beauty. There had never been such a girl, I thought, so perfect, so confident, so lovely. I felt like a troll in comparison. I was short, my face was flat, my hair was the color of straw, my eyes like gray marbles. One summer afternoon, as I pulled on my bikini bottom, Amy contemplated my muscular stomach with a cool, thoughtful air. There was a faint line on my belly, like a sepia seam, from my navel to my sex. She pointed to it and said, "You know what that means, don't you?"

"What?" I asked.

"When you were in your mother's stomach, you were going to be a boy until the *very last second.*" I looked in the mirror, at the broad muscles in my little shoulders, the round, strong thighs. I didn't look like a girl at all.

"You're a boy-girl," she said, laughing. I laughed, too, though I felt my throat constricting. I shoved her onto the bed, and we tumbled, hysterical now, screaming, wrestling. Then we lay very still beside each other, catching our breath. I propped myself up on one elbow. Amy had a chipped front tooth that glimmered inside her parted lips.

"If I'm a boy-girl, then I can be your boy-girlfriend," I said.

"No, you can't," she said dismissively.

"That way, when you have a real boyfriend, it'll be easy."

She mulled this over for a moment. "But we wouldn't tell anybody." She looked at me, her eyes narrowing.

"You think I'm dumb, or crazy?" I asked. Then I let myself tip forward, very slowly approaching her face, and kissed her. Her lips felt cool and rough. She pushed me away, laughing, but later that day she let me do it again.

We kissed a few more times that summer. I persuaded her to let me lie on top of her twice, as well. I loved feeling myself crush down on her. She struggled out from under me, though. Once, I was surprised to see alarm in her face as I pinned her down; she was clearly relieved when we heard my mother's steps on the stairs.

Years passed. Amy turned out to be a very intelligent girl. She got A's in everything but history, a subject she detested for some reason of her own. I was an indifferent student. The words in my schoolbooks held no reality for me. I consumed them reluctantly, as if they were stale bread. I spent less time with Amy now; she was always in the library with her brainy friends. She studied at a round table with those geeks, sitting up straight like a princess, her long, dark hair glistening down her back, and worked away for hours under the admiring gaze of Mrs. Underwood, the wheezing librarian. Ravaged by cigarettes, she rolled an oxygen tank with her while she was stacking books.

The kisses Amy and I had shared melted away into a childhood we both remembered like a dream. I could no more have kissed her now than fly a 747. I wouldn't have known how. I was thirteen, and I must tell you I was really something. Two compact and perfectly formed breasts had sprung up on my chest like mushrooms, overnight it seemed, disconcerting my brothers and sending my mother on an emergency shopping trip for my first bra. It took my father months to notice them. I'll never forget the look of muted surprise on his face as I bent to clear his plate and he realized what had happened to me. I was small and lithe, with copper-colored hair, padded little hands, and a face like a cat. That's what everyone said, that I looked like a kitten, with my broad, flat face and wide, slanting gray eyes, my small, cupid's bow mouth—and my lassitude. I could lie on the couch in a torpor all morning long, then spring up and bolt out the door in a pair of tiny shorts, my mother shouting after me, pleading with me to come back in and change.

As I have mentioned, I was a sexual creature pretty much from the get-go. At eleven, I found a way to achieve orgasms while doing the breaststroke, which subsequently led me to join the swim team of my junior high school and accounted for my iron thighs. In my early teens, though virginal in the extreme—I had never even kissed a boy—I developed a peculiar fantasy in which I met a faceless, unimpeachable gentleman whose pristine heart was overwhelmed with forbidden love for me. The boys in my school held no interest for me. They were all dying for it. I needed to find someone who absolutely didn't want to be seduced. But I'm getting ahead of myself. At the moment, I'm thirteen, Grandma Sally has thrombosis, and Suky is going to Delaware.

Aha!

Grandma Sally was fat. We saw her as rarely as possible. Suky could hardly look at her. But, thinking back on it now, I don't think it was disgust and embarrassment about Sally's weight that kept her sparrowlike daughter away from her. I think the reason was that Grandma Sally had the full measure of my mother. I remember, on one of her rare visits, Sally followed Suky with her hooded eyes as her daughter sped around the kitchen, sponged down the table, made individually tailored, assembly-line sandwiches for each of her children (none of whom liked the same things), then swept the floor—talking breathlessly all the while. The whites of the old lady's eyes glimmered beneath dark irises; her double chin was cradled in her hands, a half-eaten piece of pie on a plate between her elbows, two thin, blond braids pinned to the top of her head. Eventually, she sat back, crossed her arms over her chest, and drawled in pure Mississippian: "You never moved that fast when you were a kid."

"Well, Mother," Suky said with forced cheer, gritting her teeth, "when I was a kid, I didn't have five children."

"You were a lazy, dreamy kid," said Sally. "Nobody changes their tempo that way. Tempo is tempo. It's one of the basic things about a person."

"You and I just have different styles of mothering," said Suky, smiling coldly and patting her stiff nest of hair. "I like to keep on top of things, that's all."

"Mmm-hmm," said Sally suspiciously, shifting her enormous weight on her chair and poking at her pie with her fork. I couldn't figure out what Grandma Sally was getting at—but I knew it enraged my mother. Her anger made my belly tense up and ache. The discomfort was so intense, I went outside, in order to break the suction between us.

But that December, Grandma Sally seemed to be dying, and in need of her hyperefficient daughter to play nurse. So off Suky went, having left enough soup and lasagna in the freezer chest to last us a month, even though she only planned to be gone four days. The first two days of my vacation from Suky were heavenly. I'd amble home from school with my brothers, stare into the refrigerator, poke around in the cabinets, eat whatever I felt like, turn on the TV. Des spent afternoons in his study, working on his Sunday sermon, or meeting troubled parishioners. One parishioner who seemed especially troubled that week was Mrs. Herbert Orschler. I always thought of her whole name when I saw her, because she once dropped an envelope from her purse, and I picked it up. Before I handed it to her, I read, typed out, "Mrs. Herbert Orschler." I thought what an odd name Herbert was for a woman and wondered if nestled beneath her snug dress was a small, secret penis. Amy, that fountain of information, had once told me there were people who were born both male and female. This disgusted and fascinated me, and I wondered whether Mrs. Herbert Orschler was visiting my father so often because of the stress caused by her genitalia. The day after my mother left for Grandma Sally's, I was passing the door to Des's study. It was ajar; I peeked in to find Mrs. Orschler seated in an armchair, my father leaning in to hold her hand. This seemed slightly odd to me at the time, but I put it down to the duties of a pastor, which were mysterious and manifold, as my father always said.

It turned out that Suky had to stay away a whole extra week tending to her mother, whose approach to death was as sluggish as her housekeeping. (She would in fact outlive Suky by five years.) Back in the rectory, benign neglect was the order of the day. I didn't do my homework once. We ordered in pizza nearly every night and ate it in front of the television, ignoring the laden freezer. I don't think I washed much. A pact had developed between us kids and our father: he wouldn't bother us if we didn't bother him.

The caramel-colored plastic bottles of pills in Suky's bathroom medicine cabinet and nestled between the nutmeg and the cloves in the spice rack were just part of my childhood, part of the furniture, like the rough cotton drapes in the living room or the one chipped square of brown linoleum in the kitchen. I didn't think about the shiny capsules, one half blood maroon, the other a transparent little dome filled with cheerful red and yellow orbs like miniature gumballs, which my mother swallowed in the morning and the afternoon with a toss of her head, hand to mouth fast as a hummingbird, until I heard the word *Dexedrine* in a cautionary TV movie about speed-addicted beatniks I watched one rainy afternoon with my oldest brother, Chester. The word rang a bell. I stole into the kitchen and checked the prescription bottle. Sure enough, the active ingredient was Dexedrine. Speed! All at once, the manic cheerfulness, the jumpiness, the sudden bouts of deflated disconnection, Grandma Sally's suspicions—all started to make a horrible kind of sense. Even Suky's overwhelming affections seemed like drug-induced delirium. I took the bottle and ran into the living room. Chester was slumped on the couch, his long legs splayed out, a vacant look on his face as he watched TV. I showed him the label.

"Mom takes that stuff," I said, gesturing to the television. He turned toward me slowly, irritated by the interruption.

"What are you doing with Mom's medicine?"

"It's Dexedrine. See?"

"So?"

"So that's why she's so perky all the time."

"Oh, shut up. She's not a drug addict. Those people in the movie are taking it to get high."

"But what's the difference?"

"You think companies would sell diet pills full of speed? It's a tiny amount in there. I can't believe you're even saying this."

I just stood there in front of him until he kicked me out of the way. Maybe he was right. Maybe she didn't need the pills except for a diet. So I took ten of them, just to see.

Whoosh! *Wow* did I have energy! I jumped up and down on my bed for about half an hour, my heart racing, then ran downstairs and started telling Chester all these really funny things, and imitating our neighbors, and laughing, falling over myself. Des even came out of his study; I was absolutely nuts.

"What the heck happened to her?" he asked.

"I'll bet you she took Mom's diet pills," said Chester sleepily. "She was asking about them."

"Why didn't you tell me?" Des asked, springing into action. He grabbed me by the arms and pinned me down on the sofa, under the light.

"Open up your eyes!" he commanded. I couldn't stop laughing. "Goddamnit, open your eyes!" He held my eyelid open. I saw his tawny face, with the bluish cast of his shaved beard under the skin, his bushy eyebrows, the dark hairs escaping from his nose, so close it was alarming. "We're going to have to take her to the hospital," he said. I slipped out of his grasp, bolted up the stairs, dove into my room, and locked the door. Then I huddled in the corner, my mind going off like fireworks, my legs twitching. They had to pick the lock. In the end, Des decided against the hospital. I was coming down anyway and had already started crying and throwing up.

I woke up at 9:30 the next morning. The house was silent. I came down to find Des, sitting in front of a cup of tea and the paper. He smiled at me kindly. I basked in his focused gaze.

"Sleep well?" he asked.

"How come you didn't wake me up for school?" I asked.

"Your body needed the rest, after yesterday. That was a dangerous thing you did."

"If those pills are dangerous, why does Mommy take them?"

"They're not dangerous for her, she takes just a few, and she's a grown-up, not a kid."

"But why does she take them?"

"Her mother got so terribly fat," said Des. "She's afraid the same thing will happen to her."

"Is she . . . an *addict*?" I asked, using the word I'd learned from the TV drama.

"Oh, for mercy's sake, Pippa, sit down and eat your cereal. Your mother is no more an addict than . . . that squirrel out there." I looked out the window. A large gray squirrel was frantically gnawing on a seed dropped from our bird feeder. The creature did, in fact, move a lot like Suky.

When I came home from school the next afternoon, Suky was in the bath. I barged in, opened the medicine cabinet, and took out the bottle of pills. I had two more bottles in my fist: one from the kitchen and another I had found behind the tomato paste in the larder. Suky glared at me, her face tight with anger as I lined up the bottles neatly, side by side.

"So who are you, really?" I asked. There was a long pause. "I'd like to know what you're like without this stuff."

"Don't be silly," she said in a chilly, reasonable tone she almost never used with me. "That is medicine. You took enough to kill you."

"What would happen if you stopped taking it?"

"I would get fat," she announced crisply, arching her back so her pink nipples peeked out of a skin of bubbles, then sank again.

"I don't care what you look like," I said softly. She rested her feet on the end of the tub and assessed her glistening, pink toenails.

"Okay," she said in an offhand way. "Fine." But she kept looking at her feet with stubborn interest until, eventually, I left.

The next day, the pills were gone. Not a pill in the house. That was her answer to me. She seemed more focused, serene, engaged. I was so relieved. The fact that she was wiping tears away while she was vacuuming and staring vacantly out the window while she ironed—my gratitude swept it out of my mind. At least she was my real mother. I loved her intensely then and kept hugging her, kissing her. When I did, she smiled weakly and patted my arm. A week passed, and she started cheering up again. I never saw her take a pill, but she was acting like she'd drunk six cups of coffee, all day. I knew she must be hiding the drug somewhere. Whenever I got a chance, I searched. I found small stashes of pills in Baggies all over the house—in her underwear drawer, inside the freezer, taped under the couch. In the beginning, I would remove them and flush them down the toilet. But it didn't make any difference. She seemed to be taking more and more. Burying the habit had made it more important, the need more acute. Her behavior was erratic. Her pupils were constantly dilated, her reactions to sudden noises, even the telephone, were exaggerated, almost theatrical. She was prone to sudden bursts of weeping.

I tried to talk to Des about it again, but he brushed me off gruffly. They were in it together for some reason. And then I saw it—or I thought I did. With Suky out of her mind on speed, he was free to pursue the spiritual life, including consoling Mrs. Orschler, and whomever else he had tucked under his robes of office. But now I think that was unfair. I think he was simply kind enough to accept Suky for who she was and unwilling to have me insult her with a truth that could only be destructive. Or no. Maybe my father couldn't face that his wife was a drug addict because to face it would be to see his marriage and his life as a lie. So he didn't see it. Or maybe he was just plain lazy. I'll never know.

By the time I was fifteen I could barely look at Suky; her touch made my skin hurt. Each time I pulled away, she lowered her eyes, as if acknowledging her sin. I could see the glimmer of tears beneath her lids. I watched her behavior now with a coldly observant eye. She met my gaze with a strident stare. We had always known what the other was thinking, my mother and I. So, without having a single conversation, I expressed my disgust and sense of betrayal, and she, in her own way, refused to be controlled. Dinners became unbearable. She would prattle on senselessly from her station by the stove, laughing and blushing or crying and crazy, and I would stare at her, fantasizing about smacking her in the head, till I couldn't take it anymore and had to go into the bathroom, sob, and hit myself in the face. Returning glassy-eyed to the table, I would find my father and brothers eating and exchanging monosyllables, passing the dinner rolls as if nothing was the matter. Suky and I were on our own, locked cheek to cheek, dancing jerkily to a long, long number.

And Another Thing

When I was little, I had a bottle, of course, the way everyone does. Suky loved giving me my bottle. I kept it for a long time. When I turned three, four, she still made me a bottle with warm milk, or juice. And it didn't end there. When I was eleven, twelve, if Suky felt especially warmly toward me, or we'd had a fight, she would offer me a bottle. And I loved it. She would fix it for me, and I would lie down and drink, staring out the window like an infant. Even after I figured out about the pills, even once her touch made my skin ache and I had begun to daydream about her death, we could still make up with a bottle. The last one I drank, I was sixteen years old.

Good

By high school, I was angry, and that made me cool. Flanked by a few minions, I terrorized the kids that got on my nerves. Even Amy came under attack eventually. Little Miss Goody Two-Shoes was so pretty, you could eat her. She had the posture of a ballerina, carried her books level in front of her, like they were a chocolate cake. Needless to say, we moved in different circles now. But one day, as I watched her waft out of the girls' room, head held high, it occurred to me that she might tell one of her honor roll friends about our brief trip to the isle of Lesbos. If that got out, I would be ruined. I was seized by an impulse to smash her like a bug. I walked up to her and pinned her against the puce concrete-block wall, my hands squeezing her delicate wrists.

"If you ever tell anyone about us, I will beat you up," I hissed. Amy's blue eyes widened; she looked from side to side for help.

"I won't," she said. "I promise. Please." I let her go. She ran off. Tears stung my eyes. What the hell did I do that for? I loved Amy. I promised myself that the next day in assembly I would tell her I was sorry. But I was too embarrassed. And the worst of it was, after that day, Amy started fawning on me. She wanted me to be nice to her. She was lying down like a dog, letting me know I had won. She was weak and smart and beautiful and had a future, and I was strong and stupid and wasn't good at anything but scaring people. She would come up to me and make a lame joke, and I would smile with one side of my mouth, letting just a little air out of my nose. Once, I trapped her in one of the big gym lockers. I got a few of my hench-women to circle her, and we shoved her in. She was screaming, pounding on the metal. My heart was slamming against my chest; I thought I was going to faint. Afterward, she was angry, but she didn't stand up to me. She just walked away, sniffling.

Horrified at this bully I was becoming, I went to church every Sunday at nine o'clock and prayed to be a better person. My father's gruff, clotted voice ground on like a distant engine as my thoughts kneaded my sins over and over, turning them in my mind like dough. *Please, Jesus, come into my heart and change me, I am begging you, I am begging you to make me good, please.*

One summer night, it was so hot, my open window was like the yawning mouth of a dead man, emitting no puff of air. It felt like the oxygen had been sealed out of the world. I slept fitfully, my hair wet with perspiration, my legs flung over the sheets. Every few minutes, it seemed, I woke and looked around me, hoping for the dawn. The night-light emitted a sickly green glow. Each time I woke, I lay and listened to the tree frogs: ribbons of high-pitched sound layered on top of one another to create one pulsating scream that reached into my dreams like a claw, dragging me, time and again, into my room and the heat.

I heard a sound, a fluttering, thudding sound, coming from the open window. A flash of white, and then a clumsy thing, a feathered, heavy animal fell onto my floor and waddled toward me, its belly brushing the carpet. I wanted to scream, but I could not. Its webbed feet and large wings dragged along the floor, as if it was unused to perambulation. It twisted its neck to look up at me, and I saw a broad, solemn, human face, the face of a fifteen-year-old boy. The thing had shapely arms, too, which grew from the feathered trunk. With a sudden, violent flapping of wings, it heaved itself aloft and landed on my bed, its rubbery, black-skinned paddles scrambling over my bare feet. I crept back, terrified and repulsed, shrinking into the corner. The creature settled onto my crumpled bedclothes like a broody hen, then looked at me, somewhat out of breath from its efforts. It had pale, light-soaked eyes. I knew it for an angel, yet it disgusted me. I wondered if I had invoked it with all that praying I'd been doing.

"I'm sorry," I whispered. That seemed to cover everything—both the bad behavior and the excessive prayer. The great wings began to spread; the thing extended itself, stood up; it was the height of a small man, towering over me in that bed. The wings were as wide as a canopy above me. One pale, human arm floated down toward me. I felt its hot hand resting on my head. My eyes were so heavy, I strained to keep them open; the eyelids felt glued together. The thing's hand was hot, burning; heat surged through my body, then it felt like tiny insects were crawling inside my skin. When the feeling receded, my eyes snapped open. The angel had vanished. I looked around me, frightened, breathless, ran to the open window, shut it, locked it.

The next morning, I was running a fever. My mother kept me in bed. I wondered what she would think of my angel. Would she believe he was real, and if so, what would his visit signify to her? She would probably think there was something unseemly about it. Suky had a dirty mind. She always leapt to salacious conclusions, about parishioners, politicians, movie stars, using amused disapproval to mask intense interest in anything sexual. Why would my angel be any different? I yearned to tell her, but I was afraid, because I knew she would see my angel as her fault, somehow. My sins were her sins; I was a part of her. That was the way she saw it.

Mr. Brown

I sat through a lifetime of Sunday mornings, and in all that time I can remember only one of my father's sermons. I don't know if that is because it was so beautiful or because my father gave it to the congregation on the very day that changed my life. I was sitting in my usual seat in the front row, to Suky's right. She sat bolt upright, her eyes pinned to my father, eyebrows up, her small, weathered hands clamped together, one foot jiggling as my sleepy brothers slumped, inert, on the other side of her.

The sermon was about the cross, and how it is made up of both a vertical and a horizontal beam. Christ, my father posited in his growling voice, was those two things: vertical—godly; and horizontal—of the earth, a living creature. Christianity existed where the two lines met. He said that was what was so special about our God. He had been one of us, yet he was endless and almighty. Because I was actually listening to him for once, I truly saw Des at that moment. He was not a tall man. The way he held his short arms out as he described the cross, palms up, as if feeling for drops of rain in a drought, made him seem futile and precious—a man praying for order in a life governed by chaos. I felt so sorry for him. And then I turned, and it happened. I laid eyes on Mr. Brown.

He was sitting across the aisle from me and one row back, beside the Oakley boys, boarders from the local boys' prep school, in their maroon blazers with light blue crests on the pockets and wrinkled navy slacks. The campus, with its white clapboard buildings and dark green shutters, was, in fact, only a stone's throw away from my house, across the green. From the first moment, I couldn't keep my eyes off Mr. Brown. He was in his forties and seemed ancient to me at that time. But there was something about his face—a bony, veined face—that seemed deeply *good* to me. I loved his rust-colored mustache, his balding pate, his ruddy cheeks. Every Sunday after that, I situated myself in a place where I could see him; I even sat right next to him for one thrilling service. All my life till then, Suky had sat to my left at church. Once I started moving around, she was puzzled, but she didn't stop me. She rarely disciplined me anymore; when she tried, I shrugged her off with a poisonous glare.

Mr. Brown always looked straight ahead during the service, like a bird dog. His wife was an athletic-looking, serious woman. She seemed preoccupied all the time, never speaking to her husband and acting as if he wasn't beside her at all. He compulsively stroked her shoulder with his thumb, his arm around her, and occasionally he would whisper something in her ear, which she would listen to, an opaque expression on her face, and nod. I became convinced that she didn't love him. I watched Mr. Brown in church for ten months. He was my Unimpeachable Gentleman.

I got an after-school job at the Oakley Academy, working in the kitchen, just so I could be close to him. Every day at four o'clock, I would walk across the green to the enormous, steamy Oakley kitchen, reluctantly tuck my copper locks into the requisite paper bonnet, and start peeling carrots and potatoes, dicing celery, getting everything ready for the evening meal. Then it was showtime; I would serve the kids their grub. At first I was frustrated; all the contact I had with my beloved was saying hello as I spooned mashed potato and meat loaf onto his plate. But I shot him glances as I worked. He ate with his wife every night. Their conversations seemed strained yet civil. He always pulled her chair out for her. He talked more than she did; mostly she nodded, unsmiling, staring into her plate. Directly after she had finished her meal, she stood up, murmured a goodbye, and walked out. Mr. Brown would then get himself a cup of coffee and circulate around the dining hall, chatting with the boys. He seemed to relax when his wife was out of the room. He loosened his tie and sat at the edges of the refectory tables, joking with the students. He was reassuring with one, ruffled another's hair, spoke with stiff severity to another. I managed to catch his eye once or twice, but after several weeks I couldn't take it anymore. I had to speak to him.

One night, as he was walking down the hallway after dinner, I threw myself down a short flight of stairs and landed at his feet. I actually sprained my ankle doing this stunt, and he had to hold me up as I limped to the school infirmary. He smelled like talcum powder. At one point, my lip brushed his ear as I hobbled along. He blushed from his neck all the way up to his temples. That's when I knew I was getting somewhere. After that, he called me by my name and always asked how I was when I handed him his dinner. A couple of times I thought I noticed him lingering outside when I came out after my shift. But all he ever did was say "hello" in a cordial, distanced way. Mr. Brown was unimpeachable.

One night, as I left my job, my eyes dried up from exhaustion, my hands raw from chopping, I saw him walking up the stone steps to the dining hall, taking them two at a time with his long strides. He was about to pass me with a friendly greeting when I burst into tears. There was snot coming out of my nose, my knees went weak. I had to sit down. Mr. Brown took out his handkerchief and sat down beside me. I wiped my nose and put my head between my knees. I was so embarrassed, but I was in heaven, too, because I could feel the palm of his hand on the small of my back.

"What is it, Pippa?" he asked. "What's wrong?"

"I think I'm just tired."

"You must be. It seems like a lot for a girl your age, a job after school. Are you sure it's necessary?"

"It's necessary," I said.

"Can't you talk to your parents, maybe they can—"

"It's not the money," I said. "I mean, we don't have much money, but I don't have to have a job in the school year."

"Then quit," said Mr. Brown. "It's too much for you. Use the time to study, or just be a kid."

"I can't quit."

"Why not?" I shook my head then, looking around at the boys walking back to their dorms. One sped by us on his way down the stairs.

"Come with me," said Mr. Brown firmly. He led me by the arm to a building a hundred yards away. There were pillars on the front of it. He opened the door and guided me down a short hallway, reached into an open doorway, flicked on the fluorescent lights. It was a classroom with math equations written on the chalkboard. I followed him in and sat down. He sat on the desk in front of me.

"All right now. No one can hear you. Tell me what's wrong." He was being the teacher now; he had done this countless times, led the troubled kid out of the herd for a few minutes of special time. I felt stupid to have thought it was anything else.

"It's nothing," I said, looking up at him. "I was just—" He was listening to me, but he looked so weary. I was about to give up on him, I really was, but then the tears came to my rescue. I felt them, hot and thick, trickling down my cheeks.

He hopped off the desk, squatted beside me, and put his arm around the back of my chair. "It's just . . . what?" he asked softly. I tried to think of a lie. I could tell him any horror now and he would believe me to be a victim of it. My mind was blank. I told the truth.

"If I quit my job, I wouldn't see you anymore." There was a moment of silence. I looked right at him now. Telling the truth had made me powerful. I had nothing to lose. It couldn't get more embarrassing than this. He looked like the wind had been knocked out of him. And then his cheeks went all mottled. I loved the way his blood exposed him. That moment seemed to extend forever. I saw him hovering between falling toward me and retreat. I had to pull him in somehow. I had to take a risk. "I love you," I said. I knew immediately I had made a mistake.

His brows furrowed for a moment, then he sat back on his haunches. "How old are you?" he asked.

"Sixteen and a half."

"You can't love someone you don't know."

"But I do know you. I've known you for almost a year. I watch you in church. I see you in the dining room. I know you're unhappy and lonely and blue, and that you don't feel loved. You've gotten used to nobody understanding you, nobody being curious about you. You're just Mr. Brown, the guy who fixes things, just like you're here to fix me." He looked up at me, pain and surprise on his face. "You don't have to give me anything," I said. "I just . . . wanted you to know that there's someone who . . . sees you." I felt his gaze churning into me. And I cannot describe how close to him I felt. Andrew Brown, dedicated teacher and resigned husband, was in a state of acute longing and desperation, and had become inured to that condition. But all it took was one little girl who really saw him and—

Mr. Brown stood up, straightened his corduroys, and sniffed.

"You'd better go home now." He smiled at me, a kind, sad, closed-lip smile.

"I'm sorry," I said.

"Don't be, Pippa. Never be sorry for having feelings." I walked out ahead of him and ran all the way home.

The next night, as I slid three slippery slices of turkey onto his plate and poured extra gravy over his mashed potatoes, I felt his eyes on me. I looked up, and there he was, his amber irises flecked with gold; the kindness radiated out of him. His wife came next. She looked right through me. The loose skin on her cheeks, her defeated, frowning mouth, seemed like an affront against the angelic Mr. Brown. A week later, as I walked across the green at dusk after serving dinner at Oakley, I heard his voice. "Pippa." I turned. He was standing a few feet away. His breath was labored, as though he had hurried to follow me.

"Hi," I said.

"Would you like to take a little walk?"

We walked into the sparse wood that fringed the green. The moon had risen, and mist hovered between the young trees. I faltered, stepping on a rotten log; Mr. Brown took my hand. We emerged at the Depot. He let go.

The place was deserted. Pharmacy, liquor store, ice cream parlor—they looked like strange buildings I had never seen before. I was forbidden to walk through my town after dark. We walked to the end of River Road, then along the bank of the river. The moon shed cold, blue light on the faint track worn away by fishermen and kids looking for a place to smoke after school. I had come here myself on occasion. We walked along for a few yards, then he sat down on a big rock covered, I happened to know, with obscene graffiti.

We sat side by side for a few minutes, listening to the high gurgling of the little river. Mr. Brown slid his soft, warm hand over mine. I looked at him. His face was mostly in shadow, but I could see his eyes. He looked so sad. I put my palm up to his face and left it there. And then, swiftly, without warning, the unimpeachable Mr. Brown kissed me. His mustache was soft. The secret tongue inside it felt so warm and new; it was like licking a little, wet animal.

* * *

We were busted eleven months later, in the narrow attic room that Andrew Brown used as a study and a place to meet his students. We were half-dressed (Mr. Brown never allowed us to be completely naked), intertwined and sated on the couch, gazing at a spider as it glided through the air from the ceiling on its own glistening filament, when the door opened with a cursory knock, then swiftly shut. We couldn't see who had come in, but Mr. Brown immediately clamped his hands to his head, remembering his appointment with Mademoiselle Martel, a frowsy teacher visiting from Toulouse. And we hadn't locked the door! I climbed down the fire escape, ran across the green to my house, and waited.

It turned out that, though French, Mademoiselle Martel took a dim view of statutory rape. She blew the whistle, and my beloved Mr. Brown was fired. I'm sure I was, too; I never went back to find out. My parents were called, however. Suky went hysterical. I mean really out of her mind. She wouldn't stop shaking. Tears were flying out of her eyes. She kept saying, "How *could* you?" I leaned back on the wall and looked at her with false calm; behind my ribs, my heart was going berserk. Chester held her arms while my father popped a couple of sleeping pills into her mouth. I tried to laugh, but my throat was closing up.

I knew what was upsetting the pastor's wife. It wasn't her morals being tormented. It was jealousy, straight up. She was crazy with it. In fact, she was plain old crazy. They all were, really, my slow-moving, slow-talking brothers, with their laconic language and leaden eyes—they had all built their personalities up like bulwarks against her mania and neglect. Depressives, every last one of them. And my father—well, he had learned how to take care of himself. I had been eavesdropping on his phone conversations with Mrs. Herbert Orschler for a year. The two of them met every Friday afternoon, like clockwork. Poor old Suky would have no lover now. Because I was leaving. I knew it the minute she heard the news; her face crumpled like a child who's lost her favorite teddy under the wheels of a bus. Gone forever, that little stuffed bear. I couldn't stay after that performance. I mean, I didn't need a degree in psychology to realize there was something wrong between me and my mother.

It came in handy that I was so pissed off. Not just by this one episode but by the pills, by her being so needy all the time—the whole thing. I had become like one of those men you see in the movies who wear aviator sunglasses and chew gum and never get ruffled. That's what I was trying to be: Clint Eastwood if he was a seventeen-year-old girl. I packed some clothes in a duffel bag, took my savings from the job at Oakley, drove my mother's car to the bus station, and left it there with the keys in it. I never got to say good-bye to Mr. Brown. He left Oakley, without his wife. I never heard from him again, but years later I found out he was teaching at a school in Canada. I guess I sort of ruined his life. Or maybe I didn't. Maybe I just freed him from a miserable marriage and a pathetic, colorless existence. Maybe he's happy. Maybe he's got grandkids by now.

Aunt Trish

I knew Mylert Walgreen, the heavy, wheezing kid behind the counter at the bus station. He had graduated from my high school the year before. Mylert's curiosity was definitely piqued by my sudden, solitary trip to New York City in the middle of the school week. I had rarely spoken to Mylert in school; we traveled in different circles. He was one of the kids who shuffled through the halls, head down, knees rubbing together, hoping not to be noticed, not to be teased. I never bothered kids like that; I even defended them now and then against the other bullies. My prey was of a higher order: kids who thought they were cool but weren't. Mylert put on no such airs. Now that he'd graduated, however, he had a certain swagger, an air of adult authority that rankled me.

"Are you running away?" he asked.

"It's not your business what I'm doing, Mylert," I said.

"I'm not supposed to sell tickets to unaccompanied minors," he said.

I sighed, looking up at the ceiling, trying to gather my thoughts.

"So are you?" he asked. "I won't tell anyone."

"No, you dipshit, I'm going to visit my aunt Trish in New York. Now give me the ticket."

"On a Wednesday?" I just glared at him till, looking somewhat put out, he took my money and officiously handed me the bus ticket. I was sweating. Aunt Trish. So that's where I was going. And now I had confided in Mylert Walgreen, of all people! My parents would find out within an hour. Oh, well. What was so terrible about that? I wasn't running away, I was moving away. I had no legal obligation to stay in school anymore. I was starting my life, and that was that.

As the bus pulled away, I thought of Mr. Brown, his flared, delicate nostrils, the bewildered look that came into his eyes when he looked at me. I missed him so much.

* * *

Aunt Trish lived on Thirtieth Street and First Avenue, above the Fresh Day deli. I rang the bell marked "Sarkissian." The apartment was 45. I climbed five flights of wide brown metal stairs. The walls on the way up were lined with white ceramic tiles; the floors in the hallways were tiled with tiny, grimy black and white hexagons. The smell of cigarette smoke and fried onions mingled in the air.

After what seemed like half an hour, I found apartment 45. The door was ajar, and Aunt Trish was right behind it. A small woman, she was shorter than I was, but she gave me a bear hug that nearly cracked my ribs. Aunt Trish was a kind, energetic, helpful woman. She wore round glasses, had short, dark hair; a constellation of black moles dotted her face. Her body was square, short, hunched forward, as though she were always getting ready to break out for a touchdown. I had called her from the bus station.

"Your father called before you did," she said, crouching into a brown, nubbly couch with a Navajo blanket slung over the back of it. I fell into an armchair beside her, my legs spread wide. The chair had a high back and wings on either side of my head. "Apparently, you told the boy at the bus station you were going to see your aunt

Trish." She grinned at this, showing the wide gap between her two front teeth.

"What . . . did my dad say?" I asked.

"He told me you got into trouble."

"Did he say what kind of trouble?"

"Not exactly. Something about the prep school next door to you."

"I fell in love with the math teacher. And we got caught. And my mom is a pill-head." This last piece of news didn't seem to surprise Aunt Trish; it just made her go quiet, a sad smile on her face.

"So what's the plan, Stan?" she asked.

"I just don't want to live at home anymore."

"You've only got a few more months of school left, right?"

"I'm dropping out."

"You're gonna regret that."

"All I know is, I'm not going home."

Trish sighed and looked down at the mahogany coffee table for a long time. On it was a large book with a black-and-white photograph of a mountain on the cover. The scene looked cold and dreary. On the back wall of the living room was a colorful painting of mountains in a desert. There were cacti in the foreground; in the background, the sandy mountains were striped with pastel colors. I wondered what it was about mountains that Trish loved so much.

"Apparently, your mother is pretty upset," she said.

"Oh, really?" Trish caught the ice in my gaze.

"Look, as far as I'm concerned, you can stay in—um—Kat's room for as long as you need to. You're my favorite niece, you know that. But there's going to be a discussion with your parents later today, and it's not going to be pretty." Dread pulsed through me.

"They're coming?"

"They should be here in about two hours." I felt trapped. Maybe the best thing was to get out while there was still time. But where would I go?

"Who's Kat?" I asked.

Aunt Trish lit up a Marlboro from a pack in her shirt pocket. "She's my roommate," she said, inhaling.

"I didn't know you lived with someone."

"She just moved in a couple of months ago," said Aunt Trish. "So. You hungry?"

I shook my head. I hadn't eaten all day, but my stomach felt sealed. She was coming. Suky was coming. I had to hang on to this feeling of rage; I had to keep it going. If I let it collapse, if I let guilt creep in, I would end up in her arms; I would end up sucking on a baby bottle until I was twenty.

Eventually, the buzzer rang. My father's rasping voice sounded incomprehensible over the intercom. I worried about the two of them climbing all those stairs. Aunt Trish went into the hall and looked down the stairwell to be sure they found us. When they arrived, Suky looked wrung out, wan. She kept blinking really hard and smiling at Trish. Then she reached out to hug me and stopped her hands in midair. Des didn't bother taking his coat off. He sat down in Trish's wing-backed armchair and let out a long sigh. Suky and I were at either end of the couch. Trish stood leaning against the kitchen counter, a cigarette in the crook of her fingers, tilted forward, ready, as ever, for the big sprint. I couldn't believe Aunt Trish was even considering keeping me against the will of her older brother. She had always seemed so shy and easygoing to me. And in my experience, adults stuck together. But Trish was different. She rarely showed up for holidays or family gatherings. When she did, she always arrived alone and spent a lot of the time on our porch, on her own, smoking. She would call now and then, send cards and presents, but that was it.

"It's time to come home, Pippa," Des said quietly.

"I'm not going home. I'm staying with Aunt Trish."

Des looked at his sister darkly, then back at me. "You can't just run away from what you've done," he said. "You can't do that in life."

"I'm not running away," I said. "I'm just done, that's all."

"What do you mean, you're done?" he said.

"I don't want to live . . . with you." My eyes fell on Suky for a second, then away.

"Oh, so it's all my fault," she said. Her voice sounded shrill, taunting.

"What's all your fault?"

"What you did. That man has been fired. His wife is, she is . . . devastated."

"I didn't say it was your fault. Nothing is your fault, okay? I just don't want to be home anymore. I can't go back there, and that's that. You can force me to go back, but I'll leave again. I'm done, don't you get it?"

Suky's eyes were swollen and overflowing. "So you're not even coming home for Christmas anymore?"

"Mom, I didn't say that. Please. I will. Of course I'll come home for Christmas, I just don't want to live at home."

"What did I do? What did I do to make you so secretive and unhappy?"

"Nothing. Please, Mom. Please."

Des growled at Suky. "Will you stop whipping her up? For mercy's sake." Then, turning to me, he said, "Do you realize your mother was so upset she had to get an injection to calm her down?"

I looked over at her. She looked crushed; her whole body was slumped to the side of the couch, her face a mask of misery and confusion. A muscle spasm dimpled her cheek with an irregular, terrifying beat. I so wanted to make her better.

"Mommy—" I said. She brightened. A hopeful smile flickered on her face. "I'm sorry, I—I just can't." And then I got up and grabbed my coat from the peg in the entryway, flung open the heavy door, and clattered down the metal steps of Trish's building, my mother's voice echoing through the stairwell—"Pippa come back! Pippa I promise—" I looked at her standing above me. Her sticklike body, that flame of hair: she was a lit match, burning herself right out. I don't remember what she promised. I ran away from her, down First Avenue, zigzagging thirty blocks downtown as the lights changed, all the way to Houston Street. I didn't know where I was going. I turned left and walked fast, head down, imagining her behind me, grabbing at my clothes. I passed Avenues A, B, C, D, till I came to the East River. Then I just stood there on the side of the FDR Drive, cars whipping past behind me, and watched the boats go by, churning up water turned the color of fire by the setting sun's reflection. I was wearing a thin cotton peacoat, and the wind ripped through it. I turned up the collar, shoved my hands deep into my pockets.

"This is where I live"—I dared think it. Intense, surprising happiness socked me in the gut. No one knew exactly where I was at that precise moment. I was just another person in this vast city. If a truck swerved from the highway and mowed me down, I would go to the city morgue, be buried with the bums. For these few seconds, I had escaped the radar of my mother, my father, even Aunt Trish. I was just myself, connected to no one. I was free.

Shackles

When I got back to Trish's place, my parents were gone. I thought of Suky, of what she must have felt when I didn't come back. Of the long, silent car ride back home. I sat down on Trish's couch, put my hands over my face, tasted the salt of my tears.

Trish put her arm around me. "Listen, kiddo. It's tough times. Your mom has a serious problem, okay? I'm saying it. I know no one else will. It's not your fault. I think you did right getting away. It doesn't mean it has to be forever. And it doesn't mean you can't call her and tell her you love her, either." I started sobbing when she said that. Because I did love Suky. I loved her more than I could imagine loving anyone. I felt so bad for hurting her. Trish just kept her arms around me, saying, "Ssh, ssh, it's not your fault. It's not your fault . . ." Eventually, she laid me down under the Navajo blanket and turned on the TV. *Gilda* was playing. I remember thinking, Rita Hayworth had red hair, Suky has red hair. And then I fell asleep.

When I woke up, it was dark outside the window, and I was immediately aware of two people whispering in the kitchen. I turned and saw a tall, gangly woman with dark hair the shape of a Roman centurion's helmet tossing salad in a bowl. She looked down at me and winked. "Hey," she said. Her voice was low, husky. Aunt Trish reached into the oven and took out a tray of sizzling beef patties.

I ate two hamburgers and drank a quart of milk. Kat and Aunt Trish watched me with indulgent grins on their faces. Kat had a lozenge-shaped face, a broad mouth, and eyes that slanted downward. Every now and then, she would bob her head to some song she had in her mind, humming very quietly to herself.

When I finally slowed down on the ravenous eating, Trish laid down the law. "Okay, Pipps. Here's the deal I made with your parents. These are your choices." She raised her stubby thumb. "You go back to school here in the city." The forefinger came up. "You study on your own and take the high school equivalency test." The middle finger now. "You go back home."

I opted for the test. No way was I going to negotiate another high school's social life for just one semester. It wasn't worth the stress. Kat stood up now, cleared the plates, then yawned, stretching her arms high so her concave belly showed beneath her short sweater. "I'm gonna go work in my room a little, before Pippa goes to bed," she said. "Night, Pippa."

"Night," I said. Then Kat turned to Aunt Trish, bouncing from one foot to the other.

"See ya, baby," she said, and bent down to kiss her. Trish moved her head so Kat had to peck her cheek, but Kat took her chin and held it, kissing her right on the mouth. All of a sudden I knew why Aunt Trish wasn't exactly a regular at family events. Kat skipped off into her room/my room. Trish looked at me and made a gesture, a that's-the-way-it-is-what-are-you-gonna-do shrug. I smiled at her encouragingly, raising my eyebrows.

"So we're a couple of black sheep, you and me," said Trish.

Then she cracked a smile and leaked a growling, phlegmy giggle. It was the nicest, most reassuring thing anyone had ever said to me. I felt I belonged somewhere. I belonged on the outside, with Aunt Trish.

* * *

Kat and Trish slept under a shiny maroon bedspread. Over their bed hung a large painting of a naked woman with huge eyes and very long eyelashes. She looked both cute and lewd. Life with Trish and Kat was quiet at first. Kat's room, where I was staying, wasn't a bedroom; it was an office with a couch in it. The desk was cluttered with papers and an electric typewriter. Though she worked as a secretary in a wholesale textile business in Chelsea, Kat was writing a novel. At six in the morning, she would glide in with a mug of tea that smelled of warm mud and start typing. I then dragged the comforter to the couch in the living room and tried to sleep until Trish stomped into the kitchen around seven. She worked in a warehouse in the meatpacking district, carried a clipboard.

Trish made me pull my weight: every day, I took out the garbage, cleaned the kitchen, mopped the floors, studied for the high school equivalency test. And looked for a job. I hadn't had much experience, aside from Oakley, and *they* weren't going to be giving me a recommendation anytime soon. Finally, I found a restaurant on the Lower East Side, El Corazón, willing to take a chance. I didn't speak Spanish and could barely make myself understood in the interview with the enormous, somber owner-chef, Señor Pardo. I couldn't see why they wanted an English-speaking girl working in the place at all till Señor Pardo pointed at a group at one table and said, "You serve the English-speak customers." I looked over. Three young men and a woman in their twenties huddled in a booth, speaking English and smoking filterless cigarettes. There was a pudgy, blond fellow with flecks of paint on his hands, an elegant, tall one with very long black hair, a girl with a large nose and an amused-looking, painted mouth, and a skinny guy with puffy eyes and a poker face who was slumped in his seat. They all looked exhausted. "Now," said Señor Pardo, handing me an order pad. I walked over to the group. "The United States loses the war in Vietnam," the pudgy one was saying, "Greg Brady gets a perm."

"Do you know what you want?" I asked.

"There goes the neighborhood," said the thin, puffy-eyed fellow. But as he looked up at me with his poker face, his gaze stayed on me for an instant too long. They all ordered margaritas. I served this group almost daily for months, I learned their names, but I never went out with them, never saw where they lived. Until later.

* * *

I felt elated in Kat's presence. She was glamorous, in a way, always jutting out her small breasts, swiveling her narrow hips in tight bell-bottoms, making poor old Aunt Trish seem dusty and square, her dark eyes moist with devotion to the creature she shared her bed with. Once, I asked Kat what her novel was about. She flashed Trish a sly smile.

"Let's just say it's no work of art," she said.

"But what's it about?"

"Love," she said. "The mysteries of love." Aunt Trish blushed and got up to clear the table. I wanted to read that novel.

One night, the two of them had a dinner party. They invited a few women and two men. I was invited, too. I wore a lavender sundress, even though it was frigid outside. It was the only dress I had brought with me from home. When she saw me in it, Kat whistled a long, low note that made me blush. One of the women at the party was named Shelly. She was brash, had sandy blond hair and a big chest. She kept saying, "When I was in the film business," which for some reason made everybody laugh, except for Aunt Trish. She didn't laugh, she looked at her plate through her round glasses, smiling and shaking her head.

Then there was a man named Jim, small, in his forties, with yellowish skin, a handsome jawline, a cleft chin, and rotten teeth. He wore a felt fedora and an old tweed coat. He didn't drink the wine. "I'm sick," he explained to me in a breathy voice. "So you and me will be sober, okay, and we can watch all the rest of them fall apart." Jim was curious about me. "So . . . where do you go to school?" I explained that I had dropped out, left home; I was on my own now. "Very cool," he said. "Very unusual. You didn't run away. You left. I like the way you put that." His watery green eyes were constantly focused on another part of the room as he spoke to me, which made him seem blind, though I was pretty sure he wasn't. I asked him what his sickness was. He said he had diabetes. He'd already had to have a toe amputated. He removed his shoe, then his sock, and showed me a pale foot with a gap where the little toe was meant to be. "And there are other . . . side effects I won't go into, which render me harmless," he said, his lips turned up in a rueful smile. He was weird, but I liked him.

As the evening progressed, the heat from the radiators became so intense that people started taking off their cardigans, socks, stockings. Jim shed his coat and hat. His hair was very black. At one point, he leaned against the wall and left a smudge on it from the back of his head. The other guests were friends of Trish's: a drab, sad-looking couple of women who lived in New Jersey, and an acne-ridden man named Eric, who made flamboyant gestures, got very drunk, and had to lie down in the office. I hoped he wouldn't throw up in there. After the Boston cream pie, Kat shot up out of her seat. She was wearing a red, sleeveless dress that clung to her slender frame. "I say we go out on the town," she said, waving her long arms in the air like windmills, her cheeks flushed from the wine.

She turned to Shelly. "You'd know where to go," she said, jutting one hip out.

"I'm based in San Francisco now," said Shelly. "What do I know?"

"The city hasn't changed *that* much," said Kat.

"What kind of an evening do you have in mind?"

"Insane," Kat answered, winking at Aunt Trish.

Trish shook her head, smiling. She had work the next day; she wasn't going anyplace. She wanted to keep me home, too, but Kat insisted that I come along, with Jim as a chaperone.

"It's always handy to have a eunuch around," said Jim as he hung Trish's parka over my bare shoulders.

I was happy to be going out for once, but I felt bad for Aunt Trish. She seemed so nervous. But she couldn't say no to Kat, not about anything. So we all tromped down the freezing street with our arms up, trying to flag down a cab. At last, two of them stopped for us and we divided ourselves up. The dreary women from New Jersey decided to get back on the PATH train, and the flamboyant man weaved his way uptown on foot. So I got into one cab with Jim, Kat, and Shelly. Shelly sat in the front. As we bounced downtown on no suspension, the chassis slamming the pavement with every pothole, Kat kept bursting into dance songs, punching her arms in the air like a boxer. Jim called out a few points of interest to me as we passed them: Fifth Avenue, the Flatiron Building, Union Square. We stopped on West Fourteenth Street, near the river. The street was deserted. The worn cobblestones shone with the light from a lone streetlamp. There was no sign of a club of any kind.

As if remembering something, Shelly turned to look at me, then started rummaging through her purse and took out a lipstick. "We'll have to age her up," she said, twisting up the shiny, red tube and applying some onto my mouth. Then she dragged my hair from its ponytail and ruffled it so it half-hid my face. "Look," she said to Kat. "It's Veronica fuckin' Lake." I felt Kat's eyes on me then, and I stood still for an extra second, my eyes averted, so she could see me as this Veronica Lake whom I had not heard of but I knew was beautiful. She had to be, with a name like that. Shelly beckoned to us. We followed her down a short, dark stairway, through a graffiti-scrawled metal door, to a ticket booth. The man behind the fingerprint-dappled Plexiglas seemed happy to see Shelly. His gray hair was greased back into a neat ducktail, his pockmarked skin the color of putty.

"Oh hi, Suzanne, where have you been?" he asked her in a nasal baritone.

"I'm based in San Francisco," said Shelly.

"Welcome home. It's Ladies' Night! You've got one guy between the three of yous tonight? Ten dollars." Jim reached for his wallet, but Shelly slid a crisp folded bill under the window. To our right was a fringed plastic sheet, like the kind in car washes. Hazy purple light shone behind it. Loud music throbbed. We ducked our heads and passed through this fringed hymen. Upon emerging, I was amazed to see a middle-aged man wearing a fawn-colored turtleneck and glasses, naked from the waist down but for socks and running shoes. He had a drink in one hand, his half-risen penis in the other, and was masturbating halfheartedly, a bored expression on his face, while wandering around. "Keep your back to the wall," Jim suggested helpfully.

Sidling toward the edge of the room, I saw that it was lined with books. I moved closer to glance at the titles. They were all pornographic: *I Was a Teenage Sex Slave*, *Seven Amazing Fantasies Come True*. Several people were clustered around the spotlit center of the room, watching a man with a bushy mustache pour hot wax on a bound, pale woman's naked breasts. Her skin glowed in the light. A small, muscular fellow with a saddle strapped to his back trotted up to Shelly and greeted her effusively as Suzanne. Hand on hip, one leg thrust out, he asked her about a mutual friend, the leather of his tack creaking behind him. Shelly answered him with a slightly pompous affability; she was clearly a star of some kind in this netherworld. Meanwhile, Kat did a little solipsistic dance to the constant beat, occasionally throwing a few shadow punches. I tripped and fell, realizing too late that the bundle of dirty laundry I'd landed on was a scantily clad man chained to a metal pole. Jim hoisted me up with trembling arms as I apologized effusively. Just then, a petite woman being led on a leash by a skinny guy in a striped shirt came tottering up to Shelly, arms outstretched. We were all introduced. The girl had iron cuffs on her wrists, joined by a long chain. Her name was Renee; her boyfriend was Miles. Miles had a moist, boneless handshake. "Sit," he said to Renee. Renee sat down beside Shelly.

"How have you been?" she asked Shelly. "The last time I saw you was in Chicago, at the leather conference."

"Oh, God, that was wild."

"I don't think we're going this year," said Renee, widening her round, brown eyes and looking up at Miles complacently. "Miles has a new baby nephew and he's being christened, so . . ." She crossed her legs. I realized then that her ankles were also shackled. Renee looked up at Miles again. "Honey, could you get me a pop?"

"Sure," said Miles. "Anyone else want anything?" We shook our heads. He hesitated, holding the end of Renee's leash, unsure of whom to entrust it to. Finally, he settled on Jim.

"Will you hold this till I get back?"

"No problem," said Jim, his serious face filled with submerged amusement.

"Pippa, are you in school?" asked Renee.

"I'm studying at home," I said.

"I never even graduated," she said.

"When did you . . . start—"

"Oh, this?" she said, raising her bound wrists, the chain tinkling. "Um . . . we were both just kids, and one day we were making out in Miles's garage, and he tied me up, and we just really liked it!" Renee smiled, and deep dimples appeared in her cheeks. She was so wholesome. Miles returned with a bottle of Dr Pepper and handed it to Renee, thanking Jim as he took back the leash.

"That's Stan and Lisa," Renee said to me, indicating the spotlit pair in the center of the room. "They are so cute, he always says he loves her after their show is over."

I surveyed the crowd clustered around Stan and Lisa. Among them, a very young, light-haired girl, about six months pregnant, had a collar and leash around her neck, but she was holding the handle of the leash herself. She had an intent look on her luminous face as she watched Stan, who was now flicking a cat-o'-nine-tails onto the expanse of Lisa's flesh, leaving little red stripes on her white skin. I couldn't take my eyes off the pregnant girl. What was she doing here? Why was she holding her own leash?

A stern "Sit!" from Miles drew my attention away. To my surprise, Shelly and shackled Renee were now kissing! Miles let them make out for a few seconds, Renee half-standing to get a better purchase on Shelly, then he jerked back on her leash, forcing her to sit. Then it started up again.

"I don't think Trish would be too happy about you seeing this," said Jim.

"Oh, this is where you draw the line?" I asked. "Some chaperone."

He smiled widely, and I could see he was missing a number of teeth on the side of his mouth. Miles checked his watch and stood up, leading Renee from her seat. She complimented me on my sundress, indenting her dimples with a smile. As they left, I saw that Kat had her boot on the prone, shackled man's sooty head and was resting it there, conquering, immobile, like a Victorian hunter posing for a daguerreotype with his foot on a dead lion. Shelly, alone now, watched from her chair. The dead-eyed look those women gave each other intrigued and frightened me. Jim took my arm. I glanced back at the pregnant girl, but she was gone; Stan and Lisa had vanished. When I looked to Kat again, her eyes were clamped on me with an impersonal, scrutinizing stare. I returned her gaze too long, I knew—too long to be right, too long for Aunt Trish.

That night, in the dark, awake under the covers on the lumpy couch in Kat's room, I lay in wait for memories of my Mr. Brown: his long, pale fingers, the rough tweed of his worn jacket that smelled of pipe tobacco when I pressed my nose in it, the round toes of his brogans, the dull rose gold of his wedding band as it glinted in the half-light. He was so dear, so kind, my Mr. Brown. He always caressed me with tender longing, as if saying goodbye. He taught my hands and my mouth with a solemn air, an educator even in his pleasure.

Once, he drove me all the way to the shore during Easter break, our only foray outside the world of his little study. It was a warm, cloudy day in April. There were three people on the pebbly beach: a heavy man in khaki shorts and a windbreaker; a small woman with frizzy brown hair; and a tubby kid with a kite that wouldn't quite lift off the ground, though it kept making little, hopeful hops into the air.

Mr. Brown and I pulled off our clothes. We both had on our bathing suits underneath. His was baggy green nylon. His legs were thin, the hair on them reddish. I was in my shiny blue swim team Speedo suit, the only one I owned. It made my chest look flat, which I resented. But Mr. Brown knew better. We hobbled along for a while, the stones bruising our tender feet, until we came to a cluster of rocks, about fifty yards from where the people were. We sat and watched the gulls, creamy white, gliding against the ice gray sky. He turned to me and said, "You know that sand is just very finely ground rock."

"Oh," I said. "That must take forever."

"Millions of years," he said, letting some sand sift through his long, curled fingers. I put my forefinger in the elastic band of his swim trunks and watched his eyes glaze over, as they always did when desire infused him. He was sitting with his back to the beach. No one could see. I firmly stroked those nylon swim trunks until he closed his eyes in rapture. Oh, heaven.

And when our days of tenderness were over, Mr. Brown left me a virgin. Yes, after all that fuss, I lay on the couch in Aunt Trish's apartment as whole as the day I was born. I had tried to make it otherwise. I was desperate for Mr. Brown to fuck me, but he said that was a step too far. I wanted to marry him. I had it all worked out: we would live in a little house in Massachusetts, or someplace else in the liberal far north; he would get a job at one of the fancy boarding schools up there, and I would spend the day getting myself ready for him, softening my skin, brushing my hair, plucking my eyebrows. Every night, my beloved would return to me, and come close to dying of pleasure. Mr. Brown chuckled sadly when I recounted my fantasy, lowering his eyelids so I could see the veins through the papery skin, and said, "Oh, my girl, no, you're made for better things." That statement always made me feel lonely, because it implied an end to our affair but also because it hinted at some promise inside me that I was unaware of, like a tumor embedded in my flesh, making ready to bloom. I felt frightened of the future then, and huddled up against my lover's hard chest, seeking some hint of feminine softness, some extra bit of flesh to hang on to. But there was none. Mr. Brown's body was stiff as a tree.

Still wakeful on the night of the whips and chains, I mulled over my life so far. I was a botch. I could see no future. I had no plans. I saw no example I wished to follow. I didn't want to be a nurse, or a stewardess, or a secretary; I didn't want to work in the meatpacking district or be a housewife. I just wanted to prowl around. I walked the streets endlessly. Watching people. I had a ravening mind; I wanted I wanted I wanted. I wanted into people's lives. I followed couples as they scurried down the street, carrying groceries and bunches of flowers, children tugging on their arms. I followed businessmen on their way from work. I followed elegantly dressed women who marched resolutely down the street and raised their hands for taxis. They were all bustling, all running, all rushing. Everyone in New York City seemed to have a purpose, except for me. I was driven by a need with no end, no goal. I was looking for love, I think, though that's not what it felt like at the time. At the time I felt hard and cold as a knife in the snow.

Knight

One time I followed this guy. His hair was a tangled web of blond curls that fell to hunched, narrow shoulders. He made me think of a cattail reed. It was wickedly cold, but all he was wearing was a pin-striped suit and a cashmere scarf. Sneakers. I walked out of work, saw him pass me by, and followed him all the way from Orchard Street to Twenty-third and First. He ducked into a coffee shop. I walked in behind him. He sat at the counter. I sat beside him. He ordered pea soup. I asked for hot chocolate. I looked at his face. He was older than I thought. At least twenty-five. His nose was red. He felt my stare, turned. His face was pale, with a high forehead and Nordic features, like a knight, it seemed to me. He looked right at me and shivered. "Freezing," he said, blowing into his cupped hands.

"You're not wearing enough," I said.

"I thought I'd be straight in a cab," he said. "I always forget they change shifts this time of day." His eyes passed over my body. "You're all bundled up."

"I always walk home from work," I said.

His soup came, then my cocoa. We ignored each other for a few moments.

"What's your job?" he asked. "If you don't mind—"

"I wait tables," I said.

"That's a tough job."

"Have you ever—?"

"No."

I knew we would walk to his place. I wasn't thinking about making love; he was going to be my boyfriend, that was all. I was already imagining our apartment. It would have those round, paper globe shades on all the lights, and shelves filled with books. He was clearly a reader. So, after he finished his soup, said goodbye politely, and walked out, my cheeks burned with humiliation and loss.

Kitty

I knew Kat was no good for Aunt Trish. I saw she was playing her, but I was drawn to her in spite of myself. I guess I figured she was bad like me. Good people like Aunt Trish filled me with anxiety because I knew one day they would see I was just a destructive little fucker. Kat bought me clothes, tight jeans and floaty tops, platform shoes and huge hoop earrings. I was flattered by her attention. When Aunt Trish saw me in my new getups, she would click her tongue and blush, but she wouldn't say a word against Kat. All she'd say was "You better not wear that when you go back home to visit." That was her way of saying I better visit. My father called every few days to see how I was doing, and then Suky would get on the line. I missed her terribly, but when I heard that drug in her voice, I felt violence rising up in me. My voice went dead; I was abrupt, rude, horrible to her. Then I would hang up and cry, sob into my pillow, "I was mean, I was mean," and Trish would stroke my head until I fell asleep.

Kat always looked unrecognizable when she went to work in a cheap skirt suit and pumps, her thick hair teased to high heaven, lips slippery with gloss, eyelids iridescent blue. She looked like she was in drag. But one morning, after Trish left, as I washed the breakfast dishes, sponged down the table, swept the floor, Kat stood observing me in her dressing robe, her arms folded. I felt self-conscious and a little alarmed. Ever since the night at the club, when she had set her foot on that shackled man's head and stared at Shelly, I had known she was a little bit dangerous. That novel she was writing—I had read it, of course. It was full of sex. That's pretty much all it was. It was a book about a young woman named Kitty, and her adventures with other women. Kitty went prowling around hunting for pleasure. When she saw a girl she liked, she pounced. It didn't matter if her prey was a married woman of fifty or a child of twelve. Kitty always got her girl. I read the latest installment every night when I went to bed. It made such an impression on me that I committed one passage of her prose to heart:

Kitty looked at Mrs. Washington. Though no longer young, she had smoky black eyes and a long neck, her breasts were full, her hair lustrous. There was no way Kitty was going to spend one more night as a guest in this woman's country estate without slipping a finger in her pussy.

Kat made sense to me once I started reading her novel. I had seen part of a porn film once; two of my brothers, the Dim Twins, took me into New Haven to buy Christmas presents for the rest of the family. We each had our savings in our pockets—in our godly family, you were expected to save your allowance all year to buy presents for your siblings. Once we stepped off the train, Rob and Griffin, both thirteen, took me by the hand and said we were watching a movie and *then* buying the presents. I was eight. We got into the theater only because we were short enough to creep by the booth without the ticket collector seeing us. My brothers had bought me a lollipop to keep me occupied, and I, in my innocence, sat licking the thing as the opening credits came up.

In the first scene, a woman was lying on a couch in a silk nightie. There was a knock on the door. She opened it. It was the TV repairman. Within twenty seconds, the two of them were in a clump on the couch, jerking around. Griffin, the brother to my right, had his hand in his pants at this point, and I whacked him on the side of the head. The tussle that ensued, with the three of us clamped onto one another, arms flailing like some crazy octopus, me scratching and biting the twins and they spitting into my face and head-butting me, attracted an usher, who led us out fast, cursing. I came away from that incident with a bloody nose and the certainty that you had to get to the point fast in dirty movies. And Kat sure did that. Her alter ego, Kitty, didn't waste a second. No sooner did she arrive at the ornate country mansion than she was feeling up the parlor maid and pressing up against her hostess.

At first, I thought I was reading the manuscript behind Kat's back. But I think she must have noticed that it changed location, because after that first time, she made sure she left it in a neat pile right by my bed. Every morning during breakfast, she would look at me and wink. Poor Aunt Trish. I don't know how much she knew about Kat. Yet how could she not have known? There was Kat's obscene friend Shelly, the "actress," who, despite being "based in San Francisco," was in and out of the apartment every few weeks; there was the hypersexy, slightly spastic way Kat moved and spoke—not to mention what she was writing . . . Well, I guess the thing was, Trish loved Kat, and she wanted to believe she was loved in return.

That morning, as I knelt under the table, sweeping up the crumbs from under her seat, Kat contemplated me silently for a long time. And then finally she said, "What do you want to be when you grow up?" I sat back on my haunches, looked up at her, and shrugged.

"Well," she said, "what are you good at?" The thought of Mr. Brown closing his eyes at the beach, astonishment on his face as I touched him slowly and deliberately, came into my mind.

"Nothing," I said.

"You have to have some kind of talent."

I shrugged. "Not everybody has talent."

"People who don't have talent are usually nice," said Kat. "Are you nice?"

I saw Suky, slumped on the side of Trish's couch as though she had been shot. I shook my head.

"Well then, you'd better have talent," said Kat.

"What are you on my case for?" I asked.

"I believe in you, kid," she said. And then she went into the bathroom to turn herself into someone's secretary. When she came back, she pretended to have an idea on the spot. She needed some dirty pictures to illustrate her novel. She wanted me to be her Kitty. I thought about it for a few seconds. "I'll pay you, too, if the book gets published."

"Okay," I said.

Getting naked was the easy part. It was the outfits I balked at. Kat had been hoarding them in the closet of her office in a big, cardboard box marked "Kitchen Supplies." There were riding breeches with the crotch cut out, a stewardess dress with snap-on boob covers, a rubber cat suit. It was absurd. I couldn't stop laughing. Especially since Suky had basically been doing this to me since infancy: I was dressed up as Mae West at three, Jayne Mansfield at seven. Suky kept all my dress-up duds in a wooden box we called the "fun box." Even now that Suky has left me—having politely, obligingly, and without fuss stopped breathing one foggy evening—even now I believe those bizarre and slightly creepy albums are stored somewhere in Chester's basement. The pages may be disintegrating, eaten out by the acid in the cheap paper, but if you were to open one of those leatherette volumes, you would be surprised to find not pictures of four boys and a girl, a healthy, happy family of the local pastor, but the likeness of only one child, a strawberry blond, sloe-eyed girl in a skimpy dress and feather boa, staring the camera down. Pippa at one, at two, at three and five, at seven to fourteen, her expressions moving, as the years went by, from innocent cheer to a knowing, sullen stare, and finally to full-fledged hatred. So, I was a natural.

Kat couldn't believe it. I had no shyness at all in front of the camera. I looked at it as if it were a person I knew and didn't like. That's what she said, anyway. She said it was "pure Kitty." Kitty, she explained, was every woman's wild side. She was fearless.

"Don't you wish *you* were fearless?" she asked as she reloaded her battered Canon.

"I guess so," I said.

"You act hard, but you're a marshmallow. If you were fearless you wouldn't cry every time you hang up the phone after talking to your mother. You would forget the past. You would look ahead."

"Is that what you do?"

"Oh, baby. I'm the girl from Pluto. I'm the scary thing."

"How did you ever get hooked up with Aunt Trish?"

"I know, right? But she loves me. She's my Momma. Not everything has to make sense, Chicklet."

The next morning she came bouncing out of the bathroom in her sweats, shadowboxing. No work today; she'd called in sick. The doorbell rang. Shelly burst in, her naturally amplified voice bouncing around her spacious rib cage. She let out a Texan "Whoop!" then started pawing through Aunt Trish's record collection, derisively holding up a Carole King album.

"Don't even bother," said Kat, producing a cardboard box from under the electric piano. "Check mine out." They put on "Knock on Wood" and danced to Otis Redding singing "I better knock—on wood, yeah . . ." Shelly's dance was obscene, her thick pelvis thrusting forward again and again, an ugly frown on her face, her arms in the air, big, hard breasts stretching her sweater. "Let's get this show on the road!" she bellowed. Kat oozed to the downbeat, her eyes hooded, glazed, private. She touched my wrist very lightly, drawing me in. I began to move to the music, aware, somehow, of turning my back on good Aunt Trish and entering a poisonous, glimmering circle. I felt a sharp, defiant joy at my recklessness.

Shelly had been cast in the part of Mrs. Washington, the wealthy woman whom Kitty seduces in her country mansion. So this session was going to involve a certain amount of *reenactment*. In a trance of creativity, wearing a new, self-important face, Kat placed the lights, chose the costumes, set the scene: I am dressed in a pair of large white girls' underwear, a pointy black bra, and high-heeled, black fetish shoes. I am stealing Mrs. Washington's pearls. Mrs. Washington walks in, dressed in her riding clothes. She looks imperious. Infuriated by my crime, she decides I am in need of a beating. This was a still photo we were posing for, yet Kat directed us as though it were a scene in a film. Shelly got herself so worked up when she discovered me that she actually wept with rage. Kat was over the moon about her performance.

But now, having so utterly nailed this preamble, our director was confounded by a technical dilemma: when Mrs. Washington gave me my lashes, how were we to make the scene seem real without hurting me? Kat suggested that Shelly grab the rubber paddle conveniently stowed on the mantelpiece and bring it down to just above the skin of my buttocks, so it looked like she was spanking me. Shelly tried, but her aim was off, you might say. She brought the thing down so hard I let out a yelp. A little red welt rose up on my butt; I craned my neck to see it. At first, Kat rushed toward me, to see if I was hurt. But something in my astonished expression must have told her I was feeling all right. "Shall we try that again?" she asked quietly. I nodded.

So we took a little detour from illustrating Kat's book. At first, I couldn't believe it was happening. I mean, don't get me wrong; if I cut my finger, I say "ow," like everyone else. But there was something about the circumstances here, the setup, the elaborate way I was tied to the table or the bed or the radiator. The pain was different from stubbing my toe. If it went on long enough, if I was spanked or whipped or slapped long enough, my skin went cold and tingling, I was able to bust through the pain, leaving the reality of the moment, into another place where I couldn't really see anything in focus. The feeling I had there was serene, silent, empty, euphoric. My Feeling reminds me of the happiest born-agains, ones I've seen on TV, when their eyes roll back in their heads and they raise their arms, out of their minds on bliss. This particular ecstasy was limited to those few weeks with Kat and Shelly. I have never been able to pass through pain that way again. Or I haven't allowed myself to.

Fever

Here's the thing we didn't think of: one afternoon, Aunt Trish came home from work with a fever. She turned the key in the lock, heard Gladys Knight blasting out of her bedroom, hurried in, and found me manacled to the bed with the skirt of a pink crinoline gown over my head, being slapped by Shelly as Kat photographed us, shouting, "Great! Do that again. Freeze. Okay! Beautiful!" Aunt Trish was standing there, pale, shivering, and horrified, when I turned and saw her.

I moved out that afternoon, while Aunt Trish was sleeping off her flu, having called the police and watched the woman she loved flee her apartment. I couldn't bear to be there when she woke up; I was too ashamed.

The only person I knew in New York, aside from Aunt Trish, was Jim, the diabetic with the missing toe. His apartment was in a Brooklyn basement with a sizable garden. He stayed there rent free, because his old friend Roy, a drug dealer in his fifties, kept some of his supply stashed in Jim's broom closet and various other locations in the apartment. Jim also sold drugs for Roy on occasion. Kat had taken me to his place a few times. Jim always doled out shortbread cookies and black coffee, then handed Kat a brown paper bag as she was leaving. This sideline, along with disability checks for his diabetes, enabled Jim to live the life of an artist and man-about-town. Though well below the poverty line, he always had a bit of cash on hand, and he welcomed me to his modest home as if I was a visiting queen.

I had the sense, as I dropped my duffel bag on Jim's shiny floor painted the color of pomegranates, that I was slipping off the edge of what I had known the world to be and floating in dangerous space. Aunt Trish had been family. Jim was unknown territory, a new life. Suky would go crazy if she knew. My excitement was liberally spiked with guilt. I would call her soon. I would. But for now, I sat at Jim's kitchen table, sipping strong coffee brewed on a paint-spattered double burner and eating a piece of buttery shortbread. The hot coffee melted the sweet, rich cookie in my mouth. I looked out the glass of his back door, into his tiny garden, walled off by a fence of old painted doors.

Everything in the little apartment had been considered in some way, was either lovely or bizarre or instructive. The shelves were packed with books about everything from cave painting to rocket design: *Nuns' Habits Through the Ages*, *The Art of Holograms Revealed*. I spent hours that first afternoon flipping through books, learning about painters, mostly, from Piero della Francesca to Bonnard, Manet to Pollock. Jim's work was stacked neatly, facing the wall. Shyly, he turned a piece around to show me. It was a collage made up of countless shreds of paper, movie tickets, newspaper clippings, warning labels, which all cohered to make a landscape. It was obsessively constructed, but the composition reminded me of the paint-by-numbers sets I used to work on when I was a kid. Until I found the little figures hidden in the rocks or the shrubbery— incongruous beer maids peeled off of beer bottles, the man on the

Mr. Clean bottle, a naked calendar girl. Jim would Xerox the images and shrink them, so they looked like evil elves lurking in a pleasant countryside constructed out of refuse.

Jim rarely sold his work, he had no gallery, but he was ferociously dedicated. He would wake late—eleven or twelve—then perform his elaborate toilette, which included applying a light coat of Elizabeth Arden foundation makeup to his sallow skin and covering his thinning pate with black shoe polish. Only then did he begin to work, sorting through the bins of scrap paper, bits of rag, string, hair—anything to make his landscapes thrum with color and texture. In lieu of rent, I was sent out some mornings to look for material, and I would root around in the garbage, on the street, in magazine racks, for the perfect scarlet, the most acid cerulean.

At three in the afternoon, I went to work. I had found another restaurant, down the street, to hone my serving skills in. When I got off, at nine, Jim was just hitting his stride. I marveled at his ability to work all day, stop to make some inventive pasta dish for the two of us, then go back to his labors for another six or seven hours, finally smoking a joint and hitting the sack at dawn. He would do this for days at a time, then take a few days off and sleep. He was surprised the first night I came home from work bone tired, stood by him as he fitted a torn corner of salmon pink tissue paper onto the rectangle of board on the table, and said, "Can I have some?"

"Have some what?" he asked.

"Speed." He looked up at me, surprised but smiling. "How do you know?"

"That's the one I know about," I said.

"How old are you now?" he asked, crinkling his forehead.

"Seventeen."

"Did you graduate from high school yet?"

"That's what I want it for. The test is next Thursday. I have to study."

"You can have a little," he said. "But don't overdo it. By Thursday you'll be insane." So he gave me a round, white pill that he kept in a misshapen ceramic pinch pot on a shelf next to the sea salt. I swallowed it. The speed hit me hard, like the smell of ammonia. Everything in the room snapped into extreme focus; it all seemed extra clean, and bright. I hadn't felt so awake, so cheerful, so filled with purpose since the day I swallowed ten of Suky's finest back in junior high. "One thing you can't do," Jim said, "is start talking. You start talking on this stuff, you never stop." I retreated to my makeshift bedroom—a daybed blocked from the rest of the room by a swath of old pink silk—and read two entire books, one on history, one on math. Hitherto ungraspable concepts glided into my mind like melted butter into pancake batter.

I emerged from my lair to tell Jim how incredibly smart I had become, he said something in response, and we were off. We talked for six hours straight, said things so perceptive and profound that it amazed us no one in the history of the world had yet come up with them. Jim even took notes, our ideas were so brilliant. Finally, we crashed. When we woke, hours later, to read the scrawled notes he had written during our jam session, and found that they contained pearls of wisdom such as "flounder are bottom-feeders, hence should never be eaten with carrots or other vegetables that grow underground or you can develop depressions, NUTRITION IS EVERYTHING," I was dumbfounded, but Jim just nodded his head with a rueful smile. When I opened the history and math books that I had wolfed down, I recognized next to nothing, except what I had already gone over the old-fashioned, nondrug-induced way, so I went back to my old method of studying. I passed the high school equivalency test.

Surprisingly, Jim had a girlfriend: a Swedish woman named Olla. She was around forty, an artist, very kind to Jim, and she didn't seem to mind me hanging around. We would go out sometimes, the three of us, to museums or movies. Jim and Olla taught me about painting, the history of it and the point of it. I came to recognize different periods, different artists. I went to the galleries and even started forming my own opinions about the new art.

Jim had reminded me how harmless he was so many times that I figured sex was not a part of his life anymore. He would lounge around the apartment with his socks off, feet up. The smooth gap left by his missing pinkie toe made him seem curiously unreal, like an imperfect doll. But Olla was always kissing him, making much of him, and guiding him gently into his bedroom for an hour or so at a time while I sat in the garden, or did the dishes, or went out on a walk. I liked Olla, and I was determined to seem as nonthreatening as possible. After Mr. Brown and Aunt Trish I didn't want to wreck anyone's life, and I didn't want to end up on the street, either.

Crash

I still don't know the reason for what happened next. I don't understand it. I mean, I was doing relatively well. I had a job, a place to live, friends, I had finished school.

It started with a normal dose of speed one night. We were all going out dancing: me, Jim, Olla, and a bunch of their friends, hardcore bohemians in their forties, missing the occasional tooth. I hardly ever went out anywhere, so it was a big night for me; I didn't want to drag around exhausted from work. I danced all night, and in the morning I just couldn't bear the idea of going to bed and waking up with my head raw and jangled, my thoughts morose. So I swallowed some more, to keep up the happiness. Jim didn't know. He wasn't counting his stash. I went to work high and slapped those plates of eggs Florentine and Belgian waffles onto the tables so quick that whipped cream and hollandaise sauce spattered all over my arms. A few customers needed sponging down, but at least they got fast service.

That night, I decided to go out on my own and see what happened. Before I left, I got up on my tiptoes and reached into the clumsy clay speed pot like a kid filching M&M's. By now I had been levitating for forty-eight hours. I was starting to feel omnipotent. I took the 2 train into Manhattan with no idea of where I was going, jumped out of my seat at Fourteenth Street. Hot air laced with feces swirled around the platform as I hurried out of the train. There was a sound in my head, a high, metallic whistle. My movements were fluid, precise, like those of a perfect machine. My mind felt spotless, sterilized, my thoughts gleamed like stainless steel. The people and cars around me, by contrast, were pulsing in a staggered, irregular pattern, freezing one moment, then oozing by in slow motion the next, as though time had become as elastic as toffee. A gleaming scenario played and replayed itself in my head with razorlike precision; I was going to find that pregnant girl with the flaxen hair who was holding on to her own leash, the one I had seen the time I came to the club with Kat and Shelly, and I was going to save her life. I would track her down in her filthy squat and swoop in like a commando, excise her from her perverted existence, buy her a square meal, take her home to Olla and Jim. We would all live together, the five of us, a family. Her child would be fair, with violet eyes and a saintly disposition.

I searched the streets around there, trying to find the club Shelly had taken us to. All I could remember was five steps down, a metal door. At last, I found it. The sweaty, sharp-eyed woman behind the Plexiglas booth looked up from her book. She didn't know anything about the pregnant girl. She told me this was her first night of work here, and she couldn't stand the fucking heat.

I pushed the heavy plastic fringe aside, ducking my head, and emerged into the windowless library. The ceiling was very low. There was no music on. Purple and red lights flashed mutely. As I walked in, the few souls wandering around the room eyed me hungrily, like bored guests at a failing party, sizing up a new arrival. I wondered whether I was moving strangely. Music came on—a rigid beat. I walked into the back room, a kind of cave, also lined with paperbacks, and pierced with tiny cubicles. On a narrow stage, a middle-aged woman in a leather corset danced for a middle-aged man. The door of one of the cubicles swung open; a male figure emerged and walked away fast, head down. A light-haired, slender girl remained in the cubicle, her back to me, buttoning her blouse. I stood, waiting. She swiveled around and looked at me expectantly. She was young, but her face was puffy and slack. "I thought you might be someone else," I said, turning.

Back in the main room, Lisa and Stan were setting up their act. Maybe the pregnant girl would be coming in later. She had loved Stan and Lisa. Remember how she had stood, transfixed, her wide eyes unblinking, her small hand grasping the handle of her leash, as though her owner had abandoned her? A spotlight came on, illuminating the pair. I walked up to them and stood just inside that pool of light, exactly where I had seen the pregnant girl standing. I was almost close enough to touch them. Others gathered around them, too, waiting for the performance to begin, eyes glazed, hungry, and vacant.

Lisa lay on the low bed. She was blindfolded with a band of black leather. Her bare belly was pale and flaccid, a concave hammock of flesh hung between two wide-set, mountainous hip bones. Her large breasts spread out across her chest. The skin around the nipples was crowded with marks. Some of them looked like cat scratches. Others were raised, like burns, or white, old scars. Stan tipped a metal beaker of molten wax, letting a fine thread of it dribble onto her skin, precise as an alchemist. As the wax hit her skin, Lisa flinched and turned her head to the side. I gawked with the others as the pool of wax turned white and hard. Later, when Stan knelt to untie her blindfold, Lisa looked up at him adoringly with unfocused sapphire eyes and mouthed, "I love you." I felt embarrassed to witness this sudden moment of intimacy. The other observers had melted away. I stood fast, unable to budge, flashing lights throbbing in my peripheral vision. Lisa sat up as if alone, heels together, legs flopping open, and started peeling dried wax off her tits. Stan looked up at me curiously, then bent to unplug his hot plate.

A man approached me then. He was narrow hipped, effeminate, with full lips and a halo of dark curls. The first three buttons of his tight, silky shirt were open and revealed a tawny, hairless chest.

"Hey, you all right?" he asked. I told him I was looking for someone. He had never seen the pregnant girl. I smiled and talked to him, feeling so charming as I moved really fast and jerked my arms around. All I can remember of our conversation is the effeminate man saying most people thought he was gay, but he was straight—*with a twist*. He said that several times. His name was Mandy. I don't remember how it happened that I asked him to drive me to Connecticut, but there we were, at dawn, on Route 84 heading toward Danbury in his tangerine Camaro. Mandy told me about his life—how he was in auto sales with his father, how he had appeared in seven of his father's commercials, starting from the age of three. I was barely listening. I was scared to see Suky.

We stopped for a pee at a truck stop on the outskirts of Danbury. He took a little Chinese purse embroidered with a dragon out of his glove compartment, unzipped it, and held it open so I could see: white powder in a plastic bag. Feeling myself coming down slightly, I snorted a staggered white zigzag of powder off a glossy car sales brochure. As I sniffed the line through a dollar bill, felt the acidic, chemical kick in the back of my throat, I read: "200 dollars cash back with every new Nissan truck purchased!"

There was a picture of a stocky man on the brochure. He was

standing beside a red truck. He had a mustache and Mandy's full lips. Mandy's dad, no doubt, smiling up at me. I felt a little sorry for the guy, given what I was using his face for. I knew the cocaine was a mistake as I snorted it. Combined with all the amphetamines I had taken in the last two days, it clamped down on my mind like a set of iron teeth. Every noise sounded like danger to me. My chauffeur's profile, with its aquiline nose and plump mouth, seemed malign. I imagined him cutting me into lamb-chop-size chunks and tossing them gaily out the window all the way to Suky's house. At every stoplight I imagined opening the door and escaping.

We drove up to the Delton Green at twenty to seven. "I've done a lot of crazy things," said Mandy. "But this takes the cake. You said your father is a minister?" I nodded. "Yup. This takes the fuckin' cake." He made ready to get out.

"Oh," I said. "Do you mind waiting for a little, um, and then I'll . . . come get you . . . if . . ." He turned up the radio and sank down in the seat, nodding with a louche expression. Wondering what I had promised him, I walked to the side door of the house. The first birds were singing. The air smelled sweet and clean. I picked up the hollow plastic rock beside the welcome mat, ripped the silver key off its Velcro square, turned it in the lock.

The house was quiet and warm. I walked into the kitchen. The clock was ticking. It sounded so loud. The house smelled yeasty, sugary, as it always had. I was suddenly very hungry. I looked in the bread bin. There were three cinnamon donuts in there. I took one and bit into it, crunched the sandy sugar between my teeth. It felt so good to be home. Such a relief. I heard a sound on the stairs. I turned. The decline in her appearance was shocking. Her pale skin was luminous, almost translucent, the skin around her eyes dark, her red hair lank and stringy. She had lost weight. She started to scream, then she put her hand to her mouth and wept.

"Thank God," she said.

"I'm a high school graduate, Mommy," I said. My voice sounded completely foreign to me. I must have been talking very loud.

"Ssh," she said. "Your father."

I whispered now, expanding on how well I had done on the test, exaggerating my results, believing myself instantly. She hugged me. I just let her, at first, my arms dangling at my sides. After a while, though, I put my arms around her and pressed her to me. She felt so fragile, like a bird. We embraced for a long time. Then I made her put her feet on my feet. She was sort of giggling, embarrassed, but I insisted she do it, just the way I had put my feet over hers when I was little. And we danced. Her face was so close to mine. I could see the new wrinkles around her eyes. The flesh over her eye sockets was sinking. Her breath was minty. She was looking up at me with deep affection—our old intimacy, as if we were the only two people in the world, as if we were newlyweds. I glanced at the clock. A few seconds to seven. Almost time for her first dose. She never missed it. The minute hand thumped into place beneath the twelve. Seven o'clock. She gently began to release her hold on me. A spike of anger went through me then. I held my arms rigid. She put her hand on my forearm, pushing me away a little. "Okay, honey," she said.

"You have an appointment?" I asked. She must have seen murder in my face, because she looked frightened.

"Let me go," she said in her squeaky drawl.

Then I put my face close to hers. "Look in my eyes," I said. "You see anything?" She was struggling to get out of my grip now; I had her by the shoulders, I was moving her to the wall, I didn't know what I was going to do to her, but I hated her so much, I wanted to kill her. "I'm like you now, Suky, see? I'm fucking high like you wish you were right now, you little junkie!"

Her face twisted into a grimace of rage and indignation. She bared her teeth, spit formed on the edges of her mouth, her eyes narrowed, she called me a liar, a runaway, an addict. She actually looked like she was turning into an animal. It was terrifying. She wanted her dose. I had her pinned to the wall. She was hissing, "Get out, get out, get out, get out!" Her bones felt so flimsy I could have snapped them. I took a fistful of her hair, held her head back. Her eyes widened, scared, expectant. I had no idea what to do next. So I kissed her, on the mouth. Passed my hand over her nipples. I felt like I was slashing her throat with a knife. Looking back on it, it seems overdramatic, but at seventeen, a blizzard of coke and speed racing through my head, I thought I was saying it all: I was telling my mother that she had treated me like a lover and a baby, a possession, but not a person, never a person. I think she got the message. Anyway, she started screaming. She was just screaming and screaming, and Des thundered downstairs in his brown robe, growling like a grizzly. That was my signal. I ran straight into Mandy's Camaro, tears streaming down my face, wiping my mouth like there was shit on it.

By the time we got back to New York, I was curled up in a ball, staring out the window. Understandably, Mandy was sick of me. He dropped me at the entrance to the Lincoln Tunnel, saying, "You're a downer, man," and he was off to Jersey, where the girls are sunny. I walked to the subway and got back to Jim's apartment just as he and Olla were getting up. They were relieved to see me. They asked no questions. We all had coffee and shortbread cookies, and Olla tenderly laid out one of her pretty sundresses for me to wear when I woke. She put it out on a chair, where I could see it, to cheer me up. I lay my head on her lap as she stroked my forehead. I could feel the soft pillow of her bosom on my ear. I slept and slept, and when I opened my eyes, it seems to me now, it was three years later, I was twenty and living on Orchard Street.

A Brief Catalog of Sins

I remember the years after I kissed Suky in fragmented clusters, as though seen on a TV with rotten reception. I can flip through the channels as often as I like, but no narrative coheres. All I can glimpse is fixes I got myself into. Not how, not why. I see a young Finnish actor lying beside me, so thin, like a boy, except for his phallus, which stands wavering nobly. I see his girlfriend, Oxanna, sitting beside me in a restaurant as the boy hands us each a bunch of roses. I see myself on the street being slapped by a woman with short black hair and a livid face. I see myself lying on a table. A man wearing a wedding ring is standing between my open legs (somewhere in here I must have lost my virginity). And, like snowy static, I see pills—pink pills, white pills, blue pills—falling across the screen. Okay, I understand, of course, I took every pill I could get my hands on, no wonder I can't remember anything. Wait, I can see an ashtray littered with cigarette butts on a coffee table. A man—Sergei— clamps a cigarette between his thick, sensual lips, lights up, and inhales deeply, with real enjoyment, his bulging black eyes open wide. I see the man's wife, Amelia, also Russian. She is blond, very thin, exhausted looking. I work for these people. I teach their daughter English. Her name is Anya. Sergei is glowering, emphatic. The skin on his arms is very smooth, tawny, and hairless. His body is of an almost comical shape—potbelly, short, muscular legs. He is a Trotskyite and a cellist. He plays for me. Dense, dark waves of music rise from beneath his fingers. I find the sound powerful, melancholy, hypnotic. Sometimes I spend the night here so I don't have to go all the way downtown on the subway. On these occasions, Sergei reads out loud to me from *The Revolution Betrayed*. I see myself kneeling in front of the couch, Sergei's penis in my mouth, while his wife and daughter sleep next door. How much worse can this get?

At around this time, the images become so flimsy, I can't make them out. I see my hands bound together at the back. I strain to catch a glimpse of myself. I worry, What the hell am I doing now? Then a clear color image quickens: I see people holding plastic cups filled with wine, talking. I see myself in lace-up leather boots, white-blond hair, a muddy coat. My skin is pale, there are circles under my eyes. I am here with friends, ah yes, now it is all coming clear, I see better now, wait, now I'm inside the screen, I am standing next to myself, I can't believe how real this all is, I can hear the voices—it's an art opening. These are the people I used to serve margaritas to at El Corazón! Remember? The ones with paint on their hands. What are they doing here? My boyfriend, Craig, the skinny one with the poker face, is standing beside his painting, a hyperrealistic rendering of a sink filled with dirty dishes. There is a red dot beside it. Our friends cluster around us. Jed, a very tall part-Sioux sculptor from Nebraska City, his heavy work boots spread wide, checked woolen jacket flapping open, congratulates Craig. "You are one lucky fuck, man, Gigi Lee is a major collector." Jed looks over at a very beautiful woman in her forties with a nearly impossibly large bust and tiny waist, wearing a cat suit, her long black hair falling to her waist. Her lovely face is surprisingly tired looking, and her voluptuous mouth droops at the corners, as though it has been borrowed from someone else. Jed the Sioux now puts his hand on the small of my back. Have I got it wrong? Is *Jed* my boyfriend? Terry, the short young woman from El Corazón, with a soft, exposed midriff, chunky high heels, and a cartoonish, glossy red mouth, says, "She's an heiress." Now the beauty in the cat suit walks over to the ratty little clump of us and looks up at Craig with an impish smile.

"I love my painting." She has a thick Italian accent.

Craig clears his throat. "I'm . . . glad you bought it."

"I am Gigi Lee."

"I know. Nice to meet you." Craig shakes her hand stiffly.

"You like to paint from the sea?" she asks.

"I usually paint in the studio," says Craig. "From photographs."

"You must come to our house at the sea, you could make a beautiful painting of it," says Gigi. Then, turning to acknowledge the rest of us, "You must all come this weekend. Stay the night!" Craig introduces each of us. Gigi nods at us all, her tiny nose pulling itself in like a turtle seeking its shell. "Herb!" she calls. An older man walks out of the crowd. He must be in his fifties. Swarthy, with deep creases in his skin, a crooked nose, and clear blue eyes, he has an open, amused expression on his face. "I want them all to come to the party," Gigi says, opening her arms.

"The more the merrier," says Herb drily, teasing.

"It is this weekend. You can come? There is a bus if you have no car."

"I have a car," says Craig. I nod. Craig has hit a vein of gold, a big commission. And the prospect of free food and drink is something none of us will pass up.

* * *

We are all in Craig's car, a vast vanilla 1967 Riviera convertible with crimson upholstery. The car used to belong to Craig's deceased aunt Ginny. I am beginning to remember that Terry, the girl with the smirking red mouth, and I sleep with either poker-faced Craig, Jed, the elegant Sioux sculptor, or ornery Calvin, the chunky abstract painter. Don't get me wrong; this is not a free love situation. It's a rotation. Each of us is the girlfriend of one or another of these three guys at any given time. Occasionally, a third girl is brought into the group from outside, but usually it's just Terry and I, so one of the guys is single for a while and becomes neutered, essentially another female, hanging out with us girls and whining about his loveless status, until a pregnant lull in the conversation when one of us is alone with him. Eyes lock, and away we go; he's a man again. Now it's someone else's turn to be single. We have managed this game of musical genitalia for over a year without much jealousy, our friendships intact. But all that is about to change, for me anyway. As I lean my head back on Aunt Ginny's red leather seat, the wind in my mouth, I have no idea that I am driving straight out of one life and into another.

* * *

Their house was right by the sea; Gigi had told us that much in her vague directions. We drove slowly beside the long hedge that hid the big houses, looking for their name. At last we found it: "Lee," painted in light blue script on a white mailbox. We turned in to the gravel driveway and drove toward the strangest building I had ever seen. It was a huge glass box with one metal wall. Inside the box was a small, old-fashioned yellow cottage with a red door—a house in a house. It was the middle of the afternoon; there were several cars parked in the driveway. As we approached the Lee home, we could see white leather couches in the outer, modern part of the dwelling. We knocked on the tall metal door of the outer shell. A doleful looking, middle-aged man answered. His shirt was half-untucked. He ushered us in with some sort of Eastern European accent, asked us mournfully if we would like some iced tea. We said yes. He took it like bad news and disappeared. A small, dark, smiling woman in a light green uniform bustled in carrying a tray of glasses filled with amber liquid. The Eastern European man picked up a couple of our bags and made for the stairs.

"That's okay," said Craig.

"We'll get 'em," said Calvin. The man stayed them with a raised hand. "Please," he said. He had a way about him that made it hard to tell if he was kidding, as though someone had dared him to pretend to be the butler for the afternoon. "Mr. and Mrs. Lee are on the beach with the other guests," he said, gesturing to a set of French doors that looked onto the sea. "Mrs. Lee says, come down if you like, or relax up here. Whatever you prefer."

"Thanks," said ornery Calvin, grabbing a handful of salted peanuts from a large clamshell on the coffee table and looking up at a ten-foot abstract painting on the landing. "Fucking Dieter Carlson," he snarled through a mouthful of nuts. "He's everywhere. And he can't even paint."

Poker-faced Craig had ventured out onto the porch. I followed and stood beside him. I felt I was standing on the prow of a huge, beached ship. The sky stretched up from the horizon, a dome over our heads; occasional, perfectly formed clouds were frozen in the blue expanse. All below—glittering water, white-blond sand—was awash in heat and light.

"Can you imagine owning a house like this?" I asked.

"We do own it, honey," said Craig, his hand sliding down my back. "I just bought it, remember?" I leaned on the railing and surveyed the beach. Several people were having a picnic down there. A woman in a red bathing suit and long black hair—Gigi—was wading in the water. Several others reclined on multicolored bath towels. I sipped the sweet, cold tea. The best I'd had in my life. "We probably shouldn't have invited so many people with a new cook in the kitchen," I said.

"They'll be so drunk, they won't notice the food," said Craig with a convincing drawl. He took to the role of a rich man easily. In fact, he was poised for a huge success; within ten years he would be one of the highest priced artists of his generation.

The others ambled onto the porch. "I'm gonna go down to the beach," said Jed, our current odd man out. "Maybe there's a single lady down there in need of a real man." Terry and Calvin smoked in silence. Gigi was looking up at us now and waving. We all descended the splintered wooden stairs to a narrow path that led us down the dune. I clung to the fantasy of ownership, breathing in the salty air, looking back at the gleaming glass house proprietarily. "We have to get those stairs fixed," said Craig in his deadened voice. When we got to the beach, though, it was over.

Gigi was on her belly, recumbent on a cerulean towel, a cherry red bathing suit clinging to her impossible form. Her black hair was drying in brittle, serpentine waves down her back. As we approached, she propped herself up on her elbows, clamping together her cleavage. "Hello!" she said. A bronzed, lithe young man sat beside her. He had a sharp-ridged, hawklike nose, which seemed to stretch the skin on his face very taut. He gave us a surprised look from under bushy black brows. We must have looked like aliens, the druggy-pale, black-clad, sleep-deprived clutch of us standing on that costly stretch of coastline.

"This is Sam Shapiro, the novelist," Gigi announced. "Sam, this is Craig Simms, the painter I was telling you about. And these are his friends, let me see . . ." Craig introduced us all again. Gigi smiled at us vaguely, taking nothing in. I was hot in my dress, socks, and boots. "Do you have your bathing suits?" Gigi asked. I had mine on under my dress, but I didn't feel ready to reveal my pasty form to this goddess. Gigi jumped up and took Craig by the arm. "Come," she said. "Let's discuss the commission." They were off. Jed sat on the sand, legs splayed, his ancient black raincoat spread out behind him, ebony hair glistening down his back, and glared at the sea.

"It's fucking hot," said Terry, tugging off her T-shirt. Her bright purple bra encased large, soft breasts that jiggled like mounds of custard.

Sam smiled. "Don't mind me," he said.

"I don't," said Terry, leaning back on her elbows and squinting at him.

Ornery Calvin lit a cigarette. "So there's going to be a party tonight?" he said.

"There's always a party at Gigi's house," said Sam.

I got up and walked toward the water. When no one seemed to be watching me, I unzipped my tattered thrift store dress, unlaced my boots, rolled my sweaty socks off my feet, and left it all in a neat pile. My bikini top didn't match the bottom. I was hoping people would think this was intentional. My icy blond hair, fried by Terry's dubious skills as a colorist, was wound up into two little onions at the top of my head. I walked into the water, looking down at my skinny, pallid body. The water felt cold. I splashed the backs of my knees, then dove under a wave and swam a few strokes. When I came up, I was less than a yard away from two men paddling in the water, talking. I recognized one of them as Herb Lee, Gigi's husband. He had a cigar in his mouth. The other man was wearing thick, black-framed glasses. His hair was wild and graying. "I don't see how you can possibly think," he was saying, "that I should cram all that into part one."

"It's like I told you," said Herb in his deep New York yet somehow aristocratic voice. "Those scenes *belong* to the childhood."

"But I'm moving back and forth in time. That's the structure of the thing! The narrative is *liquid*."

"What I'm saying is," answered Herb, "let the sequences build up more power—less staccato. You want it to be a good read, don't you?" I had drifted a little closer to them by now and was eavesdropping shamelessly. Herb turned and acknowledged me. "Hello," he said. "Are you with our party?"

"I'm with Craig, you bought his painting? We met at the opening . . ."

"Oh yes, sorry, this is Max Kessler, Max this is . . ."

"Pippa Sarkissian."

"What kind of a name is that?"

"Swedish and Armenian." Max Kessler had paddled away and was struggling toward the shore, dragging his feet through the undercurrent, his black swim trunks clinging to his legs, shoulders bowed.

"You're very welcome, Pippa," said Herb, the laugh lines driven down the sides of his face deepening slightly, his light eyes twinkling with amusement—at life itself, it seemed. Standing in the waves now, cigar clamped between his teeth, he looked mischievous and anarchic, like some distant cousin of Poseidon, ruling his patch of sea.

"Thank you," I said, diving back into the water.

As the sun lowered on the horizon, spattering the sea with its golden, trembling reflection, the butler and the maid trudged down the path to the beach lugging a large wicker basket, each of them holding a handle, faces flushed. Inside the basket, bottles clinked against one another promisingly. Several other guests had joined us for predinner drinks. All of them cheered as the butler arrived. "Hurrah for Jerzi!" they cried. The gloomy butler allowed the corners of his mouth to turn up very slightly at this welcome. Guests hurled orders at him as he unpacked the full bar.

"Ask him anything," said Herb, "he knows it."

"Can you make a Maiden's Prayer?" asked Trudy, the wife of Max Kessler, herself a writer, who was wearing a patterned head scarf pulled tight over her hair, her mouth a fuchsia slash. The butler nodded solemnly and took a bottle of gin out of one of the baskets, a jug of orange juice. Cointreau.

"I don't believe it!" exclaimed Trudy, sipping the drink, her eyes closed with pleasure.

"And what about Pippa Sarkissian?" asked Herb. "What would she like?"

"Crème de menthe," I said.

"An old-fashioned girl, underneath it all," said Herb, chuckling.

Gigi tossed her head. "Crème de menthe isn't a cocktail, it's a liqueur," she said.

Herb turned to her. "Rubbing alcohol for you, my love?"

"A big glass, please," said Gigi playfully, plonking herself opposite Herb with a swiveling movement, her long legs folding graciously beneath her. Somehow she had managed to change into a diaphanous coral halter dress and was fully made up. Yet I hadn't noticed her leaving. Herb took out a bottle of champagne and poured her a glass. I wondered if their corrosive banter was for real or not. Gigi drank and sighed, looking around her with half-closed eyes, like a contented lioness. The sky had begun to go pink. "After this," said Gigi, "everyone can get ready for dinner and the others will arrive."

Back in the transparent box, Craig and I walked up the metal staircase, down the hall, which was open to the rest of the house, and into our room, described to us by Gigi airily as the "third door." The smell of jasmine was heavy and sweet. The drapes were shut. We flicked the light switch. Two identical lamps shone a warm light on a stainless steel bed, a quilted white bedspread, embroidered linen pillowcases. And, laid out on the bed neatly, were all our clothes, our books, and, in a small Baggie, the drugs we had brought for the weekend: a handful of pills, a lump of hash, and a singed spoon, which Terry and Jed always brought with them, just in case, though neither of them was a junkie.

Craig grimaced. "That fucking butler."

"He's a humorist," I said, bouncing on the bed and opening the Baggie. Craig clambered on top of me, jabbing me with his elbow. I wasn't in the right frame of mind for a big sex procedure, so I made him come with my mouth, then brushed my teeth, resolving to go to the party straight but for one little Valium, which didn't count, it just took the edge off, made me slightly numb. I didn't want to give that nasty butler the satisfaction of being high. But also, I didn't want Herb to see me high. I didn't admit it to myself, but in the back of my mind, I was already thinking that I wanted him to like me.

Poker-faced Craig was still showering. He was intensely vain, so it always took him ages to get ready for anything. I walked down-stairs alone, my steps echoing on the metal staircase. Sam Shapiro was standing beside Herb. They were looking out the immense glass wall, talking, drinks in their hands. Hearing me, they both turned and looked up.

"The artist's girlfriend," Herb said. I was wearing an old ballet tutu with a light blue bodice and my black lace-up boots. Bright red lipstick, shiny black nails. "Come. Talk to us."

I sat down on the couch. Sam and Herb sat opposite me. They were looking at me as though I were a specimen from a newly discovered tribe of pygmies.

"So, Pippa," said Herb. "What do you normally have for breakfast?"

Sam broke into laughter, a painful, honking guffaw.

"I don't really eat breakfast," I said.

"Does she look like she eats breakfast?" said Sam.

"Now there's your first mistake," said Herb, wagging his finger at me paternally.

"Do you go straight into the studio, then?" asked Sam.

"I don't have a studio."

"You must be an artist, dressed like that," said Sam.

"No," I said.

"What are you then?" asked Herb.

I shrugged. "I work in a clothing store."

"You must have some ambition," said Herb.

"Why?" I asked him. He looked startled, as though he had noticed something odd about my face.

"Well, I congratulate you," he said. "You are the first person who has ever walked across the threshold of this house who isn't riddled with ambition, frustrated or otherwise. Even the butler is writing a short story. He broke the news to me yesterday."

Gigi stormed out of the kitchen, flushed and upset. Herb stood and went to her swiftly. They conferred in whispers for a few moments. He put his hand on her shoulder. She wiped tears from her cheeks. Sam looked at me and raised his eyebrows, whispering: "Watch out for the wife."

The other guests trickled in over the next hour or so. Gradually, it became clear that Herb and Gigi had different tastes in people. Herb's friends were the intellectuals, an ironic, serious lot. The women, as they appeared, had no scales on their eyes and hadn't for years; they looked like they had seen it all. The men glowered at one another and huddled together, conversing intensely about matters of importance. Gigi's gang was younger, decadent. There was a theater director who arrived in a one-piece terry-cloth pantsuit; an actress who, it was whispered, had worked with Warhol; and the maverick playboy scion of a famous record label. Craig and the rest of us had clearly been invited to tip the balance in Gigi's favor.

Once it was dark, tiny torches flickered all along the path to the beach. The house was twinkling with candlelight. I milled around, a ginger ale in my hand, listening to shards of conversation. Magnificent food was displayed on various tables. Now and then, Gigi would reach into a small drawer in the dining room table at which she and a few others were sitting with their plates and pull out a little silver bell. It made a pretty, tinkling sound. Whenever she rang it, the butler or the maid would appear, and Gigi would order another bottle of champagne, or something special that had to be concocted to order. Looking up at the maid, making a face like a hopeful child, she said, "Alfonsa, could you please, please ask Maria if she could make me a little tiny chocolate mousse, just for a taste?" Alfonsa smiled, glancing at the elaborate desserts already piled high before her mistress, and walked off. The poor cook.

I glimpsed Herb here and there, conferring with the serious men or listening to Gigi's flamboyant guests with an alienated smile.

I had the strange sensation of knowing what he was feeling; I could read his face. I could tell if he was uninterested, or impatient, or delighted. After a while, though, I lost track of him. Sam Shapiro came up to me on the porch as I sat with poker-faced Craig and Terry. The two of them were laughing, hugging, and I was wondering if they wouldn't make a nice couple. I had grown tired of Craig, with his puffy eyes and frozen face, his blond hair that stuck straight up on his head. He was the most gifted of the bunch, but he was a cold person, and in bed there was a wooden reserve in him I found dispiriting.

"Beautiful night," said Sam. I turned to him and wondered what it would be like to kiss him. It was clear that he was wondering something along the same lines. But I found myself excusing myself in the middle of our conversation. The truth was, I thought, as I meandered through that house, looking up into the night sky through the great glass roof, every star visible, the truth was, I didn't want anyone anymore, or anything. I wanted to sleep for seven months. I was burned out. Exhausted. Bored. I suppose I was depressed, but I didn't think about things like that in those days. There was a light on in the little yellow cottage, I noticed. I wondered if it was all right to walk inside, or if that was Gigi and Herb's private domain, the place where they played out their mysterious relationship. The door was slightly ajar. I peeked through the window. The TV was on; a football game was playing. Men in helmets tumbled over one another, landing in a pile. On the couch, his arms spread over the back, was Herb. I opened the door and walked in.

He looked up. When he saw it was me, his face creased into a smile. "Just the girl I want to see," he said. "You like football?"

"I used to—I have four brothers."

"Have a seat. Refresh your memory." We sat watching the game for a few minutes. I snuck a look at his profile. His Roman nose and high forehead, the thick, silver hair rising from his face like a wave, made him look like an emperor. I had never seen a man who exuded such authority. He offered me pistachio nuts and a Coke from a little fridge near the TV.

"This is the most amazing house I've ever seen," I said.

"It's not a house, it's a hellhole," said Herb. "Not one comfortable piece of furniture, except this couch. It's like living in an aquarium."

"Why do you live here then?"

"My wife," he said, with a gesture encompassing the cottage, the house, the sea beyond. "I couldn't afford to live like this. Not that I'm a poor man." We watched another play. When the commercial came on, he turned to me. "So, little Pippa," he said. "Don't you think it's time to change your life?"

"What do you mean?"

"Doesn't it get dispiriting to be so aimless? I mean, I see that you're young, but a person of such unusual sweetness—"

"I'm not sweet."

"People can be experienced and sweet. I'm talking about an innate quality. It's a long time since I've seen it in a person." I was shocked to feel tears well up in my eyes. Herb was sweeping my face with his gaze, as though he were hungry for my emotion. Just then, the door swung open, and Gigi ran to Herb, giggling, and pulled him off the couch. The party was going to the beach. "Andiamo!" She led him off by his long arms and he trotted out of the room awkwardly, like a goat walking on its hind legs.

Everyone skipped or ran or shuffled to the beach. I broke up with Craig with quiet brutality on the way down the path. I explained that I needed a hiatus from romance. Not that our relationship was romantic. He was slightly morose after that, but Terry did her best to comfort him, and within half an hour he was stripping with the rest of my friends. It looked like a bluefish feed, all those people, some buck naked, some half-clothed, chopping up the water. I remained dressed and thought about sharks. I was feeling somber. Something had stirred in me. About five yards away, I saw Herb, also dressed, watching his wife as she frolicked in a bra and panties, looking like Aphrodite born out of the sea complete with lingerie. I had never seen such a perfectly formed woman. When I looked back at Herb, he was turned in my direction. I couldn't tell for sure, but I thought he was staring at me.

The next morning, we all played tennis. It was Craig and I against Gigi and Jed. Herb stood by and watched, a towel draped around his neck. He had already played singles with Sam. Gigi threw herself into the game. Whenever she scored, she jumped into the air, elated. When she missed the ball, she ran to Herb, ducking her head into his chest. At one point, after missing two shots in a row, she let her racket clatter onto the court, turned, and ran off toward the house. Herb didn't miss a beat. He ambled on with his loose-limbed gait, picked up his wife's racket, and served.

* * *

Back on Orchard Street, Terry was now shacked up with poker-faced Craig, so I got her room, which she had painted puce in a fit of jealousy years before I was adopted into the group. In the old, Jewish days of the Lower East Side, this loft had been devoted to the manufacture of ladies' girdles and crammed, no doubt, with hollow-eyed women and children, sewing their lives away elbow to elbow for a starving wage. But times had changed. The neighborhood was now given over to longtime Hispanic residents, a few artists desperate for cheap rent, and of course the junkies.

When they found the place, Jed and Craig and Calvin put up the Sheetrock walls themselves, creating a space with several bedrooms and studios. The tall, dusty windows let in plenty of light. The place was bright but filthy, with a damp towel perpetually drooped over the glass door of the jerry-rigged shower stall, hair wound around the creviced bar of yellowing soap. The kitchen was in the hall and consisted of a hot plate set on top of a small refrigerator. When you walked barefoot, you got sawdust on your feet. The air smelled of cigarettes, oil paint, and the polyurethane that Jed used to laminate his sculptures: stuffed animals set into elaborate, upholstered frames skillfully painted in the style of Tiepolo. My clothes and hair reeked of this cocktail of odors.

Since the most recent change of romantic alliance, Craig was a little bit reserved with me. I think he was sore about the abrupt breakup on the way to the beach at Gigi and Herb's house. Usually, our transfers were more seamless and unspoken, less like the ending of a regular couple. Perhaps he was insulted by my pedestrian technique, which implied he gave a shit, which of course he didn't. Jed and Calvin were both expecting me to move over in bed for one or the other of them, as I normally would have, but I was too tired. The week after we got back from Herb and Gigi's house, I slept most of the time when I wasn't at work. I think maybe I was trying to avoid my next boyfriend. I slept so deeply over those few days, it felt like I might just float away in some dream and die.

When Herb called me, it was one o'clock in the afternoon; I didn't have to be at work till nine. No one else was in the loft, the answering machine was off, the phone kept ringing and ringing. Finally I staggered out of my room and dropped to the floor as I answered, leaning against the wall, whispering "Hulluh" and struggling to light a cigarette I'd found in a crushed pack under the table. My neck was clammy, eyes unfocused. I was almost incoherent with sleep. He asked me out for breakfast. Even half-conscious, I knew that I shouldn't go out with him, so very married as he was, but I hadn't been able to get him out of my mind ever since he'd told me I was sweet. To prove him wrong, perhaps, I saw him.

He treated me like a pal. He was avuncular. He filled me with eggs and coffee, teased me about being a waster. I called him an old fart. We saw each other plenty after that. We would weave around the city, laughing and talking. He found me amusing. I found him reassuring. Once, we walked all the way up Madison Avenue. He led me into a really expensive store and made me try on this black cocktail dress. The cloth was cool and smooth against my skin. It made me look shockingly pretty. I took it off. Then, while I was dreamily sliding silk coats along their rack like the beads of an abacus, he bought me the dress. He bought me shoes, too, very high, pointy heels with straps around the ankles. I knew I shouldn't accept these things, and the truth was I found them slightly ridiculous. They were too on-the-nose sexy for the taste I'd learned back at the loft—not enough irony, not enough edge. Yet wearing them thrilled me. Gigi was away in Italy at the time. Herb asked me if I would come over for dinner.

The small elevator reeked of gardenia perfume, with an undertone of fried garlic. I sat down on the leather bench. It felt cool against the backs of my thighs, which were bare because I was wearing the cocktail dress Herb had given me. I pulled the old cardigan I was wearing around me and looked up at the walls, which were upholstered in heavy, amethyst-colored linen. I was just imagining moving into the elevator—where would I put the bed, the sink, a little carpet—when the doors opened right into Herb's apartment. And there was Herb, his emperor's face creased in a smile, his long arms open.

"Beautiful," he proclaimed. I tottered out of the elevator in the massive heels he'd bought me that afternoon. He gave me a hug. He was wearing a soft brown sweater. It felt like a rabbit. He smelled like limes. When he let go, I looked around. It was an old apartment, he said. Built before the Second World War. Gigi had decorated the place in red and blue and yellow. "It's a bit like a home for disturbed children," said Herb.

We sat down on either end of the poppy red couch, bashful now that we were alone in his apartment. A large Yves Klein painting with imprints of naked women in blue paint on raw canvas hung on the wall opposite us. Herb went into the kitchen and came out with a bottle of champagne. We drank. I was so hungry; I felt the alcohol behind my eyes immediately. I imagined what Suky would think if she saw me now, sipping champagne in *costly garments*, as she used to say. What a mix of excitement and jealousy would be sloshing around inside her. I finished my glass, and he poured me another, brought out a bag of potato chips.

"I let the maid go home, so I'm afraid it's just me tonight. You won't have the service you deserve."

"That's okay," I said. All I could think about was his broad trunk, the reassuring baritone of his voice, the way his corduroys fit him so loosely. Mr. Brown had worn pants like that. Was that why I was here? I wondered. Because of a pair of corduroys? All of a sudden, I

was overcome with sleepiness and wanted to lie down. I ate a handful of chips. "Dinner's almost ready," he said, standing up. "Don't
despair."

The dining room was all white: Lucite table, marble floor,
translucent plastic chairs, crystal chandelier. Herb pulled my chair
out, then put a big glass bowl of pasta with tomato sauce between
us. "I hope the sauce is okay," he said. "I haven't cooked anything
since I was thirty." It was the best food I had ever tasted. I ate like I
was starving. He put more in my bowl. "So, Pippa. Shall I tell you
some of the things I like about you?"

"Okay," I said, my mouth full of spaghetti.

"Well, let's see. You're not a show-off, but I think you're damn
smart. You've got an original way of living, for this town. You're in it
for the experience, is that right?" He made being utterly lost sound
like a good thing. "You're beautiful, but you're cool about it. You
don't even seem to know how lovely you are. And . . . I don't know, I
suppose there's sadness there, and I like sadness. In moderation."

"I like your corduroys," I said.

"Is that it?"

"No. I like your face. Your voice. I . . . This is going to sound
weird."

"Say."

"It's like I feel what you're feeling. If you're feeling sad, or
nervous, or happy—I feel it in my body, in my fingers."

"What a remarkable thing." He sat and looked at me for a moment. Then he said, "I don't ever want you to have to censor yourself around me. I want to know you, Pippa. I want to know who you
are. Tell me one thing about yourself. The most important thing."

I thought about that for a while. Then I took off my cardigan,
stood up, took my pasta bowl, set it on the cold marble floor beside

his chair, went down on all fours in my finery, and ate out of the bowl like a dog. I knew he could see the marks Shelly and Kat had left on my back. I have never felt so naked, before or since. After a few seconds, he gripped me around the waist, lifted me onto his lap, dipped his napkin in his water glass, and washed off my face. His eyes were glistening. "No, no, no," he said. "I don't believe it. Who did this to you?"

He carried me into a bedroom. It was not his room—he told me it was not his room. He said I was a queen. "I don't know who put this spell on you, darling. But if I'm good for anything, it's to show you how wonderful you are." When he put his hand on my abdomen, I felt a sudden, deep, pulsing ache, not pain but desire, desire in my womb. That's the only way I can describe it. I was so wet it soaked through my dress onto the sheets. That was the first night I really made love. It wasn't my pleasure and his pleasure, a transaction—"and here's your change, ma'am"—it was just wordless, thoughtless, and complete, like two waves crashing together and becoming the same water.

And that's how we buried Gigi Lee, kicked the sand over her perfect body with our bare feet as we wriggled toward each other in her very own guest bed.

Kept

Herb rented me a studio apartment on Seventieth and Lexington in a building with shining brass doors and a doorman called Nathan. I felt like an alien uptown; I was dressed wrong for everything, even buying milk. But Herb came over with something new for me to wear every few days, until I didn't feel dressed wrong anymore. I just felt like I was impersonating somebody else. Herb picked me up every afternoon at my new job in a fancy shoe store on Madison Avenue and walked me up to my little apartment. The walls were stark bluish white. There was a pine table in the kitchen, a black couch in the living room. I kept the place immaculate. I wanted it to be blank, a place for a person to change into another person. I took no pills. I got into no trouble. Herb said I was his true wife; he had found me at last.

When he told me, I was thrilled, incredulous, laughing. "What are you, fucking crazy? That's the last thing you need."

"I see something in you," he said, looking at me steadily and sweeping the hair from my eyes. "Something you don't see."

"Anyway," I said somberly. "You have a wife."

He threw himself back on the pillows. "If I have to live with that lunatic one more week, I'll hang myself. For years I've been hoping she'll have an affair so I can get out of it. But she won't do it. The bitch."

I yearned to say yes, but I was scared of Gigi, and I was afraid of what I would do to Herb. I hurt everyone I loved, everyone I met, practically. How could I trust myself with marriage?

Pivot

The doorbell rang, which was a bad sign. I hadn't ordered take-out, Herb had keys. No one else knew where I was. I said "Hello" and heard Gigi's voice. Fright flashed through my wrists. I said I was on my way down. I thought I would be safer on the street. Just as I was pulling on my jacket, there was a knock on the door. I contemplated running down the fire escape, but then I opened the door. There she was, looking over-the-top gorgeous, like something out of *La Dolce Vita*, a black dress and a fur coat, long dark hair and bangs, that drooping, voluptuous mouth, mascara bleeding around her tragic eyes. She walked around the place on stiletto heels without saying anything, looked the kitchen over, stalked into the bedroom, the bathroom. Then she stood there and took me in. I was in a tank top and sweatpants, my stringy hair scraped back in a ponytail. I looked like I should be her masseuse or maybe her tennis coach, but not her replacement. No way. "You whore," she said. That was nice.

"I'm not a whore," I said.

"Is not a whore paid for sex? What do you call this? I knew it the minute I laid eyes on you. I knew you were no good—a predator, and the worst kind, the unconscious kind. Things just 'happen' to you, don't they? And before you know it you steal my husband!"

I tried to check inside her open coat for a weapon. I thought if she was unarmed, I could defend myself. "I'm sorry," I said.

"He told me he loves you," she said.

I don't know how she ended up clutching my knees. I looked down, and she was kneeling, her coat splayed out behind her like the train of a dwarf queen. "You can stay here, see him, have a love affair, but do not take him, please, don't take him—"

I don't remember what I said. It was something like "Okay, I won't," I think, because she was out of there like a puff of smoke.

I couldn't make love to Herb after that. I knew I should move out, but I really didn't have enough money for a security deposit anyplace unless I found a roommate, and I didn't know anyone anymore. I couldn't go back to Jim or Trish or Suky or the loft. I mean, I could have gone back, but I knew it would lead to disaster. Herb was very understanding. He insisted I stay in the apartment on my own, even though that meant he had to stay in a hotel, because it was so painful to be with Gigi, now that she knew. He called and told me he loved me ten times a day, sent me flowers, sent me a necklace. I didn't want to talk to him. When I came home from work, I just curled up in bed and tried not to think about getting high. There was a Catholic church down the street, and, though I was not Catholic, I went there often. Not for Mass so much, just to sit there and pray and ask forgiveness over and over and over. All I ever did was cause misery and distress, and I was still doing it. I wrote my parents a note to say I was well and had a place and please don't worry and I think it's probably best I stay out of the way from now on, given the circumstances. I didn't intend to put a return address on the envelope, but then I did.

* * *

One morning, Herb let himself into the apartment, dragged me out of bed, dressed me, stuffed me into his Jaguar, and drove me to his beach house just so I could take a walk on the sand, breathe in the sea air. As we drove up to that glass-encased dollhouse, I was deluged with feeling for Herb, the same heady certainty that had gripped me when I watched him at Gigi's party: that I knew him, understood him, craved his company. So it was very smart of him to bring me back there.

On the way home, it was night. We were on a narrow country road. Herb's headlights raked a little fawn on the side of the road. Its legs were folded up underneath its body, and it had its ears pricked up. Herb pulled the car over. We got out. As we approached, we could see that the creature was frightened, trembling, but it didn't run; it drew its ears back and bowed its head. "Maybe his mother got hit by a car," I said.

"His legs are broken," Herb said. "Otherwise he would have run away."

"Should we bring him to a vet?" I asked. Herb lifted up the fawn's body; its two hind legs dangled, useless and bloody; its front legs made a pathetic galloping motion in the air.

"A vet can't help him," he said.

"We can't just leave him here," I said.

Herb gently laid the deer back on the ground and got back in the car. I sat next to him. He was silent for a long time. He took in a long breath, let it out again. "Close your eyes and cover your ears," he said.

"Why?" I asked.

"Just do it," he said. He backed up the car about five yards. Through the windshield, I watched the fawn, frosted ghostly white by the headlights. Herb put the car into gear, stepped on the accelerator. I screamed, but he didn't swerve. I squeezed my eyes tight, felt the thud as we hit the deer. The car had stopped. Herb backed up, got out, checked to see that it was dead. Then he steered the car back onto the road and drove us to the city.

We didn't speak on the ride home. When he stopped outside my building, he looked at me. "It would have starved or frozen or been devoured," he said. "You know that?"

I nodded. He slept at my place that night. Very early in the morning, I was woken by the sound of him weeping. I turned him over, wiped his tears away. I loved him then. To have the courage to do something that hurt you so much. A strange act of kindness. It was then that I knew, absolutely. "I will marry you," I said.

"You will?" He sounded baffled.

"How could I not?"

Bullet

Herb called me from a phone booth on Park Avenue.

"I told her we're getting married."

"How was it?"

"Horrible, and then . . . slightly less horrible."

"Come home, then," I said. He did. We scrambled eggs, toasted bagels, watched bad TV in bed till three in the morning. We were so happy.

"You need to be a little careful," Herb said, "about Gigi."

"What do you mean, she's going to try and kill me?"

"No, no, no. But she's volatile. And feeling scorned. So if the buzzer rings and you're alone here, don't answer."

"What if I ordered in?"

"Don't order in unless I'm here."

A few weeks went by. Herb gradually moved his things over: boxes of books, a couple of framed posters of old films, and his limited but high-quality wardrobe. The divorce papers were being drawn up. Gigi stayed away. We lived inside a little nutshell of contentment. We saw almost no one. Only Sam Shapiro, Herb's trusted ally, was allowed in on our secret. A couple of times a week, the three of us would go out, and Sam would regale us with stories about his disastrous love life or gripe about his new novel.

One such night, Sam got to the apartment before Herb did. He sat back on the ink black couch sipping a glass of pineapple juice, watching shivering saffron squares of sunlight appear and disappear on the wall as the sun set. His young, taut, raptor face shone with humor and curiosity. "Don't you have any hooch?" he asked me.

"Nope," I said. "But I could make you a sandwich."

"You sure have cleaned up your act," he said, looking over at me skeptically.

I laughed. "You don't believe it?"

"There are two schools of thought regarding change in human beings. Yes—and no."

"What do you think?"

"Fundamentally . . . no. But I hope I'm wrong. For my own sake." His ironic tone was shot through with wistfulness.

"What would you change about yourself if you could?" I asked softly, leaping, I knew, forward, toward him.

He thought for a few seconds. "I would be less of an observer. I'm sick of being the specter at the feast. You see, Pippa, I'm one of those unlucky beings who don't fully exist. I live off other people. But all writers are vampires, hasn't Herb told you that?"

"Not yet."

"If I find the right girl, she'll make me real."

"Do you really believe that?"

"*You're* real." He looked at me then with genuine longing. The shape of our narrative could have melted then and there; Herb might have come home to two young people falling in love. But I didn't topple. I really had changed, I realized. I wasn't going to seduce or be seduced anymore. Not even by this ravenous creature here, tempting as it was to evoke some actual passion from his ever-watchful, ever-thinking being. I looked away and stood up, aware of something having shifted inside me, some internal door closing. I had been tamed at last.

"So, Dracula, am I gonna end up in one of your books now? The little fuckup who went straight?" I asked.

"I don't think you'd fit into any of the stories in my head," he said, back to his usual, arch tone.

"How come?"

"You're too . . . I don't know, really. I was going to say primitive, but that's not it. That sad little smile, but you really do enjoy life. Winsome but naughty—you're an ingenue femme fatale—oddly calm, almost remote . . . You're hard to put a finger on, Pippa." He smiled at his own pun.

That night, in the cab going downtown, and sitting in the movie theater, I felt especially safe, wedged between these two men, protected by their solicitude and desire. Herb took Sam's crush as a compliment to him. It didn't bother him in the slightest. We all knew I was Herb's girl.

Then, one day, the phone rang. Herb answered. "Hi," he said, surprised, anxious. He listened for a long time, interjected little. When he hung up, he said, "Isn't that the most extraordinary thing."

"What?"

"Gigi wants us to go out to the beach house for lunch."

"Why?"

"She wants us to come and make the switch there."

"Make the switch?"

"She wants to be civilized, she wants to be sophisticated and show she doesn't mind losing me. I don't know."

"You mean you want to *go*? What happened to not answering the door in case she sticks a knife in my chest?"

"No, no, her voice was totally different. Calm. Gigi has a rational side, it kicks in at the damndest times." He shook his head, chuckling. "I'll bet you she has a man. That has to be it. She's going to unveil him at this lunch. Everything is about vanity for Gigi."

So, the following Saturday, we drove to the beach. The glass casing of the house glared in the sun. Inside it, the quaint little cottage looked like it was on display in a museum of the future. Beside it, there might have been a sign reading: "This is a reconstruction of an early-twentieth-century dwelling, complete with art and cooking implements." Herb sprang out of the car. I stayed in my seat as though magnetized, my limbs leaden. The skin on my face felt heavy, like clay. I was becoming very sleepy. Herb's tread on the gravel sounded brisk, optimistic. I heard the trunk click open. I opened the door, stuck my head out, and looked back at him, trying to see what he was doing.

"Can I go to the beach for a while?" I asked. I thought if I lay down in the sand, I might get my strength back. I could see only the top of Herb's face; the lid of the trunk obscured the rest. When he slammed it shut, he was holding his tennis racket. He was grabbing on to Gigi's offer of a conciliatory lunch a little desperately, I thought. He just couldn't resist the idea of a civilized finish to his second marriage. His first, dissolved acrimoniously over thirty years ago, he dismissed as the bloodless coupling of two neophyte intellectuals who mistook a shared passion for *Also sprach Zarathustra* for love.

Just as Herb was about to answer me, Gigi came out of the house. The light breeze molded the fine cloth of her orange caftan to her statuesque form, making her look like a bustier version of the Winged Venus. She held out her arms, then thought better of it and put her hands on her hips. "Welcome," she said. Now I really had to get out of the car.

We walked into the house. The sweet, full smell of jasmine hit me like heat, seeped into my brain, and conjured up a memory of my first visit—the sight of Herb and Gigi on the beach, the sweet iced tea, the brief sense of ownership I'd felt when I looked down at the sea from the porch. Let's face it: I had coveted Gigi's life at that moment. It wasn't the money—no, not exactly that. It was just that the money made everything seem all right. It made you feel safe. The smell of fresh flowers in a guest room. The taste of iced tea made by someone else. It was the opposite of chaos, the opposite of everything I had known until that time. I wanted to be sheltered at last. Yes, I confess: I wanted what Gigi had, and in a blind, unthinking, but ruthless way, I set about getting it.

As we entered, Jerzi the butler gave Herb a look of the darkest humor, his eyelids drooping, face impassive, one eyebrow raised. Herb shrugged and allowed himself to smile slightly. Seated in the glacial white leather couch was Sam Shapiro, looking awkward and surprised. I turned to Herb, who greeted his tense young friend with a hearty handshake, a quizzical look on his face. Could Sam be sleeping with Gigi? That would be too neat. Yet the way she let her fingers linger on Sam's hand when she passed him a drink, her stage whisper for him to get the cheese and salami out of the kitchen, when Alfonsa would be doing it in moments—it was all adding up. Herb paid special attention to Sam, slapping him on the back and asking him how his novel was going, when he had spoken to him the day before on that very subject, just to let him know it was okay if he *was* sleeping with his soon to be ex-wife.

Gigi hadn't managed to look at me directly. She was all smiles and bustle, flushed and seemingly happy to be doing this highly original thing. Yet there was something acted about her movements, gestures, expressions, as if she was imitating herself. I was filled with unease. Herb was grinning, teeth clenched, determined to get through this ordeal so he could have what he wanted. Sam looked like he wanted to disappear. The little ocher cottage in the center of the room had its white shades drawn demurely, as if lowering its eyes in embarrassment. It occurred to me that I hadn't really spoken yet. In fact, no dialogue seemed required of me in this play we were all enacting. It was more than enough for me to simply exist. I was, after all, the reason we were all here, in this new configuration. I needed no more lines than Helen of Troy. Pippa the Destroyer.

Champagne was poured; we each drank a glass. Gigi poured Herb a second glass, glancing up at him with impish insouciance, her tiny nose retreating into her face as it did when she was about to smile but didn't. Was it possible that she was flirting with him? The champagne left a dull weight on my forehead. Again, I wanted to lie down, to sleep, to be gone. I wished they could do it all without me. Alfonsa was looking worried as she put the finishing touches on the table set for four. She kept changing the location of the butter dish, the saltcellar, her eyes traveling back and forth over the table as if she were speed-reading. "You can bring in the food now, Alfonsa," said Gigi, gently chiding, as though encouraging a forgetful child. She ushered us out onto the porch with a sweep of her arm. "Take a few breaths before we eat," she said.

"There's oxygen in here, too," said Herb, adopting his old teasing way with her. Gigi giggled, and for a moment I thought it was all going to unravel; we would drop the scene as written, go back to our old parts. Herb and Gigi: worldly married couple; me: adoptive waif kept around as a decent-looking pet, a sort of representative of the Order of Flotsam; Sam: the brilliant friend who haunted his own life like a ghost, hunted down by his talent and sheltered, as I was, in the home of two knowing benefactors. I almost wished it were true. It would have been safer that way. I looked at Herb. He seemed impossibly old, from another world. I wanted him to hold me, to break through this web I was weaving around myself, to make us real again.

Gigi went into the house to check on the food. We all sighed at once.

"Well, this is one odd situation," said Sam.

"Sorry you got roped into it," said Herb.

"I didn't know it was happening till you drove up," said Sam.

"Listen, it's a load off my mind," said Herb, putting his hand between my shoulder blades.

"What is?" asked Sam.

"You and Gigi."

"*What?* She invited me over to lunch! That's *it*!"

"That's what *you* say," said Herb, smiling slightly at Sam's new predicament.

Sam looked over at me appreciatively and shook his head. "The mystery girl," he said.

Gigi opened the glass doors then and ushered us in. Our repast was laid out on the table like a grim offering to some vengeful god. A severed calf's head stared out at us mournfully; a leathery suckling pig had its mouth stretched wide, a too-big apple stuffed into it. Between these monstrosities, a bowl of perfectly browned potatoes and glistening salad seemed like no-man's-land.

"This lunch is in honor of telling it like it is," said Gigi, seating Herb to her right, Sam to her left, and me across from her. Herb was on edge now; I could feel it. "You know, how we all eat chops and things and we don't think of the faces, of who gets killed."

"It's lucky no one's a vegetarian," Herb said.

"In America," Gigi said, "you are very realistic. I mean to say, grand gestures have no place for you. Here is the truth as I see it. A pig for a cow. A fair exchange."

"Who's who?" Sam couldn't help asking.

Gigi shrugged, tears in her eyes.

"Sorry," said Sam, staring into his plate.

"Let's just have lunch," said Herb in a subdued tone, picking up a carving knife. "Who wants pig?"

"First," said Gigi, "a toast." She raised her wine. Sunlight streamed through the glass wall behind her and glinted off the crystal; a star of light exploded out of her hand. "To transformation," she said. We all raised our glasses dutifully, drank. Then she opened the little drawer in the table, the secret little drawer where she kept her bell, and took out a shiny, black thing, no bigger than a mouse. It was hard and perfect in the palm of her hand.

"Gigi," said Herb, standing up. "Give me that thing." He reached out. "Give it to me."

She smiled up at him, a strange smile of satiation, of victory. "Isn't it funny," she said, "how men always marry women who are easier and easier to dominate, until they end up with an imbecile?" Sam sat rigid, his face pale with terror. Gigi rested her elbow on the table, her wrist slack, the little black gun dangling in her hand like the droopy head of a fading flower. Then she turned to me. I waited for the bullet. I wondered if it would be in my chest, my head. I saw myself running to the door, shot in the back. Her eyes on mine, she parted her lips as if to speak, and wedged the tiny gun into her mouth. Herb lunged for her, grabbing her shoulder as the shell exploded. As he pulled her toward him, her head dropped to the table, and a fine spray of blood the shape of a huge Japanese fan surged out of her serpentine black hair, spattering him, all of us, like lava shooting out of an angry volcano. The glass behind her was coated ruby red. Herb was bent over his wife as if petrified, his face covered in blood. Alfonsa was screaming, running back and forth senselessly. With horrible slowness, the body slipped from the table, the chair, then flopped bonelessly to the floor.

I turned then and ran out of that bloody glass box, through the French doors, onto the porch, down the rotting wooden stairs, following the narrow path, the branches of the scrub pine snagging my dress like clawing hands. I staggered onto the beach; the sand tripped me up, it felt thick as towels. I flicked my shoes off so I could keep running, the hot sand searing the soles of my feet, and fled into the cool sea. All I remember is wanting to go under, far under, into the darkest, most frigid part of the water, where I could wash the blood off. I think I was screaming; a man came running toward me, a white dog by his side. After I went under, he pulled me to the surface and asked me what had happened as the dog paddled desperately beside me, barking. I couldn't answer him. What *had* happened? Was it a suicide, or was it a murder? And if it was a murder, who did it?

Home

A month before the wedding, Herb convinced me to invite my parents. He thought if they weren't there, the marriage might not seem as real to me. I hadn't spoken to Suky in years. I had cut her off completely, and, though I thought she was secretly grateful for it, initially I still dreamed that she would find me somehow, turn up at my apartment clear eyed and dope free, ready to go shopping or out for a milk shake. But it didn't happen that way. Any news I had from the family came in the form of fact-filled letters from my father, who told me of all the plumbing and boiler repairs, my brothers' exploits, and other local items of interest. They always ended with "Your mother sends you her love." This sentence read like a taunt; Suky had made her choice, and she hadn't chosen me. Kat's advice, to forget the past, to look ahead, only ahead, turned out to be very effective in the long run. Gradually I stopped crying about my mother. I bled the emotion from her memory until it hung lifeless in my mind, like a pig on a hook in a butcher shop window.

My oldest brother, Chester, called me every now and then to make sure I was all right, and we met in the city occasionally. Sometimes he gave me a little money. After I disappeared, Chester had gone to medical school. He was a doctor now. He still had the somber, disaffected delivery of his youth, but now it made him seem authoritative, a man you could trust. I was surprised to hear his voice when I finally got up the courage to call my parents' house.

"She's in no shape to go to a wedding," he said.

"What do you mean?" I asked.

"She's sick."

"Sick how?"

"It's complicated."

Herb and I drove up to Connecticut the next weekend. Des did what he could to discourage me from coming, but now I had to see her. As we drove up to the Green, I noticed that the paint on the house was flaking off. I wondered when my father would have to retire. We rang the bell at the front door, which felt odd; I had never used the front door growing up. But I was a stranger now. Chester came to greet us. I hugged him. Behind him, Des stood, smaller now, it seemed, the pouches under his eyes reddish, his hair gray. He had always been a calm man, but now he seemed resigned. He kissed me on the part of my hair and led me into the living room.

She was sitting on her favorite little armchair, in a quilted pink bed jacket and a dress so big for her it looked like it belonged to someone else. She had shrunk to a sliver of her former size. Always petite, she was tiny now, a wilted little thing with ankles like wrists, her thinning Lucille Ball hair pulled back in a neat ponytail, eyes glittering. She looked like an object to me. My mother was nowhere. Herb was shocked, I could tell. It took a lot to knock the wind out of his general air of removed amusement; Suky did it without trying.

She smiled politely as we walked in. Her teeth had been capped. "Would you like some tea, you two?" It was still that voice, that high, squeaky southern voice, with a slight whistle from the foreign teeth. The twitch in her cheek had become a violent, spastic tug. I felt like running away.

"I would love some," Herb said. He sat on the edge of the sofa and admired Suky's home. She beamed at him graciously as Chester poured the tea, then trembled uncontrollably as she tried to take a sip. Herb turned to Des and asked him about the real estate prices in the area. Had they gone up? How much? And his parish? Shrinking? Growing. How interesting. They kept that conversation up for about five minutes. Then, there was a pause.

"I have been very lucky," Suky said. "I have four wonderful children."

"Five, Mom," said Chester.

"Five children," said Suky in mock disbelief. "What was I thinking?" Then she chuckled, looking at me, I thought, with a sly expression entirely devoid of warmth. It seemed impossible that she no longer loved me. I had been the passion of her life! Was it possible that I looked as empty of meaning to her as she did to me? Where the hell was she? Where was my mother? I was leaking tears through the whole visit, but no one seemed to notice, and I rubbed them away like itches in the corners of my eyes.

Later, as Des helped her upstairs for her nap, Herb and I stood in the front hall to wave her off, as though she were boarding the *Queen Mary*. Halfway through her slow ascent, she stopped, her back very straight. Des looked at her expectantly. I knew she would turn around and look at me. She had to. And when she did, a shard of feeling, sharp as glass, cut through her absent stare and pierced my heart. I wanted to run up the stairs and hug her that minute. My muscles began to move. But something stayed me. I couldn't do it. The moment passed. She turned and made her way up the rest of the stairs, Des holding her wasted arm with the tips of his fingers, as if it were the fine stalk of an orchid.

Back in the living room, I slumped down on the couch, my legs weak. Chester told us in hushed tones that he was injecting her with small amounts of amphetamine combined with vitamins every few hours. The injections were keeping her alive at this point. She had been starving herself for years, he said ruefully, shaking his head. I thought about fat Grandma Sally. And about Suky, always standing by the stove eating a cup of rice pudding, never sitting with us at the table for more than a few minutes. She started taking the drug so she wouldn't want to eat, so she would have all that energy, so she could be the perfect mother, the perfect wife. Then the drug became her personality. And I had been so mean to her.

I would come back next week, I told myself. I would come back and sit with her and talk about this and that. I would hug her then. I just hadn't been ready yet. It wasn't the right time. As it turned out, I was so busy with planning the wedding, I had to put off my visit. I never saw her again. She was dead within a month, found lying on her bed, I am told, a plate of uneaten toast perched on her sunken belly. And now, if I could have one thing, one single thing, I would ask for an afternoon with my mother. I would like to let her know how much she is loved, in spite of everything, because of everything. I would like the chance to be kind.

Novice

My wedding dress was very light pink. I thought of it as white, with one drop of Gigi's blood in it. In the photographs of our wedding day, I look like a child beside him. We were married in a church. I can still smell the dust in the air, see it swirling in the orange and blue light filtered through the circular stained-glass window behind the cross. I felt like a novice taking my vows. Marrying Herb was a new skin on me, my last chance at goodness. I knew if I fucked this up, I would be fallen forever.

Early Days

In the seven years Gigi had been married to Herb, she had never bothered to change her will; upon her demise, her millions reverted to her parents and their Italian pharmaceutical empire. Herb was both relieved and puzzled to learn this. It would, of course, have been outrageous for him to inherit his spurned wife's fortune—yet why had she never changed her will? "She was always paranoid" was Herb's answer. Maybe she'd been right to be.

Not one of Herb's friends abandoned him after Gigi killed herself. Only her own old cronies, a handful of Europeans whom Herb had always deemed too boring or pretentious to socialize with, stayed away from him now—not that they were missed.

Just about everyone Herb knew had thought that Gigi was a head case, as it turned out, and, though all of them saw what had happened as a tragedy, they were also relieved that Herb was no longer encumbered by an erratic and increasingly embarrassing wife. What they thought of me— Well, they folded me in, like raisins in a cake recipe that doesn't call for them but won't be ruined by them, either. Herb could have married a llama and his circle would have accepted it. He was a truly charismatic man. He had some power in the publishing world, but it was his dynamic charm, his ferocious appetite for existence, his connection to a bigger, Titanic, preneurotic period in American literary life, when people drank Scotch with dinner and wrote unapologetic sentences and ruined each other's lives unconsciously, with the ignorance of children, that held people in his sway.

I clutched at marriage, held it like an infant, fed it, pampered it. No man was loved the way Herb was. He marveled at the genius of his choice as I fetched him his slippers, massaged his temples with scented oil, spent half the day cooking. I did not yet know how to truly be this new person. I did not know how to run a house, take care of a man, be faithful. But, like a dancer learning a new routine, I relied on repetition to teach my brain. At first I was lost in my role, feeling like an impostor as I forged checks with my new name, chose a décor for our new apartment, sold the house in a house and found a humbler place farther inland for weekends. I didn't really know how to shop for clothes or plan a dinner party. I just kept pretending, kept playing dress-up, answering the phone in a singsong voice, as I had when I was ten and married to my invisible husband, Joey. I worked at my new identity for years, until the motions of everyday life as Herb's wife were as natural to me as walking.

It wasn't until I became pregnant with the twins, though, that I really believed my own act. These two creatures squirming inside me were facts. They had blood, eyes, destinies. Unlike me, they were born perfect, male and female, complete. I thought there was something magical about boy-girl twins. It was a gift, a sign. I gave myself to them with the joy of a penitent. And gradually, through the nights lying awake between Ben and Grace as they clutched at my hair in their sleep with their warm, soft hands, sniffed my neck, held me fast with their chubby arms, strong legs clamped over my abdomen, I began to change in a deeper way. My children's limbs grew around me like roots; I became a part of them. I began to want what

I felt they needed. Using Suky as an inverse model, I made myself eat proper meals, seldom drank, took no medication.

As the twins grew up, it became clear that they had opposite personalities. Ben was kind, curious, intelligent. He loved all sports, was a good student, worked after school in the mail room of Herb's publishing house by the time he was thirteen. He was a responsible, sensible kid.

Grace was high-strung, fierce, a leader. She had strong vigilante tendencies, which became troublingly apparent at the age of five, when she knocked a boy unconscious with a softball bat for stealing her brother's SweeTart candies. As a toddler and very young child, she refused to wear clothes. I still have a scar on my wrist from a bite she gave me while I tried to wrestle her into a party dress—we were going to a wedding. In the end, I had to hire a babysitter and leave her home, because all she would wear was a string of beads. All the combs in the house had teeth missing from ill-fated attempts at taming the thick, tangled fair hair that grew in stubborn spirals around her shining, intelligent face. Grace felt everything with almost alarming intensity. She could be so possessive of me that at times I felt her affection like a plastic bag over my face. I have to admit, my feeling for her could be just as violent, and sometimes it frightened me, because I remembered Suky and the rigid clutch of her embraces, the way she held me down to kiss me, making me laugh so hard I ended up crying, feeling crushed, feeling that she would actually kill me. With Ben, it was effortless. I adored him, he adored me, that was that. But with Grace, it was a love affair, complete with sudden flashes of dislike, tearful fights, and sweet reconciliations.

One night when Grace was eight, I spied on her. I had put the twins to bed an hour before and tiptoed up to check on them. The door was ajar, and I peeked in. Ben was fast asleep. Grace, however, had secretly put on the reading light and was dancing. Her white nightgown and crazy nest of blond hair glowed in the incandescent light. The dance was both savage and graceful. She was whispering a song, or a spell, as she whirled like a dervish, round and round, her hands carving the air into arabesques. As I watched her, spellbound, through the crack in the door, I thought, *What would it take to turn this feral little creature into someone who would let herself be whipped?* In that instant, I realized that all I wanted for my daughter was that she be as unlike me as possible. I had to protect her.

Silently, I walked away, steeling myself for the coming sacrifice. From that night on, I began to both keep her at arm's length—trying with all my might to maintain some neutrality, force the drama out of our relationship, be as little as possible like Suky—and at the same time spoil her systematically, in a deliberate, thoughtful fashion. I discouraged her from helping in the house, pushed her to play competitive sports, encouraged her tendency to dress like a boy, play like a boy. I wanted her to be like a man, to have the expectations of a man—that sense of being heir to the world. I wanted to break the chain of servitude that linked the women in my family.

My system worked. Grace grew up with arrogance, charm, optimism, and total belief in herself. The fact that she came to despise me was a sad side effect of her upbringing, but I guess it was inevitable. She saw me as pathetic, a slave, a flop. I was at the kids' service day and night. I had no job and very little help in the house aside from the cleaning. Throughout Grace's adolescence, I hoped the day would come when she realized what I had done for her. She would then look at me with radiant love once more, as she had that afternoon long ago, when she'd taught herself to read and asked, "*Now* do you love me more than Ben?" But that moment never came. Her need for me had evaporated.

When the twins were small, I had a recurring dream that I was served up on an enormous platter and my children ate me. They had always loved ribs; they snapped mine off with strong, greasy fingers and consumed them voraciously, with barbecue sauce. The strange thing was, I was conscious in the dream, and I was smiling. All I could think of was how much protein the kids were getting.

In spite of all my devotion in the early days of my marriage, there were moments when, like a wolf domesticated by humans, I caught a scent of my old ways and felt hemmed in. A beautiful young man walking by on the street, the sight of teenagers high in the park, sometimes threw me off balance; I could feel myself teeter on the edge of my new existence and imagined the thrill of kissing a man I barely knew, or the sharp kick of amphetamine between my eyes. But I never strayed. Herb felt the solemnity of our vows, too, but he refused to cast a shadow of guilt on the marriage, doggedly seeing Gigi's suicide as the natural, almost inevitable, flowering of her illness. He savored his second dose of fatherhood. He had failed his first kids, angry mediocrities in their thirties by now. I was his shining ticket to happiness, new life, a second chance at youth. The fact that we had built our bliss on another person's despair—we forgot it eventually. We lived as if we deserved our luck.

Miranda

Yet I was plagued by a maddening insecurity about Herb's love for me. Almost invariably, the same poisonous daydream would infuse my mind as I pushed the kids through the park in their stroller, trying to lull them to sleep after lunch. The details of the fantasy were different, but the thrust was the same: I find a letter. I find a scarf. I find a pair of underpants. I come upon Herb with his lover in our apartment. I come upon them in the beach house. I come upon them in the park while walking the twins. She is always dark, tall, buxom, more intelligent than I. I weep. I mourn. I accuse. I confront. He leaves me.

I got so involved with these scenarios of betrayal and abandonment that I barely knew where I was. One day, I was walking along in Central Park, imagining haranguing Herb as his gorgeous lover covered herself with my guest bedsheets, when a lady in her sixties approached me. "Mrs. Lee?" I looked at her, confused. She had a sharp nose, small, dark, friendly eyes. She was English. It was then I realized I had tears on my face. I smiled, embarrassed, and wiped them away. She introduced herself as Miranda Lee. Herb's first wife! She'd seen a picture of me standing with Herb at some charity event. She wanted to say hello. She had become a psychotherapist. I should have taken her card. Instead, we chatted on a park bench while the twins slept. She was an intelligent woman with a sense of humor, especially about Herb. When she mentioned him, it was with an amused, condescending expression, as though he was a naughty child. Solitude radiated from her, but it wasn't imbued with bitterness. It just seemed like a fact of her life, something she accepted, even cherished. She had made a considerable life for herself since the divorce. She had a thriving practice, two sons who were her dear friends, she had a lively social life, went to the opera.

When we parted, she said I seemed like a lovely person. And then she said, "Take care of yourself, Pippa." She looked me in the eye when she said that. I was flustered by her warning, and slightly insulted, for Herb, and for myself, yet what she said stayed with me. After that day, I banned the fantasy of Herb's affair from my thoughts. It took a lot of discipline, but I managed to shoo it away just about every time it started running through my mind, till eventually I kicked the habit altogether. I trained myself to trust him.

Snow

I remember one winter, at the country house of friends with young children, everyone went tobogganing but the twins and me. I had stayed inside with them all morning, thinking they were too young, at two, to be on anything moving so fast. Herb came in, though, eyes shining, cheeks flushed from the cold, and said that the other kids in the party were having a great time, they were just a little older than ours. Wouldn't I come out with the twins? Herb rarely went gamboling outside, so I said yes, all right. I armed Ben and Grace against the cold with snowsuits, fat jackets, mittens, hats, and boots, and they waddled out ahead of me. The sky was clear and blue; the snow sparkled. Herb slid onto the back of the toboggan, holding the rope. Then came fearless Grace, snuggling up to her daddy, then me, then Ben, my sweet little Ben. Herb's long legs were like iron railings along the row of his family, as one of our friends gave us a little push. So fast—I hadn't known it would be so quick—and the snow! I couldn't see, there was snow flying into my face, I was blinded, out of control, clutching Ben, Grace against my back— I was terrified, flying through space with Herb bellowing, steering, and Grace screaming with joy, all of us shrieking in the white screen of no picture, till at last we slid onto the frozen lake at the bottom of the hill and slowly came to a stop. We all rolled off the toboggan. Catching my breath, on all fours, I looked up at Herb: his whole face was encrusted with snow, his eyebrows like snowy mountain peaks; the furry trim on the twins' hoods was white and glistening, their light eyes peeking out of sugary faces. We all looked at one another and laughed, we laughed so hard, turning in toward each other, a circle of people who belonged to one another, and to no one else. That was the moment I felt us become a family, a unit apart from the world. That was when I became Pippa Lee.

Part Three

Lion Turds and Potatoes

The night after her lunch with Moira, Pippa dreamed she was walking through a deserted shopping mall, chewing a wad of gum that had lost its flavor. The escalators were stock-still; rolling metal gates were clamped down over all the storefronts. She took the wad out of her mouth and started searching for a place to throw it away. She found the garbage, got rid of the gum, and was just wondering whether she could persuade someone to open the tobacco kiosk so she could buy some cigarettes when she heard a rough, breathy sound beside her. She turned and saw an enormous lion. He was serenely lapping up a puddle of strawberry ice cream from the floor. His mane was coarse and had golden hairs woven into the reddish thicket. Pippa was terrified.

The lion ignored her. He took a few bouncing steps and leapt gracefully into an enormous planter with an artificial palm tree stuck in it. Squatting, his back rounded, great haunches quivering, the lion shat onto the fake earth. He looked sheepish and vulnerable. Pippa felt sorry for the lion. Having accomplished his task, he sped off the huge flowerpot, as if disavowing his humiliation, and padded down an immobile escalator, moving as fluidly as a river, an invincible predator once again. Finding that she had a plastic bag conveniently wrapped around her hand, Pippa stepped over to the great turd and scooped it up dutifully, as she had a thousand times in Gramercy Park when walking Milo, their corgi, who'd died of pneumonia back in 1996.

"Mrs. Lee?" She heard the voice coming from inside the tobacco kiosk. She walked over to the iron gate and peered inside.

"I would like some cigarettes," she called out into the darkness.

"What kind?" said the voice.

"Those white ones," she said.

Chris Nadeau stood behind the counter of the Marigold Village convenience store, watching Pippa, who was standing in her nightgown, holding a large baking potato that she had retrieved from the bin, a plastic produce bag over her hand, her gaze fixed somewhere behind his head. "Marlboro Lights?" he asked helpfully. She didn't respond. He leaned over the counter and brushed her arm with his fingers. Pippa felt his touch as a shock from the metal gate of the tobacco kiosk, but it was enough to rend the dream. She looked down at her nightgown, the potato in the bag, her bare feet. As she looked up at Chris, his eyes filled with curiosity and concern, her mind gradually collected itself around her realization.

"Oh, my God," she said softly.

"Would you like me to take you home?" Chris asked.

She nodded, handing him the potato.

By the time they got to her place, weak light was seeping into the darkness, like a drop of ink tinting a glass of water. One bird called out. Pippa made no move to get out of the truck.

"Mrs. Lee," he said. "Pippa?" His gentleness surprised her. She felt tears on her cheeks.

"I'm sorry," she said. "This is the last thing you need. First your mother and now me."

"It's not the same," said Chris.

"It's just, I walk in my sleep. Recently, I have been. Something must be wrong . . . with me. The weirdest thing about this . . ."

"What?" he asked.

"I just feel so young," she said. "Like a very young person."

"Well, you're young for around here," he said.

"I don't mean that. When I was very young . . . I was always in the middle of some kind of drama . . . and as I got older and had a family, I gradually stopped being in the center, you know, I stepped aside, and other people were in the center; when you have kids that just sort of happens. And I got used to that. And now I am living this weird little drama and I am the protagonist, and I just feel so crazy, even though I know it's a very commonplace problem, millions of Americans are probably up buttering their stereos as we speak."

He laughed, and so did she.

"You're an unusual person," he said.

"No, I'm not," she said. "That's what I am trying to tell you. What's unusual is that I'm acting weird."

"Trust me," he said.

"Maybe you shouldn't tell anyone . . . about this," she said.

"Okay," he said.

She looked over at him and noticed his eyes for the first time. Dark as the bottom of a lake, they shone with the helpless honesty of a dog's eyes.

"Well, thank you—and good night," she said, getting out and pushing the heavy door shut.

Herb was asleep. Stark naked, legs twisted in the sheets, his arms flung out on either side of him, his hairy barrel chest exposed, he looked like he had been washed ashore, like Odysseus on Circe's isle. But for Herb, the adventure was over, Pippa thought sadly. She wished that the future wasn't so predictable, that this house was not the death house. That it wasn't just a matter of time before he had the morphine IV in, and the nurse sat in the corner reading her magazine. Eighty years old. How long did he have?

Herb opened his eyes and saw her crouching beside him. "What are you crying for?" He sounded irritated. He knew what she was thinking. He rolled over and went to sleep. She knew he was right. She had to stop being so sentimental. She needed a doctor, too. Pills, probably. She hated the idea, she never even took an aspirin if she could help it, but she was driving in her sleep, for goodness' sake. At breakfast she would tell Herb. She would tell him and he would fix it, say something dry and logical, and then she would do what he said. She didn't feel like sleeping, so she took a shower, dressed, and made coffee.

Finally, at nine o'clock, Herb came out looking sullen. He took a sip of the coffee and made a face. "This is piss," he said. Wordlessly she got up, took his cup, poured it out, and ground a new batch of beans. He sat there stewing. When she presented the second cup to him, he tasted it and said, "Let's get a new machine."

"This is a new machine."

"Let's get one that makes a decent cup of coffee. We can afford it, we sold all our real estate."

"I'll look them up," she said. "Maybe *Consumer Reports*—"
Herb got up and went to the sofa, started reading the paper. She knew better than to try to talk to him when he was in a bad mood.

"Is there anything you want at the store?" she asked.

"No thanks."

"See you at lunch then." She walked out of the house and thought about what she wanted to buy. A beautiful melon, if she could find a ripe one. And prosciutto. She walked out into the driveway and stared at Herb's car, sitting there by itself. Where was her car? Had it been stolen? Seconds passed before she remembered it was parked outside the convenience store. Probably had the keys in it! She turned to go back into the house but stopped herself. Herb would flip about the car. He was grumpy enough already. How was she going to get to the convenience store? She could walk, but it was so hot—and Herb might pass her on the way to his office. She hurried around the house and looked across the pond. Chris's yellow truck was parked in the driveway. She wondered when his shift began. It wasn't even ten o'clock. What would she say to Dot? She started walking down the road to the Nadeau house. If Dot was there, she would pretend she was just stopping by, out on a walk. If she wasn't . . .

Pippa had reached the house. The toadstool cast a purple shadow on the grass. Dot's car was gone. Johnny spent every morning at the boatbuilding club—she remembered Dot mentioning that. Her belly tight with anxiety, Pippa rang the bell. Nothing stirred inside. She tried the door. Locked. She couldn't help laughing at herself as she crept around to the side of the house, to Chris's open window, and looked in. He was asleep. Pippa tapped on the window with her fingernail. He didn't move. She knocked on the glass. His head moved from side to side, as if to shake off the sound. Then he sat bolt upright and stared at the window.

"Chris," she said. "It's Pippa. I'm so sorry to disturb you." He rubbed his eyes and swiveled around, putting his feet on the floor. He was wearing his "What?" T-shirt, and held the sheet across his lap. "I'll wait at the front door," she said. She walked to the front door and waited. This was so embarrassing, it was beyond belief. He seemed to be taking a long time. Finally, she heard footsteps. The door opened. He was dressed, but he looked exhausted.

"I'm so sorry," she said.

" 'S all right," he said, his voice weak with sleep. "Wassa matter?"

"My car," she said. "I left it at the store. I think the keys may be in it. I . . . have no way to get there and you're the only one . . ."

"Okay," he said and walked out the door, toward his truck. She got in beside him.

"I shouldn't have done this. It's terrible, you won't get enough sleep."

"Don't worry," he said.

They drove to the convenience store. Her car was still there, with the keys in it.

"Oh, thank God," she said. "Thank you so much."

"You want to get breakfast?" he asked, yawning. She realized that she was very hungry.

They went to the shingled Friendly's that was a part of Marigold Village. Pippa ordered bacon and eggs.

"This is a very strange moment in my life," she said.

"You and me both," he said.

"Yes?"

"Fired from a job I despise, I come home to find my wife on top of my best friend."

"That's horrible," said Pippa.

"The clichés were running fast and furious in Wendover, Utah, that Saturday night. But I've been thinking. Maybe there was a good reason for that layer cake of rejection."

"Really? What?" said Pippa.

"I'm an asshole."

Pippa let out a little laugh, then realized he was serious.

"I don't know why. I just always have been."

"Hm," she said.

"And what about you? Is there a reason you're potato shopping at two in the morning?"

"I don't know," she said. "I think maybe I'm . . . Ever since we moved here . . . I haven't felt right. I feel distanced from Herb and our life together, as if I were hovering above it, watching us. I wonder if it's to do with my age, and the fact that I—I don't quite know who I am these days, sometimes I'll be someplace and accidentally look in a mirror, and for a split second I think, Who's that middle-aged woman? And then, Oh, my God, it's me! It's an awful shock, I can tell you. But that doesn't explain why I've been sleepwalking."

He didn't say anything, just stared at her. Pippa felt the blood creep up her neck, her cheeks. Her whole chest was getting blotchy.

"Maybe your brain is trying to tell you something." His face was, as usual, expressionless. She could see the feathery lines of the tattooed Christ peeking out from the loose collar of his worn T-shirt.

"That tattoo you have must have hurt terribly," she said.

"I can't remember."

"My father was a minister," she said.

He nodded, then ate for a time, looking down at his plate. Pippa watched him. His narrow face seemed very angular, almost wedge shaped, as though his cheeks had been chiseled away from his broken nose and chapped lips. One strong hand curled around his plate protectively.

"I tried to enter a seminary once," he said.

"You were going to be a priest?"

"I wanted to, but—I wasn't their type."

"Do you still have a vocation?"

"Just the tattoo."

"You can have them removed."

"You'd have to take my skin off. Anyway, it's a souvenir."

"So you lost your faith?"

"I just stopped believing you could nail it all down."

"I'm curious about you," she said. And then she wondered if that was an inappropriate thing to say. He leaned back in his seat and looked at her, as if weighing something in his mind.

"Okay," he said. And then he started to talk.

Chris

When Chris was sixteen, he tried to fix the dryer. He was a handy kid, always dismantling failing machines around the house, putting them back together so they hummed. It had gotten to the point where Dot didn't even bother with electricians. She just called in Chris. He had taken an evening course in appliance maintenance at the town hall, and this, coupled with his knack, gave her the utmost confidence in his ability to figure out why the dryer was howling like a cat in heat every time she turned it on.

Up to that point in his life, Chris had been good only at repairing machinery. Every afternoon after school, he would mope around the neighborhood, on the lookout for broken equipment. At night he drove around the sleeping streets with a group of high school miscreants, committing drive-by mailbox beheadings, or playing basketball in people's driveways until lights were flicked on and the cops were called. One summer evening, he and his crew went to the nearest movie theater, took stock of a local family out for the evening, returned to the family's home, broke in, raided the fridge, and cooked an entire barbecue in their backyard. In school, Chris stared listlessly at the teacher, his thumb worrying the eraser of his pencil, jerking it back and forth until, inevitably, it crumbled off.

On the day his mother asked him to fix the dryer, Chris had

pushed the machine a few feet out from the wall and was lying behind it, curled up on his side, one leg bent, when he touched the wrong two wires together, went stiff, and started vibrating, 110 volts of electricity coursing through every cell of his body. Strangely, the boy was not afraid but awed by the power pulsing through him. A panicked Dot disengaged him from the current using a wooden broom handle. The medics arrived soon after. Chris was unconscious but alive. They had to work on him for five minutes that felt like fifty to Dot, who had her hands clamped to her face, terrified eyes staring out between spread fingers, during the whole proceeding.

When Chris woke up, his nose was filled with the smell of burnt hair and rubber; his mind was filled with God. For the first time in his life, he was on fire with ecstatic certainty: first of all, God was real as flesh. Second, the Son of God was neither meek nor mild. He was terrible as a tidal wave, merciless as a lightning bolt. He was the God of love but not mercy. His love was terrifying; it sounded like a million wings beating; it felt like being swept up by a tornado. And He reserved it for the renegades, the anarchists; those who wanted to bring the whole rotten structure of everyday human greed and insincerity to a trembling halt. Chris felt he had been chosen and warned. He started going to church daily and even brought home a woman and her two children whom he had found begging in the street, having missed the closing time of the local shelter.

Dot, who didn't even like her own family sitting on her best furniture, was horrified to find three shy, dusky strangers in her living room when she walked in, her arms gripping two bulging bags of groceries. But she couldn't exactly throw them out; the children were tiny. So she cooked them dinner in miffed silence, made them up two beds in the rec room, then took three aspirin and went to bed in tears, insisting that Johnny sleep with a revolver under his pillow.

Both Dot and Johnny were automaton Catholics; their practice was reserved for Easter and Christmas. The radical faith Chris displayed had no place in their home. His quiet, constant reading of the Bible worried and alienated them. An attempt at becoming a Jesuit novice—he offered himself to the order as a "warrior of Christ"—had his parents mildly alarmed, then humiliated when his application was rejected after a psychiatric evaluation deemed him "fervent to the point of irrationality." (One lay Ignatian Brother remarked, after Chris had left his requisite interview for the Vocations Panel, "He would have been perfect for the Crusades.")

Once spurned by the Jesuits, Chris set about giving away as much of his parents' money as possible to the bums in Jersey City, twenties and fives filched from his mother's purse, his father's wallet. He started getting into bar brawls with hypocrites; he even got himself arrested once, for screaming *Please stop lying to each other!* up and down their quiet suburban street at two o'clock in the morning. He went straight from jail to a tattoo parlor and had the Lord bored into his skin for good. The boy was driving his mother crazy. His father felt completely impotent in the face of his son's problem. "If it was drugs," Johnny said, "at least we could send him to rehab. But this . . ." He flapped his arms and let them slap his sides uselessly.

Chris left home soon after, in the Thunderbird his father had bought him for his eighteenth birthday in the hope that a vehicle would attract a girl (he sold the car a week later and gave most of the money away). His parents didn't try to find him when he left; they just sadly let him go. In the years that followed, Chris took a variety of jobs, as an electrician, mechanic, car wash attendant, all across the country. When he came to a new town, he would coast through it, searching for the poorest, most broken-down neighborhood he could find. Once there, he would seek out a rental apartment, or a room in someone's house. Occasionally, he lived in the back of his truck. Then he would find a church—be it Catholic, First Christian, Methodist, or Episcopal—pray there, help with whatever outreach programs they had going in the community, and then, after a few months or maybe a year, he would move on. Passing through Utah, he met and married a slight, bright-eyed Catholic girl. They prayed together frequently, made love seldom, barely spoke. Back home, his father, a meticulous dentist, was corroded with disappointment; his only son was an itinerant, a drifter, a religious fanatic. He kept hoping that one day Chris would come back to Jersey, finish school, find a profession. But no. The electrocution had happened nearly twenty years ago. Chris was a washout.

But Johnny and Dot didn't know the worst of it: over the years, Chris's belief in the Bible had sloughed away from him, like a scab from a healed wound. The God he still sensed with such acute certainty had somehow outgrown that good book; this was a deity too vast to be contained in a single system. There was no humility in thinking you had cracked the code. Chris stopped going to church, but he couldn't bring himself to tell his parents he had failed at being a Christian, on top of everything else. So he ricocheted around the country, his wife a stranger beside him, his faith now nameless, formless, dogging him, filling him with longing to see the Face that was veiled in darkness yet he knew was there. He was an exile, unable to stomach even the most innocuous corruption of everyday human life, to get a regular job, to settle into society, yet no longer enveloped in the golden light of dogma. He felt himself standing just outside a warm, safe, luminous circle—the circle of the Church. If only he could return to it. But it was too late: he didn't belong anywhere anymore.

Pippa listened to Chris's story, rapt. When he was done, he took a bite of toast.

"What are you thinking?" he asked.

"Nothing."

"Tell me," he said.

"I'm just thinking, you seem so bright, and it's a pity . . . that you never settled on a job you care about. It would make your life so much easier." Why had she said that? So many thoughts—of worry, recognition, admiration—had darted through her mind as he spoke. But as usual, she said the one thing that made her sound like a materialistic housewife.

Chris sat back and looked at her. Surprise, hurt, and then anger appeared on his face in a sequence Pippa found disquieting. "Okay," he said. "Well, thank you."

"I didn't mean to offend you."

"I suggest you go back to that little life you've puffed up for yourself. I'm sure you're very happy underneath all that misery."

Pippa gathered her purse to her chest, slid out of the booth, her heart pounding in her ears. He was eating again.

"You're right, you know," she said. "You are an asshole."

"Told you." He hunkered down over the last of his home fries, waved his fork. "See you in a few farts," he said cheerfully, taking a bite.

She was already behind him and stopped, turning back, her jaw dropping. Then she walked to her car, trembling. But once she got in, she started laughing. She laughed so hard, she had to wipe tears from her eyes.

When she got home, she made spanakopita for Herb, folding neat packets of filo dough around a mixture of feta cheese and spinach. Then she settled into a reclining lawn chair on the patio, sipping a large glass of pomegranate juice. Herb was in his office. It was past one, he should be home soon. Pippa looked across the pond at Dot's house. The yellow truck was there. Then she saw the front door open. Chris walked out and got into his truck. He was the strangest person she had ever met. So unpleasant, yet so touching. The yellow truck pulled away just as Herb laid his hand on her shoulder. She turned, startled. "Did you think I was a geriatric marauder?" he asked.

"I was just thinking," she said.

"I'm sorry I was a grouch," he said.

"It's okay."

"It's so hot," he said, "I'm going to take a quick shower, and then we can have lunch." She got up and put the spanakopita in the oven, tossed the salad she'd prepared. She served him out on the porch.

"Aren't you eating?"

"I had breakfast late," she said. "With . . . remember Chris, that son of Dot's?"

"The half-baked one?"

"Yeah, I saw him outside the convenience store, and he asked me to breakfast."

"That's weird," he said.

"He told me he was an asshole."

"Is he?"

"I think maybe he's just compulsively honest. Which makes him extremely unpleasant. Herb?"

"Hm?"

"I did it again."

"What?"

"Walked in my sleep. I drove."

"Oh, Jesus."

"I woke up, and I was in the convenience store. Chris works the night shift there, that's how I know him, really."

"I've never heard of driving in your sleep. How is that possible?"

"Maybe I'm an extreme case."

"We better have you looked at."

Dr. Schultz saw only old people, it seemed to Pippa as she sat in his waiting room. If they weren't using walkers, they had white slacks on. Elastic waistbands, white tennis shoes, pastel tops. The very word *slacks* made Pippa cringe. Who passed a law that old people had to dress this way? Pippa glowered at them all. She was angry with them for living past their usefulness. For being so fucking slow. Old age repelled her; that was the truth of it. Herb wasn't old-old. Not yet. He was old, but his face was still basically on. He didn't have the gaping mouth, the glassy eyes, the imprecise movements of the truly aged. She was frightened of losing her husband to this joke of time. She knew she would love him and care for him, and gradually, depending on how long he lasted in his decrepitude, she would forget his strength, his invincibility, his irony even. Oh, God, it was awful. Pippa didn't want to live too long. Just long enough, she thought. Just exactly long enough before she turned the final corner. The nurse called her name.

Dr. Schultz was a vigorous man. His bald head was shiny, the whites of his eyes luminous. He looked like an athlete—a rower, perhaps. The muscles in his powerful legs bulged under fitted trousers. His feet were enormous. And he looked cheerful. Pippa wondered how he kept that up, seeing so many revolting old bodies every day. Maybe he was a sort of leech, she thought, sucking his youth out of their age. He was asking her the usual questions. Date of birth. What did your mother die of? Heart stopped because. Because she took too much crank. No, leave that out. Father? Aneurism. Any cancer in the family? Aunt Trish. Poor old Aunt Trish. Pippa tossed her head. She was aware of keeping a thought at bay. It hadn't entered the circle of her consciousness yet, whatever it was, but she could tell it was unpleasant. It cast a jagged shadow on her mind, caused her to fidget and clear her throat, shake her head, anything to stop herself from thinking—what? What was the matter?

"So, Mrs. Lee. What can I do for you?"

Pippa started, realizing that she had drifted away as he watched patiently. "Oh," she said, smiling. "I—I have been walking in my sleep."

Dr. Schultz wrote that onto his form, his big hand curled awkwardly around a delicate silver pen. His handwriting looked like crooked teeth, Pippa thought: tiny letters crammed up against one another, slanted to the left.

"When did this start?"

"About a month ago."

"What medications are you on?"

"None."

"What about sleep aids?"

"Never. I don't take pills. I even take liquid vitamins."

He looked up at her, surprised. "Do you have a history of sleepwalking?"

"A couple of times, when I was little. But this— I cook in my sleep. I smoke, which I don't, I mean I do a little now, but that's— I drove the car! To a convenience store. I was dreaming about being in a mall and there was a lion taking a crap in a flowerpot and I went to pick it up and it turned out to be a potato. At first we thought it was my husband, but then we set up a camera . . ." Her voice had risen; she was being voluble, humorous, as if telling a funny story at a party. She didn't know why she was acting like this. She felt breathless. ". . . and, surprise, surprise, it was me!"

The doctor looked at her, thinking. "I'm not a sleep specialist, but some of my patients have problems with night mobility. Usually it has something to do with medication, or . . . dementia, which is clearly not the case here. Um . . . do you mind if I ask you a personal question?"

"No."

"Is something upsetting you, or causing you stress?"

Tears came to her eyes instantly. Irritated, she wiped them away with her pinkie.

"I don't know." An image of the beach, the day Gigi died: garnet flecks on her white dress, a flash of sky, then under bottle glass green water, swirling sand. She hadn't wanted to come back up.

"I can give you some medication which may keep you sleeping through the night. It doesn't always work. I mean, it's a sleeping pill. It depends on your tolerance."

"Oh, God, I can't start taking pills."

"You could grind them up in applesauce. Or put a lock on your bedroom door and have your husband hide the key." Dr. Schultz smiled wryly. "I know it doesn't sound very scientific, but it would keep you inside. Listen, sleepwalking is not considered a psychological problem, it's neurological. But stress can play a part, especially in adult-onset cases. I'll give you a prescription. But it seems to me that you could benefit from a short period of psychotherapy. Just to . . . get your thoughts in order. You've made a big transition and . . . you seem like you have a lot on your mind." She had her hand on the doorknob, was just about to turn it, when he asked: "Do you have any hobbies?"

"Hobbies?"

"Yes. Anything you like to do—just for yourself."

"Not really."

"Hobbies can be helpful," he said.

She thanked him and walked out the door, the image of his gleaming scalp and shiny eyes burned into her mind.

Pippa slapped her purse onto the coffee table. Herb looked up from his paper.

"He basically thinks I'm off my nut," she said. "He gave me a prescription for sleeping pills and the name of a psychiatrist." She brandished the business card in the air. "Notice it's not a therapist. That's because Dr. Schultz thinks I'm going to need medication . . . and a locksmith." She started giggling. "He suggested we bolt the bedroom door from inside, and you hide the key. Oh, and I'm supposed to take up basket weaving." She felt hysteria creeping up on her.

"You mean every time I have to get up and pee in the night I'm gonna be fumbling around looking for the goddamn key?" he said. "Some doctor." Herb looked at his wife. Two distinct red spots had appeared on her high-set cheeks, tears of laughter sparkled in her eyes. She seemed so alive.

"It's weird," he said. "Ever since we moved to the old folks' home, you look younger every day."

She drove back to the mini-mall to pick up some photographs she'd had developed and buy fruit at Shaw's. They had some organic produce. Pippa was acutely aware of how poisonous the world was these days. Cell phones, cordless phones, computers, microwaves, vegetables, meat, carpeting—you name it, it was shedding some sort of toxicity. No wonder everyone was getting cancer. Pippa bought six ripe black plums and a big bunch of grapes. She collected her photos, then stood in line in the parking lot, outside the fishmonger's truck. The man drove all the way down from Maine every Thursday; she felt guilty if she didn't buy anything from him. Today she would buy a pound of clams, make spaghetti with clam sauce. Herb loved that. It was hot in the parking lot. She took the envelope with the photos in it from her purse and started flipping through the images: Herb reading, Herb eating cereal, views of the living room. Some pictures from a month ago, when Grace had come to see the place for the first time before going off to Kabul, her intelligent eyes red from the flash, hard mouth set.

"Hey." Pippa looked up. Chris was standing beside her. "Fish tonight?"

"I thought so," she said. She was relieved to see him, surprised to be relieved.

"I'm sorry about the other day," he said.

"Oh . . . that's all right."

"I'm a jerk."

"You're not so bad," she said.

"How are you doing?"

"Oh, fine. Actually not so wonderful." She felt emotion rising in her again, waved the packet of photos in front of her face to fan it away.

"I just bought some beer," he said. "Care to join me . . . after you get your fish?"

"I can make tomato sauce," she said, waving her hand dismissively and abandoning her place.

They walked to the river. Chris's truck was parked there. He stopped at a small tree, almost entirely tented over with dense white webbing. "Look," he said, pointing. Pippa looked closely, saw caterpillars inching inside their translucent house, folding and stretching their black bodies. There were hundreds of them squirming around in there. It made her shiver. "Tent caterpillars," he said. "They're all over the place. I've never seen this many. There's going to be an invasion of moths this year." He climbed up onto the roof and held out his hand; she grabbed it and clambered up as well. They sat side by side and watched the river flow by, the current rippling the smooth, glossy water like muscle. Pippa was still clutching the photos in her hand.

"Who's that?" Chris asked, pointing to the photograph of Grace.

"My daughter," said Pippa. "She hates me."

Chris didn't say anything. He took a sip of beer, and they both looked down at the river. The sun had moved, and the water looked metallic now, a band of pure silver-white, cutting through the trees. They stared until the light changed again, and the river reappeared. Pippa looked over at Chris. She felt strangely at ease with this person.

"I bet she doesn't," he said.

"What?"

"Hate you."

"It's just . . . she's angry at me all the time. I don't know why. I wish it was different. I miss her. I wonder . . ."

"What?"

"If I got it all wrong with her."

It was getting dark. Pippa shivered. Chris took off his sweatshirt and put it around her shoulders.

"You're probably right about me," he said. "I probably should find a reasonable job. Something with a future."

"It was a silly thing to say," she said.

"No. It was . . . it was thoughtful. But. I'm beyond the pale."

"So, what do you, I mean, you . . . drive around, take up residence in places, get a job, and . . ."

"I try to be of help." He took a gulp of beer and shifted his weight. The metal of the roof let out a hollow thud as it buckled.

"What about here? Who are you helping here?"

He looked up at her, his thuggish, soulful face half-lit in the dying light, his deep-set eyes black holes. She felt her belly lurch, as though she had lost her footing and was falling.

"I'm leaving soon," he said.

She had an impulse to grab his arm, but she sat still. "Why?"

"I can't stay with my parents forever."

"Where will you go?"

"Back out west, I guess. Or south."

He jumped off the truck, helped her down, then walked her back to her car. She waved goodbye. He winked.

Every time she took her leave of him, he had to remind her that he was a crude waster. Yet she kept spilling her heart out to him. What the hell am I doing? she thought.

Back in the condo, she made the pasta. During the meal, Herb seemed to be lost in thought. He glared at his plate as if she wasn't there. She watched him, feeling awkward. She tried to remember how long it had been like this between them. Not always, no. They usually laughed so much. When had it gotten dried up like this? "I joined Dot's pottery class," she said.

"Good," said Herb without looking up.

"Why do you think it's good?"

"Didn't that doctor think you needed a hobby?" A flash of dislike went through her. *Asshole*, she thought. Irritated, she got up and went into the bedroom, leaving Herb with the dishes. She wondered if she had ever done that before.

He walked in. "Are you okay?"

"My mother used to lie on her bed like this with a plate of toast on her belly."

"I know," he said.

"I should take your blood pressure."

He made an impatient gesture. "It's fine. Okay then." He made a sort of false exit, then stood there.

"I'll do the dishes later," she said.

Backward

Pippa liked the feeling of the spinning, wet clay between her fingers, the way it rose up like a wave as she pinched it, the gray disk of the potter's wheel circling furiously between her knees. Transfixed by her power over the clay, Pippa let it grow too high, too thin. The pot listed, warped, then toppled and imploded, spiraling chaotically. It was her third class, and every effort had been a failure. The problem was, she wanted to make a vase with a long neck, not a stubby little potpourri container like everyone else in the class. She could tell her teacher, Mrs. Mankevitz, a reptilian woman with a crooked back and bohemian taste in jewelry, disliked her for this. "Mrs. Lee?" she would say. "Still unwilling to work your way up like the rest of us, I see." On one such occasion, Pippa whispered to herself, as the teacher turned her hunched back to her, "Oh, go fuck yourself."

She hadn't meant to say it out loud, but Dot's head swiveled to look at her like a magpie spotting a rhinestone. Mrs. Mankevitz halted, then turned slowly, long earrings tinkling, her toadlike face pale, her wide, lipless mouth set. "What did you say to me?"

Pippa blushed. Fifty years old and still screwing up in the classroom.

"It's just that I don't care if I end up with a perfect pot," Pippa explained. She felt the blood rushing to her cheeks, her throat tight. "I don't need more clutter in my house. All I want is to feel the clay."

"Well, if all you want to do is *play* with *clay*," said Mrs. Mankevitz, putting a veiny hand on one hip, "I suggest you take a block of it home with you and knead it on the kitchen floor. This is a pottery class, not Montessori."

Pippa looked around at the other members of the class. Six elderly women and a bearded old man, they all watched her complacently, curiously, as though chewing their cuds. Only Dot kept her eyes lowered, the coward. With a shock, Pippa realized she was being asked to leave. She felt sweat on her upper lip, her breath was shallow. She was trembling. She wiped her hands on a towel, took her jacket, her bag, and left.

Once in the parking lot, she couldn't face getting into her car. She didn't want to go home. She didn't know what to do with herself. It was eleven in the morning. Chris was asleep. Herb was in his office. She could go and see him. It was strange, Pippa felt, that she hadn't thought of Herb first. That was wrong. She must pay more attention to Herb. She walked over to the building where his office was, pushed open the door, ran up the flight of stairs to his door, knocked. She already had her first sentence formed: "I got kicked out of pottery class." There was a little laugh in it, the way she was saying it in her head; already she was making fun of Mrs. Mankevitz, her gypsy jewelry, the way the whole class had stared at her as though she had just admitted to a sex crime. Herb would crack up about it. She could hear shuffling inside his office. She knocked again.

"Who is it?" Herb asked.

"It's me," she called out. More shuffling. The door opened at last. Herb stood there, his clothes rumpled, his hair disheveled.

"Are you all right?" he asked.

"I got thrown out of pottery class," she said. But it didn't come out funny at all. It came out pathetic. She sat down on the couch and saw there was a towel spread out on it, but she didn't really take it in.

"I told the teacher to fuck off," she said.

"What did you do that for?" said Herb. His voice sounded so tired.

"She's a bitch, that's why," said Pippa. "What's this towel doing here?" There was a long silence. "Were you eating and you didn't want to mess the couch up?" she asked helpfully.

"No." He put his head in his hands.

"What?" There was a long silence then, it lasted a minute. Pippa's eyes traveled around the room until they came upon a pair of jeans. And there, threaded through the belt loops, was Moira Dulles's belt with the buckle, the silver star that she had admired. Pippa stood up, walked over to the bathroom door, and knocked. Then she tried the knob. The door swung open, and there was Moira, in Herb's teal blue V-neck sweater, sitting on the rim of the bathtub, clutching herself, her cheeks shiny with tears. She looked up at Pippa. "Oh, Pippa . . . what have I done?"

Pippa stood on the threshold, staring stupidly at her friend, unable to collect her feelings. They ran higgledy-piggledy, like a flock of sheep scattering before an oncoming truck. Shock, anger, hurt, disbelief—they scrambled in all directions within her. She was unable to harness a single one of them. She felt Herb's hand on her shoulder. She shook it off, walked back into the office, and sat on the couch. He stood before her, frowning. Moira was sobbing loudly in the bathroom now.

"When did this start?" Pippa asked.

"Sometime after we moved here." Herb sighed. "I wanted it to just be an affair, Pippa, but it . . . isn't. I know it's horrible for you. I want you to have the money. You deserve everything."

"Keep the money. You're going to marry her?"

"Oh, I don't know. At my age, it would be ridiculous. I just want to live, Pippa. It's my right. You've been burying me for the last few years. I feel the earth in my mouth. Almost like you're looking forward to it."

"How can you say that?"

"You always said old age disgusts you. Why would I be an exception? I can feel you beginning to pity me, to be afraid of me. You're already in mourning. Be honest."

"Yes, I am afraid of you getting old. Dying. It's normal to be afraid."

"I don't want to be normal, and I don't want to be mourned. I'm not a ghost. I want to live. No one knows when they are going to die. You could die tomorrow. I want to be alive. Fuck you for making me feel like an old man!"

"Herb," she said in a flat tone, "you *are* an old man."

Herb sat down hard on the couch and looked out the window, as if lost in thought. Pippa watched him become a stranger before her eyes. The transformation was almost magical in its completeness. Next door, in the bathroom, Moira started baying like an animal. Then she went quiet. Pippa heard heavy breathing, a clatter, and a thump. Herb and Pippa rushed to see. Moira was lying on the floor of the bathroom, blood all over her arms.

* * *

"Killing yourself with a disposable razor. I don't think anyone's ever done that before," said Pippa as she knelt on the bathroom floor, bandaging Moira's scraped up wrists. Moira, her face slippery with tears and snot, was sitting on the lid of the toilet, staring vacantly at the wall.

Herb stood awkwardly in the doorway. "She was in despair," he said. Pippa looked up at him sharply. He looked pale and clammy. "She loves you, you know," he added sheepishly.

"You should take a nap," said Pippa drily. She still couldn't feel anything. It occured to her that maybe she had actually stopped loving Herb without realizing it. No. That wasn't it. She remembered adoring him only this morning. Then why was she such a blank? Pippa had bought the first aid supplies only a week earlier, on impulse, to stock Herb's office bathroom. As she taped the bandages around Moira's wrists, something loosened from her mind and fell away, like a clump of earth from a crumbling dam. And all of a sudden, she was flooded with relief. It was her guilt that had fallen away, she realized, and landed right on Moira, smashed her to smithereens. Poor Moira. This was what guilt did to a person. Pippa felt time spinning back, back, back, until the bullet reversed out of Gigi's brain and she was innocent of murder, innocent of betrayal.

Pippa's luck had finally run out. She was the victim now. She had passed the guilt baton to Moira, and she felt so empty! Calm, peaceful, sad. Drained of her sin, Pippa felt herself slipping away, like a shade, no longer flesh and blood, no longer here, even. She stood up.

"That should do it," she said. Then she took her handbag from the couch and walked out the door, down the stairs. Her steps made no sound. Herb didn't need her anymore. Nobody needed her anymore. Nobody at all!

Swerve

There was only one place to go. She drove over to the Nadeaus' house, cut her engine, and sat there. Chris's truck was on its own in the driveway. She went to his open window and looked in. He was sleeping. She dragged the ceramic toadstool to the house, stepped up on it, swung her leg over the sill, then squeezed herself through the window, but one foot got caught under the sash. She had to use her hands to dislodge her shoe, hopping to maintain her balance. Finally free, she turned and saw that Chris was watching her, smiling, his hands behind his head. "Hi there," he said.

Pippa lay down on the covers beside him. "My husband is in love with a close friend of mine." She looked over at his face. The broken nose, slack mouth, and the dark, dark eyes, burning with spirit or disturbance, it had to be one or the other with eyes like that. She felt a shock of tenderness and desire. Suddenly they were kissing. His breath smelled pleasant, earthy, like a pond. There was a knock. Dot popped out of the wall, dressed entirely in white terry cloth, a big blond bunny. "Are you okay?" she asked. "I heard a sound . . ." Wide eyed, Dot looked down at them, shock and embarrassment spreading across her features.

"Hi, Dot," said Pippa. She couldn't think of anything else to say.

Blond bunny bounced out. Pippa looked at Chris, a laugh in her throat.

"I better go talk to your mom." Pippa smoothed her shirt and went into the kitchen.

"I didn't mean to upset you," she said.

"Pippa. The man is thirty-five years old. You are . . . whatever you are. It's none of my beeswax."

"I didn't think you were here."

"My car is at the shop." There were tears in her voice.

Chris was waiting outside for Pippa when she went to her car.

"I guess I'm going to pack," she said.

Pippa drove back to her house. Herb's car was there. When she walked in, he was stirring Ovaltine into a glass of milk. He looked exhausted.

"I am so sorry it went like this," he said.

"Me too," said Pippa. He walked up to her and put his arm around her. "I'm sorry. I lost control of it. I—I care for you so much."

"It's all so tired," she said.

"What is?"

"This whole . . . situation. We should just fast-forward to the divorce."

She walked back into the bedroom and packed a few things. Why couldn't she feel anything yet? Most of her nice clothes were in storage, so she took a few pairs of jeans, her favorite boots. Shirts. What clothes do you need when you're thrown on the trash heap?

He tried to help her with her bag, but she ignored him, rushed it to her car. Once she got into the driver's seat, she realized she had forgotten her car keys. She smacked the steering wheel with a curse, then ran back into the house. The kitchen was empty now. She searched the room wildly for her keys. She had to get out before Herb walked back in. At last she saw them, chucked behind her morning coffee mug. When she drank that coffee, at eight that morning, she'd thought she was a happily married woman. As she snatched the keys off the kitchen counter, she glimpsed Herb's shoe on the linoleum. His foot was in it. She walked around the island of white Formica and saw him lying unconscious on the ground, a dark stain on his trousers where he had wet himself.

* * *

Herb was in the intensive care unit of the Ford Memorial Hospital, in a curtained-off room crowded with blinking machines, his mouth covered with an oxygen mask, a long, hollow plastic thread stuck into his wrist with a needle. Clear liquid dripped into the thread from a collapsed plastic bag hooked onto a metal stand. Ben stood at the end of the bed. He had driven up from New York. His eyes were wet behind round glasses.

"So I don't understand. You were in the car and you came back in, and he was on the ground?"

"That's right," Pippa said, straining for the modulated tones of motherhood.

"Why did you come back in?"

"I forgot my keys."

"Where were you going?"

"Ben, I don't really see how—"

"I'm just trying to get it all straight."

"Does it matter if I was going shopping or to the hardware store or—"

"He just seemed really fine last time." He was weeping. Pippa put her arms around her boy. Dear Ben. When she thought of Grace, on her way from the airport, her stomach tightened. But it had to happen. Grace had to say goodbye to her daddy.

Dr. Franken came in. Only a few years older than Ben, with a round face and a slight lisp, this was the doctor they sent in to sympathize with the patients and their families, to try to stem their confusion. He had come in several times now to explain, first to Pippa, then to Ben, and to both again, that Herb had suffered a massive stroke, his brain was submerged in blood, he was living on the oxygen being pumped into him, it was the family's choice as to how long he should remain in that state and when he should be released into the stratosphere. But this time, Dr. Franken had a different message to convey.

"Ms. Moira Dulles—I believe she is a friend of yours, or of the family?"

"Of my husband," said Pippa.

"She's a friend of yours," Ben said.

"Not anymore," said Pippa.

"Well," said Dr. Franken. "She's a patient here; she was admitted with chest pains a few hours ago—" Pippa just about stifled a laugh.

The doctor looked up.

"Sorry," she said. "Go on."

"I think she got a call, or someone told her, about your husband's stroke."

"Mmm-hmm."

"She wants to visit Mr. Lee. She wants to visit your husband. Now. I actually saw her today, because I am a cardiologist. She is . . . extremely distraught. I am sorry to bother you with this, but I had to ask."

"She can come in for five minutes," said Pippa.

Moira walked in and tossed herself on Herb's bed like a sack of sour laundry. Ben looked at Pippa, perplexed. Pippa rolled her eyes.

Later, in the visitors' lounge, she found herself fetching a cup of sweet tea for Moira, who, in her hospital gown, wrists bandaged, looked like she was fit for a lunatic asylum.

"Oh, Pippa," she said, taking the steaming cup of tea. "It's like the gods are punishing me."

"Stop being such an egomaniac and drink your tea."

"Please, please, please forgive me."

"Forgive you for what?" asked Ben, sitting down in front of Moira.

"I . . . I can't," said Moira.

"Ben, your father and Moira were in love. That's why I was leaving."

"*What?*"

"Oh, Pippa, I swear to God I will jump out a window if you don't forgive me. I was so stupid, so blind, so selfish, so—" Moira had gotten off her chair and was kneeling now. "Please!" she said. People were staring at them over their newspapers.

"Okay. I forgive you. Get up," hissed Pippa.

Moira got up and flung herself onto the nearest couch.

"You do not forgive her," Ben said.

"You're right," Pippa said. "I don't." She sat back and sighed. "Why do I always end up with the crazy women?"

"How could Dad do that to you?"

"He was afraid of dying. He fell in love. It made him feel alive. I was . . . not altogether there at the end. I don't know."

"Don't you even care?"

"How can I compete with *that*?" She waved her hand at Moira.

It was then that Grace appeared, far down the hallway. She ran toward them, looking young and frightened. Ben walked up to her, and they embraced. "Where is he?" asked Grace, casting a curious eye on Moira.

As Ben led his sister into Herb's curtained room, a nurse whispered to Pippa that she had a phone call. She went to the high desk at the nurses' station.

"Oh, Pippa." It was Sam.

"Hi, Sam."

"I don't know what to say."

"How much do you know?"

"Herb had a stroke. He was having an affair with Moira. She called and told me the whole thing this afternoon. Of all people, you are the last one this should be happening to."

"Thanks, I guess."

"I just want you to know that I love you."

"I love you, too, Sam."

"I mean, really."

She sucked in her breath. So strange to hear him say it out loud. Exhaling, she said: "Oh, Sam . . ."

"I'll come to see you later."

"Okay." There was a pause. Through it, Pippa saw her life with Sam skidding toward her inevitably, like a runaway sled: the intimate outdoor wedding, a violet halo of flowers balanced on her head. In Sam's big, country kitchen, Pippa bending down to heave a large leg of lamb out of a steaming oven while Sam paced in his study. The artist's wife at last. It felt like something soft and heavy had been laid on her chest. A large bag of sand, perhaps.

"Sam?" she said quickly.

"Yes?"

"I don't want to make butterflied lamb . . . anymore." There was a silence. "Do you understand what I mean?"

* * *

Hours later, Pippa and Grace got into Pippa's car. There wasn't room for all three of them to stay overnight in the room with Herb, and Ben wanted to be the one. The idea was to have a few hours' rest, then return to the hospital.

"But why did Ben get to stay?" asked Grace.

"I don't know," said Pippa. "He seemed to want it the most."

"Oh, really?" asked Grace. "How did you measure that, exactly? Do you have some sort of love-o-meter?"

"We'll rest for a few hours, and then we can—"

"Who's been smoking in this car?" asked Grace, a suspicious look on her face.

"I don't know," said Pippa vaguely, feeling as though she'd been caught.

"Yuck." They drove in silence for a while. Then, in a whisper, "Was it Daddy?"

"No, no . . ."

"If he started smoking again, maybe that's why he . . ." She folded in on herself, knees drawn up to her chest. "So his brain's just dead, just completely dead?"

"That's what they're saying, honey."

They arrived at the house. Pippa opened the car trunk and took out the bag she'd packed that morning. It was so light. A moth fluttered by Pippa's face as she walked to the front door. It made her think of those sticky white tents, like cotton candy with worms in it. The larvae must have popped. Pippa remembered Chris. She missed him.

"Good night," Grace muttered the moment they walked into the house. She walked down the hall, to Herb's study, and shut the door without looking back.

In her room, Pippa pulled on a pair of sweatpants and a T-shirt. It was better to be dressed in case she needed to go straight back to the hospital, she thought. Then she lay down in the bed. The fine cotton sheets felt noxious to her now. She thought of all the lying that had gone on in this bed in the past weeks. Why had he bothered to lie? She got out of the bed, sat in the small armchair in the corner, and lit a cigarette. She heard a soft knock and looked up. It was Grace.

"My God, you *are* smoking."

"I'll stop soon."

"But I've never seen you smoke in my life," said Grace, coming into the room and sitting on the bed.

"I know," said Pippa. She took another drag and inhaled defiantly, then stood up, took one of the decorative plates off the wall, and stubbed the cigarette out on it. Grace looked at her mother as though she'd gone insane. Pippa shrugged and sat in the chair again, her legs folded beneath her. For once, she wasn't afraid of Grace's disapproval. She felt she'd been dismissed and was remaining in the family as a consultant. No, of course. Motherhood is forever. But what about if your child can't stand the sight of you? Do you just linger on, simpering, hoping for a change of attitude?

Grace sniffed. She was weeping. Pippa walked over to her and sat beside her. To her surprise, Grace leaned in to her, buried her head in her chest, and sobbed. Pippa stroked her daughter's head. "I'm so sorry this had to happen to you," she said.

"That's not why I'm crying," said Grace. "I'm crying because I'm mean to you all the time, and I hate it. I don't want to be, I really don't."

Astonished, Pippa took her girl's face in her hands, kissed her cheeks. "I love you so much," Pippa said. Poor girl, she didn't know what sickness had been passed to her through the women in her family. Mother to daughter in a line as long as Pippa had lived, and maybe farther, maybe past Grandma Sally, to Sally's mother, and her mother before her; the chain of misunderstandings and adjustments, each daughter trying to make up for her mother's lacks and getting it wrong the opposite way. Some families were cursed like that. "There is so much," said Pippa, "I wish I could tell you, but . . . I really don't know how."

Grace put her finger to her mother's lips. "Not yet," she said. "I just want to be your friend, Mom, while we still have time."

"I would be honored to be your friend," said Pippa.

"Not honored," said Grace. "Just happy."

"Okay. Just happy."

"Can I sleep with you?" Grace asked. Pippa felt a wave of almost excruciating happiness flush through her. She felt dizzy with it. "Of course, sweetheart." Pippa lay beside her daughter as Grace's eyes closed, her breathing deepened. Grace had wept in her arms. Imagine! The unfamiliar certainty of her daughter's love filled her with ecstatic disbelief. An hour passed. Pippa wasn't tired. She felt she should go back to the hospital. She would wait another hour. They would call if anything changed. She gazed at Grace, her young face so intent, even in sleep. Her brave little girl. She hoped there was still time to mend things between them. She heard a car pass by the house. Then it backed up, and white light swept through the bedroom. She looked out the window to see who it was. It was Chris. She switched off the bedroom light, walked into the kitchen, and opened the door. He was already standing there.

"I saw your light on; I wanted to see if you needed anything. My mother has a friend who works in the ICU; that's how we found out."

"My son is with him. The idea is I'm supposed to be sleeping, but I can't."

"I could drive you around a little bit."

"Don't you have to work?"

"I'm off till five."

"Maybe just for half an hour." She went into the house, tiptoed down the hall, and peeked into her bedroom. Grace was asleep, huddled under the duvet. Pippa wrote a note, propped it up on the bedside table beside Grace, took her cell phone out of her handbag, drew her sweatshirt off the back of a kitchen chair, and walked outside. Chris was already in the driver's seat.

They drove around Marigold Village for a while. Pippa called the hospital to check on Herb, made sure they knew to call her cell. Then she looked out the window and stared at the wooden houses with their slanted roofs, the American flags drooping sleepily, as if resting for the night. "I can't believe I ever lived here," Pippa said.

"It's a weird place all right," said Chris. He drove her past the convenience store, through the mini-mall parking lot where the fish man parked, to the river. He turned the engine off but left the headlights on; immediately, hundreds of white moths were whirling inside the columns of illuminated air, their wings flapping desperately, as if feeding on the light.

"They hatched," said Pippa. They sat like that for a long moment, looking out at the moths.

"You said your father was a minister," said Chris. "Did he ever pray with you?"

"No. I went to his church every Sunday. But he wasn't praying with me."

"Do you . . . anymore?"

"Yes. I don't know if I believe in anything, but I still pray. It's sort of automatic."

"What do you pray for?"

"To be good." She laughed. "It sounds so childish when I say it out loud."

"It's the only thing to pray for. The rest is wish lists." There was something about him—so hard to put into thoughts—something genuine and transparent that she had only seen in children.

"Come on," he said. He reached over her to pull open the latch of her door, then pushed the door ajar. His arm brushed the tops of her thighs. She got out. He came around to her side, took her hand, and led her to the back of the truck. There was a little door there. He opened it and drew her inside the orange shell. A match flared. He was lighting a candle. She could see now that there were several candles fixed on saucers along the wall and windowsills of the low plastic dome. He lit them, one by one. She shut the door so the candles wouldn't go out. The floor was covered in brown plush carpeting. A thin mattress was rolled up neatly and made a tidy couch. He patted it. Pippa sat down on the mattress ticking. He knelt in front of her.

"Do you want to pray for your husband?"

She felt irony pressing in on her.

"It's hopeless. His brain is dead."

"Not for his brain. For his soul."

"Oh. I don't know how to do that."

"I don't, either," he said. "Let's try." Chris took off his shirt. She had forgotten his tattoo. Jesus was in the room with them now. His fierce black eyes burned out of Chris's chest; his intricately drawn wings arched up over Chris's shoulders. Chris closed his eyes, clasped his hands, and looked at the ground. Pippa stared at the image on her friend's chest, and it stared back at her, unblinking, all seeing, awesome. This was not any Christ she had known. This was elemental, crushing divinity. She felt as though this truck was standing at the edge of space; she could not imagine anything beyond this moment, so foreign and yet so familiar, repellent and irresistible.

At last, Chris looked up at her, his face above the other face. He moved toward her. With deliberate, calm movements, he guided her off the rolled up mattress, pushed it so it flopped flat. She crawled over to him. She lay down. As he kissed her, she felt her mind fill up with him and nothing else. Candles glimmered behind his head. His hands were very warm. Her eyelids were heavy. There was a slowness in her now, a torpor, like a drug in her veins. She was slipping further and further into the moment until she felt herself at its very pit, where there were no images, only one color, only red, behind her closed eyes. She felt his hand on her sex. She opened her eyes. The tattoo loomed over her; the wings of the Christ seemed to spread wide and real above her, pulsing up and down, making the sound of two dry hands rubbing against each other as they brushed the sides of the plastic shell. This can't be real, she thought. And then, out of nowhere, a pleasure ballooned from her sex, swelled to fill her body until it burst, the sensation running down her legs, and she cried out, her head falling lifeless on the mattress, her body lank as the neck of a dead swan. Sadness trailed behind the pleasure like the tail of a comet. Grief and rage shot out of her mouth like flames. He held her head between his palms as she sobbed.

She did not know how she had gotten to the other side of the shell. She was zipping up her sweatshirt. "I have to go back to the hospital," she said.

She said nothing on the drive; words seemed distant as the stars. She didn't dare look at him, now that he had regained his human form. When they arrived at the hospital, she ran out of the truck; the glass doors slid open to let her in, then glided shut behind her.

Herb was breathing deep, difficult breaths, the plastic elephant's trunk strapped to his face, eyes closed. Ben was sleeping, curled up on the narrow cot by the window. Pippa shook him awake. Clutching the pillow, he jerked his head up to check his father. "It's okay," Pippa said. "It's just time now. Go call your sister."

Ben pulled on his jeans, his shirt, and padded out into the hall in his socks. Then he turned. "I'll go get her."

"She can take my car," said Pippa.

"How did you get here?"

"Just call her, sweetheart."

He walked off.

Pippa sat with Herb for a moment. "I love you anyway, you know. I'll always love you, you bastard." She stroked his head. Husband. Always and forever.

Ben came back in the room. He sat on the other side of Herb's bed, and they each held one of his big hands until Grace came in. She was already crying. She knelt and put her face on her father's arm.

A figure opened the curtain, a stocky lady with teddy bears printed all over her nurse's smock. "Are you ready now?" she asked gently. Pippa nodded. The children were keening. The nurse removed the oxygen mask from Herb's face. His lips were blue. He took in a long breath, his chest straining. Another breath. His eyes snapped open, seeing something distinct, it seemed, just ahead. He began breathing hard, terrible breaths, as if he was in a battle, as if it was very difficult to die. His hand pawed the drip in his arm. He wanted it out. He wanted his dignity, Pippa knew. He wanted to go out whole.

"Can the drip . . . come out?" Pippa asked. The nurse gingerly eased the needle from Herb's arm, leaned in very close to his face, looked into his eyes. He focused on her, expectant. She held his arms and said firmly, "It's okay." Pippa squeezed his hand. The nurse moved to the corner of the room. A long moment of quiet. Then, finally, one long, gushing exhalation, as if a great animal were breathing his last. The nurse set the stethoscope on his chest for a moment. "He's gone," she said. "I'm sorry." Then she slipped past the curtain. Ben and Grace came to Pippa and held her and wept. She kept her eyes on Herb's face. It was already changing, becoming sharper, meaningless, a mask.

Chris was waiting outside the hospital when they walked out, after Herb had been taken away to the crematorium and the papers had been signed. He was standing by his truck. Pippa halted, seeing him, and Ben looked at him curiously. Then she got into her son's car, deeply embarrassed by what had happened in the truck. A fifty-year-old woman, fooling around in a pickup truck with the strangely spiritual, feckless son of her neighbor in the old folks' home! How Herb would have laughed. The whole thing was grotesque. She wished she could erase it.

"Stephanie and I want you to come stay with us," Ben said.

"Hm?"

"We want you to live with us, Mom, Stephie and I. For as long as you want. We're going to take care of you."

"Oh. Thanks, honey," she said vaguely, imagining the clouds of cat hair that would rise up as she opened the foldout couch in their study, made ready to lie down. There you go. Yes. She would pack up their things as fast as possible, she would sell that death trap of a house, and she would stay with Ben and Stephanie, find a little place near them. Wait to be a grandmother.

Hopper

That night, Pippa dreamed she was driving into a dense cloud of white moths, thousands of them beating their wings against the windshield. Then she woke up, and she was driving inside a cloud of white moths. She felt blinded, claustrophobic. She stopped the car. But how would she get out? What if she was in the middle of the road? Someone would crash into her. She crept along, panicking, disoriented, trying to see the edges of the road so she could figure out where she was. She wondered if this could possibly be real. Had she gone insane? Was she dreaming? Or maybe she was dead.

At last the creatures were thinning out. She could see through the fluttering wings, into the night. She was driving along her own narrow road, toward the intersection. She could see the convenience store across the road. It glowed with the cool blue light of a Hopper painting. So that's where she'd been headed. She tapped the gas pedal, rolled the car across the road tentatively, pulled in, and parked. She could see Chris inside. He was alone, leaning back, arms crossed, staring out the window, his skin stark white under the fluorescent light. She looked down at what she was wearing. Sweats and a T-shirt. Thank God, no nightgown. She got out of the car. The sound of tree frogs outside was shrill, continuous. She walked up to the store, swung the glass door open. As he saw her, his eyes followed her, but he didn't move, his expression didn't change. She walked up to the counter. They looked at each other. "I'm awake," she said.

Part Four

Yellow

Pippa stood at the threshold of the door to the bedroom and watched the children down the hall in the kitchen. They were sitting across from each other on stools, elbows on the counter, speaking softly, so as not to wake her. Grace was weeping, shaking her head. Ben was talking, looking out the window. He was telling her about Moira, Pippa was sure of it. To think they had once been inside her, those two people. She picked up the canvas bag at her feet and walked down the hall. She couldn't remember when she had packed such a light bag. Ben and Grace looked up at her.

"Hi, Mommy," Grace said softly.

"Hello, my darling," Pippa said.

"What's the bag for?" Ben asked.

"I'm going on a little trip," Pippa said.

"A trip?"

"Yes I—I was wondering if you would mind—just go through the house and take whatever you want, then call these movers here." She took a card from a drawer. "They'll pack up the rest and take it to Goodwill." The kids were watching her carefully. "I left a check for them on the desk in my room. I don't want any of it," she said.

"What about the memorial service?" Ben asked. Pippa hooked the Rolodex with her index finger and let it swing there. "Pick a date and invite everyone on here. Except for Moira. Or invite Moira. What the hell."

"Mom. You're actually leaving right now?" Ben was looking at her with a mix of disbelief and concern.

"Sweetheart. Your father was about to run off with a woman I cooked for practically every other night over the past four years. I gave her advice on her love life, listened to her endless, egomaniacal complaining until I thought my head would explode, and then it turns out she's crying about my husband. I am not organizing his memorial service. I mean, I'll come to it. I'm just not buying the flowers." Righteous outrage felt exhilarating and unfamiliar. Pippa took a breath and saw that Grace was staring at her with a trace of a smile, something dawning. Could it be—admiration? Just then, Chris's truck drove up.

Ben stood and went to the window. "Who *is* that guy?" he asked, turning.

"My friend," Pippa said.

"Your *friend*? What is going on here?"

"I'm sort of . . . hitching a ride," Pippa said.

Ben put his head in his hands.

"I'm not driving off into the sunset, sweetheart," Pippa said. "I'm just . . . seeing what happens next."

"I don't believe this," Ben said.

Grace turned to him. "She gave us half her life," she said. "Don't you think she deserves a vacation?"

Filtered through the dusty glass, the landscape looks smeared and faint, like a yellowing photograph. I roll my window down and watch the picture go vivid: flat, sandy land the color of rust; great, hulking slabs of brick red cliffs against the deep blue sky. I am skimming over pure planet, cut loose again. I glance over at him staring ahead into the clear distance as he drives. I feel as though he is driving me across a bridge of rock and sand. I don't know what is on the other side. I see little towns along the way. As I pass each one, I wonder, Could I live here? I try to imagine my other life, the one I left, but it is evaporating from my mind. I can remember images—Herb, the house in Marigold Village, my favorite vegetable knife—but they are bloodless and unreal. I will go back, of course. Ben, Grace, the memorial service. But I feel an unfamiliar story unfurling in me. I have no idea how it will go, I don't know who I will be in it. I am filled with fear and happiness.

Acknowledgments

Thanks to my editor, Jonathan Galassi, for his subtlety and intuition; to my stalwart friend and agent, Sarah Chalfant; to my first readers: Cindy Tolan, Julia Bolus, Mary Ellen Peebles, Michael Blake, and Honor Moore, for their honesty and time; to David Turnley for lending me his experience; to Jane and Tom Doyle for getting lost with me; to Robert Miller for his memories; to the Jesuit Brothers of New Jersey for their kind help; to the Galway Literary Festival for giving me a chance to present Pippa to an audience; to Claire Hardin, Kate Brady, Charissa Shearer, Emma Wilkinson, and Angela Trento for giving me the peace of mind to write; to Ronan and Cashel for the lines, and all they've taught me; to my mother and father.

Little Farm
in
the Ozarks

THE LITTLE HOUSE BOOKS

By Laura Ingalls Wilder

Illustrated by Garth Williams

Little House in the Big Woods

Little House on the Prairie

Farmer Boy

On the Banks of Plum Creek

By the Shores of Silver Lake

The Long Winter

Little Town on the Prairie

These Happy Golden Years

The First Four Years

THE ROCKY RIDGE YEARS

By Roger Lea MacBride

Illustrated by David Gilleece

Little House on Rocky Ridge

Little Farm in the Ozarks

Little Farm *in* the Ozarks

Roger Lea MacBride

Illustrated by David Gilleece

HarperCollins*Publishers*

Little Farm in the Ozarks
Text copyright © 1994 by Roger Lea MacBride
Illustrations copyright © 1994 by David Gilleece
All rights reserved. No part of this book may be used or reproduced in any
manner whatsoever without written permission except in the case of brief
quotations embodied in critical articles and reviews. Printed in the United
States of America. For information address HarperCollins Children's Books,
a division of HarperCollins Publishers, 10 East 53rd Street, New York, NY
10022.

Library of Congress Cataloging-in-Publication Data
MacBride, Roger Lea, date
    Little farm in the Ozarks / Roger Lea MacBride ; illustrated by David
Gilleece.
        p.   cm.
    Summary: Laura and Almanzo Wilder and their eight-year-old daughter
Rose continue to work to make Rocky Ridge farm in Missouri their new
home.
    ISBN 0-06-024245-0. — ISBN 0-06-024246-9 (lib. bdg.)
    1. Wilder, Laura Ingalls, 1867–1957—Juvenile fiction.   [1. Wilder,
Laura Ingalls, 1867–1957—Fiction.   2. Frontier and pioneer life—
Missouri—Fiction.   3. Missouri—Fiction.]   I. Gilleece, David, ill.
II. Title.
PZ7.M12255Lf   1994   93-23688
[Fic]—dc20   CIP
                                                                  AC

1   2   3   4   5   6   7   8   9   10
❖
First Edition

For my daughter Abby,
who shares with me the legacy of Rose.
In them both, God got it right.

Contents

Little Farm
in the Ozarks

Thief!

Rose was sitting at the table in the little log house on Rocky Ridge Farm, finishing a letter to Grandma Ingalls, when she heard snarling outside in the dark, snowy woods. Fido, the little white terrier with black and tan spots, raised his head from the hearth and growled deep in his chest. His ears lay flat against his head.

"What was that?" Rose asked.

Mama closed her book and looked at Papa.

"That's a new one on me," he said. "Might be it's just a bobcat, but I'd best check the horses." He set down the leather horse collar he was oiling and wiped his hands on a rag.

Papa lit the lantern and pulled on his heavy buffalo coat. Fido followed him to the door. Papa took his gun down from its rack. "Stay here, boy," he told Fido. "I can handle this."

Mama laid more wood on the fire and hugged herself against the chill air that blew in when Papa opened the door.

Rose read the letter to herself by the light of the lamp:

"Dear Grandma," she had written. "Thank you very much for the good, warm socks, and for sending us the *De Smet News* every week. I am reading the story about poor General Custer.

"It is not so cold here as South Dakota, but my feet get cold sometimes. It snowed today. But Papa said spring will come soon, even if it is just Febuary! I like Missouri, but I miss everyone so very much. Your loving granddaughter, Rose."

"Mama, how do you spell this month?"

"Feb-ru-ary," said Mama. "How does it sound?"

Thief!

Rose saw her mistake and squeezed a small "r" in between the "b" and the "u."

They both looked up when they heard Papa open the outside door to the lean-to and kick the snow off his boots.

"Everything seems to be in order," he said. "The horses are quiet and I don't see any strange tracks in the snow."

Papa went back to oiling the collar.

"I was thinking, Bess," Papa said to Mama. "It's getting on toward spring and I'll be needing some help around the place. Reynolds at the general store told me this morning that here in the Ozarks folks plant their peas in February and their potatoes in March."

"I can scarcely believe it, Manly," Mama said. "We never planted anything before April in South Dakota. Are you sure he wasn't pulling the wool over your eyes?"

"I wouldn't have believed it myself," Papa said. "But Reynolds has his onion sets and seed potatoes in stock already, and he just put his plows and hoes out as well. Some fellows were in today signing their crop liens."

"What is the interest?" asked Mama.

"Fifteen percent," Papa replied.

"Why, that's as bold as thievery!" Mama complained. "How can we ever get ahead when we must wait four more years for the apple trees to bear fruit?"

"We've been through all that," Papa said calmly. "We have acres of good timber to hack into railroad ties and fence rails that we can always sell. But I can't do it alone and still raise our own corn and grain."

"I'm just not accustomed to waiting so long for a crop to come in," said Mama. "In South Dakota, we had the wheat crop to count on every summer."

Suddenly Fido barked. They all heard a burst of cackling.

"The henhouse!" Mama cried out. Rose's heart fluttered in her chest.

Papa and Mama jumped up at the same time. They threw on their coats and shoes. Papa grabbed his gun again. Mama lit the lantern and they both rushed out the door with Fido leading the way.

Thief!

Rose shivered in the doorway and watched the lantern light throw trembling shadows among the trees as Mama and Papa ran. Then the light disappeared into the henhouse. She could hear their voices, but she could not tell what they had found.

Finally they came walking back. Someone else was with them! When they drew close, she was shocked to see it was a boy. Papa gripped him by the arm. The boy jerked his shoulder, trying to pull away. His hat fell to the ground and Mama picked it up. Rose backed into the house and they all came in.

"All right, son," Papa said in his most sober voice. "Now just you calm down a spell. Have a seat over there, by the table."

The boy sat down with a huff. He tucked his hands under his elbows and scowled. His thin, pale face poked out of clothing that looked like a pile of old rags. His coat was a man's threadbare suit jacket that hung to his knees. His pants were too big also, man's pants that had been cut off and patched. They were so big the pockets hung on the inside of his legs. His patched shirt was made of flour sacks, sewn with twine. The soles of his shoes flapped loose. A white feather clung to one of the pant legs. He glared at Rose and stuck his chin out defiantly.

Rose didn't know what to think. She had never seen such a stern look on Papa's face. Mama's face was grave and furrowed.

"Now, son," Papa said. "Let's have your name."

The boy stared at the floor in silence. Papa watched him, waiting and stroking his chin.

"We're going to straighten this out, one way or another," he said. "Stealing is serious business. We can go into town and talk to the sheriff if you like. Now why don't you tell us, who are your folks?"

"Ain't got none," the boy muttered in a raspy voice. He shivered and hugged himself.

"Come sit by the fire," Mama said. "You must be cold."

The boy got up and moved his chair over by the fireplace. He held his palms out to the flames and then rubbed them together. Rose sat on the big bed. She couldn't take her eyes off him. The boy looked about her age, which was eight, or perhaps a bit older. His face was plain. His ears stood out, and his nose was too big. His blue eyes seemed to show nothing at all. Rose noticed a bad smell had come into the house.

"Everybody has folks somewhere," Papa said. "Are you from these parts?"

"I ain't from nowhere," the boy said defiantly. Rose thought she saw his mouth wobble in the flickering firelight. Mama and Papa looked at each other over the boy's head.

"You must be living somewhere nearby, son," Papa said. His voice was softer now and his eyes shone with a gentle warmth. "If you're hungry we might be able to scare up a bite or two."

The boy looked at Papa for the first time.

"Are you hungry, son?"

The boy nodded. Papa let him sit warming in front of the fire while Mama put up some beans and cold potatoes in the spider-legged skillet to heat in the fireplace. The food began to sizzle and the room filled with the warm smell of cooking. Rose spotted a tear glittering on the boy's cheek.

"Now, just you relax. We aren't going to harm you," Papa said. "But you must tell us who you are. We can help, if you're alone."

"I ain't alone," the boy said. "I got my big brother. He's out a-working, is all."

"I'm Mr. Wilder," Papa said. "This is my wife, and our daughter, Rose."

"Hello," Rose said softly. The boy looked at her, but his face was blank, like a clock without hands. She could not tell what he was thinking.

"I'm Swiney," the boy finally said. "Swiney Baird. It's just me and my big brother, Abe."

"What about your folks, your ma and pa?"

"Dead," Swiney said simply.

He licked his lips and swallowed. His eyes followed Mama lifting the skillet out of the fireplace and spooning the steaming beans and potatoes onto a plate on the table.

"All right, Swiney," Mama said. "Come and eat."

Thief!

Swiney pulled his chair over, sat down, and spooned the hot food into his mouth as fast as he could. Mama wrinkled her nose and frowned as she watched him. In an instant he was mopping up the plate with a piece of corn bread. Rose had never seen anyone eat so fast.

Mama took the empty plate away. Swiney stood up and looked around the little log house, as if to leave. But Papa motioned with his hand to sit back down.

"Now, then," Papa said. "Let's see if I have this right. Your folks have passed on, and you live with your brother. Where is that?"

Swiney pursed his mouth and stared into his lap. "Yonder," he said after a long pause, jerking his thumb. "On Kinnebrew's place. In the tenant house."

"Kinnebrew," Mama said slowly. "I've heard that name in town. Aren't they the folks who moved here from Illinois last fall?"

Swiney nodded his head.

"And your brother," Mama said. "He left you nothing to eat?"

"The latch busted on the door. Raccoons got in and stole every bit."

"But surely the Kinnebrews would take you in for a meal."

Swiney shook his head gravely. "Abe says they're city dudes. They don't like us country jakes." Then he looked at Mama, his eyes suddenly wide with fear. "You ain't a-going to tell them, is you? There wasn't no real harm in it, honest. I was just a-looking for eggs is all."

"Don't you worry about that," Papa said. "The important thing is that you don't have to steal from us to eat, Swiney. We'd never let a boy go hungry if we had a crumb to spare. Now, when is your brother coming home?"

"I ain't sure," said Swiney. He wiped his nose with the back of his dirty hand. His nails were chipped. "He drove a load of timber to Cabool."

"Cabool is a good two days' wagon trip," said Papa. "You must stay here with us tonight."

"But I cain't," Swiney whined, standing up. "I got to be going, mister."

Thief!

"You'll stay here, son, and that's final," Papa said. "We'll fix a pallet for you to sleep on, by the fire, where it's warm. After a good breakfast we'll go to your place and see about fixing that latch."

Swiney's shoulders slumped and his face puckered as if to cry. But he sat quietly as Mama got out extra quilts and made up his bed.

When they were all settled for the night, Mama and Papa in their big bed and Rose in her trundle bed, Rose couldn't sleep. She listened to the crackling and hissing of the fire. She could hear Swiney tossing and turning under his covers. It frightened Rose to think a stranger would sneak into their henhouse and steal their eggs.

She did not think she liked Swiney very much. He was a thief, he was dirty, and he hadn't thanked Mama for his supper. But she was sorry he had no mother or father to make sure he had food to eat.

And it *was* something new to have a stranger in the house. Their first winter in Missouri had been lonely. Mama had kept Rose home from school until they could get a little money ahead. There were taxes to pay, and Rose needed new shoes.

Mama had said Rose could start school in July, when the next session began. By then the chickens would be laying again and Mama would have eggs to trade at Reynolds' store for necessities like new shoes and slate pencils.

"Besides, I have been a schoolteacher and I can certainly keep you up with your studies here at home," Mama had said.

It had been too cold, and the days too short, to explore outdoors or play with her friend Alva, who lived nearby on her father's farm. Her only other friends were Paul and George Cooley, who had come with Rose's family to Missouri from South Dakota. When they weren't in school, Paul and George helped their mama and papa run the Mansfield Hotel in town. Mr. and Mrs. Cooley were best friends with Mama and Papa. Rose saw Paul and George only on Sunday, when the two families went to their new church in town.

Thief!

Rose's restless thoughts were interrupted by Swiney crying out in his sleep, "Mumphster fluff!" Rose was curious about him. She wondered about his life, and how he got such a funny name.

Peeping Frogs

When Rose woke up in the chilly dawn, Mama was gathering up Swiney's bedclothes. Swiney was gone. He had slipped out of the house before the first rooster crow.

"Phew!" Mama said, making a face and holding the quilt away from her. "That boy smelled as skunky as an old dog. We might as well do a wash today, Rose."

"Why did he leave?" asked Rose.

"I expect he was afraid we would change our minds and turn him over to the sheriff," said Papa. "That little shaver's as bold as a sparrow. I'm sure last night wasn't the first time he found himself in a fix."

"Will he have to go to jail?"

Papa laughed. "Little boys don't go to jail for stealing eggs. There isn't a boy alive hasn't done something as bad or worse. He might be put in an orphanage, if we complained to the sheriff. But I wouldn't anyway. It's no crime to be hungry. I'll ride over to Kinnebrew's after breakfast and see how he's getting along."

The day dawned warm and soft. To look at the snow-covered ground was to be in winter. But when the sun rose high, its light fell strong on Rose's face. The sky was brighter than it had been in a long while. Before dinnertime the snow had turned mushy. In the bare spots the earth softened to reddish mud that clung to her shoes and made squishy, sucking noises when she walked.

While Rose helped Mama hang the sheets to dry in a sunny spot, she noticed a strange noise coming from the direction of Fry Creek. It sounded like a multitude of tiny bells, or many people whistling.

"I hear it, too," said Mama. "I wonder what it could be? It's too early for grasshoppers and crickets."

After dinner, when she was done with her laundry chores, Rose walked down toward the creek to explore. The whistling sound grew louder and louder. It seemed to be coming from a marshy place near the creek. But she couldn't see what was making such a racket. She walked toward the marshy spot. When she got close to it, when the sound was at its loudest all around her, it suddenly stopped.

Rose stood there for a long moment in confusion. There was nothing to see but swampy water full of dead leaves and the dead stems of last year's grass and reeds. Then she heard a single peep close by her. *"Peent,"* something said. She stood very still, trying to see what had made that sound without startling it into silence. Farther away, there was an answer, *"Peent. Peent."* In no time that whole swamp was alive with the noise of all those *peent*s.

Rose took a step. A fallen branch crackled under her foot. Immediately she saw several splashes in the water and the noise stopped again. She squatted down at the edge of the swamp and looked closely into it. All she could see at first was decaying leaves and bubbles and twigs.

Then she spotted some bubbles close together that seemed to move. She stared at those bubbles for the longest time, until finally she saw that they were a tiny pair of frog's eyes and a little frog's nose floating in the murky water. But as long as she sat there, no frogs would peep.

She walked a little way from the swamp and waited. In a minute, it started again. *"Peent. Peent. Peent."* But no matter how hard she tried to sneak up on the frogs, they would not peep when she was close. So she backed far away and just listened. It lightened her soul to hear those frogs singing their hearts out. Rose realized with astonishment that even though it was still winter, this was a sound of spring, the very first sound of spring.

Rose was telling Mama about the peeping frogs when Papa came riding home on May.

Behind him, riding together on a mule with notched ears, were a young man and Swiney.

"We have company," Mama said with a sigh, "and I can't think what we have to feed them. Draw a pail of water from the spring, Rose. At least we can make tea."

When Rose brought the water, Mama and Papa were talking to the young man, who held his battered hat in his hand. Swiney stood beside him, staring at the ground and kicking at a clump of snow.

"This is our daughter, Rose," Mama said. "Rose, this is Abe Baird, Swiney's big brother."

"Hello," Rose said politely.

"Pleased to make your acquaintance, Rose," Abe said in a warm, deep voice. His face was young and smooth, like a boy's. But it was also strong and bony, like a grown man's. A great shock of black hair fell across his forehead. His thick eyebrows met in the middle. Rose couldn't help staring at him. He didn't look anything like Swiney at all.

"It's like I was a-telling Mr. Wilder, ma'am," he said to Mama. "Swiney's and me's ma and pa passed on when Swiney was just a pup. Ma died birthing our baby sister. I reckon she was wore out after a-bringing twelve little ones into this world. The apoplexy carried off Pa just six months after."

"Twelve children," Mama said in wonderment. "However did you manage? Where are the rest?"

"We stuck together for a spell," Abe said. "But we durn near starved. In time all us kids just flew off like a bunch of quail. The little ones was a-taken in here and there. The older ones went out to find work. Swiney here always was a fractious little hornet, so I kept him on with me.

"But I ain't been much of a pa. I'm real sorry about last night. I told Swiney, stealing ain't no path to go."

He turned his head and spat a stream of amber tobacco juice onto the ground.

"Well, you must stay to supper," Papa said. Mama cleared her throat. "We haven't much," Papa went on. "But what we have . . ."

"I ain't a-aiming to put no burden on

you'uns," Abe said. "No sirree. I brung you some meat in this here poke, to show no harm meant." He reached into a sack at his feet and pulled out a dead raccoon by the tail. Rose had seen the skins of raccoons that her friend Alva had trapped.

"I don't think . . . " Mama began. "I mean, I wouldn't know the first thing about cooking a . . . what is it?"

"Coon, ma'am," said Abe. "You folks ain't tasted no coon yet?"

"No," Mama said firmly. "I'm not sure we're quite ready for that."

"Ain't nothing to it," Abe said heartily. "Why, coon's some of the best eating meat we got in these here hills. Swiney and I'll skin it, and I can tell you just how to cook it."

Mama looked at Papa. The color drained from her face. But there was nothing more she could politely say. Abe would not take no for an answer, and Mama would never argue against the generosity of strangers.

Tree-Topping

Abe and Swiney stayed to supper of roast raccoon and turnips. After they had ridden away on their mule, Mama scraped her full plate onto a slab of wood and put it outside for Fido.

"I just couldn't eat it," she said, making a face. "I have never seen so much greasy fat on an animal."

"I liked it," Rose said. "It tasted like rabbit."

"I wouldn't have guessed it myself, but it was delicious, Bess," agreed Papa.

"It did smell good," Mama admitted with a chuckle. "But that's the last time you are going to find a raccoon in my oven."

"It won't be the last we see of Abe and Swiney," Papa said. "Abe is going to be our hired man."

"Are you sure he's reliable?" asked Mama. "Isn't he sharecropping for Mr. Kinnebrew?"

"He is," Papa said. "But he's also cutting railroad ties and fence rails on his own. He's a good strong boy, just a little young and rough around the edges is all. And Swiney can help with the chores around the place."

"Very well," Mama said. "You can never tell through what door Providence may walk."

After breakfast the next morning Abe and Swiney came back.

"You listen to Mrs. Wilder same as if she was our ma," Abe told Swiney before going off with Papa to the woodlot.

"Now, Swiney," Mama said. "First thing we need to do is get you a good hot bath."

"A bath?" Swiney said in a whining voice. "But why? Abe don't make me take no bath."

"I'm not Abe," Mama said, "and you've got skunk scent in all your clothes. Don't you smell it?"

"No, ma'am," said Swiney, wrinkling his big nose. "I did catch me a skunk a little time back. But I cain't smell nothing now."

Rose giggled. Swiney glared at her.

"So long as you are going to be part of this family, I'll thank you to leave skunk business to the skunks," said Mama.

"Awww," Swiney grumbled.

But he took his bath anyway, in a corner of the house behind a sheet Mama had hung from the rafters. While he splashed around in the tin tub, Rose helped build a fire under the big cast-iron pot outside. Then Mama scrubbed his threadbare clothes with soft soap. She gave him Rose's extra flannel union suit to wear while he sat in a chair and his things dried, hanging from the fireplace mantel.

When he was dressed again, Swiney still looked shabby, but his face shone pink and clean, and his dark hair glistened. Then Mama said Rose could show him around the farm.

The weather had turned wintry again. Silver-gray clouds pressed down upon the hills. A pair of jaybirds, crying out in shrill voices, flashed across the open space in front of the house to hide in a bush. Rose shivered against the cold and pulled her woolen fascinator tight around her head.

The surface of the snow had frozen to a crust as hard as a plate. The horses' hooves had left holes in the mud, which had frozen into little pools of ice. The ice crackled when they walked on it.

Rose kept her thoughts to herself as they walked by the henhouse. Swiney stared at the ground until they had passed it.

Then Rose showed Swiney the new barn that their neighbors had helped Papa build one day in the fall. They looked at the mares, Pet and May, in their stalls. They were fat and sleek from having so little work to do in the winter.

Then they fed handfuls of oats to the colts, Little Pet and Prince. Papa had been breaking and gentling them all winter. Soon they would be old enough to sell. Rose hated to think of it. But she knew they couldn't keep the colts forever, and someday the mares would have new ones.

Swiney hardly spoke a word as Rose told him about their long trip to Missouri from South Dakota in the wagon. She told him about her friend Alva, and how she sometimes went with Alva in the darkness before dawn to check Alva's trap lines for rabbits and raccoons.

Swiney threw rocks at squirrels and the little black-capped chickadees that flitted from branch to branch singing, "Day-day-day."

It was wicked to hurt or kill anything that one didn't need. But Rose did not know Swiney well enough to scold him.

Swiney pulled out a folding knife and began to sharpen it by scraping it on a whetstone he carried in his pocket. He spit on his arm and shaved off a tiny patch of the fine, damp hair.

"Why did you do that?" Rose asked.

"To see if it's right sharp," Swiney said. "That's how to tell."

"Can I try it?"

"Girls ain't supposed to play with knives," Swiney scoffed. "Besides, this here was my pa's knife. Abe gave it me and I ain't never let nobody else touch it." He wiped the blade on his pants, snapped it shut, and dropped it back in his pocket.

They walked to the apple orchard. Fido sniffed for rabbits around the brush piles left from Papa's clearing the land. Papa had felled forest trees all winter. As soon as the ground had thawed enough, he would replant all of the slender young apple saplings that came with Rocky Ridge Farm when they first moved there in the fall.

"When I am thirteen years old, all those trees will bear apples," Rose explained. "Then the apples will go on the trains to big cities, where people will buy them to bake pies."

Then, Rose added to herself, Mama and Papa will have everything they ever wanted. Those fragile young apple trees were their whole future. Mama and Papa had brought Rose here from South Dakota to get away from a drought. For as long as Rose had been alive, too little rain had fallen on the prairie and the wheat crop failed year after year. Finally they could live there no longer.

So they had packed all their belongings into

a little black wagon and driven to Missouri, to The Land of the Big Red Apple, with the Cooleys. They were starting a new life in a place where good water pours right out of the ground all year long and the winters are short.

The Land of the Big Red Apple was a name the railroad companies gave the Ozark Mountains, to persuade people to come there, buy land, and grow apples to ship on the trains.

Mama and Papa had come to Missouri to make a new future. They bought the little run-down farm, called it Rocky Ridge, and began to fix it up. They had been very lucky. The farm came with nearly a thousand apple saplings all heeled in, waiting to be planted. In a few years those apple trees would begin to bear fruit that Mama and Papa could sell. They would never want for anything again.

But for now, Rose knew they must make do with what they had.

Rose and Swiney were walking through the woods around the apple orchard when Swiney suddenly stopped and peered up at a particular tree.

"Want to play tree-topping?" he asked.

"What is that?"

"You ain't never tree-topped?" Swiney said, his eyes wide with amazement. "Just you watch."

Swiney climbed up the tree as quick as a squirrel. When he got near the top, it began to bend under his weight. He grabbed hold of a thin branch over his head. He let his legs swing out. Slowly, with a little groan, the tree bent down until Swiney's feet touched the ground.

Then he began to jump up and down, still holding the top of the little tree. Each time he came back down he bounced a little higher. The tree limbs rattled and shook wildly. Finally he bounced so high that the tree stood straight up and then bent all the way down on the other side until his feet touched the ground. Swiney had ridden that tree all the way over the top!

Rose had never seen anything like it. Swiney bounced way up in the air and then down the other side of the tree, back and forth, back and forth. Fido raced around the tree, barking excitedly. Rose shrieked with delight.

"Let me try!" she shouted.

Swiney stopped bouncing, but he held on to the branch. "Come and grab on," he said. Rose took it and held on as tight as she could. She felt the springiness in it.

"Now start a-jumping, is all," Swiney said. "Don't let go."

Rose took a little jump, but her feet barely left the ground.

"Come on," Swiney said. "Jump high, and keep a-jumping, high as you can."

Rose jumped higher and higher. She felt herself starting to fly. She laughed.

"Higher!" Swiney shouted. "Higher!" Each time she came down she saw his grinning face looking up at her, and then up she went again, higher and higher. But she still wasn't over the top.

Finally she pushed off with all her might, and she knew she was going to go over. She felt herself going up and up, as if she would never come down. Up and up, into the sky.

Just as she felt her feet swinging out from under her, she heard a sickening crack, like a gunshot. The branch she was holding didn't feel springy anymore.

Now she really *was* flying, spinning sickeningly, away from the tree. Then she was falling and falling, for the longest time. She heard herself crashing against branches as they flew by. She felt twigs whip her face and legs.

In an instant, everything came to a stop with a horrible thud that stole her breath. Lights exploded in her head. The back of her neck hurt. The side of her face burned. Her ears rang. Tears stung her eyes.

Rose tried to get up, but she could not move her arms and legs. She was in a peculiar, misty place of no sound, no time, and no color. There was only a warm stinging in her face, and the ringing in her ears, like bumblebees trapped in a jug.

Faintly, through the buzzing, Rose heard Swiney calling her name.

"Wha-what happened?" Rose asked in a quavering voice.

"That old tree broke right off," said Swiney. "You sure went a-flying."

Rose slowly got up, brushing off her coat. Her legs wobbled at first, but then she felt like herself again and laughed.

"That was fun," she said. "I want to do it again. I mean, without it breaking."

Swiney picked another tree. He bent it extra hard to be sure it wouldn't break. Then they took turns tree-topping. Rose lost her grip at first and tumbled to the ground. But soon she understood how to do it and she was flying again, watching the forest floor zoom away as she went up and up. Then she watched it come rushing at her as she came back down on the other side, Fido's pointy little face barking at her. Rose thought nothing could ever be so much fun.

Finally they were tired of tree-topping and walked quietly back to the house.

Rose still did not know if she liked Swiney. He was rough, and she could not forget that he had tried to steal from them. But they had had fun playing together.

"What on earth have you been up to?" Mama exclaimed when they got back. "Your face is scratched, your braids are all undone, and your coat! It's torn."

"I was running. And . . . and I fell," Rose fibbed. She didn't want to tell Mama about tree-topping. She was afraid Mama might forbid her to do it again. She *had* been running, and she *did* fall. Rose stole a sideways glance at Swiney. He was grinning at her. Rose struggled to keep her face straight.

"You were just running and fell?" Mama asked. She wiped her hands on her apron and raised an eyebrow doubtfully. She looked at Swiney and then back at Rose. "That's a mighty lot of scratches for running and falling. And look at that tear. It will need mending."

Rose held her breath. She was just about to tell Mama the truth when Mama sighed. "All right, then," she said. "Come sit while I dab some coal oil on those scratches. Then you two wildcats can gather some firewood. Abe shot two rabbits today. He and Swiney are staying to supper."

Abe's Wolf Story

Rose loved company. The little house rang with the warm sounds of rattling plates and lively voices. The everyday fire in the hearth seemed festive, and the everyday food tasted as good as Sunday's.

Rose especially liked Abe. She enjoyed the full sound of his deep voice, and his curious way of speaking.

"Yes, ma'am," he answered to a question of Mama's. "Our pa, he had no care but to build him a cabin and get his meat from the bounty of the forest. From day's ending to day's ending he was a-relying on the Providence of God. But Pa, he's gone to his reward, and poor Ma also, and them times are buried with them. It's the peaceful way of living that is past and gone."

"The whole country is pretty well settled up," Papa said, nodding. "Even on the open prairie, where we used to live, the game is mostly hunted out."

"When I was a little girl, the wolves would sometimes come at night and serenade our little house," said Mama.

"There's still wolves a-roaming these here hills," Abe said. "You don't see but a few now and then, but they are surely about. I recollect Pa a-telling wolf stories such as would put your hair straight up."

"Tell us one!" Rose blurted before she could stop herself. Abe laughed a great hearty laugh. Even Mama chuckled. She did not mind that Rose had spoken out of turn.

"Yes, Abe," Mama said. "We do so like to hear stories. I'm afraid Rose has heard nearly all of mine."

"Let me study on it a spell," Abe said, pursing his lips in thought. The whole house seemed to listen as they waited. The lamp purred peacefully on the table. Far away they heard the mournful whistle of a train. The coals in the fireplace settled with a crunching sound.

"Now this here's a story Pa told me when I was a sprout. I never could forget it," Abe began. "Pa, he was a fiddler. Now and again he'd fiddle here and there, at a frolic or a wedding. There always was music about him, a-singing or a-fiddling."

"My pa played the fiddle also," Mama said, her face shining in the warm light. "I think sometimes we never could have gotten through the hard times without his music. I miss it still."

"I am surely glad to hear of it," said Abe. "Pa left me his fiddle, you see, and I fiddle myself.

"Well, Pa was on his way home from a-fiddling one night. It was dark as a poke full of black cats. He'd left his gun home, a-thinking it weren't a far piece to walk and him a-having his hands full with the fiddle and all. But when he'd gone down the road a lick, he heard a terrible howl a-coming up the hollow at his back.

"Pa weren't afraid of much, but that howl put spring in his step. He knowed it were a wolf, and where there's one wolf, there's surely a pack. Soon enough, he heard more howling."

Abe got up and walked to the fireplace. He stood with his back to the fire, warming his hands behind him.

"Now Pa recollected there was an old empty house in the woods nearby, so he lit a shuck for it. He could hear them wolves a-crashing through the woods, a-getting mighty close. By the time he broke out into the clearing, he could hear them a-breathing on his heels.

"Them folks he was a-fiddlin' for that night had given him a poke full of leftover corn pone, so he throwed it on the ground, a-hoping them wolves would hold up to eat it.

"Pa ran into that empty house, a-thinking he were finally saved. He weren't too pleased to find the door busted clean off, and it being too dark inside to find a chunk of wood to block it up. He did find a ladder up to the loft, so he climbed it, quick as a squirrel and none too soon at that. The wolves come a-pouring into the house."

Rose's skin tingled with excitement. Everyone was very still, even Swiney, listening to Abe's every word. The only sound was the clock, clearing its throat to chime the hour.

"Them wolves—there must of been four or five—was bold with hunger, being they was in a pack and all. They was a-licking their chops, and a-snarling down there on the floor, and a-looking for a way to get up into that there loft.

"Pa figured he'd make out fine just a-setting up there. But then the biggest of them wolves, the leader of the pack, stood up, a-putting his paws on the wall. Then he jumped, and got his front paws hooked on one of them rafters. He slipped off, but them other wolves got the idea and the whole pack was a-jumping.

"Pa felt around in the loft and found himself a stick of wood. He started a-swinging it at them wolves, and a-kicking with his feet, a-knocking this one back, and that one. But he could see it was a losing fight. Them wolves weren't a-giving up.

"Pa was a-swinging that stick when once he missed and busted a place clean through the roof shingles where they was rotted. He got the idea he might fare better on the roof. So he broke him that hole bigger, grabbed his fiddle, and slung it by the cord over his back.

"He was a-pulling himself up through the hole, them wolves a-scratching and a-snarling just a few feet below, when the fiddle got snagged on the strings. He pushed and that there fiddle let out with an awful screech. Pa eased himself back down, and tried again. *Screech!* that old fiddle cried out.

"All of a sudden, Pa noticed them wolves was a-getting real peaceful like. He quick pushed the fiddle through the hole and climbed out onto the roof.

"Now he studied on his fix a spell and got himself an idea. He took up his bow and scratched himself a long note on the fiddle. Then he listened. It was quiet down below. So he started a-playing a slow tune. Them wolves either liked it, or it scared them. But they was real quiet, like they was a-listening. He looked down through the hole and them wolves was a-sitting there like a church full of mourners.

"So Pa kept right on a-playing, one tune after another. He played slow, then fast; loud, then soft. If he stopped, them wolves would stay still a spell, then they got restless and started a-snarling and a-jumping again.

"Some songs set them a-howling, low and sorrowful. Sometimes they just sat there polite as can be.

"It was a long night, but Pa played and played, a-laughing at them wolves. Finally the first light came a-creeping into the clearing. The big wolf slunk off into the forest. Then, one by one, the rest of them gave up and slipped away. Pa waited a good long while till it was sunup, and then he climbed down and walked on home."

Rose clapped her hands with delight when he was done. She loved scary wolf stories. "Tell another, Abe!" she cried out. "Please."

"That was a wonderful story, Abe," Mama

said, getting up to wind the clock. "But I think that's enough for tonight, Rose. We don't want to tire Abe out."

Rose was sorry to see Abe and Swiney leave. But it had been a wonderful evening. It left her eager to meet the next day, and all the days that would follow. It was a feeling, like the peeping frogs and the lengthening days, of newness and change. Rose felt it rushing through her veins. The rustle of spring was everywhere, even in Abe's voice.

Fresh Greens

Gentle spring rains fell all the next week, slowly melting the snow. Gray mist often hung in the air, or gathered in little wisps of clouds that settled in the valleys. The rain and gathering warmth began to soften the earth.

Abe did not come every morning. Sometimes he had spring chores to do for Mr. Kinnebrew. On those days Swiney stayed with Abe.

One day Papa hitched the mares and began to plow the new ground he had cleared for the garden, the orchard, and the crops. But almost as soon as he started, Papa came back to the house with a frown on his face. His shoes were balls of mud, and his overalls were spattered with it.

Mama and Rose were scrubbing the floor, so Papa stood in the lean-to.

"This beats all," he said. "It's as if the bottom dropped out of the earth! Nothing but mud. You could walk the whole forty acres and your feet never leave the ground. And the worst of it is, the horses' hooves sink right into it. They hurt themselves trying to pull out."

"Surely you can wait a bit, until the ground dries some," Mama said.

"I can but I shouldn't," said Papa. "There's too much plowing and logging to be done. We'll have to trade the colts for a pair of mules. They work better, and they have narrow feet that won't hurt the garden or get stuck in the mud.

"Spence at the livery stable was just saying the other day that he could use a good pair of young horses, to pull the buggies he hires out."

Rose sighed heavily. A hard lump jumped into her throat.

"But surely a pair of colts are not worth two full-grown mules," said Mama. "How will we make up the difference?"

"Spence knows my way with horses," Papa said. "He has been asking me to break some colts for him. I bet I can talk him into letting me work off the difference."

"It was bound to come to this sooner or later," said Mama. "We had to borrow Mr. Stubbins' mules last fall, to plow the ground for the garden. The colts are broken now, and there's no sense wearing out the poor mares."

So Papa put leads on Little Pet and Prince and walked them away from Rocky Ridge Farm, to a new life at the livery stable in town. They tossed their graceful heads and whinnied to their mothers as they went. Pet and May answered from the barn with troubled neighs. Papa had locked them in so they couldn't follow.

Rose could not stifle a sob as she watched them go.

"You mustn't cry," said Mama, hugging Rose to her. "There is no work for the colts here anyway. They will be happier pulling a buggy and getting some exercise."

But Rose could not make herself feel better. She remembered how the little colts had trotted alongside their mothers all that hard, dusty trip from South Dakota. She remembered how Prince would nuzzle her arm asking for a carrot or a bunch of clover. She remembered the time Papa had let her sit on Little Pet as he led the colt around the barn. Now she would never ride him again.

Rose went to the barn and stroked Pet's nose, and then May's. But they were fidgety. They kept sticking their heads out of their stalls into the hallway, looking this way and that for their colts. Across the open hallway the still-warm stalls stood empty and silent.

When Papa came back with the mules and put them in the barn, Rose did not go to look at them. The mules were not beautiful and graceful like horses. Mules were bred for work, not for riding. They didn't toss their

44

heads gaily, like horses. Their necks were short and thick and their bellies low-slung. Their coarse coats did not shine, their ears were too big, and their mossy faces looked at everything with discontented eyes.

The next day Papa hitched up the mules and plowed the garden. He had broken the ground in the fall and hurt himself when the plow point struck a root. Now he knew to be very careful not to stumble. The ground was still full of roots, and rocks, too. The mules had to fight every inch of the way. The soil was as sticky as pudding. Everywhere Rose walked there was reddish-brown mud.

The new ground Papa had cleared was all stumps and piles of dead brush, surrounded by the bare trees. The world was brown and gray and muddy. Rose thought the farm looked as desolate as a cornfield after the harvest, bristly broken stalks.

When Papa finished plowing the garden, Mama and Rose went to work, clearing the rocks and hoeing it smooth. Pools of water stood in the holes where Papa had taken out stumps. For days and days they picked stones out of the mud, and Swiney came to help.

Swiney made a game of it, hurling stones at tree trunks and squirrels until Mama scolded him. But picking up those rocks was no game for Rose. The mud got on her clothes and under her nails. Her back ached from stooping over, and her hands became raw and chapped.

"Where did all these stones come from?" Rose asked with a weary sigh. They had picked stones out of the garden in the fall until the soil was clean. But now it was full of them again.

"I don't know," said Mama, pushing her hair from her face. Her cheek was streaked with mud. "The earth here is very thin. It just seems to grow them."

The days were often cold and damp. But it felt good to be out of doors after being cooped up all winter like a possum in its den.

The melting snow told the story of winter in the woods. On the forest floor she found skeletons of animals and scatterings of feathers where an owl or hawk had eaten a bird. Tiny nests told where mice had raised their litters.

On neighboring farms she could hear newborn calves bawling for their mothers. Flights of geese, crying joyfully in their harsh voices, circled the valley at sunset and landed in last year's fields to look for forgotten kernels of corn. Groundhogs sunned themselves on rocks, or waddled through the fields to feed along the streams.

Shyly at first, then more boldly, the forest birds rehearsed their spring voices. The simple chipping and aimless twittering that Rose had heard all winter gave way to new songs, clear and sweet and hopeful. "Cheerio! Cheerio! Cheerio!" the robins sang. Brilliant red cardinals cried, "What cheer! What cheer! What cheer!" Little white-throated sparrows called out, "Old Tom Peabody, Peabody, Peabody."

Rose whistled those songs as she worked. All the woods seemed to be a bustle of mysterious affairs.

Rose was resting from picking up rocks and throwing them to the side of the garden when she saw someone coming through the trees. At first she did not know who it was. But then she saw it was a little girl with fiery red hair sticking out from under her bonnet.

"Alva!" Rose cried out. It was her first friend in the Ozarks, Alva Stubbins. She had not seen Alva since before Christmas.

"Hello, Rose," Alva said. "Hello, Mrs. Wilder."

"Hello, Alva," Mama said. "What a pleasant surprise. What brings you visiting?"

"My ma sent me over with some sassafras," Alva said.

Alva handed Mama a bundle of small tree roots tied up with a string. Rose could smell the pungent odor from where she was standing.

"That's very nice," Mama said. "But I don't know what to do with it."

"It makes tea," Swiney piped up. "To thin your blood. Everybody takes sassafras tea in the spring."

Alva frowned at Swiney. "Yes," she said. "It perks your blood up when it gets too thick in winter."

"This is Swiney Baird," Rose said. "His big brother Abe is my papa's new hired man."

Alva looked at Swiney, but she did not say anything.

"Can Rose come and play a spell?" Alva asked Mama. "I found some pokeweed down by Wolf Creek. We could pick you a mess for salad."

"Pokeweed?" said Mama.

"It's greens," Swiney piped up again. "And cow parsley. We always eat greens in spring."

"I don't see why not," said Mama. "Are you sure you know what's good to eat, and what isn't?"

"Yes, ma'am," Alva said. "I help my ma with the picking every year. We ain't never got sick yet."

Rose took a pail from the house and walked down to Wolf Creek with Alva. Swiney trailed behind. Rose told Alva about the wonderful wolf story Abe had told at supper one night.

All through the story, Swiney kept interrupting to tell parts of it. Just as she was about to tell the ending, about Swiney and Abe's father playing the fiddle all night, Swiney shouted it out.

Then Rose frowned at Swiney, too.

At Wolf Creek, Alva showed Rose a clump of pokeweed. Rose had seen green leaves pushing up here and there in the forest, but she didn't know which ones she could safely eat.

"You take the little soft leaves," Alva explained. "But not the root. That's the bad part."

"I got a knife, so I'll be the cutter," Swiney announced. He took out his knife and started sharpening it.

"Who says?" said Alva. "We don't need no cutter anyway. We can just tear them off."

"Can not!" Swiney shouted. Rose was surprised at how foolish Swiney was being.

"Can too!" Alva shouted back. "You can just go find your own poke and cut it if you like. We don't care."

"Humph!" Swiney grumbled, shaving a little patch of arm hair. Then he began carving his name in the trunk of a tree.

Alva showed Rose how to check to make sure there weren't any bugs or insect eggs hiding on the undersides of the bright green leaves. They tore the tenderest leaves off and dropped them in the pail. Then Alva showed her lamb's-quarter and cow parsley. On the edge of the creek, growing right out of the clear cold water, they found watercress. "Try it," said Alva. "It's real good."

Rose pulled some of the tiny leaves from the stem and put them in her mouth. Nothing had ever tasted so fresh and tangy, like radishes. Rose had not realized how hungry she was for fresh vegetables. Swiney brought some pokeweed to put in the pail, but after a while he stopped helping.

Alva and Rose were busy picking when Swiney called out to them: "Watch me! Look! Bet you can't do this!" he shouted. He was standing next to a fence. He climbed up and began to walk shakily along the top rail, holding his arms out for balance.

"That's nothing. We don't care, anyway," Alva sniffed. Just as Swiney got to the end of the section, he tried to turn around. But he lost his balance. He fell, head first. Rose gasped. But just in the instant before Swiney's head would have hit the ground, one of his pant legs got tangled in the fence. He stopped short, hanging upside down, just above the ground.

"Ow!" he screamed. "I'm stuck!" He wriggled and tried to lift himself back up with his arms. He twisted and turned, and huffed and kicked. But try as he might, he couldn't unstick himself. His face turned bright red and the veins stood out on his neck.

"Ha, ha, ha," Alva shouted gleefully. "Now I know why they call you Swiney. You got your snout into everything. Now you look like an old hog at butchering time. Maybe we ought to take your knife and cut you up for sausage."

Rose giggled. She hadn't thought of it before, but Swiney really did get into things like a rooting hog.

"Get me down," Swiney pleaded. "Help me!"

"Maybe we ought to just leave him there," Alva said, putting her hands on her hips. "It would serve him right, sticking his swiney snout into everything. Whiney Swiney!" she shouted in singsong.

"No," Rose said. She didn't like Swiney as well as she liked Alva, and she could laugh at how foolish he looked. But Rose could never be truly mean, and especially not to poor Swiney, who had no mother or father. His face puckered up.

"Come and help," she said to Alva. Together they lifted Swiney up until his pant leg came loose. Then he fell to the ground in a heap, like a pile of old clothes.

Swiney got up and brushed himself off. His face was crimson, and pinched with anger.

"I guess you're really something," Alva said mockingly.

"Are you all right?" asked Rose.

"Awww, never mind!" Swiney shouted. He stomped off toward the house, and they followed him.

When the bucket was full of greens, Alva

went home. Mama cut the sassafras roots into short pieces and put them in a big kettle of water to simmer. The house quickly filled with a strong, spicy smell.

Then Rose brought pails of fresh spring water and helped Mama wash the greens, three times to be sure they were good and clean. Mama parboiled the greens in a pot. Then she drained off the water and added them to the salt pork that was frying in the skillet.

When everything was cooked, they sat down to eat it with chunks of fresh corn bread to sop up the delicious pot liquor. The greens were a little bit bitter, but it was a refreshing kind of bitter for tongues tired of beans, salt pork, and corn bread three times a day, six days a week.

Then Mama served them the sassafras tea, sweetened with molasses. It was tart and spicy and sweet, all at the same time. Rose liked it better than grown-up tea.

"That was delicious," Papa said, wiping his mustache with his napkin. "Sure whets a fellow's appetite for real garden food. I'd say it's about time to start planting."

"Yes, the garden is about ready and it's coming up on a full moon," said Mama. "After that will be time to put in the ground crops. Rose and I will go with you tomorrow to town and I'll pick up some onion sets and seed potatoes. And some seed to start my hotbeds."

Rose had hardly been to town since they first moved to Mansfield, only to church on Sunday when everything and everyone was quiet and sober. Each day on Rocky Ridge she heard the trains whistle as they arrived and left the station. She watched their ribbons of smoke unfurl above the trees and hills. She heard the school bell ringing and imagined all those children running not to be late for their lessons.

But she had never gone to town with Papa on his errands. Now she looked forward to seeing the town on a market day, full of life. It would be fun to see something different for a change.

Market Day

The next morning's chores were all done in a rush. Rose was in such a hurry, she spilled the water Mama had warmed for the chickens. It didn't do for them to drink water cold right from the spring, but Mama said there wasn't time to heat more. The hens would have to make do.

Rose scrubbed her face, hands, and feet in the washbasin in the lean-to. Mama washed where she had missed, the back of her neck and in her ears.

Then she brushed Rose's hair and plaited it tightly into two braids. When she was done she tied on Rose's yellow hair ribbons. Rose wriggled into her blue calico school dress. When she put her arm into the tight shoulders, she heard a ripping sound.

Rose looked at Mama and made a face.

"Never mind," Mama said. "I had hoped it would last till summer. We'll just have to get some goods today for a new one. No one will notice with your coat on."

Then Mama and Papa washed and dressed themselves. Mama put on her second-best dress, a calico that beautifully set off her long, shimmering, roan-brown hair. Then she wove her hair into one wide braid and wound it, lady-like, into a bun.

Papa combed bay rum through his hair. The rich scent always made going somewhere seem special. He put on a fresh pair of overalls, his jacket, and his felt hat. Mama and Rose tied on their bonnets. Then they were ready to go.

Mama and Rose carried their shoes to the wagon so they wouldn't get soiled.

Pet and May stamped their feet impatiently. Papa had brushed them so their coats shone brightly in the early light.

Patches of thin mist floated above Wolf Creek as they splashed across the ford to the other side. Then the wagon rumbled alongside it, through the little valley that lay between Rocky Ridge Farm and Mansfield. The creek chuckled to itself. The horses' hooves clattered on the flinty stones. The strong sun lay like a weight on Rose's shoulders. She wanted to take off her coat, but then she remembered the ripped shoulder of her dress.

A pair of crows flapped past them, diving and twisting playfully in the bliss of spring. A tufted titmouse called out from a bush as they passed, "Wheedle! Wheedle! Wheedle!" never stopping to catch its breath.

"Do you think Reynolds will give us credit enough to get all our spring provisions?" Mama asked over Rose's head.

"Can't see why not," said Papa. "Folks know me now, from my winter job, delivering coal oil for Mr. Waters. And I've sold our stove wood to half the houses in town. Anyone can see we're honest, hardworking farmers."

"It just makes me uneasy, Manly," said Mama. "It was hard enough on the prairie, praying all summer for the wheat harvest to come in only to see it blown away by cyclone, or burned up by drought.

"At least the prairie gave us free grassland to feed the livestock. Now with taxes and the mortgage, and this land so thin and stony, it's a wonder we can raise enough just to—"

"Now, Bess, you're putting the oak before the acorn," Papa interrupted. "Besides, you forget all that timber we have to be made into fence rails and railroad ties. Nothing can take that away. It's cash money we can always count on.

"And the hens will be laying again soon. We've always made out somehow. We always will." He smiled and reached over to squeeze Mama's hand.

Mama sighed and looked out across an orchard of grown apple trees they were passing. Rose prayed that their orchard would hurry and grow.

The bumpy, muddy wagon tracks turned

away from the creek and climbed a steep hill. The railroad tracks curved toward them and then ran alongside. When they crested the ridge, they could see the whole town spread out before them. The horses began to trot down the long, gentle hill into the center of town. Papa had to rein them in to keep their hooves from kicking up clods of mud.

Town was crowded. Farmers streamed in from all directions. The square swarmed with wagons and horses. Children raced shouting and laughing across the steaming muddy streets. Papa had to drive around the square twice to find an empty hitching spot.

Some men waved and called out to Papa, "Howdy, Wilder!"

While Papa hitched the team, Mama and Rose brushed off their feet and put on their stockings and shoes. Then they all walked on the gravel path around the square. Mama put her hand through Papa's arm, and held her skirt up from the muddy ground with the other. Rose thought Mama and Papa looked lovely together, walking like that.

Rose's senses were keen in the strong sunlight. It was exciting to be among all those people, to hear all the strange voices calling to each other. The loneliness of the cold, gray winter melted away.

In the middle of the square was a park, with trees and a bandstand. Around the square were the stores that all those people had come to trade in. The signs read "Newton's Groceries," "Coday's Drugs," "The Bank of Mansfield," "Opera House," and "The Mansfield Hotel," where Paul and George lived. The railroad tracks made one side of the square, with the depot for the Kansas City, Fort Scott, and Memphis Railroad. Some men were unloading boxes onto the platform with bumping sounds.

"Mama, can we visit the Cooleys? Please?" Rose pleaded.

"No," said Mama. "A hotel is a business. It is not a place for visiting."

Now they came to Reynolds' Store. Some men sat in tipped-back chairs on the wooden sidewalk. They were spitting tobacco juice and carving pieces of cedar wood into little piles of reddish-brown shavings. Sacks and boxes were piled on the sidewalk waiting to be loaded onto wagons. Two boys were playing, taking turns pushing each other off the sidewalk. Rose took Mama's hand.

As they passed from the bright sunlight to the darkness inside the store, Rose's eyes could see only shadowy shapes. But her nose instantly filled with a delicious riot of scents and smells. A tingle ran all through her body and settled in her stomach.

"Wait here, Rose," said Mama. Then she and Papa walked all the way to the back of the store to speak with Mr. Reynolds.

Slowly Rose's eyes began to see. She looked at what made all those smells. And she looked, and looked.

The store was a wonderland. Everywhere she turned were tables, shelves, rolls, bins, barrels, kegs, and boxes of every imaginable made thing in the world, all piled up every which way.

On the floor around her were sacks marked

Flour and Corn Meal, and bags of potatoes with the tops turned down. There were barrels brimming with pickles, and crackers, and raisins, and kegs of horseshoes and nails.

The dark wooden counters had moldings that seemed to frown down at her. On top there were piles of overalls, socks, pants, and men's hats. On other counters there were coffeepots, dishes, pitchers, and washbasins. There were boxes of seed packets painted with beautiful pictures of shiny red tomatoes, and dark green watermelons, and pale green cabbages.

The walls of the store were all made of shelves. Some drooped with great bolts of colored calicoes, gaily checked ginghams, dotted swiss, sleek silks, and shiny ribbons. There were boxes of different-colored sewing thread arranged like a rainbow, and piles of pencil tablets, schoolbooks, and slates.

There were rows of metal tins lined up like soldiers, and bottles of every size and shape, full of colored liquids, with brightly colored labels.

Even the ceiling had been used to hang water buckets, and tools, and horse collars.

Rose walked farther back into the store. Waves of scents washed over her and made her giddy. She took deep breaths of nutmeg, and coffee, and tobacco, and pickle brine, and onions, and coal oil, and paint, and leather.

A young man in a crisp white shirt was cutting a wedge from a big wheel of cheese. He pulled a sheet of paper from a long roll and tore it off to wrap the cheese. Then he pulled some string and cut it to tie the package up.

A woman was giving her order to another clerk, and he was writing it down on a piece of paper.

Rose stared as she passed jars and kegs crammed with brightly colored candy. She could smell the peppermint and it made her mouth water. There were perfumed candy bananas, and licorice sticks, and striped hard candy, and lemon drops.

"Hello there, young lady," a man's voice boomed out close by. "What can we do for you today?"

A man with a big belly stood with his hands on his hips, looking down at her. His big teeth grinned at her from under a bushy mustache.

"Which one do you like?" he asked.

Rose was startled. Her ears warmed. She didn't know what to say. The man laughed.

"It's all right," he said. "I'm Mr. Reynolds. This is my store. Your ma and pa are right over there, giving their order. How about these lemon drops. Do you like them?"

Rose nodded. She had never eaten a lemon drop, but she just knew she would like them.

The man pulled a little brown bag with red stripes on it from a rack. Then he took a tiny shovel and scooped up a whole scoopful of the sunny lemon drops. He poured them into the bag, folded the top, and handed it to Rose.

Her heart fluttered so, she almost forgot to say, "Thank you, Mr. Reynolds."

"You bet," Mr. Reynolds said. He called out to a customer and walked away.

Rose weighed the bag in her hand. It was heavy with lemon drops. She wanted to eat one right then, but she would wait to share with Mama and Papa on the ride home.

Mama was holding up a piece of cloth, brown calico with white polka dots.

"How do you like this, Rose?" Rose looked at the fabric. Then she looked at the other bolts of cloth on the shelves. Her eyes rested on a bolt of pale blue and pink gingham.

"I like that one," Rose said. The brown reminded her of mud. The gingham made her think of flowers.

"It's very pretty," said Mama. "But I don't think it will wear as well as the brown. It will show when it's soiled."

Rose had always worn calico. She thought she would like gingham, for a change. She looked at the blue and red, the blue and black, and at a dark blue and deep lavender.

"That one," she said, pointing to the blue and lavender. The clerk took down the bolt, measured out five yards, and cut it with a big shears. Watching him do it, Rose felt a wave of happiness. She had not had a new dress in almost a year, since Mama had sewn up the sprigged blue calico.

Rose wanted blue hair ribbons to go with her dress, but she knew not to ask. She could have new hair ribbons when Mama said so.

Finally they were finished and it was time to go home. Papa backed the wagon up to the sidewalk and loaded everything in. Rose's mouth watered when she saw the big bag of flour. They would have light bread again after a long winter eating corn bread day in and day out.

On the short ride home they ate some of the puckery-sweet lemon drops. The day had turned so warm that Rose had to take off her coat, now that no one would see the rip. The sky was clear and blue. A lone white cloud rose from the horizon in front of them.

In the wagon behind them were new shuck collars for the mules, spring onion sets, packages of seeds for the garden, seed potatoes, the coal oil can filled to the top with coal oil, a sack of sugar, a sack of flour, a box of salt, a tin of tea, a big piece of salt pork, a tin pail of molasses, the gingham for Rose's new dress, thread, a large piece of denim, and chambray for shirts. Mama said she would sew Papa a new shirt and pair of overalls. She would make a shirt and pair of overalls for Swiney, too.

"You see, Bess," Papa said. "Reynolds treated us square. We'll have everything we need to get through till settling up time in the fall, and then some."

Fighting Mules

As they came to the crest of the hill, the lone cloud seemed to grow taller, and to billow. It was a strange-looking cloud, Rose thought. It seemed to be coming from the ground, right on the wooded hill where the house and barn stood.

All at the same time, Papa whipped the reins and Mama cried out, "Manly, fire!" The horses jumped forward. The coal oil can shot backward through the wagon and crashed against the endgate. Bits of mud hit Rose's cheek.

The wagon flew down the bumpy tracks.

The horses' shod feet struck sparks on the stones. Rose's teeth clattered as she bounced on the hard seat. Mama stared at that cloud of smoke. Her face had gone white. Papa's mouth was set in a pale, thin line. Rose's stomach flip-flopped. No one spoke a word.

In no time at all the horses were grunting up the hill. Fido pranced down the wagon tracks to greet them, his tail wagging. As soon as the house came into view, Mama breathed a big sigh. Then they could see the barn as well. Everything looked as normal as could be.

"Praise be," Mama said in a trembly voice. "It's not on our place. It just looked that way. The smoke is coming from farther off."

"I'd best take a look," said Papa. "It's downwind from us, but you never can be too careful."

Papa unhitched May and rode into the woods toward the smoke, toward Mr. Kinnebrew's farm. Mama unhitched Pet and put her in the barn. Then Rose helped unload the wagon.

They watched that cloud of smoke every

minute. It grew smaller, and smaller, and paler. Finally only blue sky remained. Then Papa returned.

"It was only Abe, burning off one of Kinnebrew's brush piles," he said. "There was never any danger." But worry lines darkened his forehead.

"That's a relief," said Mama. "My heart was in my mouth when I saw that smoke."

"That's not all," said Papa. "He was also burning off the fields and even the woods, too. Just letting the fire burn through perfectly good timber."

"Whatever for?" Mama asked.

"It's the most confounded thing I ever heard. He says folks here always burn off the underbrush and new fields in spring. They just let the fires go till they burn themselves out."

"But why?" asked Mama.

"They say it improves the soil, and clears out the weeds and stump sprouts. But I don't like it," Papa said. "It's a crime to treat good land that way!"

The roughness in his voice startled Rose. It

was always so calm and patient. Even horses trusted Papa when he spoke. But fire was a monstrous thing. They were all terribly afraid of it. Rose still remembered the fire that had burned up their house in South Dakota many years before.

"We'll just have to be on our guard, is all," he said. "We can be thankful at least that the land here is good and wet. A fire can't travel far and do too much harm."

Now began the hard work of planting the garden. First Papa got out the harrow he had made during the winter. He sharpened the wooden teeth with his knife.

Then he hitched the harrow to the mules and they dragged it back and forth, breaking up the clods of earth into smaller and smaller clumps. Finally, after many passes, the garden was smooth and soft. Then he hitched the mules to the plow and plowed deep rows in the garden, leaving high ridges of dirt on either side.

Rose helped Mama cut the potatoes into small pieces, making sure each piece had at least two eyes. Then they carried them to the garden in a sack and buried the pieces in the ridges of dirt. They made sure the eyes were facing up. That way they could see the sun and sprout properly. They buried the bits of seed potatoes deep, where they would be safe and warm in case of a late frost.

Then they planted the onion sets and the turnip seeds. Mama planted the tomato seeds in soil she put in wooden hotbeds Papa had made. On warm days she brought the hotbeds out of the house and set them in a sunny place. She always made sure to bring them in before supper, so the cold nights couldn't hurt them.

Every day fires burned on farms all around them. The air was always full of wood smoke. No matter what she was doing, Mama would stop every so often and look around, through the trees at the columns of smoke. If she was inside, she would come outside to look. If she was crouched down in the garden, she would stand up, shield her eyes from the bright sunlight with her hand, and sniff the air. At night they could sometimes see the orange glow of a neighbor's burning brush pile or field.

"I just can't get used to the idea of it," Mama said to Papa at breakfast one morning. "I can't forget those terrible fires on the prairie, and how hard we fought to make the little cottonwood trees grow. People here treat trees like a nuisance."

"But you can't keep piling up the cut brush forever," said Papa. "There'd be no room for planting before long. We have to burn some of our brush piles, as well."

One day, after a soaking rain, Papa told Mama and Rose and Swiney to meet him in the orchard. He and Abe poured some coal oil on the great mounds of branches and stumps that had collected all winter. Then they lit them.

Papa told Rose and Swiney to watch that no sparks fell in the woods and started another fire. But the rain had wet everything down. No fire could start anywhere except where Papa wanted it.

So Rose and Swiney played around the great bonfires, watching them grow until long tongues of scorching orangey-red flame licked the sky. Terrified rabbits scurried out from where they had been living under the piles and bounded off into the woods with Fido chasing after them. Rose and Swiney tried to catch them, too. But the rabbits were too scared and too fast.

Papa did not try to shoot any of the rabbits. It was spring, when all the wild animals have their babies. There would be no more fresh meat until fall, when all the woods creatures had grown up.

Rose and Swiney threw sticks into the flames and watched them burn. They listened to the roaring and the popping and hissing. Then they pulled the sticks out and drew smoke pictures in the air. Their faces turned pink from the searing heat, and Rose burned her fingers playing with her stick. But she was having too much fun to care.

The fires burned all day. They took turns going back to the house to eat, so that someone always was watching. The fires burned into the night, too. Papa stayed to watch until

the coals had cooled and no sparks came out.
The next morning, all that was left was piles
of ash and a few blackened tree limbs and
smoking stumps, sticking up like the bones of
a skeleton.

One beautiful, warm Sunday, after they got
home from church and ate dinner, Mama said
Rose must be good and watch the farm. She
and Papa were going back into town, to see
the Cooleys.

"Can't I go, too?" Rose pleaded. She never
got a chance to play with Paul and George in
church. They had to sit still and be quiet.

"No," said Mama. "Paul and George are
staying behind also, to watch the hotel. We are
going for a buggy drive, just Mr. and Mrs.
Cooley, Papa and I."

Rose sat on one of the trunks by the bed and
sulked while Mama quickly changed out of
her good black cashmere into her white lawn.
It was pretty and light, with a collar crocheted
in pineapple shapes.

Rose pouted while Mama put extra wood in
the little stove in the lean-to kitchen. Then

she put in two loaves of bread to bake. They would be ready when she and Papa came home.

Papa saddled the mares, and Mama and Papa rode off toward town.

"Be good, Rose," Mama called out. "Don't wander off, and watch the stove."

Rose was bored. The first thing she did was take off her stockings and shoes. At least if she had to stay home alone, she could go barefoot. She put her shoes under the bed. Her feet were pale from being cooped up all winter. She wiggled her toes. They were happy to be free again.

"I'm not wearing shoes anymore till winter comes again," Rose told herself out loud.

Then she went outside and sat on a stump in the yard. She listened to the wind sighing in the trees. Far away a train whistled, grew close, and passed. The first tiny leaves were sprouting, tender and blushing pale pink and yellow and green. The air smelled fresh with the scent of newly turned earth.

Little white butterflies fluttered here and

there in the new grass. Bumblebees butted and buzzed, starting their nests. They landed on purple violets, bending the delicate flowers with their weight and nosing in them for nectar.

Goldfinches fluttered from tree to tree, calling out their spring cheer. A robin snatched up a tiny twig and flew away to the nest it was building high up in a tree.

Rose was bored again, so she decided to look at the mules. Papa had told her to stay away from them. But Rose thought she would just give them a little salt. The mules loved salt almost as much as they liked the tender young blades of new grass that were pushing up everywhere. Rose got a handful of salt from the house.

One of the mules was bay-colored, and the other was gray. Papa had named the bay mule Roy, for his big brother Royal. Mama named the gray mule Nellie, after a little girl she had known a long time ago.

When Rose walked into the hallway of the barn, the mules did not come to the stall gates to see her. They stood at the backs of their stalls, eyeing her suspiciously. Rose climbed up on the log wall and laid the salt on top of the low wall that separated their two stalls.

Both of the mules went straight to the salt. Nellie got there first, and when Roy tried to lick some, Nellie squealed horribly, wheeled around, and kicked at the log walls with all her might. Little chips of wood flew into the air. Roy backed up, his ears laid back, snapping at the air with big yellow teeth. Then Nellie wheeled around and started licking again.

The sound of their fighting and braying and squealing was horrible, but it struck Rose as funny, and she shrieked with laughter. She had never seen anything like it.

The mules fought and fought, each getting a little lick of salt now and again, until finally all the salt was gone. Rose had been terribly naughty. She blushed just to think of what Mama would say if she knew. But of course she wouldn't.

Rose was trying to think of something else to do when Swiney came riding up on Abe's

mule, Old Guts. Rose could hear Old Guts'
stomach rumbling as he walked. That was
why they called him Old Guts.

"Howdy, Rose," Swiney called out, sliding
off Old Guts' saddle. His foot got caught in
the stirrup and he tumbled to the ground.
Rose giggled. Swiney got up and brushed himself off. "What are you doing?"

"Nothing," said Rose. "Mama and Papa
went riding. I was playing with the mules.
They were fighting over salt. Do you want to
see?"

"You bet," he said.

Rose got another handful of salt. This time
the mules smelled the salt and started fighting
before she even put it down for them. Swiney
and Rose laughed and laughed. Then, when
the salt was all gone, Swiney showed Rose how
to imitate their squeals and braying. It made
the mules fight again because they thought
there was more salt.

While they were watching the mules fight,
Swiney spat a stream of brown juice onto the
ground.

"Abe lets you chew tobacco?" Rose asked in surprise. Chewing tobacco was a thing done by grown-up men. Mama did not approve of a man chewing tobacco. She said it was a disgusting habit, and once she had told Papa he'd better think twice before he ever took it up.

"Sure he lets me," said Swiney. "Abe lets me do anything. He ain't my pa."

"What does it taste like? Is it good?" Rose asked.

"It's all right, I reckon," Swiney said with a shrug. "It's just a thing to do."

Finally they tired of the mules. "Mules are mean," Rose said. "I like horses better. Does Old Guts fight?"

"Naw. He's tame as a kitty-cat. I been a-riding him since I was a baby. Want to ride him?"

"Could I?" Rose asked eagerly.

Swiney untied Old Guts and turned him so Rose could put her foot in the stirrup. Papa had let Rose sit on the mares a few times, and had led her around with the halter on Little Pet. But she had never ridden by herself.

Rose knew how to pull herself up. She

scrambled up on top of Old Guts and settled into the saddle. The mule turned and looked at her with baleful eyes.

"Go on," Swiney said. "Give him a kick."

Rose kicked her heels a little against the mule's sides.

"Aw, come on," Swiney said. "Kick him good."

Rose kicked harder, but Old Guts ignored her and nibbled some grass.

Swiney picked up a stick and swatted Old Guts on the backside with a *whap!*

The mule leaped into the air, tossing his head. Rose pitched forward and her forehead hit him hard between the ears with a clunk. Old Guts galloped a few steps, his stomach rumbling, and then stopped short. Rose's head spun. She climbed trembling down from the mule's back. She wobbled a few steps and then sat down hard.

Swiney came running. "What happened?" he shouted.

"I hit my head," Rose groaned. Everything was spinning.

"Uh-oh," Swiney said. "You're looking kind of puny, Rose. I'll fetch some water."

Rose sat there as still as she could for a long time. Swiney brought the wooden water bucket. Rose drank a dipperful. The cold, clean water refreshed her. The spinning slowed down, and then she just felt a little woozy.

"You look like a ghost, Rose," Swiney said.

Rose grinned weakly. She stood up on wobbly legs. Swiney picked up the water bucket and followed her to the house. Just as she got to the lean-to door, Rose smelled smoke. She remembered Mama's bread cooking in the stove. Out of the corner of her eye something made her look up.

She glanced at the chimney pipe coming out of the lean-to roof and gasped. Little flames were licking up from the lean-to roof, around the chimney opening. The roof was burning! The house was on fire! Rose's mind went black with horror.

Her breath snagged in her throat. Her legs turned to stone. She stood there in frozen terror, staring at the tiny orange flames that danced in the breeze. They were growing bigger even while she watched.

Then, suddenly, Rose snatched the bucket from Swiney's hand.

"Say," he shouted. "What's the idea?"

Rose raced around the back of the house. She ran to the edge of the gully where the spring was. She tripped on a root and tumbled down the path, splashing into the water. She got right up, scooped a bucketful, and scrambled up the slippery, muddy path. Her eyes stung. A sob jerked from her throat.

Swiney stood on the roof. He had taken off his shirt and was beating the fire with it.

"Quick, Rose!" he shouted. "Hand that bucket up. Hurry!" He squatted and leaned over the edge of the roof. It was low, but not low enough. The bucket was too heavy for Rose to lift all the way to Swiney's hand. Another sob strangled her breath.

She poured some water out. Then she lifted the bucket with all her strength in both hands. Swiney barely caught the bail in his fingertips.

He heaved the bucket onto the roof with a loud grunt. Then he poured the water all around the chimney. Steam and smoke mingled in the sunshine.

Rose peered inside the lean-to. Water ran sizzling down the outside of the stovepipe. It splashed and hissed on the top of the stove. It crackled inside the stove, where it put out the coals. The bread was ruined.

Rose sighed a great shivery sigh. There was no fire in the house. Only the roof had burned, and only a little.

She slumped against the doorway and sat on the sill. She put her face in her hands. She began to shake all over. Then she cried.

Swiney sat down next to her. They sat there a long time, Rose crying and Swiney saying nothing. Finally Rose snuffled up the last of her tears. She wiped her face with the hem of her skirt.

"I better go," said Swiney.

Rose walked with him to Old Guts, who was scrunching up some grass. Swine climbed up into the saddle and looked down at Rose.

"You shouldn't cry none," he said. "It's all right now."

"Thank you," said Rose. "You saved our house. If you hadn't gone up on the roof. . . . I don't know how you did it . . . I . . . I couldn't have reached it by myself." The thought of what might have happened brought tears welling in her eyes again.

"I just climbed up the logs," Swiney said, grinning. Rose had to smile a little herself.

Now Rose waited for Mama and Papa with a dreadful sinking feeling. They would be upset about the fire. And Rose had been very naughty, teasing the mules. A little bit of her even thought the fire might have been her own fault.

Rose was afraid she would cry when she tried to tell them. But she didn't.

"The roof caught fire from the stove," she said as soon as Mama and Papa rode close enough to hear. "But Swiney was here. He helped put it out."

Mama and Papa jumped down from the horses at the same time, their faces lined with worry.

"What! How in the world . . . " Mama blurted. She looked at the roof. Then she looked inside the lean-to, and inside the stove.

"Are you all right, Rose?" Papa asked.

Then Rose told Mama and Papa the whole story of that afternoon, except the part about feeding salt to the mules. She flushed hot with shame. She promised herself she would never do such a terrible thing again.

When she told about knocking heads with Old Guts, Papa guffawed loudly. Mama frowned at him. Rose didn't know what to think.

"Now, Bess," said Papa. "I'll bet you were some kind of shaken up, weren't you Rose?"

Rose nodded. Her forehead ached a little.

Mama bit her lip. Her eyes glimmered with tears, and she gave Rose a hug.

"It's my fault," Mama finally said. "Trying to save a little time by leaving that flimsy stove hot like that. The pipe sections must have come apart, letting the sparks get to the roof."

"Now, Bess, don't you fret so. It's just like your ma used to say, there's no loss without some gain. First thing, I'm going to tear down that old lean-to and build you a real kitchen, with a proper chimney."

The New Room

The next day Papa took the little stove out of the lean-to. Then he and Abe tore the lean-to away from the house, log by log. When they finished, there was nothing left but the hard bare ground that had been the lean-to floor, and the doorway into the house. Papa and Abe began to build a new, bigger room on that spot which would be the kitchen.

First they made a low stone wall, in the shape of a large box. One side of the box was the log house. The stone wall was the foundation. Rose and Swiney helped find stones that

Papa could fit snugly together to make it solid and level.

On top of the foundation they made another box by laying down four heavy squared-off logs of white oak. That was the sill. The sill must be good and sturdy to hold up the floor, the stove, and the walls. The stone foundation would keep the wooden sills from touching the ground, so they would stay dry and season hard.

Next they laid heavy joists across the sill, to hold up the floor.

But instead of building the walls out of logs, like the walls of the house, Abe helped Papa split logs into hewn clapboards. The clapboards were rough like shingles. They were thick on one edge and thinner on the other like shingles, too. They weren't as fine and smooth as sawed boards. But Papa said, "Abe is a mighty fine wood cobbler. Those walls will stand as long as time lasts."

"How long is that?" Rose asked.

"Nobody knows," said Papa.

While they worked, Abe sang and whistled

songs that Rose had never heard before. He called them frolic songs.

> *"Lips a-like a cherry,*
> *Cheeks a-like a rose,*
> *How I love that little gal,*
> *God A'mighty knows!*
>
> *"Get along home, Cindy, Cindy,*
> *Get along home, Cindy, Cindy,*
> *Get along home, Cindy, Cindy,*
> *I'll marry you sometime."*

"Why is it called a frolic song?" Rose wanted to know.

"On account of it's played at a frolic. Why else?" Swiney chimed.

"What's a frolic?"

"It's a time when folks get together and dance," Abe said, holding a board so Papa could nail it in place. "Of a Saturday night, some folks will clear the beds out of their house, wax the floor up real slick, and bid their neighbors and friends come by for a frolic. Some fellow, like me, comes up and fiddles, or picks the banjo. Then they all dance till their toes are a-twiddling in their boots."

Rose laughed and twiddled her toes.

"You never seen the like of it," said Swiney. "If it's a real good frolic, them big boys get to fighting over some girl."

A frolic sounded like fun. Rose wanted to see one, although she didn't think she wanted to see any fighting.

"Can we go, just one time?" Rose begged. "Just to see?"

"I think that a frolic is not something for little girls," Mama said politely.

In no time at all, the walls were up and the roof was on. Papa left two square holes, one in the east wall and one in the west wall. He made two wooden doors for those holes and hung them on leather hinges. When they were closed, the room was very dark.

"In the fall, when it gets cold again, we'll get you proper glass windows," Papa told Mama. "But for now, while it's warm, we can leave the shutters open during the day when you want the light."

"It's just beautiful the way it is," said Mama, her eyes bright with pleasure.

There was a hole in the roof, too, where the stovepipe would go. Papa said he would line the hole with tin, so the roof could never catch fire again.

Next Papa and Abe laid down the floorboards on top of the heavy joists. Rose noticed for the first time that the floor went right out the door and made a shelf outside, in front of the kitchen.

"The part outside is the porch," Papa said. "Now Mama can sit out outside like a lady and cool off on a hot summer day."

The last floorboard Papa laid down was short, and it was in the middle of the floor. The board had a hole in it, too, big enough to stick your fingers in. That board was a trapdoor. Mama could pull it up and store vegetables and eggs in the cool space under the kitchen.

Then, the last thing, Papa took the old door from the house and fitted it to the doorway of the new room. Finally Rose could walk all around the new room. She was sorry to see dirty footprints on the bright new floor. But it was beautiful and clean-smelling inside.

Rose noticed light peeking between the clapboard walls.

"Won't the wind come through when it's cold?" Rose asked Mama.

"We'll batten the walls with thin strips of wood," said Mama. "But the stove will warm it up when we're using it, and when we aren't, we'll be cozy in front of the fireplace in the house."

Mama and Rose swept all the dirt and saw-dust out of the kitchen. Then they moved the table from the house into the kitchen, and laid one of the rag rugs over the trapdoor. Papa gathered up his tools and began to put them away.

"What about the stove?" Mama asked.

"It's getting late and I've got to feed and water the mares and mules," said Papa. "The weather's good. Why don't you cook outside? We'll move the stove tomorrow, after break-fast."

"Very well," said Mama. "But it isn't a very big job. It's just a small stove."

The next morning after breakfast, Papa said he had a load of fence rails to deliver in town. He was gone most of the morning. Mama and Rose hoed the garden to make new rows where they would plant beans and squash. Crows had been digging in the potato hills, eating the seed potatoes. So they had to cut and plant more.

"I wonder what can be keeping him?" Mama said as they worked. "I've got my dough ready to bake. But I don't want to start a fire in the stove if we're going to move it."

Finally, just as Mama had decided to go ahead and start dinner, they heard the wagon splashing across the ford on Wolf Creek and rumbling up the hill. Fido raced down the wagon tracks to meet it. The mares were grunting and slipping on the flinty stones, trying to pull the wagon. Papa had draped the oilcloth covers over something in the wagon-box, which rode low on its springs.

"I wonder what that could be," said Mama,

mopping her forehead with the hem of her apron. She laid down her hoe and followed the wagon.

Papa drove right up to the kitchen porch and *whoa*ed the horses. He set the brake and jumped down. A grin crinkled his mouth.

"I can see you've got something up your sleeve," Mama said. "What is it?"

Papa climbed into the wagon-box and pulled off the oilcloth covers. Mama's mouth flew open. Sitting there, still half in its crate, was a brand-new cast-iron stove. Papa crossed his arms and waited for Mama to speak.

"Oh, Manly!" Mama cried out finally. Her hand flew to her mouth.

"It isn't the best stove money can buy," Papa said proudly. "But when I do a thing, I do it right. It's got a hot water reservoir. Now you can heat water and cook at the same time!"

The stove was beautiful. A pattern of sprigged flowers and leaves spread all over the doors. The nickel knobs and pins gleamed in the sunlight.

Rose waited for Mama's face to melt into

happiness. But her mouth was tight, and her forehead furrowed. Finally she said, simply, "No."

Papa's eyes widened. "No?" he said.

"Yes," said Mama, more firmly this time. "I mean no. I mean, you must take it back."

"What in tarnation?" Papa said.

"We cannot afford the expense," said Mama. "It's that simple. I couldn't bear to cook on it knowing we had gone into debt for it. You know how I feel. You will just have to take it back. I'm sorry. I know you only meant to please. But no."

Papa stared at Mama in disbelief. Rose held her breath. She had never heard Mama speak so to Papa.

"Now just a durn minute," Papa said, jumping down from the wagon. "I went to no end of trouble trading with Reynolds for fence rails and railroad ties. Prices are high now. There's never been a better time. One way or another, I'll pay for the blasted thing. Now quit this foolishness and let's get on with unloading it."

"Manly Wilder, you won't talk me into

anything by cussing," Mama said. Rose flinched. "You can unload it yourself. You can install it yourself. But I'll cook in the fireplace like my ma did before I'll cook on that stove. It's a sinful, wasteful extravagance for folks as poor as us.

"I have a perfectly good stove already," she said, pointing to the little tin stove sitting near the porch. "How can we ever get ahead if we keep going deeper and deeper in debt?"

Now Papa's face was deeply creased between the eyes. He stared at Mama for a long moment.

"Dash it all, Bess!" he shouted. "Hang the expense. What's the difference if we owe an extra twenty dollars? It may as well be two hundred. If we can't pay it, Reynolds will give us more time. But I gave my word and I don't aim to take it back."

Mama took a step back. "I just—" she began to say. But Papa's earnest voice drove on.

"See here," he said, "it's been more than fifteen years since I set out to find my fortune on the frontier. We can't live like sodbusters all our lives, letting the land grind us down year after year. I wouldn't wear out a dumb horse that way, not for any reason.

"Why should I let you wear yourself down, bending and slaving over a flimsy stove, worrying yourself half to death about fire? By jiminy, sometimes I . . . "

Then Papa ran out of words. He took his hat off and threw it to the ground, hard as he could. It landed with a puff of dust. Then he took a big breath, picked it up, and brushed it off.

"I've got work to do," he muttered. He turned and stalked off to the barn, forgetting to unhitch the team. Mama looked after him with a long face. Her hands wrung each other. Then she walked slowly into the kitchen.

Rose was dumbfounded. She had never seen Mama and Papa quarreling so. She had never heard Papa speak so forcefully. She didn't know what to think, or do, or say.

Even the horses seemed stunned, standing still as statues. Fido looked at Rose, his head cocked in a question. Then he trotted off to the barn after Papa. The yard filled with a terrible silence.

A gloom thickened around Rose and pressed down on her. She yearned to go off somewhere where she could be alone, and think. But she knew she shouldn't. Now was a time to be extra good, and quiet as a mouse.

She gathered kindling to cook dinner. She laid it next to the little camp stove where it sat outside near the porch. The sound of rattling pots came from the kitchen. Presently Papa came and unhitched the horses. After he led them away, Mama came out and lit a fire in the little stove.

Chickens

Dinner was dreadful. Mama and Papa did not speak to each another. Rose could not enjoy the beautiful new kitchen. The cozy clatter of dishes and utensils could not defeat the silence. Papa ate quickly and left to go work in the timber lot. Mama sighed after he had walked out the door.

"Well," Mama said after they had washed and dried the dishes. "It's time we cleaned out the henhouse. Two of the chickens have gone broody and I think one of them has stolen her nest out somewhere. Maybe you can find it for me."

Rose called Fido to help. She looked in the bushes near the house first. When Rose got down on her hands and knees to peek under them, Fido thought it was a game. He sniffed around the other side from where Rose was peering, a quizzical look on his face.

Then she hunted around the outside of the barn, and under a pile of brush that was left from when the barn had been built in the fall. But she found no nests.

It was wonderful to be outside. In the cabin the hearth fire had gone out for the last time. There were no more ashes to carry or wood to gather in the slushy mud and snow of winter. The door and windows stood wide to the spring. The log walls were no longer a shelter, but a prison opening to freedom with every dawn.

Spring was hazy on the Ozark hills. The skeletons of the trees were covering themselves in leaves. The brown slopes were burying themselves under drifts of green. White-oak leaves hung in rich masses. Black-jack leaves glittered in the morning sun. Little nuts were forming on the tufted walnuts.

The ground had finally begun to dry out. The dust of the path by the spring branch was velvety cool to Rose's bare feet. In the sunshine the flints were warm.

Papa had fenced in a small pasture, and the horses and mules had been turned out to graze. Baby quail were hatching. Squirrels and rabbits had their little ones.

Rose could not find the hen's nest.

"Either way, she'll show up one of these days with her babies," said Mama. "She's got awfully good sense. She has never lost a single chick for me. And Fido is such a good dog, he will watch out for her as well."

Next they cleaned out the henhouse. They swept out all the dirty litter from the floor. They emptied all the old straw out of the nest boxes that hung on the henhouse wall. Mama took out the roosting perches. She dabbed coal oil on the perches and in the cracks in the walls of the henhouse to kill lice and mites.

Then they put down a blanket of fresh leaves, mixed with wood chips and sawdust.

Mama put fresh straw in all the nest boxes. She showed Rose how to make sure each nest had a cozy little hollow in the middle.

"It should be deep enough so the eggs won't roll off to the side and get cold," Mama explained. "But not so deep that a clumsy hen will step on the eggs and break them."

Then she brought two white china door-knobs from the house that she had kept in one of the trunks. She set one in each of two nests. The hens would think they were eggs and lay their eggs in with them, instead of hiding them in the woods.

"That old rooster is starting to wear out," Mama said, looking over the flock as she fed them their ration of corn. "I'll have to find a young one. Maybe I can trade some chicks with Mrs. Stubbins. She has such nice Leghorns."

Rose thought chickens were not very smart and, except for roosters with their shimmering colored feathers, not pretty to look at. She couldn't play with them, or teach them tricks.

"Mama, why do you like chickens so well?"

Rose asked. "They take so much care."

"A chicken is a miracle of nature," said Mama. "And the salvation of any farm. A hen asks very little: a dry, safe place to sleep at night, sunlight, fresh air, water, some mash every day, and a place to scratch for worms and bugs and grasshoppers.

"In return, she is a factory for food. She gives us eggs for nearly two years. She gives us young pullets to fry up for Sunday dinner. And when she is old and tired, she cooks into a delicious stew with dumplings.

"Just think of it; a good chicken will lay an egg every day. Now I have twenty hens. If they lay a dozen eggs each day, and Mr. Reynolds will give nine cents the dozen, how much is that after a week?"

Rose was better at reading and writing than at arithmetic. She had to think a minute before she answered, "Sixty-two cents?"

"Sixty-three cents," Mama corrected. "Now, how much do you think that is after a month?"

That was too complicated a problem. "Two

dollars and more than four bits," Mama said. Rose looked at her in surprise.

"And in a year," Mama said, as she showed Rose how to multiply again, "that makes about thirty dollars."

Rose thought for a moment. Then she cried out, "Mama, that's more than the cost of the stove!"

The shadow of a frown flickered in Mama's blue eyes. Then she brushed away the numbers she had drawn in the dust.

"Yes, it is," she said. "But chickens are not predictable. They get sick, and remember last winter when that owl carried off my best layer? There are hawks waiting to carry off the spring pullets, and snakes to steal the eggs. And besides, we have many other things to pay for.

"Well, never mind about that now. Let's get back to work on the garden. We need to get those fence rails up if we're to keep the chickens from eating it up."

While they were working, Papa came back to the house with Abe. They climbed up into the wagon where it still stood by the porch.

Rose tried not to stare, but she couldn't help it. Papa and Abe slid the cast-iron stove out of the wagon. Then they dragged it across the porch, into the kitchen.

After that, there was nothing to see. But Rose heard the sound of metal banging, and hammering. After a time, the round chimney pipe poked up through the roof hole Papa had made and lined with tin. Rose stole sidelong glances at Mama, but Mama never looked up at the house. She just kept working, lifting fence rails and fitting them together.

When it was time for supper, Mama built a fire in the tin stove outside. Supper was almost as quiet as dinner had been. Only now, sitting in a corner of the kitchen was the shiny new stove. Rose dared not open the heavy iron doors, or lift any of the four covers on top.

When she had finished helping Mama with the dishes, Rose went to the barn in the gathering twilight to watch Papa doing his evening chores. He pitched fresh straw into the stables.

"How's my little prairie Rose tonight?" said Papa. "How do you like that new stove?"

Rose's face grew warm. She stammered from not knowing what to say.

"That's all right," said Papa, setting down the pitchfork. "I must have given you quite a fright, carrying on so. Were you scared?"

"A little," Rose said. "You never did that before."

"No, I never did," said Papa, his eyes wrinkling into a smile. "Hopefully never will again. Your mama's strong-willed, is all. Always was. Fact is, it's what I liked about her from the first. She's got spunk and spirit."

Then Papa looked at Rose with mirth in his eyes. "If you can keep it a secret, I'll tell you a nickname your grandpa used to call Mama."

"What!" Rose shouted with a giggle.

"Shhhh!" Papa shushed. "You must keep it a secret."

"I will," Rose whispered loudly.

"Just between us?" he said.

"Yes!" Rose nearly squealed.

"Flutterbudget," Papa said.

"What?"

"Flutterbudget," said Papa again. "When

your mama was young and she'd get her dander up, your grandpa teased her by calling her Flutterbudget."

Rose giggled. She couldn't imagine anybody calling Mama such a funny name. But she thought it sounded a little like Mama. Rose liked it.

"All right, now," said Papa with a wink. "That's the last word on the subject."

"But can we keep the stove?" Rose asked.

"That's for Mama to decide," said Papa. "We must wait and see."

Rose walked back to the house. Just as she was about to walk into the kitchen, she heard the metal clank of a stove door closing. When she walked in, Mama was patting down her apron and looking around as if she had lost something.

"Here, Rose," she said, snatching the broom from its place in the corner. "Sweep out the kitchen. Then it's time for your lessons."

Rose's heart grew lighter with each swish of the broom. Having a secret with Papa made her feel grown-up. She understood that everything would turn out all right.

Going Fishing

Rose woke in the fresh dawn to a chorus of birdsong and clattering stove lids. She smelled wood smoke, coal oil, and coffee. She heard the crackling sound of a fire. Her eyes popped open.

Rose leaped out of bed and threw off her nightgown. She wriggled into her dress and peered around the corner of the door. On the table, sprouting from a glass jar, was a beautiful bouquet of flowers.

Mama was bent over in front of the new stove, poking a stick of wood into the firebox. Sour-milk biscuits sizzled in a hot greased pan. Rose's heart jumped for joy.

"Good morning, Rose," Mama said cheerfully. "Look at the flowers Papa picked this morning."

The bouquet was lovely. There was a thin, twisted tree branch of white cross-shaped flowers. The outer edge of each petal was tinged reddish-brown, and the middle had a cluster of tiny seeds. "What's that?" Rose asked.

Mama said it was a kind of tree. "I've never seen it before," she said. "Papa said it grows down in the woods, on the other side of the timber lot."

There were tiny purple violets in the bouquet, and pink-edged spring beauties, and delicate yellow buttercups, and blushing purple blossoms of some sort, and sweet williams. The flowers and birdsong and the cozy warmth of the new stove in the corner made a merry breakfast. Mama and Papa did not speak of the stove, but when Papa came in to eat, he looked at Rose and winked.

After breakfast, Mama put a dried-apple pie to bake in the oven. They would take it with them to church the next day. Mama was also going to bake a chicken pie, the next morning.

Sunday was Decoration Day and there would be a church picnic. Rose jumped for joy. A picnic, with Paul and George!

"It isn't just for having fun," Mama said. "Decoration Day is when the church members weed and tidy up the graveyard. But it will be fun, too," she added.

Papa helped Mama and Rose finish the fence around the garden. They wove sticks through the lower rails to keep out rabbits and groundhogs. The sun was bright, and soon the day grew warm and smothery like summer.

Papa made a little log gate for the garden fence that fastened with a loop of rope on the top. When they were done, the garden looked very safe. No wild hogs could get in to root up the tender young plants.

Then Mama stretched pieces of string between the fence tops, across the garden. She tied scraps of cloth to the strings. The fluttering scraps would scare away crows and other birds.

At noon, when it was time for dinner, they

were all hot and thirsty. When they sat down to eat, Papa had a surprise.

"How would you girls like to go fishing this afternoon?"

"Fishing?" Rose had never been.

"Abe says he knows a good spot up on Wolf Creek," said Papa. "I could do with some fresh fish for a change."

So Papa hitched the mares to the wagon and they drove past the Kinnebrews' farm. Abe and Swiney were waiting for them at the end of the lane, by the wagon track. Abe was carrying his fiddle. As soon as they had climbed into the wagon box, he plucked the strings, tuning it up. Swiney got out his knife and sharpened it. Fido sat on Mama's lap where he could see everything better.

"I thought you folks might fancy a bit of music to pass the while," said Abe.

"That would be wonderful," Mama said. Abe drew the bow and began to play a lively song with simple words they could learn right away.

Going Fishing

"Lark in the morning, sailing from her nest,
Lark in the morning, sailing from her nest,
Lark in the morning, sailing from her nest,
Dew-drops falling from her snow-white
breast.

"The higher she flies the sweeter she'll sing,
The higher she flies the sweeter she'll sing,
The higher she flies the sweeter she'll sing,
And we'll all turn back to the green fields
again."

Their voices rang out through the bare trees. The strong light made a lacy pattern through the tiny spring leaves. If Rose squinted her eyes, the woods looked like fall. But the gentle warm breeze and drowsy scent of the growing earth spoke only of the coming summer.

On the limbs of the still-bare oaks the wise squirrels ran fearlessly, frisking tails and cocking saucy eyes. Fido's ears perked up, and the squirrels scolded, "Chit! Chit! Chit!"

Then the wagon passed trees blooming a

purple haze. Those were the same flowers in Mama's bouquet. Abe said it was redbud. The little blossoms were bunched up all along the branches. Up close they looked like swarms of little purple bees with delicate pink wings.

Here and there in low places stood a few short trees with twisting branches, lighting the forest with snowy drifts of blossom. Those were the white flowers in Mama's bouquet.

"That there's dogwood," said Abe.

Finally the road ran by a large, deep stream and the wagon stopped. That was Wolf Creek. Great tall trees lined the banks. Their tangled roots, like gnarled toes, stuck out of the mud at the water's edge. A flock of brown birds that had been pecking in the mud flew up into the trees. Their bottoms flashed white. Their open wings showed golden yellow.

In a swampy place next to the creek, Abe showed them where a grove of cane grew. Swiney used his sharp knife to cut everyone one of those slender trees. The cane stems had little knuckles on them, and they were hollow inside.

Going Fishing

They stripped all the delicate branches and feathery leaves from the cane. Papa and Abe tied long pieces of heavy sewing thread on the ends. Close to the ends of the threads they tied little bits of wood. Then they tied hooks on the ends of the threads.

Swiney showed Rose how to find bait. That was a game. They peeked under old rotting logs and found pale grubs, and slithery worms, and small slippery salamanders. Fido played, too. He pawed through the rotted soil, sniffing and sneezing.

Swiney took a worm and poked his hook through it. The worm squirmed and fought to get away, but it was stuck there.

"Here," Swiney said, giving Rose a worm. "Stick your hook in real good."

The worm waved and writhed in Rose's fingers, making itself short and fat, then long and thin. She hated the feel of it. She hated to hurt the worm by sticking the hook through it. She tried, but the worm kept slithering away. It stretched and stretched until it was impossibly skinny. She jabbed at it, but the hook

stuck her finger instead.

"Let me help you with that," said Papa. He took the worm in his hand, and with a flick of his fingers the worm was wriggling on the hook.

Now they spread out along the bank to fish. Mama sat on an old log, pushed her bonnet back, and watched. "It's so peaceful here," she said. "I'm perfectly content to sit and enjoy it."

Rose stood on the bank, at the edge of the water, and dropped her line in.

"Not like that," said Swiney. "The fish can see you. You got to be sneaky or they ain't going to bite. Come on."

They walked a little way upstream along the broad deep creek, hiding like Indians behind the bushes and logs along the banks. Then Swiney told Rose to hunch down. When they were almost flat on the ground, Swiney said, "Just crawl up close, but keep your head down. Then whip your pole over and let the hook fall in."

Rose flicked her pole back, and then forward. She felt something pulling right away. She peeked to see if the hook had fallen in the creek. But the thread was pointing behind her. Then she felt it, tugging in her dress. Swiney unstuck her and showed her how to cast her bait.

Finally, they were really fishing.

"How do you know if you caught one?" Rose asked.

Swiney laughed. "You'll know," he said. "The little hunk of wood starts to bob. Then the fish yanks your line like he's a-going to drag you right in the water." Rose grabbed the pole tightly with both hands.

They lay there in the leaves. Rose was impatient. She peered over the edge of the bank. Her line disappeared into the water. The piece of wood floated calmly. She lifted up, to see if there were any fish on the hook. But there was only the worm, still wriggling. She sighed and dropped it back in. Then she picked it up again. Still no fish. Downstream she could hear the low voices of Papa and Mama and Abe. She checked again. Nothing but the worm. Now it was limp.

Rose noticed a blood blister on her wrist that had not been there a moment ago. The blood blister wriggled a little. It had legs! Rose had to scrape and scrape at it to scrape off that flat brown bug. Swiney said it was a tick.

Rose scratched a bite on her leg. She watched spots of sunlight dancing on the water. Dead leaves floated lazily by. A breeze stirred, roughing up the water's surface.

Rose lifted her pole again. This time something pulled back. She jerked the pole hard. Something was holding it down.

"I got one! I got one!" Rose shouted. She could hardly breathe, she was so excited. She stood up and yanked as hard as she could. Then Swiney helped. He took the pole and pulled.

"Wait a minute," he said. He waded into the creek and fished around in the water with his hand. Then he pulled up Rose's hook. At the end was a stick, covered with dead leaves. The worm was gone.

"Let's go upstream, where that old dead

tree is hanging out over the water," said Swiney. "Them fish cain't look up and there won't be no sticks out there."

Now they sat out high over the water and dropped their lines into Wolf Creek. Rose liked fishing better when she could see the whole creek. She could see Abe and Papa fishing way downstream. In a shallow place, Fido was catching a fish that was trapped on a gravel bar. He grabbed it in his mouth and trotted off into the woods to eat it.

Abe had caught a fish and was taking it off the hook. Then he held it up by its tail. The dripping silver fish flashed like a knife blade in firelight.

Rose could see the dark shadows of fish swimming in the creek. She could even see fish come to look at her hook. But none of them wanted it.

She looked out on the creek. A fallen log on the far bank was covered with bumps. The bumps were turtles, lined up in a row, sunning themselves and catching flies.

Suddenly, right behind them on the bank,

Going Fishing

Rose heard a loud splash. A long, slinky brown creature climbed up on the mud. It had beautiful shiny-wet fur on its arched back, and a pointed face, and whiskers. It shook itself like a dog. Then it looked around and scampered off into the woods.

"What was that?" Rose asked.

"Mink," said Swiney. "He's scared the fish away. Maybe we can catch something by noodling."

"Noodling?" Rose asked.

"I'll show you," said Swiney.

He climbed down from the dead tree and walked along the creek bank to a log that had fallen into the water. Rose watched from her perch.

"Sometimes the fish hide in here," he said. Swiney rolled his pants up and waded into the water along the log. When he got to the hollow end, he climbed up and sat on the log. Then he leaned over and stuck his hand under the water, into the hollow part.

He reached around inside for a moment.

"Cain't feel nothing," he said. "Wait! I

think there's something in there!"

He leaned over, to get his hand farther in. "Something's in there!" he shouted. His head was almost in the water, he had to reach so far in.

Then he shouted, "Got it!" He pulled his hand out of the water. Something was writhing in the splashing water. It was long and . . .

"Look out!" Rose shouted. "It's a snake!" Swiney had it by the tail.

"Jiminy!" Swiney screeched. He flung the snake away from him. It landed in the water with a plop. Then it swam wriggling away across the creek, its head poking out of the water.

Swiney stumbled and splashed out of the creek. He clambered up onto the bank, his eyes big and round. He was shaking. He looked at his hands and his arms. But the snake had not bitten him.

"Jiminy!" he said again. "I ain't never noodled no snake before. Jiminy!"

Rose was watching Swiney so intently, she didn't notice the tugging on her fishing pole. Then, all of a sudden, it nearly jumped out of her hands. She grabbed tight.

Her line slashed the water, this way and that. She could see the shadow of the fish. Its bright belly sparkled as it turned and fought the hook.

"I got one!" she shrieked.

She yanked on her pole, but that fish fought hard. The pole bent way over until she thought it might break. The fish dashed out into the middle of the creek. Rose gripped the tree trunk with her legs to keep from falling off.

"Don't jerk so hard!" Swiney shouted. "The hook will come out."

The fish fought and fought, but soon it tired and floated near the surface. Then Rose swung her pole over by the bank, where Swiney grabbed the line and unhooked it. It was a big fish with beautiful gold and blue scales and wide surprised-looking eyes. Swiney strung it through the gill on a piece of vine.

Rose ran downstream, carrying the still flopping fish by the piece of vine. "Papa, Mama, look!" she shouted.

"You got yourself a pretty little smallmouth there," said Abe.

Rose showed the fish to Mama and Papa.

"That will make good eating tonight," Papa said. Rose beamed. He took the fish and strung it with the fish he had caught. Rose counted. She and Papa had caught seven fish! And Abe had caught five fish for himself and Swiney. Swiney hadn't caught any.

Rose was proud as a gander. It made her feel good to help put food on their table.

They all fished a little while longer, but the fish had stopped biting. Finally Papa said it was time they got back to do chores.

He put all the fish in the keg he had brought, with water to keep them fresh. Then they all climbed back in the wagon and drove home. Great piles of white clouds mounted in the hazy blue sky. The air seemed to press down, hot and sticky.

"Looks like we might get some rain," said Mama. "We could use it, too. The garden is drying out."

"Most likely it'll be a gully-washer, too," said Abe. "I seen a couple snakes heading for high ground this morning. And the rocks in my corn patch was a-sweating dew. Them is sure signs a good rain is a-coming."

"We had better hurry and get the chores done soon as we get home," said Mama.

Rose pulled the string of fish out of the barrel of water, to see her fish again. She knew exactly which was the one she had caught.

"Sakes alive. That's the fourth time you've looked, Rose," Mama said. "You're going to wear those poor fish out before I get a chance to clean them."

Abe tuned his fiddle again and began to play and sing. The song was a story.

> *"Down in the Missouri mountains*
> *Far from the cares of the world,*
> *Stood Dan Kelly's son and he leaned on his*
>   *gun,*
> *Thinking of Zeb Turney's gal*
>
> *"Dan was a hotblooded youngster,*
> *His paw raised him sturdy and right.*
> *A gun he had worn since the day he was*
>   *born,*
> *To shoot every Turney on sight."*

The sky darkened and the wind picked up as they dropped Abe and Swiney off at the Kinnebrews'. Papa hurried the horses, to beat the coming storm home.

The Flood

Papa unhitched the team and put the horses in the barn. Then he brought the mules in from the little pasture.

The sky closed in, shutting out the last rays of sunlight. The forest grew dim and murky with an early dusk. The undersides of the dark clouds boiled. Thunder grumbled in the distance. Rose's heart beat with a strange excitement, and she felt feverishly hot. The sound of beating wings startled her. She looked up to see a flock of crows fleeing before the storm.

"It smells like hail," Mama said. "Let's get

the chickens inside."

She rattled a spoon in a bowl the way she always did at feeding time. The chickens came running with their necks stretched out, flapping their wings. Soon the yard was alive with scratching, quarreling, cackling chickens.

Rose helped Mama herd them into the henhouse. Just as the last chicken went in, Fido burst out barking from behind the large rock at the head of the spring. A moment later, Mama's missing hen strutted into the yard, all ruffled and cackling loudly. Behind her, running to keep up, was a little parade of fluffy chicks, eleven in all. Behind them was Fido, herding them toward the henhouse!

"What a good dog!" Mama exclaimed. "The rain might have washed the poor things away. But the baby chicks are too little to sleep in the henhouse."

She caught the hen and put her in the wire coop. The hen growled and pecked Mama's hand. But when the little peeping chicks crowded in around her, she sat down and preened herself.

The Flood

Mama laid down old newspapers in a corner of the kitchen. Then she set the coop on top of the newspapers. She put in a bowl of water and another bowl with cornmeal. The chicks crowded into the bowl, trampling the cornmeal and peeping excitedly.

"We will keep them in the kitchen until the weather clears up," Mama said.

The black clouds tumbled and rolled. The wind began to bend the tree branches and thrash the young leaves. The first drops of rain spattered dark spots in the dust as Rose raced to bring in extra stove wood.

Papa tipped the rain barrel over to dump out the old, stale water. Then he put it where it could catch rain running off the roof. Mama did not like to wash with spring water. Rain made better suds and it took less soap.

When all the animals were safe and snug and there was plenty of stove wood piled up on the porch, they all went inside and shut the door. Fido turned around three times and curled up next to the stove.

Rose peeked out the glass window in the

house. A tongue of lightning licked at Patterson's Hill just across the valley. The thunder boomed loudly. It seemed caught among the hills, unable to escape, rolling and echoing. Then the rain came rushing into the valley. It drummed loudly on the roof and poured off like water from a boot.

It beat so hard that Rose barely heard Mama call her to help with supper. Then hail fell, rattling as though someone were throwing rocks on the roof. The wind howled through the trees. It clawed at the walls and rattled the shutters in the kitchen. It shrieked down the chimney. It banged the damper in the stove.

The wild sounds of the storm made Rose shiver. She wanted to climb into bed and pull the covers over her head.

"It's just a rainstorm, Rose," Mama nearly had to shout. "Come and help me clean these fish."

Mama cut off all the heads. There were two perch, four fat catfish with long whiskers, and Rose's smallmouth bass. Mama showed Rose how to clean out the insides. Then she let

Rose scrape the scales off the bass she had caught. The scales sparkled like jewels in the lamplight.

Mama sprinkled cornmeal on the cleaned pieces and fried them in drippings in the skillet. When they had turned golden brown, she put them on the serving plate and sprinkled a few drops of vinegar over them. Then she fried the wild greens she had picked that day at Wolf Creek. The last thing she did was make a flour gravy to sop up with corn bread.

Finally they ate the delicious, delicate fish. It melted in Rose's mouth. She was hungry, and she ate and ate to fill the emptiness inside her.

The hail stopped and only rain pounded on the roof all through supper. The dampness made the house stuffy. But the wind was blowing too hard to open the door or the shutters. They could hear broken branches and twigs rattling and sliding down the roof.

It was Saturday, so after dinner they took their baths. Rose always bathed first. Mama set the tub near the stove and filled it partway with warm water. The splash of the water pouring into the tub and the splash of the rain pouring on the earth were one sound in Rose's ears.

Papa went into the bedroom to read a letter he had gotten from his sister, Rose's Aunt Eliza.

When Rose was done and Mama had checked her neck and ears, Mama freshened the bath with warm water from the reservoir. When she had finished bathing, she freshened it again for Papa. Papa always took his bath last, because he was the dirtiest.

While Papa bathed in the kitchen, Rose looked out the window of the bedroom again. She rubbed a little clear spot in the fog that had collected on the glass. It was pitch black outside, except now and then when a flash of lightning showed the trees bending and flailing in the wind. After that all she could see was running drops of rain, and light reflected from the lamp on the mantel.

Rose noticed a new sound, a roaring.

"What is that?" Rose asked.

The Flood

Mama listened "It must be the spring, flooding from all the rain."

When Papa was done bathing, Rose played with the baby chicks. She cupped one of the tiny trembling creatures in her hand. It peeped loudly for its mother. Then the warmth of her hand made it drowsy. It blinked sleepily and looked up at her, its little head bobbing. Rose could feel its fragile, bony body and its rapid breath through the downy ball of its feathers.

Then she kissed its head and set it on the floor. The chick peeped and tottered about comically. It walked right in front of Fido's head, which was resting on his paws. The chick looked at Fido and peeped at him. Fido's ears perked up and he sniffed at it. Just then the chick pecked Fido's nose. Fido jerked back in surprise. He looked at Rose with a startled face that made Rose laugh.

"That bullheaded sister of mine is trying to talk my whole family into moving to Louisiana," Papa said. "She's so determined, she just might do it, too."

"I suppose Eliza Jane is a bit lonely, down there by herself with a new husband," said Mama. "And now with a baby due."

"She's already talked my little brother, Perley, into it. He's on his way there now by boat down the Mississippi, from Minnesota," said Papa. "He's going to be a rice farmer. Now she wants the rest of us to move down there as well."

"We're staying where we are," Mama said firmly. "I have moved enough times, and left behind enough gardens for the rabbits, for three lives. Wherever would she get the idea we would even consider it?"

"You know Eliza," said Papa. "She was your teacher once. Nobody has to give Eliza Jane any ideas. She's got plenty all on her own. I wouldn't be surprised if my mother and father took her up on it, too."

Just before bedtime, Papa lit the lantern and went to check the barn. It was still raining hard. When he came back he had a worried look on his face.

"This is a bad storm," he said. "The whole

ground is running like a river. There are a lot of tree limbs blown down. Fry Creek is over its banks."

They went to bed with an uneasy feeling. The rain lashed the window. The roaring of the spring and the creek was loud now. Rose was tired, but the drumming on the roof kept her awake.

She had just drifted off when the squeak of the lantern globe woke her up. Papa struck a match to light it. Mama was looking out the window. Her forehead was knobby with worry.

"Is it morning?" Rose asked.

"No," said Papa. "I heard a noise. I'm going to take a look."

Papa had been gone only a few moments when he came back in. His shoes were muddy and water poured off his hat. He shook himself like a sparrow.

"It's the henhouse," he said in a grim voice. "A tree fell on it."

"Oh, no!" cried Mama. "Is it bad?"

"I'm afraid so," said Papa. "We'll have to move them into the barn. Otherwise they may drown in this downpour, or catch a chill at the least."

"Get dressed, Rose," Mama said quickly.

Rose hurriedly pulled on her dress. Then she and Mama followed Papa out the door, into the driving rain and the inky blackness. Big drops of rain stung her face, like bullets fired by the wind. In an instant she was soaked to the skin. The wind howled in the trees. The rushing water of the spring roared in her ears.

She could feel mud squishing between her bare toes. The air smelled like newly plowed earth and freshly cut wood.

It was just a few steps to the henhouse. When the circle of lantern light fell on it, Rose gasped. A great tree had toppled over, right onto the roof. The sturdy little henhouse was crushed in half. The tree trunk blocked the door. She could hear the chickens squawking inside.

Papa fetched the ax and two-handled saw from the barn. Rose held the lantern while he and Mama sawed the tree in half. When they had cut almost all the way through the trunk, there was a loud cracking sound. The trunk twisted and began to roll off the henhouse toward Mama. The chickens squawked in fright. The henhouse leaned as if it were going to fall on her.

Rose tried to shout, "Look out!" But the water ran off her hair, down her nose, and into her open mouth. Nothing came out.

"Watch it, Bess!" Papa shouted.

At the last moment, Mama jumped out of the way. The tree trunk splashed in the mud right at her feet. The henhouse walls sagged. Now it was not a henhouse anymore. It was an old pile of wet logs.

Papa and Mama began to pull loose logs away, one at a time. When they had made a hole in the pile of logs, Papa took the lantern and looked in. Over his shoulder Rose could see some chickens huddled in a pile.

Papa began to hand chickens out to Mama, one at a time. Mama gave the first two to Rose.

"Take these and wait for me," she said. The chickens were soaked and muddy and they smelled rank. They were too terrified to struggle or flap their wings. Rose took one in each arm. Then Mama took three in her arms, and Papa picked up three more.

Then he held up the lantern and they walked through the squishy mud and pools of water to the barn. The wavering light lit the faces of the horses and mules and shone in their dark eyes as they poked their curious heads over the stall gates to see.

Papa set the wet hens in the damp straw on the hallway floor.

"We had best put them in the loft where they'll be safe and dry," he said. He climbed partway up the ladder. Then Mama handed him the chickens and he set each one in the soft, dry hay.

Then they went back for more. They made three trips altogether. They saved seventeen of Mama's hens. The old rooster was dead, and so were six of the young chickens.

"Thank goodness we kept the baby chicks inside," said Mama. "They never would have gotten through it."

When they were finished they walked by the spring to look. The lantern light was too weak to reach across the gully, but they could see foamy water boiling halfway up the sides.

"Be careful!" Mama shouted. "It's slippery here." She pushed Rose away from the edge with her hand. Rose was astonished to see how high up the thrashing water reached. The rain had turned the purling little spring into an angry torrent.

Then they walked down the wagon tracks toward Fry Creek. Rose could not see into the blackness. But when they had walked only halfway, she heard an even deeper, more terrifying roar. She noticed a wet, slapping, gurgling sound. Then, suddenly, her feet were in water!

"Mama! Papa! Look!" Rose cried out.

Fry Creek, which Rose could usually walk across in her bare feet, had climbed all that way up the wagon tracks toward the house. They stared into the darkness. All they could see in the lantern light was the black, rippling water. It lapped against the nearest tree trunks and foamed around the bushes. Rose could not picture it, but she knew the valley must be one great river! They would never get to Decoration Day now.

Somewhere out in that horrible flood they heard the piteous bawling of a cow. Rose shivered.

"Do you think we're in any danger?" Mama shouted. "It's awfully high. Maybe we should move the livestock up the ridge."

"No," Papa said. "We're safe up here. But I better check on the neighbors when it's light. I reckon some of them will need help."

Baby Birds

Mama made an early breakfast in the dark. As soon as the first smudge of light showed in the window, Papa saddled one of the mules and rode off toward Kinnebrew's.

"If anybody needs a hand today, it'll be the folks downstream," he said. Mr. Stubbins' farm was upstream, on higher ground.

Mama and Rose hurriedly washed the dishes. Then they went outside to look at the flooded land. Shattered tree limbs lay everywhere on the ground. It was still raining, though more gently now than during the night. The rain barrel overflowed. Fog and mist hung in the treetops. The voice of the wind was stilled.

The henhouse was ruined, a pile of rubble. Mama fed and watered the chickens in the hallway of the barn.

"This is a bother," said Mama. "They were so stirred up last night they probably won't lay for a week."

The garden was all piles of mud and pools of water. Little rivers had cut swirling paths through the middle, washing away some of the seeds and tender shoots. Here and there seed potatoes, their tender shoots sticking up, peeked out of the wet ground. A large limb had fallen on the fence and broken it down.

"We have our work cut out for us," Mama said with a weary sigh. "I reckon we'll have to replant. The potatoes will rot in this dampness. At least we have the tomato plants still in the hotbeds. We can plant them as soon as the soil dries out."

All over the ground, little brown toads were hopping. There were so many the earth seemed alive and moving. Fido chased one, trying to catch it in his mouth. Rose caught one in her hand. Its tiny eyes looked without blinking. Its frowning mouth bulged underneath and puffed with every breath. Its brown skin was covered with warty bumps.

Rose looked up to see Fido sitting in front of her. He cocked his head quizzically and raised an ear. Rose looked at him. His face had an expression Rose had never seen.

"What is it?" she asked him.

Fido's other ear perked up. Then he opened his mouth. Out jumped a toad!

Then she and Mama walked down the wagon track to the flood's edge. Water rippled around the tree trunks. Beyond the trees they could see the brown plain of the flood. The swirling water was the color of dirty cream, spreading out as if poured from a pitcher. It boiled in places like stew.

Mama shook her head slowly. "Land sakes," she finally said. "The railroad must be washed out as well. I never heard the whistle of Number Six this morning. I wonder how the Cooleys are doing. Decoration Day must certainly be rained out."

"At least there isn't a drought anymore," Rose said, remembering the years of dry weather where they used to live, in South Dakota.

Mama chuckled. "Just think. Last summer we were choking on dust. Then the fires, and now this. As Papa says, if it isn't chickens, it's feathers."

Waves of churning, roiling water raced by. Fry Creek, only yesterday sparkling peacefully among the rocks, had vanished. Rose could not tell where it flowed.

In its place, the flood covered everything. You couldn't see an inch into the murky water. No one could ever cross it alive. Rose stared at the flowing water so long it made her dizzy. When she looked away the earth seemed to slide backward.

Everything the flood had stolen from the land hurtled past them on the waves: brush, boards, chicken coops, a drowned muskrat, fence rails, railroad ties, split wood, bottles.

Rose wondered about all the little creek creatures. Where did the crayfish go in the flood?

A cow stood bawling on a little island of land surrounded by swirling water. A mud-smeared chicken clung to a board, its feathers plastered to its body. The chicken squawked every time the board bounced over a wave.

Then Rose heard a man's voice shouting. Across the flood, on the town side, some people were standing.

"I see them, too," said Mama. "It is the Cooleys! They must have come to see how we are."

They listened and Mr. Cooley shouted again. But they could not understand him over the sound of the flood. Now Rose could see Paul and George. She waved. Mama shouted back, "We're all right!"

But her voice was too small to reach. They all waved to each other, and then the Cooleys walked back to town.

On their way to the house, Rose spied something moving in a pile of leaves. She looked closer. It was a fallen nest, with four baby birds in it.

"Look, Mama!" Rose shouted. The baby birds' eyes were barely open. Their tiny naked heads wobbled. When Rose touched the nest, they stretched their scrawny necks and opened their delicate pink mouths to be fed.

"The poor things," said Mama. She looked about in the trees, but there was no mother bird to be seen. "She must have been killed, or flown off in the storm. They will die for certain if we leave them. Let's bring them inside and see if we can save them."

Mama carried the little nest carefully in both hands. In the house she took an old feed sack and rolled down the sides to make a cozy place to cuddle the nest in. Then she set it near the stove, where the little birds would stay warm.

"What can we feed them?" Rose asked.

"They are very young," said Mama. "I don't know if they are grown enough to eat worms and such. Let's try giving them cornmeal. I'll soften some in water."

Then Mama showed Rose how to feed the trembling chicks. She dipped a hollow stem of straw in the corn mush to pick up a little of it. She poked the stem in the mouth of one of the nestlings. The baby bird grabbed at the food greedily and gulped. The others made chattering noises and opened wide their trembling mouths.

Rose fed them all, again and again. She made sure to give each bird the same number of turns. After a long time they began to settle down. Then they huddled together and fell asleep. Mama carefully tucked the top of the feed bag closed to make it more cozy for them.

Rose and Mama spent the rest of the morning cleaning up. They moved the chicken coop into the barn. Then they pulled the tree limb off the garden fence and put the rails back in place. The rain stopped and the creek began to go down. The gray sky lightened.

Finally, just in time for dinner, Papa came riding back. He was soaked and muddy.

"It was pretty bad all right," he said. "We had to rescue a couple of Kinnebrew's cows from the creek. He lost three of his best milkers. They were standing under a tree when lightning struck it.

"But here's some good in it, anyway," he said, handing Mama a sack. "He butchered one of them and gave us a nice piece of beef."

There wasn't time to cook the beef for dinner. Mama said she would make a good stew of it for supper, with onions.

When Rose went to feed the nestlings she found one of them outside the nest, curled up in the corner of the feed bag. She touched it, but its fragile little body did not stir. It was dead. Rose's heart ached to see it.

"Perhaps it was injured," said Mama. "The others look quite healthy."

Rose fed the three nestlings again. Their tiny pinfeathers had dried out and stood up from their naked bodies. When she was done, she asked Mama if she could bury the poor dead bird.

"We'll do it together," Mama said.

She got the shovel and dug a little hole where Rose asked her to, under the big oak tree near the barn. Rose laid the tiny creature's body in the bottom. She crumbled up some muddy soil and covered it. She jabbed a stick in the ground, to mark the spot. Then they walked slowly back to the house.

Rose fed the three little birds many times, every chance she could, all afternoon in between helping Mama hoe the garden.

By supper the creek was almost back inside its banks. All in the woods and across the creek the land was covered with a layer of mud. Close by the creek the tree trunks wore necklaces of twigs and muddy grass above Rose's head, showing how high up the water had come. Across the valley some buzzards picked at a dead animal.

The dark clouds had moved on, and white ones filled their places. The lowering sun was a great, yellow eye sending a shaft of sunlight to fill the valley with a hazy glow. Then the light faded and a mist rose over the creek.

"We can thank our good fortune we didn't buy bottomland," said Papa over supper. The savory beef stew was delicious, the best meal they had eaten in a long time. "This may be a poor rocky ridge, but at least we know it'll never flood."

Rose fed the three baby birds every chance she could. Each morning she jumped out of bed and ran to the feed sack to see them. Each morning their pinfeathers had grown a little. Their voices were stronger, and they ate more hungrily. They could not seem to eat enough.

Sometimes the little birds stretched their tiny wings, like babies trying to walk for the first time. Rose put in little sticks for them to climb up on. She was so happy to see how well they were doing. Rose felt like a great mother bird. She would protect the babies and feed them until they were strong enough to fly away on their own.

But after three days, Rose noticed that the birds were not getting any stronger.

"Perhaps they need something different to eat," said Mama. "Why don't you catch some bugs and worms?"

Rose caught tiny grasshoppers and ants. She

dug worms up in the garden. But the nestlings did not know how to eat those things. The grasshoppers and ants crawled out of their mouths. The birds shook their heads to spit out the worms. Rose tried everything she could think of, bits of grass, oats, leftover beans.

But the little birds began to weaken. Their chattering hunger calls grew softer. More and more slowly they raised their open mouths to be fed. Rose became frantic with despair.

Then, one morning when she got up, she found the littlest one outside the nest, in the bag. It was barely breathing. She put it back in the nest, but it would not eat any of the corn-meal. By dinnertime, it was dead. Rose buried it under the oak tree, next to the first one.

That afternoon, when she went to feed the two that were left, one of them was outside the nest. She put it back in. An hour later, it was out again, but it would not open its mouth to eat. At suppertime, it was dead, too. Now there was just one nestling left, the largest.

Rose's spirits fell. She picked at her supper

and answered when spoken to only as much as she must. She wanted to do something to save the last little bird. She prayed for it to live. But her hope was melting away.

In the morning, Rose could not stifle a tiny sob when she looked inside the feed bag and saw the lifeless little body huddled in the corner.

"I'm sorry, Rose," Mama said, hugging her gently. "That is the nature of wild creatures sometimes. Only a mother bird can properly raise its young."

Rose knew Mama was right. But she could not stop thinking how small and weak those little birds had been, yet how bravely they had struggled to live. All the rest of that day her eyes stung with unshed tears.

Visiting Alva

Now every day was summery warm. The garden dried so quickly after the flood that the potatoes were saved from rotting. Weeds sprang up every-where. The alfalfa and oats that Papa had planted in the ground between the apple saplings seemed to grow inches overnight. Even the oaks, the slowest of all the trees, began to unfurl their leaves. All the woods were bathed in a soft green light.

Papa rebuilt the henhouse. Then he plowed up a patch of new ground for corn. After it was harrowed smooth, he plowed long furrows with the mules. Then, when the oak leaves were the size of squirrel ears, Rose helped plant the corn in the furrows, four grains of corn together in each spot.

Each time she did it, she sang a ditty Mama had taught her:

"One for the blackbird,
One for the crow,
And that will leave
Just two to grow."

Sure enough, crows and other birds came to steal the corn as soon as they had dropped them in the furrows. Papa shot two crows and hung them from tree limbs to scare away other crows.

When all the corn had been planted, Papa hitched a log sideways behind the mules. The log pushed the soil along, covering up the kernels. But the crows still came to dig them out. Papa had to stay in the corn patch a long time, shouting and shooting at the thieving crows. Then at night the woods creatures came to steal the corn. But Fido barked and chased them away.

Abe and Swiney did not come to help very often now. They were busy helping Mr. Kinnebrew plant and hoe his crops.

When the corn was laid by, Rose had more time to play. She often went for walks in the woods with Alva. They hunted bobwhite nests along the fencerows. They were hard to find because the hen always covered her eggs with leaves when she was away. They counted thirteen of the tiny, pointed eggs in one nest.

They waded in Fry Creek, capturing crayfish and finding tiny Indian arrowheads along the banks. A frowning kingfisher dove into the water to catch fish. Rose stood in a small pool and watched the minnows going like flights of tiny arrows over her insteps. When their slithery bodies touched her skin, they tickled. Now and then a little belly flashed silver.

They tried to trick buzzards into coming down to earth. Rose and Alva flopped in the grass and lay as still as they could be.

"You cain't even twitch your little finger," said Alva. "They won't come down if they see we ain't dead. Buzzards only eat dead things."

They lay there in the grass the longest time. Rose opened her eyes just a little to peek now and then. The great birds soared and circled high above them in the sky. Each time she peeked, they were a little bit closer. But Rose couldn't be still so long. Ants crawled on her skin and made her itch and squirm. Right away those buzzards sailed off until they could see them no more.

Rose loved the woods. All the forest creatures were busy eating and nesting and raising their young. Beautiful flowers bloomed everywhere she looked. And now there were patches of blackberries to eat.

One morning Rose was helping Mama scrub the wash in the yard when Alva came tramping up the hill. She invited Rose to come to her house for dinner. Rose had never been to Alva's house. She was very excited and begged Mama to let her go.

"Very well," said Mama. "Remember your

manners, and thank Mrs. Stubbins. I will expect you home in time for evening chores."

The Stubbinses' house was a log house, too. But it was very big, with two whole floors of rooms. The first floor was two rooms, with an open-air hallway between them. Alva said that was the dogtrot. Two lanky, bony hunting dogs came loping out to greet them, panting and pleading with their eyes to have their heads scratched.

On the porch were a spinning wheel and a loom. Under an oak tree stood a quilting frame. The week's washing hung in the morning sunshine. There was line beyond line of sheets, overalls, shirts, underwear, and dresses.

Dozens of hens scratched in the yard. Geese walked statelily on the banks of a little spring branch. Ducks swam in a pond below the stone milkhouse. Rose could see pigs rooting in the woods above the spring. There was a summer kitchen, and a little smokehouse, and corncribs and cattle sheds, and a large ash hopper, and a pasture with a herd of beautiful Jersey cows, and horses and mules, too.

Rose had not known that Alva's family was so rich.

"Howdy, Rose," Mrs. Stubbins said heartily as she came out of the house. "We're right proud to welcome you. It's about time you was a-visiting. Alva's all the time bragging on you."

A wisp of gray hair fell across Mrs. Stubbins' smiling face. Rose liked her very much. She remembered meeting her last fall when all the neighbors came to help Papa build the barn.

Dinner was a merry feast. She sat next to Alva at a long table with all of Alva's brothers and sisters, six in all, her mama and papa, and a hired hand. Mrs. Stubbins had fried a big plate of chicken and another plate of ham. There were boiled potatoes and hominy and biscuits with butter to spread on them. Rose split open a biscuit and laid it crumbly side down in the fried-ham gravy. Then she carefully ate the biscuit halves, making four bites of each. She couldn't remember when she had eaten so well.

Mrs. Stubbins even gave Rose a big glass of delicious cold milk to drink.

On the other side of Rose from Alva sat Alva's oldest sister, Effie. Two of Alva's sisters were older than Alva, and one of her brothers was a grown-up man. Alva had a little sister and a baby brother. Everyone was talking and laughing, all through dinner.

"How do you find it here in the Ozarks?" asked Effie.

"I like it very much, thank you," Rose said politely. "Except for snakes and chiggers."

Everyone laughed good-naturedly.

"Yep, we got ourselves a mess of snakes and other pests in these hills," said Mr. Stubbins, spearing another piece of ham with his fork. "You young 'uns got to watch out, running around barefoot all summer. Most snakes are harmless. But we got some that are right poisonous. Say, now, you ain't seen none of them hoop snakes about, have you?"

"No, sir," said Rose. "What kind of snake is that?"

Mr. Stubbins looked around the table with a twinkle in his eye. Effie giggled.

"Well, now," he said. "The hoop snake is

one of God's strangest creatures. He only lives here in the Ozarks and not many folks has ever seed one.

"He climbs uphill like any sneaky old snake, slithering and sliding on the ground through the leaves and bushes." Mr. Stubbins wriggled his arm to make it slither like a snake.

"But when he wants to come back down the hill, he bites his tail in his mouth, makes himself into a wheel, and rolls down, just like a hoop. And fast as lightning, too."

"Oh, Emmett!" Mrs. Stubbins said. "Filling their heads with such nonsense."

"Oh, it's true, all right," Mr. Stubbins went on. "Now that old hoop snake is ornery. He likes to chase folks. The thing about it is, he's got a horn on his tail that is right sharp and mighty poisonous. Worse than a rattlesnake, or even a copperhead.

"His aim ain't too good, though. A hoop snake most always runs into a tree before he can hurt you. Then his horn gets stuck in the bark. And do you know what happens then?"

"What?" Rose said, her fork paused in midair.

"The leaves of that old tree curl right up, and in a few days, the tree dies."

Rose giggled uncertainly. Mrs. Stubbins rolled her eyes and got up to clear the dishes. Rose looked at Alva, but Alva was looking at her father with wondering eyes.

Then it was time for the grown-ups to go back to work.

"Thank you, Mrs. Stubbins," Rose said. "It was a very good dinner."

"Don't you even mention it," Mrs. Stubbins said. "You come any old time you please. And tell your ma and pa to come a-visiting of a day, too. There's always room at our table for good neighbors such as you'uns."

Rose began to pick up plates to help with the dishes.

"You ain't got to do that," said Alva. "My sisters do the washing up. Come on. I'll show you around our farm."

Rose thought Alva was very lucky to have big sisters to help with the chores. At home

Rose helped with everything. She was almost as busy as Mama, all day long.

Alva and Rose went into Mr. Stubbins' great barn and played with the baby calves. They let the calves suck their fingers. Alva showed Rose how to milk a cow, but Rose's hands weren't strong enough to make the milk come out.

They found one of the barn cats nursing her kittens in a hollow place in the hay. The mother cat was rust-colored, with a white spot around one of her eyes. She raised her head and blinked dreamily at Rose. The kittens were as tiny as mice. They paddled around with their little paws and sucked at their mother's stomach.

Rose picked one up and cuddled it in the palm of her hand. The kitten nosed between her fingers and mewed softly.

"When they get older, you can have one if you want, Rose," said Alva.

"Could I!" Rose shouted.

"Pa said we got too many cats," Alva said. "Which one you want?"

They all looked the same, with softly striped orange fur on their backs and velvety white fur on their bellies. Their tiny eyes were shut tight, and their tiny ears lay close to their heads. Their short, pointy tails stood straight up and trembled as they nursed. Only one had a black foot, and it was a little smaller than the rest.

"That one," said Rose. "I like that one because I can tell it from the others."

"I'll tell Pa and when he says it's old enough, you can come and take it," Alva said.

Rose clapped her hands with joy. "Thank you, Alva! Thank you so much."

They played away the rest of that afternoon. They watched Mr. Stubbins and the hired hand cutting hay and pitching it into stacks. They made a little dam in the branch of the spring and watched the water spiders darting on the water's surface. They made mud pies and left them to bake in the warm sun.

Alva noticed some bees drinking water from a rock. They tried to follow the bees when they flew away.

"If we can course them, we can find where the bee tree is," said Alva. "Then Pa can chop it down for the honey."

The bees took off one at a time, loaded down with water, and spiraled up into the air. But hard as they tried, Rose and Alva could not see where they flew off to.

Then it was time for Rose to go home. She went back to the barn to peek at her kitten one last time. She decided to name it Blackfoot.

Rose ran home, full of excitement. She ran through the Stubbinses' pasture, startling the cows chewing their cuds in the shade. She skimmed bushes and leaped over stumps. She laughed out loud when a frog she had startled *kerplunk*ed into Fry Creek.

But when she got close to home, she slowed down and walked. And she thought. It had been a wonderful day. She was very happy about her kitten. But a part of Rose felt hollow. She liked Alva's family. She had enjoyed all those people around to listen to and talk with.

Rose wished she had brothers and sisters to

play with. She wished she could visit Alva's house more often. She imagined how wonderful it must be to live at Alva's house, to be Alva and have so many wonderful things to do every day. Rose wished Mama and Papa had a cow, so she could have milk to drink, and butter for her bread.

Then she blushed hot with shame at her thoughts. But she could not stop from having them. A long time ago, when Mama and Papa had decided to move to Missouri from South Dakota, Mama had told Rose they would have sheep and cows again. Soon it would be a whole year since they had left Dakota.

Rose could see it would be a long while before Rocky Ridge Farm looked anything like Mr. Stubbins' wonderful farm. When the apple trees came into bearing they would have everything they ever wanted. But that was years and years away. Rose did not know how she could ever stand the wait.

Off to School

A kitten?" Mama said in surprise. She stood over the kitchen table, ironing Rose's new dress, which she had just finished sewing up. "But where is it?"

"It's too little yet to leave its mother," said Rose. "It's orange and white, with a black foot. Its name is Blackfoot. I picked it."

"We certainly could use a good mouser," Mama said, changing the iron for a freshly hot one that sat on the stove. "When we get the crops in this fall we will need a cat to keep the rats and mice out of the corn and oats.

"There," she said, holding up the dress. "All

168

done. Let's put it on you so I can pin the hem."

Rose wriggled into the new blue and lavender gingham. The cloth was stiff with ironing and newness. Mama had tatted a lace collar for it.

"Your hands are soiled," Mama said. "Try to keep them away from the cloth." She stepped back to look at Rose, chin in hand. "That was a good choice you made. The blue matches your eyes. You look very pretty in it."

Mama's eyes shone as she looked. Rose fidgeted happily. She couldn't wait for a chance to wear it.

Rose stood on a chair so Mama could pin up the hem. Rose told her all about dinner at the Stubbinses', and about trying to milk the cow, and about hoop snakes.

"Are there really hoop snakes here?"

"I've never heard of one," said Mama. "I expect Mr. Stubbins was playing a little joke on you."

Rose was quiet for a moment as Mama worked her way around the hem. Then she asked, "Mama, can we have a baby brother, or a baby sister?"

Mama stopped pinning and looked at Rose with searching eyes. A shadow seemed to pass across her face, and then she sighed.

"I don't think so, sweetheart," she said softly. "Are you lonesome?"

"A little, sometimes," said Rose. "Why can't we have a baby? God brings babies to everyone else."

"You can take your dress off now," Mama said. Rose slipped back into her soft, cozy everyday dress and sat on the chair while Mama fed wood into the stove.

Finally Mama came and sat down at the table. "Do you remember, when you were a baby, when Papa and I were sick and you stayed with Grandma?"

"A little, I think," Rose said. She remembered living with Grandma.

"And do you remember right after that, the baby boy we had in South Dakota who died before we could give him his name?"

"Yes," Rose said in her smallest voice.

"Well, Papa and I wanted to have another baby, and we prayed for another baby. But I think that when I was sick, God decided we won't have one. We cannot do more than pray. After that, we must accept God's judgment. Do you understand?"

"I think so," said Rose. "But . . . why does God bring babies to some people and not to us?"

"God brought you, Rose. That was the greatest gift of all for Papa and me. To have you is enough, if that is His will. No one can know why God decides anything.

"And as for feeling lonesome, you won't be for long," Mama said. "School starts next week. Just think of the friends you'll make!"

Rose's mouth flew open to speak, but nothing came out. She had not thought about school for a long time. She had loved her school in South Dakota, but she didn't know if she would like it in Missouri.

The first day of school, Rose had to get up early to have time for all her chores. First she gathered stove wood from the woodpile and put it on the porch. Then she carried buckets of water from the spring for the horses and mules. She carried warmed water from the reservoir in the stove for the chickens.

She fed the chickens their mash and collected the eggs. Then she washed up and set the table. As soon as breakfast was done, she helped Mama wash the dishes.

Finally, she put on her new dress. The crisp new fabric felt smooth and cool against her warm skin. Mama buttoned up the back. Rose tried out the arms by hugging herself. The fabric didn't bind in the shoulders like her old dresses. Her body felt as free inside it as if she were wearing nothing at all.

Mama plaited Rose's hair tightly into two braids and bound the ends with thread. She tied on Rose's yellow hair ribbons. Then she went to the trunk and got out Rose's ruffled pinafore.

"Don't make a face, Rose," she said. "I know it covers up the cloth, but you must wear it to keep the dirt off. That dress must last until school finishes, at harvest time."

Then Mama took out of the trunk her old copy of *McGuffey's Third Eclectic Reader.* Mama had been a schoolteacher. While Rose was waiting to start school, Mama had taught the lessons at home using her old textbooks. Rose was all the way through the Third Reader and she knew it practically by heart.

Mama gave Rose her slate and a new slate pencil. She slipped the pencil in the pocket of the pinafore. Then she handed Rose an old molasses tin with a lid on it and a handle for carrying. That was her dinner pail.

"There's a surprise in it for you," Mama said. "Don't you peek or nibble before Teacher calls dinner. Promise?"

"I promise," said Rose. Now she was ready. Suddenly she saw that she really was going to school. Something churned in her stomach. "Mama, would you walk with me to school?"

"Why, Rose! You're a big grown-up girl now. I have chores to do, and Papa needs help in the woodlot. You know the way."

Rose sighed. "Can Fido come?"

"School is no place for a dog, and we need him here, to keep the snakes and hawks away from the chickens. Don't fret so, Rose. School will be fun, and Paul and George will be there. You best hurry now or you'll be late."

Mama kissed Rose and watched from the porch as she walked down the wagon tracks toward Fry Creek. Fido bounded alongside her, but Mama whistled for him to come back. Fido looked at Rose and cocked his head. Mama whistled again and he scampered away, back up the hill.

New Girl

Rose waded across the creek, holding up the hem of her dress so it wouldn't get wet. The cool water tingled on her bare feet and washed away the dust.

The footpath that went over Patterson's Hill started on the other side. Rose trudged up the hill past Williams Cave, where she had explored with Alva. They were going to play there again, but now that Rose was in school, she would have no time. The ringing of Papa's ax in the woodlot echoed in the valley. A train whistled loudly as it chugged into town.

The sun was already high, and the air was

shimmery warm. Rose pushed her sunbonnet back off her head. She could hear the voices of farmers as they went to work, shouting at their horses. Yellow daisies with black centers speckled the hillside as if someone had dusted it with yellow powder. Little white and yellow butterflies fluttered among the wildflowers.

Finally she reached the top of Patterson's Hill, from which she could see the back of the tall brick schoolhouse. Children were walking up the road from town. Other children were playing on the bare ground to the side. Three little girls rode a horse up to an open shed. Then they got down and tied up their horse with the other horses that were already hitched there. Rose looked for Paul and George, but she did not see them.

She walked slowly down the slope toward the school. Her heart pounded in her chest. Just then the bell began to ring and all the children raced toward the front door. Rose hurried not to be last.

Then she was in a crowd of children who were pushing, jostling, and laughing. At the head of the crowd, children were pouring through the big double doors. Rose caught a glimpse of Paul as he was swallowed up by the doors.

Finally Rose reached the entryway. A tall bald man with a long beard called out, "Fourth Readers upstairs to the left, Fifth Readers upstairs to the right. First and Second Readers to the left, please. No pushing. Third Readers to the right.

"You there, little girl in the plaid. What reader are you in?"

Rose stood just inside the door, not knowing which way to turn. A stream of children poured in around her.

"Which reader?" the man said again, impatiently. He tapped Rose on the shoulder.

Rose didn't know what to say. Then the man saw her book. He pointed, "Third Reader, to the right."

Rose walked through another door. A boy rushed past her, knocking her dinner pail to the floor. She picked it up and looked around. The room was full of double desks, four rows of four desks. The floor was bright yellow wood and shiny. The room smelled of linseed oil.

There were many great tall windows all around on three walls, and a large heating stove against one wall. The opposite wall from the stove was partly painted black. That was the blackboard. All the other walls were painted a pale sickly green.

On some of those walls were pictures of old men with long beards. In between the pictures were sayings, printed on large cards. One said, "Kind Words Can Never Die," and another said, "Be Diligent, Prompt, and Truthful."

Children were racing about the room, shouting and arguing over seats. Rose stood uncertainly next to the wall by the door. Then the tall man with the beard was talking to her again. "Have a seat, please. Put your dinner pail on the shelf and sit anywhere on the girls' side."

Rose put her dinner pail up and looked around the room. It seemed every seat was taken. Then she spotted an empty one at the front, next to a girl with beautiful curly black hair falling in ringlets. She wore a lovely lawn dress and shiny black shoes. Rose liked to sit in the front in school, so she went to sit in that desk. But when she put her book and slate down on the desktop, the little girl turned and frowned at her.

"You can't sit here," she said quickly. "It's my friend's seat. She's coming in a minute."

Rose flushed hot. She stood in front of all those desks of strangers, not knowing what to do or where to go. Several children were staring at her. Two girls sitting together whispered to each other and pointed at her.

Finally Rose spied an empty seat in the back row. She almost ran down the aisle and quickly sat in it. She was relieved to be where no one could stare at her.

Then Rose looked at her seatmate. Her head was resting on her hands on the desk, her face turned the other way. Rose couldn't tell if she was resting or sleeping. Her faded brown calico dress had a large patch of gingham sewn on the front. Her brown hair fell limp and unbraided over her shoulders. Her feet were dirty. Then she sniffled loudly.

"Hello," Rose said politely. "My name is Rose Wilder."

The little girl looked at Rose blankly with weary eyes.

"I'm tired," she said. Then she wiped her nose with the back of her hand and laid her head down again.

Rose's heart began to sink. There was no sign of Paul or George. They were older, so they would be upstairs in the Fourth Reader.

Now the teacher began to speak.

"My name is Professor Kay," the man said. He wrote his name on the blackboard in chalk. "You may wonder why I have such a long beard. Well, it is to cover my shirt so I do not have to wear a tie."

There were giggles all around the room. Rose could not tell if Professor Kay was making a joke or not.

Then Teacher took the roll. He called out many names. Rose had seen some of the last names on stores in town. "Blanche Coday," he called out. Rose remembered Coday's Drugs.

The girl with the beautiful black hair called out, "Present, sir." Her seatmate was very pretty, too. Her blond hair hung in a silky braid down her back. Her white dimity dress had a butterfly pattern on it. A gold bracelet hung from her wrist. She was looking around the room with bright, curious eyes and whispering to Blanche.

"Quiet in the classroom," Professor Kay said. "Maude Reynolds, Hattie Talbott, Tarah Tarbutton, Clella Rippee, Ida Goss, Oscar Hensley, Harry Carnall . . ." And everyone answered, "Present, sir," or "Here."

Rose listened anxiously so she wouldn't miss her turn. One by one, the students answered to their names. Her throat grew so choked with expecting to speak that she could hardly breathe. Finally, all the names were called, including Irene Strong, the snuffling girl sitting next to Rose. All the names had been called except Rose's.

"Is there any scholar here whose name I did not call?"

Rose raised her hand.

"Stand up, please," Professor Kay said. He pointed a long stick at her. Everyone in the room turned to look at Rose. Her neck blazed hot under all those eyes. "What is your name, please?"

"Rose Wilder," Rose whispered.

"Speak up. I can't hear you." Titters rippled around the room.

Rose said her name again.

"Very well," Professor Kay said, writing it down. "Be seated."

Rose hated being stared at, and laughed at. Irene Strong smelled like a barnyard. She snorted and sniffled.

The desk seat was too tall. Rose's legs ached from dangling. The room was stifling hot. A trickle of sweat ran down the back of her neck.

Rose had never had a teacher who was a man. She had loved Miss Barrow, her teacher in South Dakota. Miss Barrow was pretty and she had a beautiful voice; she liked to lead the class in singing. Rose had loved her classes there, and she had had many school friends to play with.

Now Rose had only one thought in her mind, to run out of that school and all the way home. She would go home and she would never come back. But she did not budge from her seat. She was too shy to run away.

Then the lessons began with recitations. Professor Kay called on the boys first.

"Harry Carnall, recite, please, the first paragraph of 'George's Feast.'"

A boy in overalls stood up and read slowly from his reader, "George's mother was very poor. 'Stead of havin' bright blazin' fahrs in winter, she had nothin' to burn . . ."

"Ing!" Professor Kay barked. "No-*thing*." He stood up and wrote on the blackboard, *having, blazing*, and *nothing*. The chalk jabbed and scratched angrily as he wrote. After *nothing* he wrote ten times, *ing, ing, ing*.

He turned around, folded his arms across his chest, and glared at Harry Carnall.

Harry giggled nervously and looked around at the other boys. Professor Kay just stared at him. Finally Harry said, "What's the *ing, ing, ing* doin' up thar a whole passel of times?"

"I am glad you asked that question," Professor Kay said. Then he wrote out what Harry had said on the blackboard, with spaces between the words.

"I wrote the *ing* up there ten times so you won't forget it. I have hardly heard anyone pronounce *ing* since I came to this school last winter. We are going to learn it now. Let us all say *ing* together, ten times."

Everyone sang out a chorus of *ing*s. All those *ing*s together sounded like a pondful of spring peepers. Rose kept her mouth shut. She did not need to learn how to pronounce *ing*. The lesson was stupid.

"Now," Professor Kay said. "The word is *fire*, not *far*. And it is *there*, not *thar*."

Everyone took turns reciting. One boy could not read at all.

"Do you at least know your ABC's?" Professor Kay asked.

"Heck no!" the boy shouted out in amazement. "I ain't been here but a few minutes."

The room erupted in laughter. Even Professor Kay cracked a small smile. Then he sent the boy to the First Reader across the hall.

Rose grew bored waiting her turn. She was the last to recite.

"Recite, please, the first two paragraphs of 'Johnny's First Snowstorm.'"

Rose knew her whole book almost by heart. She recited easily:

> "*Johnny Reed was a little boy who never had seen a snowstorm till he was six years old. Before this, he had lived in a warm country, where the sun shines down on beautiful orange groves, and fields always sweet with flowers.*
>
> "*But now he had come to visit his grandmother, who lived where the snow falls in winter. Johnny was standing at the window when the snow came down.*"

"Very well done," Professor Kay said. "Please be seated."

Rose knew she should have been pleased

with Teacher's praise, but she didn't care. She knew all of her Third Reader. She had even read the Fourth and Fifth Reader as well. She had read *The Adventures of Robinson Crusoe*, and she often read *The Chicago Interocean*, a newspaper Papa brought home.

So she sat there, legs aching, prickly hot, listening to Irene's horrid snuffling, looking at the ugly green walls, and watching Professor Kay. He tipped back in his chair against the blackboard. He looked out over the class through steel-framed spectacles. He carried a long stick that he poked down the back of his soiled shirt to scratch himself.

Finally Professor Kay rang a tiny bell that he kept on his desk. That meant to put books away. He rang it a second time for everyone to stand up. The third time he rang it was dismissal.

Rose could hardly wait to see Paul and George. She raced outside with all the other children and waited by the doors. Paul came clomping noisily down the stairs with two other boys. His face lit up in a wonderful way when he saw Rose. His bright smile was like the sun coming up.

"Hey, Rose!" he shouted. "Finally came to school, huh?"

"Yes," said Rose cheerfully. "But I don't like it very much. I wish I could be upstairs where you are."

"It's not so bad," he said. "At least you don't have to stay home and do chores. And then you can play at recess and dinnertime."

Just then another boy cried out, "Two-cornered cat and one my bat!"

All the boys raced around to the boys' side of the schoolhouse to play a game.

"See you later!" Paul shouted. Then he dashed off to follow them.

George came racing out of the schoolhouse. He shouted hello to Rose and ran off to play two-cornered cat.

Rose was by herself. She watched four boys carrying water buckets down to the spring at the bottom of the hill. A group of town girls in pretty dresses, including Blanche Coday, were playing house with some rocks. But they did not invite Rose to join them and she was too shy to ask.

Some other children were playing crack the whip. But Rose's spirits were so low, she did not feel like joining. She looked longingly at the crest of the hill that stood between her and home.

Recess was over in fifteen minutes. The bell rang and all the children crowded through the door again. Inside they pushed and shoved to get a drink of water from the bucket before they had to sit down. Two boys wrestled over the dipper, knocking it to the floor.

Rose waited until everyone else had gotten a drink. But when she looked in the bucket, there was not enough water left to get even a dipperful.

The rest of the morning dragged on. Professor Kay wrote on the blackboard, *Exercise in verbs. Insert words in the following sentences: The dog_____at the cat. The horse_____the wagon.*

Rose stared out the window at the trees rustling in the breeze. A bluebird flashed past the windows. Rose wondered what Alva was doing today. Probably she was helping her papa bring in the hay, or playing with the kittens, or just about anything that was more fun than sitting in that stuffy schoolroom.

Afternoon Lessons

At noon, Paul and George went back to the hotel to eat dinner with their mama and papa. The children who stayed at school gathered in groups of friends, or sisters and brothers. Rose ate by herself under a tree at the edge of the playground.

In her molasses tin she found two pieces of brown bread with bacon fat spread on them, a boiled potato, and a dried-apple turnover. That was Mama's surprise.

Rose ate the turnover first. The sweet, crisp taste melted in her mouth. Eating it made her feel a bit better. Then she slowly ate her bread and the potato. Two girls who were twins sat near her. They were dressed exactly the same, in sprigged green calico. Their hair was fixed exactly the same, arranged in a tidy bun on the tops of their heads. Out of their large tin they each took a piece of fried chicken and a biscuit.

"You're a new girl, aren't you?" one of the twins said. "Come and eat with us. We like to meet new girls."

"Thank you," Rose said gratefully. She picked up her things and sat down next to the twins.

"My name is Dora," one of the girls said. "This is my sister, Cora. We're the Hibbard twins. Have you heard of us? Everybody knows us in town. What's your name?"

"Rose Wilder," said Rose.

"You aren't in the Fourth Reader," said Dora.

"I'm in the Third Reader," Rose said. "This my first day in school. I used to live in South Dakota."

"I know where that is," Cora said proudly.

"It's very far. All the way north. Almost to Canada."

"Are Paul and George in your reader?" Rose asked. "Their mama and papa brought them here from South Dakota, too."

"Paul and George? Are they brothers who live in the Mansfield Hotel?" asked Dora.

Rose nodded.

"We don't like George very well," said Cora. Dora nodded in agreement.

"He is in our class," said Dora. "He teases the girls by putting bugs down their backs. Boys are pests, anyway."

"And he pulls their braids," Cora added. Rose thought Dora and Cora were like one person, split in half. Even their voices were exactly the same. She wondered how anyone could tell them apart.

"Would you like a piece of our chicken?" Cora asked. "We have lots."

She held out a crisp, golden-brown chicken leg. Rose's mouth watered at the sight of it. She wanted to accept. She loved chicken and Mama only made it sometimes, when a hen got too old to lay. But she thought it might be impolite to take food from strangers.

"No, thank you. I'm full."

"We love school very much," said Dora. "The first day is so much fun. We like to see our friends again, and everyone is so excited."

"We hate it when school ends," Dora said. "There's nothing to do until it starts again."

"I liked school in South Dakota, but I don't like it very much here," said Rose. "The girls are not very friendly. I mean, except for you. And the teacher is a man. I like a woman teacher better."

"So do we!" Dora said cheerfully. "We like Miss Pimberton so very much."

Rose chatted with the Hibbard twins until they had finished their dinner. Then they all joined some other girls who were playing cat and mouse.

All the children held hands in a circle. One person was the cat and another was the mouse. The mouse started in the middle of the circle. The cat prowled around the outside. Then the cat chased the mouse, darting into the circle under clasped hands. The mouse dashed out and the cat chased her around and through the circle until the mouse was tagged.

Then the mouse became the cat, and it was someone else's turn to be the mouse.

Rose liked cat and mouse. The sound of other children giggling and shouting, and the excitement of all that running and shrieking, cheered her up. When it was her turn to be mouse, her legs rejoiced to be running and free. Soon she was laughing as hard as anyone else.

When the bell rang for afternoon books, Rose went to say good-bye to Cora and Dora, but she hesitated.

"Good-bye, um . . ."

"I'm Cora," Cora helped. "Would you like to know how to tell us apart?"

"Oh, Cora," Dora moaned, making a sour face.

"Just look at Dora's left ear. See, she has a fawn's ear."

Dora's ear was pointed. But the twins' names were so much alike, Rose thought she would never get them straight. On her way back to her seat, Rose wondered what it would be like to have a sister who looked and sounded exactly like her. Twins were lucky, she decided. They always had a best friend to play with.

When Rose sat down in her seat, the two girls sitting in front of her were whispering excitedly and looking at one of the boys. Rose looked at the boys' section. There was a great deal of giggling and snorting among them, but Rose could not tell what it was about.

Professor Kay had just rung the bell to take up books when Harry Carnall jumped to his feet.

"*Ow!*" he shouted. Then he began jumping and writhing in the strangest way, as if he were having a fit. All the children burst out in noisy laughter.

"What's the meaning of this?" Professor Kay demanded.

Harry didn't answer. He was jumping about and digging his hands in his pockets, trying to pull something out of them. Suddenly, from the bottom of his pant leg, a blacksnake slithered out and raced across the floor.

The room erupted in shrieks and shouting and stamping as everyone tried to frighten the snake away or stomp on it. Rose stood on her seat. She would never shriek at a snake, but she didn't want one crawling on her.

Finally Teacher took his stick and picked up the snake. He threw it out the window.

"Harry Carnall," he said in a terrible voice. "I will not tolerate such disruptions in my classroom. Step to the front."

Harry's face was scared and flushed, but he could not stop himself from giggling.

"Hold out your hand," Professor Kay said sternly. Harry held out a hand. Professor Kay took it and bent the fingers back. Then he whipped the open palm of Harry's hand with his stick five times. Harry winced in pain.

Finally, Teacher went to the blackboard and drew a small circle in chalk.

"You will stand here until recess with your nose pressed on the board in the middle of this circle," he said. "And you will remain in at recess."

No one could concentrate on lessons with Harry standing there, his face pasted to the blackboard. When Professor Kay rang the bell to put down books, Harry was finally allowed to go to his desk. His nose was red and there was a damp spot on the blackboard where it had been.

After recess was spelling. Professor Kay drew a long, straight chalk mark on the floor at the front of the classroom. Everyone stood on it in a line, in alphabetical order, facing Professor Kay. No one's name started with an "X" or a "Y" or a "Z," so Rose's name was last. She must start at the foot of the line. Then Teacher called out words and each student took a turn spelling, beginning with the person at the head of the line.

Spelling was Rose's best exercise, and she knew all the words.

"*Frequently,*" Professor Kay said when it was her turn.

"*Frequently,*" Rose repeated. "F-r-e *fre*, q-u-e-n-t *quent, frequent;* l-y *ly, frequently.*"

Rose felt a tingle of excitement every time

she got a word someone had misspelled and she could move up one place in line. Soon she had spelled down two students, and she was third from the foot.

All afternoon they spelled. Rose moved up the line, closer and closer to the head, closer to Blanche Coday, the girl who wouldn't let Rose sit with her. Blanche was a good speller, and she had spelled down the two boys who were ahead of her.

Finally, Rose stood next to Blanche and Rose was only one word away from being the best speller in the class that day. Her stomach quivered, her hands were cold, and her palms were damp. She wanted more than anything to spell down Blanche Coday.

But Blanche was a good speller, too. Every word Professor Kay gave her she spelled correctly: *curious, purpose, material, cautiously.* Every time she got one right, Blanche looked at Rose smugly. But every word Professor Kay gave Rose, Rose spelled correctly as well: *reminded, including, constructed.*

The next time it was Blanche's turn, Professor Kay said, "*Chiefly*."

Rose knew that word, too. She crossed her fingers behind her back.

"*Chiefly*," Blanche said, tossing her head so her curls shook. "C-h-e-i-f *chief*." Rose trembled with joy. "L-y *ly*; *chiefly*."

It was everything Rose could do to keep still. She knew by heart the rule "'I' before 'e,' except after 'c.'" Blanche had got it wrong! Rose's whole body poised to pounce on that word.

"Wrong," said Professor Kay. "Next."

Blanche shot a hard, pinched look at Rose.

"*Chiefly*," Rose said with confidence. "C-h-i-e-f *chief*, l-y *ly*, *chiefly*."

"Very good," said Professor Kay. He wrote Rose's name on a corner of the blackboard and put a mark next to it. That was a headmark, for Rose had gotten to the head of the line by turning down all the other scholars.

"That will be all for today. Class is dismissed."

Everyone scrambled to leave. Rose picked up her book, her slate, and her molasses tin, and bounded out of school. Girls like Blanche might laugh at her, but she could beat any of them in spelling. She flew home, running down Patterson's Hill and splashing carelessly across Fry Creek.

Fido ran down the wagon track to meet her, barking with joy. Rose was never so happy to see him, and Mama, too, when she came to the kitchen door, drying her hands on her apron.

So much had happened that day that Rose didn't know where to start the telling.

"First things first," Mama said. "Change your dress and gather in some kindling for the stove. Then you can help Papa feed and water the horses. You can tell us all about school when we sit down to eat."

Mama untied the sash of Rose's pinafore and carefully pulled Rose's dress off over her head. Then she hung it up behind the curtain in the corner, so the wrinkles would hang out for tomorrow.

The whole house seemed to smile at Rose, glad she was home. The warm, moist smell of fresh bread hung in the air. Salt pork sizzled cheerfully on the new nickel-plated stove. Mama whistled as she rattled a stove lid to check the fire. Rose could hear the mules braying in the barn as Papa fed them their supper.

When Rose finished her after-school chores, she washed her hands and face and set the table. Finally, Papa came in to wash up. It was wonderful to be home.

She told Mama and Papa that the town girls in her reader were very pretty but they were rude. Her seatmate was awful, she smelled bad, and her nose ran all the time. She didn't like Professor Kay very well, either.

"He's dirty and he's the stupidest teacher in the world," Rose complained. She knew it was wicked to say, but all her feelings from that day just came tumbling out before she could stop them. "And he gives the stupidest lessons. 'The dog barked at the cat.'"

"That's enough of such talk, Rose," Mama said firmly. "Besides, people aren't stupid. They are just more or less foolish."

"He is more and more foolish," Rose said.

Papa chuckled, but then stopped when he saw that Mama was not smiling.

Then Rose told Mama and Papa that the schoolroom walls were painted an ugly green that gave her a strange feeling in her insides. The walls made her sick.

"You are just imagining it," said Mama. "You must not be so silly. Besides, you would not be looking at the walls if you were studying like a good girl."

"But the lessons are dull," Rose said. "I know them all. I know all the spelling words, too. I made head in spelling."

"That's very good," Mama said. "I'm proud of you."

But Rose did not feel proud. It had been too easy.

They sat down to supper as the sun was setting. A cooling breeze came in the doorway. A mockingbird that had nested in a tree by the log house began its long, sweet song from the chimney top. The sound floated down the chimney and echoed inside. Katydids and tree toads began their nightly chorus, shattering the quiet with their shrilling songs. From Fry Creek came the chuckling songs of frogs.

"You must have seen Paul and George," Papa said. "How are they doing?"

"I saw them," said Rose. "But they are in the Fourth Reader, on the second floor. At recess they play with the boys. They go to the hotel for dinner."

As they ate supper, Rose told Mama and Papa about the Hibbard twins and about Harry Carnall and the snake. Papa laughed so hard he nearly choked on his food.

Then Rose fell silent in thought. Mama did not understand how unhappy she was in school. Rose could not bear another day sitting next to Irene, staring at those walls, and watching Professor Kay scratch himself. She simply couldn't.

When they were done eating and Papa sat back to light his pipe, Rose finally screwed up her courage to ask, "Do I have to go back? Can't I stay home and study my lessons here, like before?"

"Why, Rose, it's only the first day!" Mama

said, getting up to clear the dishes. "You mustn't give up so easily. In time the other students will catch up to you, you will make some friends, and then it will be more fun."

Rose frowned.

"Don't pout," said Mama. "What must be done is best done cheerfully."

In Trouble

R ose woke the next morning with a terrible feeling of dread. She would have begged Mama to let her stay home, but she knew it would not change a thing.

She dawdled so long on the way to school that she was the last to take her seat. Irene did not speak to her again. At recess she watched Paul and George and the other boys playing. Morning recitation dragged on, and Rose stared out the window.

She listened to the birds singing and watched cloud shadows moving across the hillside. She thought about Alva, and about Blackfoot. She wondered if the little kitten had opened its eyes yet. Rose wished she were a bird. She would fly out the window, over Patterson's Hill, up Fry Creek, right to Alva's barn, where she would sit in the hay and play with her kitten.

Rose was startled from her thoughts when Irene nudged her in the ribs.

"Rose Wilder!" Professor Kay called out impatiently. "I said, please rise and recite."

Rose sprang to her feet, knocking her reader to the floor with a thud. Blanche chortled and some of the other children giggled. Rose's cheeks burned hot.

She picked up her book. "I . . . I'm sorry," she said. "I lost my place."

"Please recite the first three paragraphs on page thirty-one, 'The Beaver.'"

Rose found her place and recited those paragraphs perfectly.

Noon finally came. Rose dashed outside and wolfed her dinner down in nothing flat. When she was done she put her tin back on the shelf in the classroom. Then Rose left school. She couldn't fly to Alva's, but she could run.

She ran all the way to the Stubbinses' farm. She must hurry to have time enough to get back before afternoon books. Alva was just coming out of her house from dinner.

"How come you ain't in school?" Alva asked.

"I am," said Rose. "I just wanted to see Blackfoot."

"Come on, then," Alva said. "Their little eyes are open now."

Sure enough, all the kittens' eyes were wide and shining and looking curiously at everything. They had grown so in just a few days. Now they played with one another, gnawing each other's ears and tails, pouncing, and kicking with their tiny back feet. Rose and Alva laughed at how comical they were.

Rose picked up Blackfoot. He climbed up her pinafore onto her shoulder. He sniffed tiny breaths that tickled in her ear, and batted at her hair ribbon. Then he mewed softly to get down.

"Oh, Alva," Rose said. "I hate school so."

"I'm glad my ma and pa don't make me go to no school," said Alva. "My pa says you don't need no schooling to know how to milk cows and hoe corn. I just know I couldn't sit in those old seats for a minute."

Then they left the kittens and walked out into the yard to get a drink at the spring.

"Look, Rose!" Alva shouted. "The bees are back drinking water. Let's follow them and see if we can course the nest."

"I don't think I ought to," said Rose. "I might be late for afternoon books."

"We won't go far," Alva insisted. "Come on, there goes one now."

A bee had taken off from a moss-covered rock. It circled around and around until it was high in the air. Then it took straight off in a beeline into the trees, flying slowly.

Alva took off running and Rose followed. "I can still see it!" Alva shouted. They ran through the woods, a long way. Rose could never see the bee, but Alva kept shouting, "There it is! Hurry up, Rose!"

But then she lost sight of it. "It don't matter

209

anyway," Alva said. "'A hive in May is worth a load of hay, but a hive in July ain't worth a fly.'"

On the way back they passed by the horse pasture. They watched two colts racing each other back and forth across the field. Then they hunted quail nests along the fence. They found a blackberry patch. Alva took a stick and beat the bushes first, to scare away snakes. Then they plucked and ate all the ripe berries they could find.

Rose remembered school, but she was sure she still had time to get back for afternoon books. She had not heard the bell, and it wasn't so far if she ran.

Along the spring branch they hunted crayfish. Then they built a dam and watched a little pond form behind it. Brilliant blue dragonflies hovered darting to catch bugs.

Finally Rose said she had better go. She ran all the way back to school. The sun seemed much lower in the sky now. She had better hurry not to be late. When she got to the top of Patterson's Hill, Rose gasped. The schoolyard was empty! She slowed to a walk, catching her breath. Then she noticed that there were no horses tethered in the shed. Her stomach flip-flopped.

The last thing she noticed made her heart skip a beat. There was a wagon standing by the front of the school. She recognized Pet and May, Papa's horses.

A great weight settled around Rose's shoulders. She walked very slowly down the hill, around the front of the school. She climbed the steps, one at a time. Her feet were as heavy as stones.

As she got to the top of the stairs, she heard Mama's voice, and Professor Kay's.

Then she stood in the schoolroom doorway. Mama was sitting in a desk with her back to the door. Papa stood next to her. Professor Kay looked up at Rose from his desk. He nodded toward her and looked at Mama with raised eyebrows. Mama turned and looked at Rose. Her mouth was tight and her eyes glared fiercely.

Professor Kay cleared his throat. "I best be going," he said. "I expect you have the matter in hand now."

Then he left without another word.

"Where have you been?" Mama asked sternly. Her voice had never had such a hard edge.

Rose could think of nothing to say. She stared at the floor.

"I asked you a question," Mama said. "You weren't in school all afternoon, and Teacher dismissed class an hour ago. Papa and I have been worried sick. *Where have you been?*"

Rose flinched.

"I went to Alva's," Rose said meekly. "I'm sorry, Mama. I only wanted to see the kitten. I didn't know it would be so long."

Mama said, "To think, you could have been lying hurt somewhere, and Papa and I with no idea where to begin to look. I can't imagine where you got it into your head . . ."

"Now, Bess," Papa interrupted. "There's no need to get too stoked up. She's here now, safe and sound. Just some childish foolishness. But you mustn't ever do anything like that again, Rose."

"Yes, Papa," Rose said softly.

Mama said, "We have told Professor Kay to keep you in during recess and dinner as many days as he sees fit, until you have learned your lesson. You must obey him the same as you obey Papa and me."

"Yes, Mama," Rose said.

The silence on the ride home crashed in Rose's ears. She wanted to cry, but she didn't dare. She hated causing Mama and Papa to worry.

Every day for the rest of that week Professor Kay kept Rose inside during recess and dinner. At first it was torture to be still and listen to the high, light voices of the other children playing outside.

But Professor Kay chatted pleasantly with Rose while they ate their dinners.

"You are a very good student, Rose," Professor Kay said. "I don't blame you much for being bored. By rights, you ought to be in the Fourth Reader. Your mother taught you well."

"Thank you," Rose said, trying not to speak with her mouth full. She munched on a carrot that Mama had put in her lunch. Raw carrots were Rose's favorite vegetable.

"I expect it takes some getting used to, coming into these hills for the first time," said Professor Kay. "A lot of these folks have never been out of the Ozarks. Just a few miles from here there are people who have never seen a railroad train."

"A man told Papa that once," said Rose. "When we drove here last summer. The man said people here had never seen an organ or a train."

Professor Kay's beard crumpled into a smile. "I'll tell you a story. Once there was a young fellow who lived back in the hills who had never seen a train. He had to go to town for the first time, and it was several days' journey. One night he slept on the ground, and along around daybreak he woke up to a tremendous roaring sound. He looked up and saw the biggest thing he had ever seen come running out of a hole in the hillside, near where he was sleeping.

"He was scared. He took off and ran away. He just ran and ran. Finally he saw a woodsman splitting rails. He stopped to catch his breath, and the woodsman asked him what he was running from.

"After the fellow got his wind back, he told the woodsman that he had just seen the worst thing in his life. It was some kind of beast, huge, that was snorting and raging something fierce. The thing was black and it had one great big shining eye and fire and smoke were coming out of its head. He said it just came tearing out of its den in a hillside, and it was making a terrible racket and letting out a great yell now and then."

Rose giggled.

"Now that woodsman told this young fellow that he'd seen a train, is all. He told him, 'It won't hurt you. You can even ride on it.' And this hill boy said, 'It'll have to catch me first.'"

Rose burst out laughing. Professor Kay chuckled, too.

Then Rose had a new thought.

"Could I go into the Fourth Reader, Professor Kay? My friends are in that class. Paul and George. I promise I would be good and study hard to keep up."

"I am sure you would, and I wish I could say yes," Professor Kay said. "But Miss Pimberton's room is full and you are a bit young for her class. I'll tell you what, though. There is a library of books in her room that have been donated to the school. If you wish, you may pick one out to read. Would you like that?"

"Yes, sir," Rose said. "I would like it very much. Thank you."

When they were done eating and Rose had put away her tin, she walked upstairs with Professor Kay to Miss Pimberton's room. In the corner was a bookcase with four shelves. The bottom part was where the erasers and the boxes of chalk were kept. Above it were three shelves behind glass doors. Two of the shelves were almost full of books.

Professor Kay said Rose could look through those books. He opened the glass doors so she could pull them out and see if she would like to borrow one.

Rose had never seen so many books. There were books of poems by Alfred, Lord Tennyson and William Clement Scott; Prescott's

History of the Conquest of Mexico and *History of the Conquest of Peru*; *The Green Mountain Boys*, and *John Halifax, Gentleman*, and another true book, the biggest of all: *Ancient, Medieval and Modern History*, full of beautiful colored maps and pictures.

There were many storybooks, too: *Afloat in the Forest*, *Five Little Peppers and How They Grew*, *Five Little Peppers Grown Up*, and important-sounding books: *Sense and Sensibility*, *Pride and Prejudice*, and *The House of the Seven Gables*.

Rose loved the feel of the cloth covers and the rich weight of the books in her hands. She couldn't decide on just one. She wanted to read them all, to learn the secrets hidden in all those hundreds of pages of words. Finally she picked a big book called *The Leatherstocking Tales*. It had been written by a man named James Fenimore Cooper many years before. Rose picked it because she liked the title. Professor Kay said it was a book of stories about the beginnings of America.

At noon the next day Rose sat at her desk,

ate her dinner as quickly as she could, and read. She began at the beginning. The first part was called *The Pioneers*.

She read about Leatherstocking, a nickname for an old man called Natty Bumppo who lived in New York State and who hunted deer in the wild forests. Rose did not understand some of it, and there were quite a few words she had to ask Professor Kay to explain.

But the more Rose read, the more she wanted to read. It was very pleasant to sit quietly in the empty classroom. In no time at all she was carried away from school. She forgot about the green walls and about Irene. Instead, she was tramping through the winter snows of New York many years ago, hunting deer with a smoothbore rifle, and wearing a deerskin coat with the hair still on.

When the bell rang for afternoon lessons, she hated to put it down. Rose thought the people in books were more real than the people she saw every day.

In the afternoon each day there was spelling. Every day Rose started at the foot and ended at the head. She always turned down Blanche Coday. But even though they ended up standing next to each other, Blanche did not speak to Rose, and Rose was too shy to speak to Blanche.

On Friday, Professor Kay let Rose take the book home with her. On Saturday night and Sunday afternoon, Mama read aloud from it to Rose and Papa. Mama liked that book very much.

"It reminds me of when I was a child, growing up in the Big Woods of Wisconsin," she said. "Your grandpa used to hunt deer and bear, just as Natty Bumppo did."

On Monday Rose took *The Leatherstocking Tales* back to school. Her punishment was ended and she could go out with the other children. But she would still read it. She propped herself up against a tree at the edge of the schoolyard and opened the book on her knees.

But before she could sit down to read, Professor Kay gave her a chore. He asked Rose to clean the erasers. That was a special chore that he only gave to the best students. Rose was surprised that after she had been disobedient he would give her a special chore. But she was even more surprised when Professor Kay picked Blanche Coday to help her.

At dinnertime, she and Blanche took two erasers each and walked quietly to the edge of the playground. They clapped the erasers together to get all the chalk dust out. A fog of chalk dust floated on the breeze, making them both sneeze. They must clap and clap those erasers until no more dust came out of them.

They did not speak a word to each other. Rose could not think of anything pleasant to say to Blanche, and Blanche turned her back to Rose.

Rose stole as many looks as she dared at Blanche's beautiful lawn dress, her shimmering, curled black hair, her shoes and stockings. Rose hated to wear shoes, but all dressed up that way, Blanche was simply beautiful. And she seemed to wear a different dress every day of the week. Rose could not imagine owning as many school dresses as there were days in the week. She had one dress, and it must last the whole school term, until fall.

Blanche's father was rich. Rose had heard some other children say it. He owned Coday's Drug Store. Rose wondered what it must be like to be rich. She would have liked to own any one of Blanche's dresses, and she would like to eat chicken every day, and have butter on her bread instead of bacon fat.

The next day, as they were clapping the chalk dust out of the erasers, Blanche startled Rose by asking her in a haughty voice, "Where are you from? You aren't from around here. Anyone can see that. You don't talk like girls from around here."

"My mama and papa brought me here from South Dakota," Rose said. "We drove last summer in a covered wagon all the way."

Blanche clapped her erasers a few more times. Then she said, "You haven't been in school here before. How did you learn so many spelling words?"

"My mama taught me," said Rose. She did not like the tone of Blanche's voice, but she tried to be polite anyway. "She was a school-teacher once. I like to read, too. I learned many words from reading books."

"Well, anyone can see that plain as day," Blanche said tartly. "It's all you do, is read and stare out the window and be teacher's pet. But don't think we can be friends just because you are so smart. After all, you're a country girl."

With that, Blanche flounced off to return her erasers. Rose's face stung as though it had been slapped. She stared hard after Blanche, boiling with anger. Alva was right, Rose thought. Town girls are stuck up.

Rose decided then and there that she would never, ever let Blanche Coday spell her down.

Summer

Every day in spelling Rose turned down Blanche and ended up at the head of the line. Every day Professor Kay put a headmark next to Rose's name on the blackboard. And Rose remembered each time her promise to herself and studied her spelling harder.

Irene took sick and stopped coming to school. Irene's older sister said Irene had caught diphtheria. The word echoed in Rose's mind like a thunderclap. That was the terrible illness Mama and Papa had once had.

The doctor had been to visit Irene, and now

the rest of her family could not leave their house because they were quarantined. Only Irene's sister could go out to school and to town on errands. But she said she must sleep in the barn, so she would not catch it, too.

Rose felt sorry for Irene, but she was glad to have the seat all to herself now.

Summer flowed on, slow, lazy, and stifling hot. Specks of dust hung in the still air, catching the sunlight and shimmering in the heat. The hot weather pressed down like an iron pot lid.

It was prickly and sticky sitting inside the classroom, even with all the windows opened. Everyone was glad to dash outside at dinnertime and sit in the cool shade of a tree to eat. Most days Rose ate by herself and read. Paul or George visited with her sometimes. Sometimes she played cat and mouse, or sat and talked with other students. She liked Cora and Dora best of all.

But Rose did not make a best friend at school. Many children had brothers and sisters in school. The families ate and often played together. The town girls snubbed her. Rose did not want to be friends with other country girls like Irene whose mothers sent them to school unwashed in shabby dresses. And the boys played rough games and kept to themselves. Rose did not fit in anywhere.

But she was mostly content. She had grown to like Professor Kay. She enjoyed watching Paul and the older boys playing two-cornered cat. And Rose had been an only child all her life. She was used to pleasing herself.

At home, the whole farm was growing. The garden was rows and rows of different shades of green. Mama liked to keep a neat garden. She and Rose hoed and chopped weeds every other day until the soil was smooth and soft and clean between the lush columns of leaves. There were radishes, lettuce, onions, and carrots. But the carrots did not grow like any carrots they had seen. They were crooked and thin from struggling to reach down through the stony soil. The tomatoes had blossomed, and now there were shiny pale-green tomatoes hanging from thin stems.

Baby melons clung to the melon vines, and potato leaves sprouted all along their heaped rows.

The corn had sprung up almost overnight. It was growing taller every day, unfurling bright new leaves that fluttered in the breeze like ribbons. Already the stalks reached Rose's waist. She could almost watch them grow, the corn was shooting up so fast.

In the same soil with the corn Papa had planted the pole beans. The thin tendrils of their stems trailed along the ground, crawling straight to the corn. Then they hugged the cornstalks and began to climb them. The cornstalks were the poles. Before they picked the corn in the fall, the beans would be ready to harvest. That was a way to get two crops out of one piece of ground. Rose wondered how the beans knew to climb the cornstalks.

In the orchard the young apple trees were filling in with new growth. Slender, bright green fingers reached out from the end of each gray branch and twig. Papa brought home wagonloads of wood ashes from town and spread some around each tree. The ashes would sweeten the soil and keep away wood-eating bugs that might hurt the trees.

One Sunday Alva came by, carrying a sack that meowed loudly. She opened it and out jumped Blackfoot. He shook himself, blinked in the bright light, and rubbed, curving, against Rose's leg.

"He remembers me!" she cried. Blackfoot was even more beautiful than she recalled. And he had grown so big. His short, straight tail had become long and wavy.

When Fido came to sniff at him, the kitten batted the dog's nose playfully. Fido gave a short surprised bark that sent Blackfoot skittering behind Rose. But in a moment he came back out, sat down, and licked his paw, keeping his bright eyes on Fido. Soon after that they became friends and even played together.

It was often too hot to sleep at night, even with all the windows open. Some nights Rose's legs itched so from chigger bites that even if she could fall asleep, the burning and itching kept her awake. And it was noisy, too. Katydids, crickets, frogs, and other night creatures made such a clamor in the dark woods that when Mama read aloud she almost had to shout to be heard. Only in the wee hours before daybreak did all those creatures finally go to sleep.

One night at supper Papa said, "It's too blamed hot for cutting wood. The crops are laid by, not much hoeing and plowing to be done. Why don't we gather up some folks and throw ourselves a picnic?"

"That would be lovely," said Mama. "After all, we were too busy with the corn to go to town on Fourth of July. We could all do with a change of scene. Do you think the Cooleys would come?"

"Don't see why not," said Papa. "I'll ask them when I'm in town tomorrow."

"Perhaps we could ask the Kinnebrews as well," Mama suggested. "We haven't all met them yet."

In a day it was decided. The three families would meet on the Ava Road south of town and drive down to Bryant Creek.

The morning of the picnic they woke up in the false dawn, hurriedly did their chores, ate a cold breakfast, and loaded the wagon. Papa pitched a pile of hay in the back to sit on and for the horses to munch. The picnic food was packed in a basket with a clean white towel tucked over it. A jug of sweetened ginger water sat under the wagon seat.

Rose gave Fido's head a good scratching and explained to him that he must stay behind and guard the farm. He whimpered in disappointment.

Then they were off in the first gray light of dawn. They met the Kinnebrews in their wagon and the Cooleys driving the hotel hack. There were many shouts of hello, and they drove off into the fresh morning with Papa's wagon in the lead. The wagon track twisted and turned through the hills under a canopy of branches heavy with leaves. Rose tingled with excitement to be going somewhere different, and to have a day away from school.

It had been a whole year since they drove to Missouri from South Dakota. That had been a great adventure, and now that it was summer again, Rose remembered the wonderful, new things they had seen along the way. Going somewhere made her feel like singing. She hummed, "Oh Susanna."

Right away Mama began whistling it, and then they were all singing as the sun peered over a ridge and lit the tops of the trees.

The wagon rattled past many small farms along the way, with log houses and barns tucked away in little hollows. Horses and cows munching the dew-fresh grass lazily watched them pass. Farmers waved from their corn patches. They passed small white churches and a schoolhouse. Rose could see children inside studying their lessons. They stopped often to let the horses rest and have a drink from the little streams and springs they crossed all along the way.

Nits and horse flies buzzed around the team. Papa had to keep the lines tight in case they suddenly bolted from being bitten and tried to run away.

Finally, when Rose was getting fidgety and

the air was turning muggy, they came to a wide stream, bigger than Wolf Creek. That was Bryant Creek.

They set themselves up on a gravel bar, right next to the water. Rose helped Paul and George gather wood for a fire. Mama and Mrs. Cooley hung an old sheet between two trees for a private place to change into the old dresses they had brought for swimming.

Mr. and Mrs. Kinnebrew had brought two big watermelons for everyone to eat at dinner. Rose's mouth watered just looking at them. Their two sons, Coley and Claude, carried them to the creek's edge and set them in a quiet pool to chill. They weighted them down with stones to keep the watermelons from floating away. Mr. Kinnebrew scolded the boys to quit fighting over how to pile up the rocks.

"I'm going to wear you two out if you don't behave," Mr. Kinnebrew said irritably. "It's bad enough we're missing a day's work without having to listen to you two scrapping all the time. Now give a hand unhitching the team."

There were three Kinnebrew children in all. Coley was a big boy, a year older than Paul, who was eleven. Then there was Ernestine, who was nine, the same age as George. Claude was the baby of their family. He was seven, a year younger than Rose. Rose had seen all of them at school, but they were in different classrooms for lessons.

Mrs. Kinnebrew was a very proper-looking lady. She wore a beautiful lawn dress, and her hair was pinned up in a tight bun. She carried a dainty white parasol, with ruffles around the edges.

"I don't like to wear a bonnet if I don't have to," she told Mama. "It's too hot in this country."

"You came here from Illinois, didn't you?" Mama asked.

"Yes, and a prosperous little town it was, too," Mrs. Kinnebrew said, puffing up like a hen that had just laid an egg. "I often wonder what Mr. Kinnebrew could have been thinking of when he dragged us all down here. This is lovely country from nature's point of view, of course. But it is a mighty poor excuse for a place to try to dig out a living."

"The ground's a bit thin and stony," agreed Papa. "But you can't beat it for fuel and the best water that ever flowed out of Mother Earth."

"And the people are so friendly," Mrs. Cooley said. "So neighborly and helpful."

"I suppose, although they are somewhat poor-folksy, don't you think?" said Mrs. Kinnebrew, smoothing the front of her dress. "And there are so many pests and varmints in the timber that try to destroy our livestock. We have had a wolf carry off two of our pigs. And last fall the rats killed eleven of my young chickens, and two turkeys, too."

"A wolf?" Mama said, casting a worried glance at Papa. "I hadn't heard of that. Why, your place isn't a mile away from ours."

Then Coley chimed in, "They call this Missouri but they ought to call it the state of Misery, right, Ma?"

"I wish you would stop making fun of this fine country," Mr. Kinnebrew said. "We should use our own judgment and push ahead and not let discouraging words alter our course.

"I never saw a place yet that wouldn't raise a fair crop if farmed right, and I'm going to give this country a good tryout before I give up. I'll work till doomsday but what I'll succeed. I know we can make a good living if we don't lose our ambition."

"It is never easy to start over," said Mama. "We are doing it ourselves."

Finally, when the wagons were unloaded, the horses tied up in the shade with buckets of water to drink, and the food assembled for dinner, the children were free to play.

Picnic

First they threw rocks into the creek. Claude said he wanted to scare away all the cottonmouth snakes in the creek so they could swim.

"I hate snakes," he said. "There are too many snakes around here."

"You're afraid of everything," Coley scoffed. He was tall and blond. A shock of his blond hair covered his forehead and shook as he hurled a skipping stone. It skipped almost all the way across the creek. That stone somehow went into the water and popped right out again, time after time. Rose had never seen anything like it. She tried to make stones skip, but they only plopped and sank.

"You think there's a bear behind every tree," Coley said with a smirk. "Just waiting to jump out and eat you. You're afraid of your own shadow."

Claude turned red-faced and punched Coley in the side. "I am not either," he shouted. In a second they were on the ground wrestling. But Claude could not possibly win against Coley. Coley was a big grown-up boy. He sat on Claude's chest and pinned Claude's arms with his knees. Then he tickled the inside of Claude's nose with a grass stem until Claude cried, "Uncle!"

"I'm tired of you two fighting all the time," Ernestine huffed. "I'm going to go sit with Mother and help with dinner."

Rose thought the Kinnebrews were not a very happy family.

The creek was very wide. They stopped in a place where two streams flowed together. In the middle where the streams met was a point of stony land. It was like an island, or the bow of a boat. The water made a rushing sound as it ran around it.

Rose wanted to explore the island. But the current looked swift, and in the middle of the creek was a large pool. It was dark there, too deep to see the bottom even through the clear water. The creek looked so fresh and inviting that Rose wanted to jump right in and get her whole skin wet. But Mama said she must stay dry until after they ate, so she wouldn't have to change twice.

But even if she had been allowed to, Rose did not know how to swim.

"Stay close to the bank," Mama called out, as if she had heard Rose's thoughts. So Rose only waded along the creek bank, hunting crayfish and Indian arrowheads with Paul and George and talking about school.

Then they chased grasshoppers to fish with after dinner. Every minute Claude was hollering, "There's a snake!" But there never were any. He was just imagining them.

It was very hard to catch grasshoppers. They were the same color green as the grass.

The only way was to scare them up and then watch one flutter away to see where it landed.

Then Rose crept up behind that grasshopper. When she was close enough, she swooped her hand down to grab the grass stem where the grasshopper clung. She tried many times before she finally caught one. The grasshopper kicked and fought in her fist, giving Rose's palm a queer tickly feeling.

They put all the grasshoppers they caught in a sack.

When dinner was ready they all gathered together to eat. The men had dragged logs near the fire to sit on. In the trees around them, cicadas shrilled in the warmth of the day. Their raspy sounds rose and fell, like knives being sharpened on lopsided grindstones.

There were pickles and steaming potatoes that had been roasting in the fire. Mama had brought hard-boiled eggs. Mrs. Cooley had made a big batch of biscuits with snowy white insides, and she passed them around. Everyone admired and enjoyed them.

"It's nothing, really," Mrs. Cooley said.

"When you feed a hotel full of guests you are accustomed to making big batches."

"How is it, living in town?" Mrs. Kinnebrew asked. "It must certainly be more civilized than living on a farm in the middle of nowhere. I suppose you see many interesting people in the hotel."

"Yes, but we are too busy to visit," said Mrs. Cooley. "It seems all we do is work. And the noise! When it isn't the trains and the trade coming into town, there are fights that break out at the saloon. And just the other day some farmers tipped over one of the boxcars on the siding."

"Whatever for?" Mr. Kinnebrew asked.

"It was parked right where the tracks cross the road," Mr. Cooley said. "The town asked the railroad to move it three times, but they never did. Folks got tired of bouncing their wagons over the rails and ruining their wheels. I guess some fellows took it in their own hands to show the railroad company a lesson."

"That reminds me of the story about Mr. Arnold's hog," said Mama with a twinkle in her eye. Rose perked right up. She had never heard this story.

"It was in Walnut Grove, Minnesota, one fall at butchering time when a freight train ran over Mr. Arnold's fat hog about halfway up the hill east of town. He couldn't save the meat, but he rendered the fat into soap.

"Mr. Arnold tried to get the railroad people to pay him for the hog, as they should have. But they refused. He had no money to go into a lawsuit and the railroad knew it.

"So one day, before the freight came through, he went and soaped up the rails. He smeared the soap all up and down the track. When the train came along its wheels spun and spun on the slippery rails and it couldn't pull up the grade. The train crew used up all the sand they were carrying and had to get out and throw dirt on the tracks to get going again.

"Every day after that, the freight train never could get up the grade without sand and trouble. The passenger train went through all right, but when the freight came, it slipped and fell behind schedule.

"The railroad people were suspicious, but they never could catch Mr. Arnold in the act. Finally, the railroad sent a man out to Arnold's one day and paid him cash money for his hog. Sure enough, the very next day the freight went through without any trouble.

"After that, Mr. Arnold bragged in town that he'd given most of that hog to the railroad company, bit by bit on the rails. But he had a little of the soap left over, so he figured he had beat them out of that much of it anyway."

Even Mrs. Kinnebrew laughed when Mama finished.

When they had eaten their dinner, they cut and ate the sweating watermelons. The melons were deliciously sweet, and the children competed to see who could spit the seeds farthest.

Finally Rose and Ernestine and Mama and Mrs. Cooley changed into their oldest calico dresses to go swimming. Mrs. Kinnebrew sat on a log and watched. The men and boys went swimming right in their overalls.

Papa swam far out into the deep water. He

dove down and disappeared with a splash. Rose held her breath. She waited and waited for Papa to come up again. No one could stay under water so long. Rose was just about to scream for Mama when Papa's head popped out of the water, far away downstream from where he had vanished.

Rose wanted to swim with Papa and go under the water. She wanted to see what it was like down there. She walked deeper and deeper into the water.

Rose squatted down until the water came to her chin. She felt herself rising up, light as a leaf. Her dress blossomed up around her. Then it got wet and sank, sticking to her all over. Her whole skin drank up the refreshing coolness.

"Don't go in any farther," Mama said.

Suddenly, Papa's dripping wet head rose up out of the water, right in front of her. He laughed a great laugh that echoed from the creek bank.

"Will you take me in the deep water, please, Papa?" Rose begged. "I want to disappear under the water."

Papa laughed again. "I think you need a lesson first," he said. "Give me your hands."

Papa took Rose's hands in his own and gently pulled her away from the shallow water. Rose's feet lifted right off the gravel bottom. Then she was floating like an angel. The bank looked very far away. The water flowed over her skin like a cool breeze.

"Now kick your feet," said Papa. "I'll hold you up, and you kick with your feet." Papa towed her into the deep water. Rose kicked as hard as she could. Papa towed her around and around.

She stopped kicking to see if she could touch bottom. But there was nothing there, nothing solid to touch. Only deep dark water. And it was colder down there, too. The coldness on her feet scared Rose. If Papa let go, she would sink down and down in that cold darkness and nothing could stop her.

"Keep kicking," said Papa. His smiling face was always in front of her, going backward. "Now I'm going to let go of your hands. You must paddle with your hands, as if you are climbing up a slope, or crawling. And keep kicking, too."

Then Papa let go. Rose paddled as fast and hard as she could. But she could not make her hands and feet go at the same time. When she paddled with her hands, her feet stopped. When she kicked with her feet, her hands stopped. Then Rose felt herself sinking. Her head went into the dark water and she gasped, swallowing a great mouthful of water.

In an instant, she felt Papa's hands lift her up. Rose sputtered and coughed until she could catch her breath.

"Now you know what can happen if you go into deep water without knowing how to swim," Papa said. "I think that is enough for now." He towed Rose back to the shallow water.

"Can we do it again, Papa?" Rose begged.

Papa laughed. "I have a better idea," he said. "You can hold on to that old fence rail over there. It will float and you can paddle around. But only so long as I'm watching."

Rose kicked around the creek after that, her arms draped over the fence rail. Sometimes Paul or George would grab on to it, too. They were a ship, sailing on the ocean. The current carried them downstream to a wide shallow place. Then they got out and pushed the fence rail back upstream along the bank and floated down again.

All afternoon they played. There were horseshoes to throw. They cut cane and fished for a while. But the fish would not come to the grasshoppers. Papa said it was so hot even the fish weren't hungry.

Coley and Paul played lap jack. They locked their left arms together by hooking their elbows. Then they swatted each other with switches they held in their right hands.

Coley was taller than Paul and he landed the best blows. Rose laughed to see them both trying to get away and hit each other at the same time. Soon their shoulders were covered with red welts, but the boys were laughing loudly.

They stopped when Mr. Kinnebrew scolded Coley for waking him up from his nap in the wagon. "How is a poor farmer to get a little rest with all this commotion!"

Finally all the play was drained out of Rose.

She lay down on her back on a wide, flat stone that was big enough for her whole body. The heat from the stone warmed her wet dress. She looked up into the sky, at piles of fat, white clouds floating above the trees.

She gazed at the shapes the clouds had made. They were always changing, but she could never actually see them change. She stared at one cloud, hard as she could. It was a great tower of whipped cream. She stared at the folds and bulges and nothing changed. Then she looked away for a moment. When she looked back, the shapes had begun to dissolve, ruffled by the wind like tousled hair.

Each time Rose looked away, the cloud had changed, tearing itself apart in shreds and dissolving into a new shape.

She turned over on her stomach and yawned. She stretched her arms out to the side and felt the warmth of the rock soaking into her body. That rock was alive. The heat of its life was flowing into Rose. She hugged it. Rose felt as if she were hugging the whole beautiful living earth and the earth was hugging her back.

She loved that rock and she loved that summery day. The warmth on her skin, the rich odor of the damp soil, the peaceful chuckling of the water, the lazy buzzing of insects, and the murmur of grown-up voices all filled her with peace. She could not possibly have an unhappy thought. It seemed to Rose that summer could soothe every care and heal every hurt.

Jungle of Green

They went picnicking two more times that summer, with Abe and Swiney to Wolf Creek. By the last time Rose had learned how to use her hands and feet together. Now she could swim in deep water. But she never did unless Papa was with her. Deep water still frightened her.

At school, Rose stayed at the head of the line in spelling, although often it was very close. Blanche was a good speller and she only missed the hardest words. Some days when Rose sat reading her book at dinner, she noticed Blanche studying her reader.

Rose learned her times tables as well. Professor Kay had taught the scholars how to sing the tables to the notes of "Yankee Doodle Dandy." On the way home Rose skipped to the beat and sang to herself, "Five times five is twenty five, and five times six is thirty, five times seven is thirty-five, and five times eight is forty."

One morning, before they took up books, Professor Kay stood before the class with a grave look on his face.

"I have an announcement to make which is very sad," he said. All the rustling and fidgeting in the room stopped. Every head snapped to attention as if they were all connected to Professor Kay by strings he had pulled.

"Irene Strong, who has been out of school these many weeks with diphtheria, has crossed to that other shore from which no traveler returns." One of the girls choked out, "Oh!" All around Rose children were looking at each other with open mouths and big, scared eyes.

Rose was confused. She leaned across the

aisle toward the boy sitting in the next row. "What did he say?" she whispered.

"She's gone and died," the boy hissed. "Irene's died."

"We will bow our heads now for a minute of silent prayer," said Professor Kay.

Rose was too stunned to think of praying. Her mind skittered about like a water spider. The only person she had ever known who had died was her little brother. But she had been only a baby then herself. She didn't really remember anything at all.

Irene had not been Rose's friend, but she had sat right next to Rose. Rose remembered how unkind she had been to Irene in her thoughts. She remembered how she had complained to herself about Irene's sniffling and shabbiness. Rose's whole body blazed with shame.

Then she had a new thought. What if she caught diphtheria? Would she die? Did it hurt to die? And what would become of Mama and Papa if Rose died? They would never have other children. Mama had said so. Who would help on the farm?

The thought of Mama and Papa alone was the most unbearable of all. Tears flooded her eyes and fell from Rose's bowed face, splashing on her folded hands. She fought back a sob. She could hear some of the other children muttering their prayers. Someone was sniffling.

Professor Kay did not need to raise his voice or punish anyone all the rest of that week. Rose wished she could move her seat, but all the other seats were full. She could not help thinking of poor Irene whenever she looked at the empty spot beside her.

The days flew by and summer grew old and dusty.

"Seems as though it has been weeks since we had a good rain, Manly," Mama said at breakfast one morning. "The garden soil has just about dried all through. It's cracking at the surface. If this keeps up much longer, I'll need to haul water."

"It's the rocky soil, Bess," said Papa. "It's too thin and porous to hold the moisture. It drains right away. But the weather evens up in the end. This is the best time for a dry spell, just before the harvest. Too wet and the corn could go moldy."

"Yes, and the dryness has kept the bugs down in the garden," Mama said thoughtfully. "I just can't help remembering all those years of heartbreaking drought and stunted crops in South Dakota. How many times the weather robbed all our hard work at the last minute."

Papa only nodded in agreement as he got up to go cut wood in the woodlot. There wasn't anything to be said about the terrible hardships of the prairie that had not been said a hundred times before.

The corn had grown very tall, and now it was heavy with the ripening ears. The beans had climbed up the stalks. Bulging pods hung everywhere. In between the rows, here and there, pumpkins grew. Soon they would have their first harvest from the new farm.

The flat, empty field Rose had helped plant with the pitiful little seeds in the spring had grown into a wonderful, mysterious place to explore. In it Rose found another world, far away from Rocky Ridge Farm, where she could lose herself without being afraid. Sometimes she liked to go into the corn patch and just sit and listen. It was a jungle of green, rustling with life. The waxy corn leaves shone in the sunshine. In the early morning, sparkling beads of dew clung to the leaves and trickled down into their dark throats.

Rose liked to walk down the shady rows between the stalks, listening to the whispering leaves and imagining that she was Natty Bumppo stalking wild animals in the deep, dark forest, or Robinson Crusoe exploring a deserted island. Sometimes when Swiney came they played hide-and-seek there. Fido and Blackfoot tagged along as well.

September came, and the last day of the summer school session drew near. Professor Kay announced on Monday that there would be a special spelldown on Friday after supper. Then there would be no more school until after harvest time, in December.

"Each classroom will have its own spelldown," Professor Kay explained. "Your mothers and fathers are invited to come and attend and see how well you are all getting along. There will be refreshments after and a prize for the winner. I advise you scholars to study well if you are to make a good account of yourselves before your families."

Rose was terribly excited and jittery all that week. Every time she thought about the spelldown, her insides quivered. She knew she could win. She had gotten almost all the headmarks in the class. But Blanche was getting better and better. She had gotten three headmarks when Rose made mistakes. All that week during recess and dinnertime, Rose stole anxious glances at Blanche studying in her reader.

After dinner on Friday there was no spelldown. Instead the students scrubbed the whole classroom until it shone. Rose helped wash the blackboard and sweep the floor. The windows were washed as well.

Then they all cut pieces of red, white, and blue paper into strips. They glued the strips into little rings and strung the rings together to make paper chains. Professor Kay stood on a chair and tacked the paper chains around the windows.

When the classroom was spotless and decorated, school was dismissed. Rose dashed home to do her chores and get ready. Mama had washed and ironed Rose's best calico. After supper they all washed up, got dressed, and walked to school.

When they got to the top of Patterson's Hill, Rose and Mama slipped on the stockings and shoes they had been carrying as the sun began to melt into a puddle of gold. Rose swallowed hard as they walked down the hill into the schoolyard.

Spelldown

The schoolyard was teeming with wagons and horses. People were streaming in from every direction, dressed up and in a festive, friendly mood.

At the door of Rose's classroom, Professor Kay greeted Mama and Papa and invited them inside.

"Good to see you folks again," he said. "Come on in and have a seat."

School looked very different with all those grown-ups milling about. Rose spied Blanche, standing with her parents. Blanche's best dress was even more beautiful than the dresses she wore every day. It was made of red serge trimmed with satin that shimmered in the light of the setting sun.

Finally Professor Kay asked all the parents to be seated. There weren't enough seats to go around, so many people had to stand along the walls. Lanterns were lit, and the air filled with the smell of coal oil smoke. Rose took her place at the foot of the line of scholars standing against the wall. The grown-ups looked funny sitting in the tiny seats, their knees crowded. They looked like giant children. Professor Kay rose to speak. He had dressed up as well. He was even wearing a tie.

"We are honored to have all the parents here this evening," he said as the scuffling and murmuring faded away. A baby cried out in the back and everyone giggled nervously. Rose could hear voices and feet moving upstairs in the other classrooms, where the older children were having their own contests and recitations.

"We will begin the program with a few words from one of our patrons, Mr. Elliot Hoover, who, being the town livery man, a member of the school board, and the father of one of our students, hardly needs introducing."

Mr. Hoover stood and talked for a long time. Everyone was very polite and listened solemnly. But his voice was a blur to Rose. She was thinking of words she might have to spell.

"We are proud of our scholars studying so diligently . . ." Mr. Hoover said.

"*Diligently,*" Rose thought. "D-i-l-i *dili*, g-e-n-t *gent*, l-y *ly. Diligently.*"

Mr. Hoover was a tall, thin man with a drooping mustache. His enormous Adam's apple stuck far out of his neck and bobbed up and down so much when he talked that it was all Rose could do to keep from staring at it.

Mr. Hoover droned on and on until Rose's legs ached from not bending. He talked about the school board's business, how much money was spent and how much was collected in taxes. Finally he looked at the scholars and said, "In conclusion, students, the town is pleased to provide you this opportunity to improve the shining hours of your youth, just as I did with mine. For I was once only a schoolboy like any of you, and look at me now."

Professor Kay led the audience in singing a song. Then there were recitations by two other students. Finally, the spelldown began.

"We will begin with two warm-up rounds," Professor Kay said. He sat down at his desk, pulled his gold watch from his vest pocket, and opened the spelling book.

The words in the warm-up rounds were easy, and Rose began to relax. Anyone could spell them—*kettle, beyond, mouse.* Rose looked at Mama and Papa and smiled.

Then the real spelldown began and the words got harder, and trickier.

"*Counsel*," pronounced Oscar Walters, the boy standing ahead of Rose. "C-o-u-n *coun*, s-i-l *sil. Counsel.*"

"I'm sorry. That is wrong," Professor Kay said. Oscar shrugged and hung his head as he shuffled out of line to go sit with his mother and father. Rose liked starting out at the foot of the line. It gave her heart to hear other students making mistakes.

"Next."

"*Counsel,*" Rose said confidently. "C-o-u-n *coun*, s-e-l *sel. Counsel.*"

Papa winked at her. Mama smiled.

One by one, the students were spelled down and left the line to join their families. The line became ragged, like an old comb with teeth missing.

"*Constructed,*" Blanche said slowly, as if she were confused. "C-o-n *con*, s-t-r-u . . ." She hesitated. Rose's heart fluttered. "C *struc,* t-e-d *ted. Constructed,*" Blanche said with a little sigh.

"That's my girl," a man in the audience whispered loudly. It was Blanche's father, Mr. Coday. Blanche blushed brightly and stared down at her shiny black shoes.

Soon there were only three students standing, Rose, Blanche, and a redheaded boy named Oscar Hensley.

"*Sheaves,*" Professor Kay said.

"*Sheaves,*" Oscar repeated. "S-h-e-e-v-e-s, *sheaves.*"

"I'm sorry, Oscar. That is wrong. Well, ladies and gentlemen," Professor Kay said,

"we are down to the two best spellers in the Third Reader. May the better of them win."

Rose felt every eye in the room on her. Blanche got the first word. Then Rose, then Blanche. Blanche spelled every one correctly: *pendulum*, *conquer*, *locomotive*, *portrait*. Each time she spelled so slowly that Rose was certain she was about to make a mistake. But she never did.

On and on they spelled, into the evening. Clapping and a commotion upstairs in one of the other rooms told Rose that some of the other spelldowns had ended. Her mouth had grown dry, and she desperately wanted to sit down.

"*Occasion*," Professor Kay said.

"*Occasion*," Rose repeated. She opened her mouth to spell when suddenly her mind went blank. "*Occasion*," she said again. Her thoughts raced. One "c" or two; one "s" or two? Her chest tightened and she felt herself gasping for breath.

She looked at Mama and Papa. Papa was twirling his mustache. Mama twisted her handkerchief in her hands.

"*Occasion*," she said a third time. All the shuffling and fidgeting in the room came to a stop. Everyone was staring at Rose. A chair creaked in the awful silence as someone leaned forward to hear better.

Rose was too terrified to speak. She didn't know which it was, two "c"'s or two "s"'s! Or two "c"'s *and* two "s"'s. Which was it?

Professor Kay cleared his throat. Rose's heart began to pound in her ears.

"Do you wish me to repeat the word and define it?" Professor Kay said gently.

"No," Rose croaked. She must try, even if she got it wrong. She closed her eyes tight, trying to see that word in her mind.

"*Occasion*," she said slowly. "O-c *oc* . . . c-a *ca*, s-i-o-n *sion. Occasion.*"

"Good girl!" Papa called out rather loudly. Nervous laughter broke out in the room. Mama's hand flew to her mouth.

"Correct," Professor Kay said. Rose let out a shivery sigh.

There were four more rounds of perfect

spelling. Then Professor Kay gave Blanche the word *precipice*.

"*Precipice*," Blanche said slowly. Rose thought she saw Blanche tremble, but she wasn't sure.

"P-r-e *pre*, c-i *ci*, p-i . . . s-e *pice*. *Precipice*."

"Oh!" someone in the audience cried out. Papa slapped his hand on the desktop. Mama turned and shushed him.

At first Rose did not understand what had happened. Then Professor Kay said, "Wrong."

Rose could hardly believe her ears. She knew how to spell that word. Blanche had got it wrong!

Professor Kay looked at Rose. "'Precipice,'" he said.

"*Precipice*," said Rose. "P-r-e *pre*, c-i *ci*, p-i . . . c-e *pice*. *Precipice*."

The room erupted in a swirl of shouting and clapping and confusion. Suddenly everyone was on his feet, moving about and talking. Oscar clapped Rose on the back as he ran past. Professor Kay was shouting something about lemonade on the second floor. Then Mama and Papa came pushing through the crowd up to Rose. Papa gave her a big hug. Mama smiled her biggest smile.

Rose realized with a shock that she had actually won the spelldown.

"That's our smart girl," Papa said. "You did it! You beat 'em all hollow."

"We are very proud of you," said Mama.

Then Professor Kay was there. "Very well done, young lady," he said. "Here is your prize, well deserved I must say, close as it was."

He held out to Rose a book. She took it in her hands. It was heavy and thickly covered with plush. The plush was deep red, soft as moss. Inscribed on the cover in shiny gold lettering was the word "Autographs."

Inside that book all the pages were blank, with beautiful curlicue borders printed in pale blue. Mama said it was an album, for friends and loved ones to write little sayings and poems in. It was a place to keep memories of good friends and special times.

"Every girl must have one," said Mama. "I did."

Rose looked at all those blank pages. How would she ever fill them up? She didn't know very many people she could ask to write in it. But she trembled with excitement to think of those empty pages filling up with words no one had thought of yet.

Rose was jumping with joy inside her skin, but she said politely, "Thank you, Professor Kay." She ran her hands over the velvety cover. It was so smooth and silky it could have been alive.

But when Rose spotted Blanche across the room, her joy began to melt into something else. Blanche stood slump-shouldered with her face buried in her mother's bosom. Her father was patting her on the head and saying something to her.

While Mama and Papa talked to Professor Kay over her head, Rose stared at Blanche's heaving back. The more she looked, the worse Rose felt. Yet she could not tear her eyes away. She thought about how close she herself had come to losing.

Rose looked at her beautiful new album,

and then back at Blanche. She tried to think of something to do. Blanche had been unkind to Rose, but Rose did not hate her. She didn't really ever hate anybody. She just thought they were more or less foolish, as Mama said.

But Rose did hate to be the cause of Blanche's tears. She thought and stared and thought some more. Then, in a flash, she knew what she must do.

Rose walked across the schoolroom, right up to Blanche's family.

"Why, hello there, young lady," said Mr. Coday. "You really gave us quite a show here tonight."

Blanche turned from her mother to look at Rose. Her cheeks were damp and her face was blotched. Her reddened eyes flashed and her mouth pinched itself into a frown.

"Please don't cry," said Rose. "I'm sorry you lost. I almost lost first. I couldn't remember if *occasion* has one 'c' or two. I only guessed. I was just lucky."

Blanche's frown softened. She looked down at the autograph album in Rose's hands.

"Professor Kay gave me this for winning. It isn't fair to give only one prize when we are such equally good spellers," said Rose. "We can share it, if you like."

Rose held out the album.

Blanche stared at it with disbelieving eyes.

"Well, isn't that something?" Mrs. Coday said. Then she nudged Blanche with her elbow. "Have you lost your tongue?" she said sharply.

"Thank you," Blanche murmured.

"That's a fine gesture, young lady," Mr. Coday said quickly. "You are an example to us all. But a memory album, now, that isn't a thing easily shared. Besides, you did win it, fair and square, luck or no."

"Yes," Blanche said, the storm clearing from her face. "It is your prize. You must keep it for yourself. But thank you. You are very nice to offer."

"We can take turns keeping it," said Rose.

"It wouldn't be right," said Blanche. "Thank you very much."

Rose thought for a moment. Then she had another idea.

"Will you write in it, then?" Rose asked. "Since we are both the best spellers, I would like you to be the first one to write in it."

"I . . . I wouldn't know what to write," Blanche stammered. Then she blushed.

"Take it home with you," said Rose. "Then you can think of something."

Mr. Coday said that since the school session was over, he could give it to Papa when he came into the drugstore.

"All right," said Blanche softly. She took the album from Rose, ran her hand over the mossy cover, and tucked it under her arm. Now she looked at Rose with shining eyes and smiled. She snuffled up the last of her tears. "I'll take good care of it. I promise."

"Good-bye, Blanche," Rose said.

"Good-bye, Rose," said Blanche.

Rose skipped back to be with Mama and Papa. They were still talking to Professor Kay and some other parents. People were leaving the room and going upstairs for lemonade. Rose tugged Mama's skirt and whispered in her ear, "*Lemonade.*"

Mama laughed. "Very well," she said. "But where is your album?"

"I gave it to Blanche. She is going to write something in it. Mr. Coday said he will give it to Papa when he goes to town."

"That's very sweet, Rose," said Mama. "Now I have two reasons to be proud of you tonight. A good winner is a gracious winner."

Blanche did not come upstairs to drink lemonade. Rose did not see her again the rest of the evening. But as she walked home in the dark between Mama and Papa, the lantern throwing its quivery circle of light on the path, Rose remembered Blanche's grateful smile. It made Rose happy to think she could make someone smile.

Rose wondered what Blanche might write in her autograph book. She couldn't wait to see.

Harvest Moon

The first cool breaths of autumn stole into the Ozarks at night, pulling heavy blankets of fog over the hills and hollows. Each day the sun rose strong and golden to chase off the gray dawn.

Rose bounded out of bed each morning, delighted she didn't have to dress for school. While she fed the chickens and poured their warmed water into a pan, she took deep breaths of the spicy autumn air. Everywhere Rose looked there were spiderwebs in the grass, sparkling with dewdrops. Puffy white clouds floated in a deep blue sky.

The leaves of the trees had begun to fade. Rose noticed that many of the leaves had jagged holes and edges where insects had been chewing, and brown spots. It was a sure sign that summer was getting old.

Woolly brown and black caterpillars crawled across the barnyard, looking for a good safe corner to spin a cocoon and rest until spring. You could pick one up and put it facing the other way and it would always turn around and crawl rippling off the way it had been going. The wind could bowl them over and they would right themselves and march off in the same direction.

Rose even tried shaking one up in her hand. It curled up into a tiny round pincushion. She carried it to another part of the barnyard. When she set it down, it uncurled itself and started crawling in the very same direction it had been going before. How did it know?

But there was no time for play. This was the month of the harvest moon. They must hurry to gather in the crops before frost.

Mama said they should pick the potatoes.

first. "They could wait, but the market is high now. Two and a half cents a pound! And this Ozark weather is almost too good to believe," she said, bent over and huffing as she dug with her hands. She brushed the dirt off a large one and weighed it in her hand. "Two potato crops in one summer! We'll have almost a wagonload to sell and enough to winter over. And we have second plantings of turnips and carrots, yet."

Harvesting potatoes was a treasure hunt. Papa walked along the rows with the shovel and loosened up the hardened hills of earth. Then Rose dug with her hands into the loose soil until she found the pale yellow potatoes clinging to the roots. She made sure to get every one, even the tiniest buttons. They would keep the smallest for eating and trade the big ones at Reynolds' Store.

They stacked the potatoes in piles between the rows. Mama separated the good ones out to sell. When they were done, she and Rose put the graded potatoes into sacks. Then Papa loaded the heavy sacks onto the wagon and drove into town. Rose and Mama stood outside and watched him go. Rose swelled with pride to see the food she had helped grow going off to market.

That night after supper Papa went to the mantel and got down a little book he often wrote in. He sat by the fireplace and scribbled some numbers in pencil. Papa called it his accounts book. He wrote down everything they bought, traded, and sold.

"Why?" asked Rose.

"Any farmer worth his salt keeps his records," said Papa. "It tells how we're doing. See here," he said, showing her the page he was writing on. It had blue lines printed on it, and three columns. The first column had writing, "375 lbs potatoes @ 2 ½¢." In the second column he had written a number, $9.38. The third column was blank.

The book was pages and pages of writing and numbers.

"Every time we trade at Reynolds', I write that down in the third column," Papa explained. "That's a minus. Every time I sell a load of stove wood, or fence rails, or railroad ties I made, or potatoes, or Mama sends in eggs, I write it down in the second column. That is a plus.

"When it comes settling-up time, after the harvest is all in, I will add all the minuses and all the pluses and I can see which one is greater."

"What does it say now?" Rose asked. "Are we plus or minus?"

Papa laughed. "Too soon to say for sure, Rose. But we're getting by."

Papa's account book was a little confusing, but Rose understood that it was very important.

Next Papa dug a shallow pit in the ground in a little clearing between two trees, close to the house. He began to line it with small stones.

"Why, Papa?" Rose wanted to know. "What's it for?"

"Curiosity killed the cat," Papa said. "Run and fetch some straw from the barn."

Rose made several trips, gathering up as much straw as she could carry in her arms. Papa spread the straw over the stones until they were all covered.

He drove the wagon up to the pit. It was piled with the keeping potatoes and the keeping onions that had been hanging from rafters in the barn to dry.

"Now you can help me put all this treasure into the pit," he said.

Papa used the shovel and Rose carried as many as she could in her hands.

"Don't take too many," Papa said. "They mustn't be dropped or bruised. One bad potato will spoil all the rest."

They kept piling up potatoes and onions until Papa said the mound was high enough. Then he sent Rose to fetch more straw. He spread a thick layer of it on top, and shoveled a thick layer of soil on top of that.

The pit had grown into a small hill. Papa dug a hole, just big enough to stick an arm through, on each side. He stuck his hand in to make sure he could reach the potatoes and onions. Then he covered up the holes with some stones and straw. He laid some boards on top of the mound, to make it harder for raccoons and other animals to dig into it and steal the food.

Finally, he stood up and brushed the dirt from his hands.

"All tucked in for winter," he said. "The soil and straw will save them from rot and frost, almost until spring. Anytime we want potatoes or onions, all we have to do is stick an arm in and pluck them out."

The rest of the potatoes and onions went into sacks that Mama stored under the kitchen, through the trapdoor in the floor.

Then they dug up the sweet potatoes that Papa had planted in a corner of the corn patch. They brushed off the dirt and set the gnarled roots out on planks to dry in the sunshine. Rose sorted out the long stringy ones that weren't good for eating. Mama would save them to use for seed next spring.

When the sweet potatoes were dry, Rose and Mama wrapped each one in a scrap of old newspaper. Then they put all the wrapped potatoes in a wooden box in a corner of the kitchen.

They gathered chestnuts that had fallen

from a chestnut tree near the orchard. Mama packed them in layers of salt in a big pickling jar. She tucked the jar away in one of the trunks where they wouldn't be tempted to eat them. She was saving them for Christmas.

One night at supper, after Papa had been to town to pick up some liniment for his sore shoulder, he laid Rose's autograph album on the table. Rose opened it at once and looked on the first page. Blanche had written something there in blue ink. Mama peered over Rose's shoulder and read:

Too wise you are, too wise you be;
I see you are too wise for me.
Your friend, Blanche Coday. October 3, 1895.

Rose tingled with excitement when she read the words "Your friend."

"That's very sweet," said Mama. "I suspect your book will fill up quickly when you go back to school in December."

"I want you and Papa to write something, too," Rose said.

Harvest Moon

When the dishes had been cleared, Papa took Mama's pen, twisted his mustache for a few minutes, and then scratched away at the page. Rose fidgeted impatiently. Then Papa carefully blotted the page with Mama's blotter and showed it to Rose.

To my prairie Rose:
Be faithful in all things,
Superficial in none,
And always remember,
that home is home.
—Papa.

Mama said she must think of what to write. The next Sunday she spent a long time writing in Rose's book. When she was done she showed it to Rose. It was a poem Mama had composed.

There were some naughty flowers once,
Who were careless in their play;
They got their petals torn and soiled
As they swung in the dust all day.

They went to bed at four o'clock,
With faces covered tight,
To keep the fairy, Drop O'Dew,
From washing them at night.

Poor Drop O'Dew! What could she do?
She said to the Fairy Queen,
"I cannot get those Four o'Clocks
To keep their faces clean."

The mighty Storm King heard the tale;
"My winds and rain," roared he,
"Shall wash those naughty flowers well,
As flowers ought to be."

So raindrops came and caught them all
Before they went to bed,
And washed those little Four o'Clocks
At three o'clock instead.

Mama's poem was beautiful, as good as any in Rose's *McGuffey's Reader.* She read it over and over again, and liked it better each time.

Beans were the next crop to harvest. Abe

and Swiney came to help. They would get a share of the harvest for helping.

For days and days, from morning to night, they picked bean pods off the vines that had climbed up the cornstalks. Rose and Swiney picked the pods that were closest to the ground. Mama and Papa and Abe picked up high.

They all wore tow sacks tied around their waists with string. The tow sacks were long and narrow. Rose's drooped on the ground, and she kept tripping over it. When it began to get full, it was very heavy to drag.

Picking beans was hard work. But Abe made it fun by teaching them a song. They all sang it as they picked, their voices rising from different places in the field.

> *"My papa came from town last night*
> *As sad as a man could be,*
> *His wagon empty, cotton gone,*
> *And not a dime had he.*

"Huzzah! Huzzah!
'Tis strange, Ma did declare!
We make the clothes for all the world,
But few have we to wear."

One morning before the first rooster crow, Rose woke up with a start. A sound had disturbed her sleep, but she didn't know what it was. The soft, slow sighs of Mama and Papa sleeping came from their bed in the corner. A square of bright moonlight from the window lay on the floor at the foot of her bed. The wind was still and the woods quiet, as if they were listening, too.

Rose heard water dripping outside, like rain. But it couldn't be raining if there was moonlight. It was so bright inside that Rose could read the clock face. It was three o'clock.

Then Rose heard the sound again. At first she thought it was a train whistle. It was a wild howling, far away. Then more howling and baying, in different voices. Rose had never heard wolves crying before, but she thought for sure that was what it must be.

She crept out of bed and tiptoed across the cold floor into the kitchen. Fido got up from his sleeping place by the stove and stretched with a tiny moan. Then he tapped across the floor and stood at Rose's feet.

Far away the voices howled again. It was a wild sound that sent shivers up her back. She opened the shutters of one of the windows and looked out. The cool night air flowed over her skin like water.

The whole world was bathed in the bright light of the harvest moon. Heavy dew dripped from all the trees. It gently splattered on the leaves. Moonrays fell like dark sunlight, dappling the ground with shadows. Down toward Fry Creek, fingers of morning mist were starting to creep up among the trees.

Far away the howling took up again. One of the horses snorted in her stall in the barn. The spring purled quietly in the gully behind the house.

Rose went to the front door and opened it. It complained with a tiny squeak. She stepped out onto the porch and looked up at the moon through an opening in the trees. The bright circle of light was clothed in a fuzzy halo that was brownish around the edge.

Rose looked at the moon for the longest time, trying to see the man's face. But it was a harvest moon, when the moon is so bright farmers can work into the night gathering the crops. It was too bright to see the dark spots of its eyes and nose. She had to look away.

She sat down on the porch and stared hard at the trees. She thought she could see the green in the leaves, but only just barely, and only just the darkest green. But even then she wasn't sure. She could just barely see the brown of the soil and rocks. The shadows seemed as crisp as daylight, but the harder she looked the more they were smoothed and softened, the way moss softens a rock. Her eyes kept playing tricks on her.

The gathering mist made the air glow in places. She could see the dark outlines of spiders asleep in their webs in the eaves of the porch, waiting for the earth to warm up and send them a morning meal. Rose felt herself part of the night.

A creaking floorboard in the kitchen startled her. Mama appeared in the doorway, ghostly white in her nightgown.

"Is something the matter?" she asked sleepily. "I heard the door creak."

"Something was howling in the woods," said Rose. "I thought it was wolves."

"I heard it, too," said Mama, sitting down next to Rose on the porch's edge. She yawned. "But it isn't wolves. I think it is just some farmer out hunting a raccoon with his hounds."

They sat in silence for a moment. Rose shivered against the cool morning air. Mama put her arm around Rose's shoulder and squeezed. Then the ghostly shape of Blackfoot came padding toward them across the yard from the barn where he had been sleeping. He mewed softly and rubbed against their legs, purring loudly in the stillness.

"The moonlight is lovely, isn't it?" said Mama. "It's as though you were inside a dream. You can see everything, but you can't see it either."

Rose sat cuddled up against Mama for the longest time, watching the mist floating quietly into the moon-washed yard. She wished that moment could go on forever.

But just then the rooster crowed. A new day was about to begin.